THE UNION BELLE

THE UNION
BELLE

GILBERT MORRIS

BETHANY HOUSE PUBLISHERS
MINNEAPOLIS, MINNESOTA 55438

Cover illustration by Brett Longley,
Bethany House Publishers staff artist.

Published by Bethany House Publishers
A Ministry of Bethany Fellowship, Inc.
6820 Auto Club Road, Minneapolis, Minnesota 55438

Printed in the United States of America

Library of Congress Cataloging-in-Publication Data

Morris, Gilbert.
    The union belle / Gilbert Morris.
        p. cm. — (The House of Winslow ; bk. 11)

    I. Title. II. Series: Morris, Gilbert. House of Winslow ; bk. 11.
PS3563.08742U5   1992
813'.54—dc20   91–43430
ISBN 1–55661–186–2   CIP

To Bobby Funderburk

How strange a thing friendship is! We live in the midst of throngs, yet know most people so little. But from time to time one person out of the hundreds we meet will open a door, admitting us into his very life—and we in turn will open ourselves up to that one. This transformation that makes strangers into friends is one of the miracles of human existence. We touch so many people, yet so rarely does the alchemy take place that turns cold knowledge into the warmth of friendship!

Well does the old Book say, "There is a friend that sticketh closer than a brother," and since I have no brothers in the flesh, I am grateful that I have found one in the spirit—Bobby—a fellow pilgrim along the way who makes the path pleasant and life far richer.

BOOKS BY GILBERT MORRIS

THE HOUSE OF WINSLOW SERIES

★ ★ ★ ★

1. *The Honorable Imposter*
2. *The Captive Bride*
3. *The Indentured Heart*
4. *The Gentle Rebel*
5. *The Saintly Buccaneer*
6. *The Holy Warrior*
7. *The Reluctant Bridegroom*
8. *The Last Confederate*
9. *The Dixie Widow*
10. *The Wounded Yankee*
11. *The Union Belle*
12. *The Final Adversary*
13. *The Crossed Sabres*
14. *The Valiant Gunman*
15. *The Gallant Outlaw*
16. *The Jeweled Spur*
17. *The Yukon Queen*
18. *The Rough Rider*
19. *The Iron Lady*

THE LIBERTY BELL

1. *Sound the Trumpet*
2. *Song in a Strange Land*

CHENEY DUVALL, M.D.
(with Lynn Morris)

1. *The Stars for a Light*
2. *Shadow of the Mountains*
3. *A City Not Forsaken*
4. *Toward the Sunrising*

TIME NAVIGATORS
(For Young Teens)

1. *Dangerous Voyage*
2. *Vanishing Clues*

GILBERT MORRIS spent ten years as a pastor before becoming Professor of English at Ouachita Baptist University in Arkansas and earning a Ph.D. at the University of Arkansas. During the summers of 1984 and 1985 he did postgraduate work at the University of London and is presently the Chairman of General Education at a Christian college in Louisiana. A prolific writer, he has had over 25 scholarly articles and 200 poems published in various periodicals, and over the past years has had more than 20 novels published. His family includes three grown children, and he and his wife live in Baton Rouge, Louisiana.

CONTENTS

PART FOUR
The Golden Spike

THE HOUSE OF WINSLOW

★ ★ ★ ★

THE
HOUSE OF WINSLOW

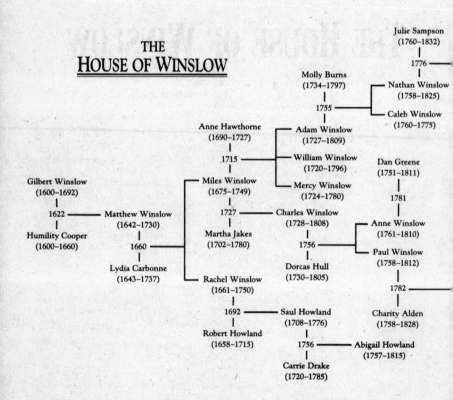

Julie Sampson
(1760–1832)

1776

Nathan Winslow
(1758–1825)

Caleb Winslow
(1760–1775)

Molly Burns
(1734–1797)

1755

Adam Winslow
(1727–1809)

Anne Hawthorne
(1690–1727)

1715

William Winslow
(1720–1796)

Dan Greene
(1751–1811)

1781

Mercy Winslow
(1724–1780)

Miles Winslow
(1675–1749)

Gilbert Winslow
(1600–1692)

1727

Charles Winslow
(1728–1808)

Anne Winslow
(1761–1810)

1622

Matthew Winslow
(1642–1730)

1756

Humility Cooper
(1600–1660)

Martha Jakes
(1702–1780)

Paul Winslow
(1758–1812)

1660

Dorcas Hull
(1730–1805)

1782

Lydia Carbonne
(1643–1737)

Rachel Winslow
(1661–1750)

Charity Alden
(1758–1828)

1692

Saul Howland
(1708–1776)

Robert Howland
(1658–1715)

1756

Abigail Howland
(1757–1815)

Carrie Drake
(1720–1785)

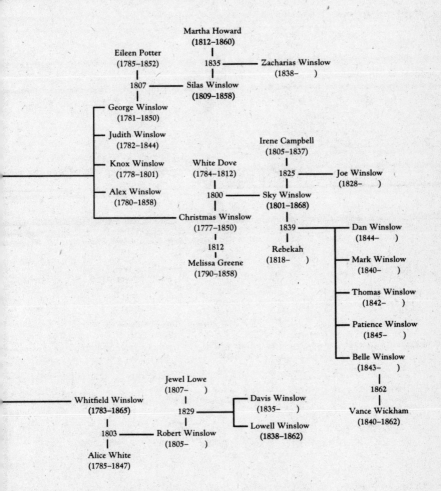

PART ONE

ESCAPE FROM TEXAS

★ ★ ★ ★

CHAPTER ONE

GUNFIGHT AT LA PALOMA BLANCA

★ ★ ★ ★

Lola came out of a coma-like sleep with a violent start the instant she felt a hand touch her. She opened her eyes to find Ramon Varga, her brother-in-law, pawing her, and instantly jerked away, rolling across the narrow bed to avoid him. The door of her small room stood open, but as soon as he saw her eyes light on it, Ramon quickly moved to block the opening.

"Get out of my room!" she said at once. "I told you to stay out of here!"

Varga was a tall man, powerfully built, though beginning to show fat. His hatchet-shaped face was dark, and his flat black eyes gleamed as he maneuvered around the bed. For all his size, Lola knew he was very quick, and she retreated until her back pressed against the wall.

"I was worried about you, Chiquita," he said. "You've been asleep for almost twelve hours."

"Next time, Ramon, knock on my door before you come in here."

His eyes suddenly glowed with anger, and he reached out and seized her shoulder. His fingers cut into her flesh like steel hooks and she could not conceal the grimace of pain that touched her face. "You never learn do you?" he said, making no attempt to conceal the pleasure that her gasp of pain gave him. "If you had any sense, Lola, you'd know by this time I'm never going to let you get away from me."

Despite the pain, Lola threw her head back defiantly, and staring straight into his face, she said, "You're a yellow cur, Ramon!" She tried to pull away, but moved too slowly to avoid the ringing slap that caught her full on the cheek. She closed her eyes, waited until the pain and the ringing in her ear subsided, then gave him a steady glance, saying, "You can hit me, but you'll never have me!"

Anger blazed in Varga's eyes, and with a curse he threw her away from him. The bed caught her behind the knees, and she fell across it, but in a quick, reflexive motion came to her feet and moved across the room to stand by the open door.

"Get out of here, Ramon," she said, her eyes filled with disgust. "Or maybe you want me to scream and let Maria know you've been after me?"

Ramon stood across the room, studying her, his expression a mixture of violent anger and admiration. He was accustomed to having his way with women, and Lola Montez's resistance both angered him and whetted his appetite. He studied her as his anger subsided, his eyes wandering over her. She was, he saw, still half exhausted, for there were faint circles under her large eyes. Those eyes were her most prominent feature, a visible inheritance from her American father. The jet black hair that fell in lush profusion over her shoulders and the olive complexion, unbelievably smooth, were gifts from her Castillian mother. Although she was barely five feet five inches in height, her carriage was so erect that she seemed tall. The plain brown cotton dress she wore did not conceal the full-bodied figure that at the age of nineteen was mature in the manner of Mexican girls. Her eyes were the darkest of blue, and the curving lips and smooth oval face made a striking combination, imparting a rare beauty that had brought her the unwelcome attention of men since she had been fifteen years old.

Even now, Ramon watched her with a look in his eyes she had grown to hate, but he was baffled by her defiant stubbornness. "You didn't learn anything the last few days, did you?" He slapped his hands together in an angry gesture, adding, "You can't run away from here—don't you see that?"

Lola thought of her abortive attempt to run away with a sinking feeling. Three days earlier she had left Eagle Pass, Texas in the middle of the night, taking what little money she had. It had been a desperate effort to get away from Varga, for he was getting bolder in his attention to her. She had known better than to get on the stage, for Varga would check that first. Her hope had been to walk north along the Rio Bravo as far as Del Rio where the stage stopped once a week. But Ramon had been too clever for her, for as soon as he discovered her flight, he had known she would either have to cross the Rio Bravo and try to hide in Mexico, or take a stage into the heart of Texas. Varga had rightly guessed that she would not cross the border, so he had sent Sid Marsh, the deputy sheriff of Eagle Pass to Laredo, while he himself had gone to Del Rio.

Lola thought of how she had walked through the cold all the way to Del Rio. The memory of the brief thrill of victory when she had gotten on the stage came to her—quickly followed by the bitterness she had felt as Ramon Varga had opened the door just before the stage pulled out for San Antonio. She had fought him, but he had the sheriff of Del Rio with him.

"I've done nothing!" she had cried. "He can't force me to go back with him!"

But the sheriff, an elderly man named Johnson, had said, "Sorry, Miss. He's got a warrant signed by a judge. It says you're charged with grand theft. You'll have to return with him."

Varga had brought her back, and now as he stood looking down at her, he seemed to read her thoughts. "Yes, I dragged you back, Chiquita, and if you run away again, I'll let them put you in the women's prison at Brownsville." His thin lips curled in a cruel smile, and he shrugged. "You may not like me so much—but you'd like that a lot less! You'd come out an old woman—and I don't want to waste all those good looks."

Fatigue from the long miles on the road had worn her down, he saw, and he stepped beside her, laying his hand on her shoulder in a soft caress, saying in a silky tone, "Chiquita—I'm not such a bad fellow. Why don't you try to like me a little? It'd make things nice for both of us."

"You're married to my sister," Lola said wearily. She had gone over this with him many times in the past, but Ramon had a morality not far removed from that of the skinny cats that roamed the town. He had been, everyone knew, the lover of Delores Montez, the owner of the cantina and the mother of Lola and Maria. Varga had been a useless vagrant, but in her loneliness, Delores had let herself be drawn to him. He had asked her to marry him many times, but she had refused, knowing that he cared nothing for her; it was her money he was after. She had died a bitter woman, burned out by her trade of dance hall girl and saloon keeper, leaving La Paloma Blanca to her daughters. It had been a simple thing for Ramon to shift his "affection" from the mother to the daughter. He had attempted to court Lola, but when she had coldly repulsed him, he had turned to Maria, five years older than Lola and already hardened beyond her years. They had been married, and it had been Ramon's next move to get Lola's half-interest in the cantina.

That was on his mind as he stood there stroking Lola's shoulder, and he murmured in answer to her statement, "Maria knows better than to question anything I do." He took her other shoulder, pulled her against him, and before she could protest, kissed her.

Lola broke away and shook her head. "Ramon, just leave me alone!"

"I'll never do that, Chiquita! I've got to have you!" He moved toward her, but she drew back, and he shrugged. Turning, he moved to a chair beside the door and picked up something. "Here's a nice dress I bought for you in Del Rio. I want you in the bar tonight."

"I have to do the cooking." La Paloma Blanca was more or less a hotel—rooms upstairs with a bar and a restaurant downstairs. Three girls—including Maria—worked the bar, but Lola had for the most part managed to avoid that duty by doing the cooking for the diners.

"I hired a cook. From now on, you help with the bar. We'll be busy tonight," he said as he turned to go. He paused at the door and added, "Play your guitar—and be nice to the cowboys. They'll all be anxious to spend their money." He gave her a knowing look, and added, "We'll talk about us later."

He stepped outside and shut the door, almost running into his wife who had evidently been standing there. "What have you been doing in Lola's room?" she demanded instantly. She was shorter than Lola, and had a different father, an Indian who had left as soon as Maria had been born. Once she had been a shapely girl, but her liking for rich spicy food and liquor had thickened her body, and though she still had a coarse attractiveness, it was a fading bloom that no longer excited Varga.

"I took her the dress she's going to wear tonight," he said carelessly.

"It's a bad idea—her working the bar. And letting her deal blackjack is worse." Maria's voice was thick, for she had been drinking. "She don't know how to act. Keeps herself away from men like she was something special." She shook her head stubbornly. "I'm going to fire that cook and let Lola do the cooking."

She gave a sharp cry as his strong fingers closed on her arm, her eyes suddenly opening with fear. "You get down to the bar, Maria," he said sharply, "or I'll give you some of what I gave you last time."

"Ow! Don't, Ramon!" she gasped, and the resistance fled from her face. "You're breaking my arm!"

Varga tightened his grip on her and raised his other hand, causing her to cower, as the tears streaked her heavy make-up. "Go fix your face," he ordered, "then get to the bar."

She stumbled down the hall, and he watched her go with satisfaction. He regretted that he had had to marry her to get an interest in the business—but he had taken steps to remedy that. He had forced her to sign her interest over to him, and someday, he knew, he would rid himself of her. The thought pleased him, and as he glanced at Lola's door, he smiled and moved down the hall toward the steps descending to the bar downstairs.

★　★　★　★

The cold February wind cut through the thin, worn coat of the rider who appeared at the end of Front Street, causing him to halt his horse long enough to turn up his collar. Realizing the futility of the gesture, he shrugged and spurred the horse, an undersized roan with ribs showing like a picket fence. The animal groaned and plodded slowly down the street until the rider recognized a stable and pulled him up. He stepped off stiffly, opened one of the large doors, and led the horse into the dim interior.

"Señor, I will take your horse."

"He's about worn out. Give him some grain."

He responded in Spanish to the small Mexican who came out of one of the stalls to take the reins, then said in English, "I need something to eat and a place to sleep."

The stable hand nodded. "Try La Paloma Blanca, Señor. Two blocks down the street." He shrugged and added, "The rooms are dumps, but the food's not bad. You staying long?"

"No. Just tonight."

"This horse won't make it far."

The tall man made no answer. Pulling his bedroll off the horse, he turned and left the stable, walking down the main street. He moved slowly, as if he were very tired, and from time to time, a cough shook his body. Eagle Pass, he noted, was somewhat larger than most border towns, and by the time he got to the cantina with the faded sign that read LA PALOMA BLANCA over a pair of swinging doors, he was breathing hard against the cold gusts of wind that swept along the sidewalks, sending small bits of paper whirling along the street.

A blast of warm air welcomed him as he stepped into what seemed to be a lobby, and the smell of food awakened his starved senses. He took off his worn hat, noting that a large barroom lay beyond the open door on his left. To his right was a fairly large room with tables, which he entered at once. He took a seat beside a window, and although it was only four in the afternoon, about a fourth of the tables were occupied mostly by roughly dressed men.

A young Mexican boy wearing an apron came to his table. "Señor, what will you have?" The boy paused for only a moment before hastening to add, "We only offer frijoles, steak and chicken."

"A steak and potatoes—milk if you've got it, and some kind of pie."

"Sí. We have some apple pie."

A pot-bellied stove stood in the center of the room radiating waves of warmth. He had gotten wet crossing the Rio Bravo, and his feet began to throb as the heat thawed them out. He thrust them out toward the stove and slumped over the table, finding it an effort to keep his head up. He nodded, caught himself, and shook his shoulders. Getting to his feet, he walked slowly over to the stove and held his hands out to catch the heat, aware that he was being watched by some of the customers.

They saw a tall man of twenty-six, half an inch over six feet, with hair and eyebrows black as a crow's wing. He had a broad forehead, smoky gray eyes and a heavy nose. His hair was shaggy and his clothes tattered and worn, his boots run down at the heels. There was a suggestion of strength in his body, but he looked thin and there was a hollowness in his cheeks, as well as a red flush that gave him an unhealthy look. His hands were large, and he seemed to have been heavier at one time than he appeared. He wore a Colt on his right thigh, an ancient weapon, worn with use, and the tips of his fingers brushed it as he moved away from the stove back to the table where the boy was setting his meal down.

He ate slowly at first, then faster, forcing himself to chew thoroughly. He called for more milk twice, and asked for coffee to wash the pie down. It was very mediocre fare, but the young waiter noticed that he ate with enjoyment, cleaning his plate, then sitting back to nurse his coffee, sipping it with the satisfaction of one who has been long without such comfort.

Finally he stood up and moved to where the boy was wiping off a table. "How much do I owe you?"

"One dollar."

He reached into his vest pocket, pulled out some money, and selecting a coin, handed it over. "You have a room?"

"See Ramon, Señor. In the bar."

"Gracias."

He moved out of the restaurant, crossed the foyer and entered the bar. It was beginning to grow dark outside, and a barkeeper was lighting the lamps that were mounted on the wall. "Ramon?" he asked. The barkeep nodded toward a large Mexican who was leaning against the bar. "That's him."

Mark Winslow moved across the sawdust floor. "I need a room."

"Why, we can fix you up. Be two dollars for one night." The man added, "I'm the owner here, Ramon Varga."

Mark nodded, but made no reply.

"Little bit early for bed," Varga suggested. "Have a drink on the house."

Winslow took the drink that the barkeep brought at the wave of Varga, swallowed it, and nodded. "Thanks." He pulled his shoulders back and said, "Guess I'm pretty tired. Which room?"

"Take number four, head of the stairs, turn right," Ramon nodded. "Be a game tonight. Come and try your luck after you get rested up."

"Maybe I will."

Ramon waited until he left, then said to the barkeep, "Just come out of Mexico, I think. Probably with the Federales after him." He weighed Winslow, then shrugged, "No money. Looks like he's getting out with nothing but the clothes on his back."

Winslow climbed the stairs slowly, found number four, and entered. It was not much—merely a closet-sized cubicle with a sagging bed, one chair and a table with a basin and water pitcher. He threw his bedroll on the floor, moved to the stand, and took a drink of stale water from the pitcher. The room was cold, and after taking a look at the worn blanket on the bed, he bent and unfastened the one he'd brought. His teeth were beginning to chatter, and he took off his gunbelt, then fell on the bed, wrapping the blanket around him. He fell asleep instantly and slept for four hours without moving.

He awoke slowly, his mind thick with sleep, the sound of raucous music below slamming harshly against his ears. He unwrapped the blanket, left it on the bed and got to his feet. The fading evening glow threw his shadow across the bare wall. His head ached and every thread of clothing he had on was drenched with sweat. "Must have sweated the fever off," he muttered, and moving to the washstand, he drank thirstily from the pitcher, then filled the basin and noisily washed his face and hands. There was no towel, so he briskly wiped the water off with his hands. Removing his shirt, he tossed it on the bed and took the lone shirt that remained in his bedroll and put it on. He buckled on his gunbelt, started to leave, then thought of his bedroll. With no lock on the door, anyone could step in and steal it. Then he smiled cynically and murmured, "They wouldn't get much anyway," and left the room.

A hard rain was falling on the roof as he came down the stairs. The dining area was dark, so he moved through the doorway into the bar. The barkeep nodded and asked, "What'll it be?"

"I could use some coffee."

"Help yourself." The man picked up a mug from the shelf behind him, then pointed to a large stove over by one wall with a huge black coffee pot on top. "You buy as many as three drinks, you get the free lunch," he commented while pointing to a tray of sandwiches.

Winslow got his coffee, came back to the bar and waggled his fingers at the bartender. "Give me a bottle," he said. When it was placed in front of him, he drank off half the coffee, poured whiskey in to replace it, and stood there sipping it slowly. Finally he picked up two of the sandwiches and carried them with the bottle and the mug to an empty table. The cantina was crowded, with cowpunchers making up the bulk of the customers. They lined the bar and there were two poker games going. A thin American was dealing faro at a table to Winslow's right. At a table against the wall a dark-haired young woman with a clear olive complexion was dealing blackjack. She lifted her eyes and gave him a steady stare, then looked down at the cards again.

He ate slowly, not really hungry, but knowing that he had a long way to go and needed the energy the food would provide. Twice he filled his cup half-full of coffee, then topped it off with the raw whiskey, and once he went back and got another sandwich. He chewed on it slowly, only half conscious of the loud laughter that filled the room. A Mexican woman came to stand before him once, invitation in her eyes, but he shook his head and she left for more likely company. The dark-haired woman dealing cards stopped to play the guitar and sing in a clear alto voice, and the customers stomped and yelled, clapping their hands for more. Winslow gave her a closer look, noting that she had almost no paint on her face and seemed to be alienated from the crowd. Several men pushed up to ask her to dance, he noticed, but she shook her head and busied herself waiting on tables.

"Like to join us?" Winslow's attention focused on two men at the table next to his. The one who had spoken was a tall, skinny man of thirty with a heavy moustache and shaggy brown hair. "Name's Lonnie Brinks—this here is Joe Simpson," he said, nodding at a short, muscular fellow with fair, sunburned skin and wearing a broad-brimmed Mexican sombrero. They were both obviously cowhands, and seemed more sober than most of the crowd.

"Thanks," Mark said. "I'm Mark Winslow. I'm not too well heeled at the moment."

"Aw, we're just playing penny ante poker," Brinks shrugged. "We done spent all our pay on a big bust. Got to go back to work now and lay in for the next trip to town. Might as well join us."

Winslow got up and moved to the table, and for the next thirty minutes the three of them played a leisurely game. Brinks did most of the talking, and soon revealed that both of them worked for Faye Hunter at the Box M Ranch. It was, according to both Brinks and Simpson, the biggest and lowest paying ranch in southern Texas. Their dislike for their employer was muted, but plain from their talk. Both of them, Winslow noted, carefully avoided asking any personal questions, but broad hints revealed Brinks's curiosity.

The pretty girl who played the guitar had come over to bring the pair fresh drinks, when Brinks said innocently, "Guess if a fellow was going to travel far, he might run into some snow up north, wouldn't you say?"

Mark grinned and nodded. "Hope not, because that's where I'm headed."

"Going up as far as Dallas, maybe?" Lonnie asked, leaning back to let the girl pour his drink.

"Farther than that, Lonnie," Mark shrugged. "Going all the way to Omaha." He started to say more, but the girl had lifted her head suddenly at his words, spilling the whiskey on the table.

"Hey, Miss!" Lonnie exclaimed. "Don't want to be baptized in the stuff—just like to have enough to drink."

"I'm sorry," she said quietly. She quickly mopped the whiskey from the table and refilled his glass, then moved to the next table and began cleaning it.

"Omaha, you say?" Lonnie picked up the conversation again. "Why, you'd have to go right through the Indian Territory to git there—and in the middle of winter! You shore want to go there more'n I do!"

Winslow shrugged his shoulders, and a wry smile crossed his broad lips. "Got to go where the work is."

"Railroad man?" Simpson asked. "I hear they're trying to build a railroad all the way to California. Been working on it a year, ain't they?"

"That's right." Winslow hesitated, then added, "I was working on a railroad down in Mexico until the Revolution caught up with me."

"Heard about that. Guess you picked the wrong side, hey?" Lonnie asked, giving him a sharp look. Both punchers had noted the pallor of Winslow's face and the poor shape he was in. "They stick you in one of them blamed prisons down there?"

"Just got out three days ago," Winslow said slowly.

"I hear that ain't no Sunday School picnic," Simpson said after a pause.

Winslow looked up and his lips compressed tightly at the dark memories rising in him. "No, it's not," he said quietly.

"If it was a little earlier, we could maybe get you on at the Box M," Lonnie said. "But most of the hands is laid off now." He motioned across the room where several men were playing poker. "That's Boyd Hunter—the big one with the vest. He's the owner's son. I could maybe ask him if he could take you on."

"No, thanks, Lonnie," Winslow shook his head. "I've got to be in Omaha by spring, and it'll just about take that long to get there on the scarecrow of a horse I'm riding."

The three of them played a few more hands, and Mark found himself growing tired. "Looks like I owe you a dollar and fifty cents, Lonnie," he said, getting to his feet.

"Aw, forget it," the tall puncher said. "You can make it back . . ." A sudden commotion across the room caused all three of them to turn their gaze on the poker game. The piano player stopped abruptly, and Mark saw that two men were standing facing each other, one of them the man Lonnie had identified as Boyd Hunter. Hunter had the girl who had brought the drinks by the arm, and she was struggling futilely to get away.

Lonnie said under his breath, "Larry ought to know better than to get Boyd all stirred up when he's drinking."

"Looks like they're havin' it out over that purty Mex gal," Simpson murmured. He shook his head, and added, "Larry better pull out of it. Boyd can pull that gun mighty fast."

Mark decided that he wanted no part of the thing. He turned and began walking toward the door. He was halfway there when suddenly he saw Hunter draw his gun and with one quick movement smash the man called Larry across the head, driving him to the floor.

Varga stepped in between the men to bend over the limp form, then stood up, announcing, "He's not dead." Licking his lips nervously, he said, "Let the girl go, Hunter. You've got her scared."

Boyd Hunter was no more than twenty-three, but had a blatant arrogance in his slate-colored eyes. "She's a saloon girl, ain't she, Varga?" He pulled the girl closer and grinned, "Well, I'm a customer and she's here to entertain me."

Mark would have left the room, but as Hunter finished his sentence, he gave the girl's arm such a squeeze that she cried out. The agonizing sound tugged at Winslow, and he stopped abruptly, wheeling to face the group. Hunter caught the motion out of the corner of his eye and half-turned to face him. His eyes went small as he focused on Mark, and he snapped, "We're doin' right well without your help. Move it out!"

A stubborn streak ran through Mark, and he did not move at the command of Hunter. He stood there making a sorry figure in the worn clothes and run-over boots, and his gaunt form looked ineffectual as he faced the angry ranch hand. A silence had fallen over the room, and the blood was beginning to throb in his temples, just as it had before he had plunged into battle during the war.

Something told him he was a fool, that he'd wind up in another jail—or else dead on the floor, but there was a rashness that characterized Mark Winslow. The Mexican guards had seen it, and it had meant a hard time for him as they tried to extinguish the defiance in his eyes. It was something that made him get up when he was knocked down, that drove him forward when other men refused to go, and it had left scars on his body over the years.

Deliberately, he turned and moved across the floor until he

stood no more than five feet from Hunter. He said softly, "You're hard on a woman, aren't you?"

The words were quiet, but Hunter flared up, his face reddening with anger. He was a man who could not refuse a challenge, and he saw something in the eyes of the shabbily dressed stranger that made him stiffen and loosen his grip on the girl's arm. He tilted forward on his toes, cursed Winslow, and threw a hard right at Mark's face. It would have ended the fight, for Hunter was a big man with the full weight of his body behind the punch, but Mark threw up his left arm, deflected the punch, and in one motion caught Hunter by the shirt. Using the man's own force, Mark gave a tremendous jerk that sent the larger man flailing across the room. Hunter failed to catch his balance and went crashing into a table, pulling it over with him as he went down in a crash of broken glass and wood.

He was not hurt, and kicked a chair in anger as he struggled to his feet. With a roar he flung himself at Mark, his face flaming. The cowboy's left fist caught Mark in the temple, a disaster that brought a crimson curtain over his eyes for a moment. He grabbed Hunter and hung on blindly until his head cleared, taking several wild punches around the head. Then he suddenly lifted his boot and stamped on Hunter's foot with all his might. Hunter let out a yell of pain, and when he involuntarily stepped back and lifted the injured foot, Mark leaned back and drove home a smashing right hand that caught the man square in the mouth.

Hunter's cry was cut off short, and he was driven back once more. His eyes were blank as he sat down abruptly on the dusty floor, and Mark thought the fight was over. He waited until Hunter's eyes cleared, then asked, "Any more?" The cowboy shook his head, and Mark turned and started toward the door.

A shout caught him—"Look out!" It was a woman's voice, and he whirled to see that Hunter had drawn his gun and trained it on him! Before he could move, a shot thundered in the room, and he felt a fiery streak of pain rip through his left side. He turned sideways, drawing his Colt, and another explosion rocked the room. His hat shifted as the bullet touched it, and then he lifted his gun hip high and pulled the trigger.

The slug caught Hunter high in the chest, and he threw his

hands up in a wild gesture as he was driven back. His gun flew through the air, striking Ramon Varga on the leg before clattering to the floor. A heavy-set Mexican woman began to scream and Varga said sharply, "Shut up, Maria!" Then he went to bend over the fallen Hunter. He straightened up and said, "Better get Doc Wright, Juan." The barkeep scurried out of the room, and Mark suddenly felt the presence of the Box M men behind him. He started to turn, but had no chance. He felt a hard object in his back, and a voice said, "Just take his gun, Sonny." A young puncher stepped forward and Mark had no alternative but to hand it to him. When he moved as if to leave, he turned and saw a hard-bitten older man staring at him, his gun fixed on him.

"It was self-defense," Mark said. "You all saw it."

The Box M man shrugged. "You'll have your chance to prove it. But if I let you go, Faye Hunter himself would shoot me. Come on."

The muzzle of the gun gave Mark no choice. He walked unsteadily toward the door, gripping his bleeding side. Accompanied by four other men, including Brinks and Simpson, the group moved outside.

"Where you taking me?"

"Have to put you in the lockup until we see how she floats. Head down that way."

The cold wind bit at Mark's lips as he marched along the board sidewalk. He said nothing, nor did any of the Box M men. The only sound was the keening of the wind through the cracks of the buildings. A despair began to settle in Winslow, and he cursed himself for not walking away from the scene.

The jail was a log building, and when they walked inside, Mark saw a fat man asleep on a cot beside the wall. The only other furniture was a battered desk. Two cells spanned the width of the building, one of them occupied by three men, the other empty.

"Wake up, Sid," the leader said tersely, and the fat man woke up abruptly, his eyes growing large at the sight of the small crowd.

"What's up, Max?" he said, getting to his feet.

"Lock this fellow up, Sid."

The deputy stared at Mark. "What for?"

"He shot Boyd," Max said.

Sid's eyes opened, and he clucked, "That's too bad. He dead?"

"Not yet—but you hold this bird until we can get word to Mr. Hunter."

"Sure." With alacrity, the deputy seized a set of keys and opened the empty cell. "In here." He shut the door and asked, "What's his name?"

Max shrugged. "Don't know. Who are you, fellow?"

Mark shot a quick glance at Lonnie and Joe, then took a breath and lied, "My name's Frank Holland. I come from Missouri." He waited for one of the two men to speak, but with glad appreciation saw that Lonnie elbowed his friend in the side and remained silent.

"If you let him get away, Sid, Faye Hunter will roast you over a slow fire," Max said. Then he turned and said, "Potter, you ride to the ranch and get Mr. Hunter. The rest of us will stick around town."

They all trooped out, and Mark fought down a rising fear. He could face any situation better than he could face being locked up, and it took all his will to force himself to go over and lie down on the bed after the cell door clanged shut. His nerves clawed wildly, and he stared at the ceiling, willing himself to be still. He heard the prisoners in the next cell asking him about the fight, but he did not respond. Finally Sid came to stare into the cell, and after looking at the still form of Winslow, he shook his head and said mournfully, "Son, I shore do wish you'd have picked somebody else to plug!"

Mark moved his head to look up at the deputy. "He didn't give me much choice. It was self-defense."

Sid rocked back and forth on his heels. "Well, that'd be fine and dandy with anybody else in Eagle Pass—but not with old Faye Hunter. He's a bad one, that man is!"

"No jury would convict me. Everybody in the room saw Hunter draw first!"

"And how many of them was Box M punchers?" Sid shrugged his fat shoulders. "Faye Hunter ain't much for courtroom justice, anyhow. If that son of his dies, he's got enough men on his payroll to pull this jail down and string you up on the nearest tree." He had a sad bulldog face that had seen more than its share of trouble, and he stood there staring down at Winslow with a fatalistic cast.

"Sure wisht you'd put that slug in a Mexican 'stead of Boyd Hunter," he sighed, then moved back and took a bottle out of the desk. He drank the liquor eagerly, and in twenty minutes was asleep.

Mark lay there for over an hour, trying to think of some plan to escape, but none came to him. The door suddenly burst open, and a short, thin man wearing a black suit and carrying a small bag came in. He had a pair of sharp black eyes and said with irritation, "Marsh—open the cell!"

Sid came awake fuzzily. "Whazzat?" His eyes focused with difficulty, and he said, "Oh, it's you, Doc." He reached for the keys, and asked, "Hunter dead?"

"Not yet." The small man moved into Mark's cell, and the deputy slammed the steel door behind him. "Let's see where that slug took you," he said briskly.

Mark stripped off his shirt, and after a quick look at the raw furrow, the doctor said, "That won't kill you." He opened his bag and washed the wound out with antiseptic. "By the way, I'm Doc Wright." He pulled out some bandages and was making them fast when the door opened again, and Mark looked over Wright's shoulder to see a huge man fill the opening. He was so tall he had to duck his peaked hat beneath the door frame, a great florid Texan with leathered skin, massive jaws and eyes of marbled agate.

His voice bellowed out, "You—Doc Wright! How's my boy?"

Wright, busy bandaging Mark, looked over his shoulder without pausing his fingers as he said, "He's alive, Faye."

The huge man came and grasped the bars of the cell as if he wanted to tear them down. "Fellow, you'll hang for shooting my boy!"

Mark didn't answer, but he felt the hate oozing from the man, and knew that Faye Hunter would never be satisfied until he tasted revenge.

Wright finished the bandage, stood up and put his things back into his bag. "Boyd's not dead yet, Faye. And even if he dies, I hear it was self-defense. Sid, let me out of here."

The deputy opened the door, giving an apprehensive glance at the huge Hunter, who took a step toward Mark as the door opened.

"Come on, Faye," Wright said quickly. "Let's go see how Boyd is doing."

"All right, Doc—but you keep this fellow jugged tight, Sid, you hear me?"

"Sure, Mr. Hunter," Sid said nervously. "He ain't goin' no place." He waited until the pair had left, then turned to face Mark. Pulling a soiled handkerchief out of his pocket, he wiped his brow, saying mournfully, "Holland, I shore do wisht you'd had better judgment! If Boyd dies, you ain't got no more chance than a snowball in perdition—and even if he lives, I ain't puttin' it past Faye Hunter to string you up. He's jest that kind of a man!"

Mark turned and moved to stand beside the small barred window. It faced the north, and the wind whipped through it. Somewhere in that darkness, hundreds of miles away, was Omaha. But the longer he stood there, the less he believed that he would ever see it.

CHAPTER TWO

SHEDDING THE PRISON WALLS

★ ★ ★ ★

"The gringo is lucky!"

Lola paused on her way out of the bar, halting long enough to hear Ramon continue speaking to one of the Bar M riders. "He would be swinging from a tree right now if Hunter had died."

"Yeah, Faye would have lynched him then all right," she heard someone answer, "but he'll still make certain Holland does five years in the pen." Lola cast a look at the pair, recognizing the foreman of the Bar M, a man called Max, leaning against the bar. "I heard Mr. Hunter spell it out to Judge Hardesty this morning." Hardesty was the circuit judge, and it was universally understood that he was a puppet for Faye Hunter, the most powerful man in that part of the state.

"That's pretty raw, Max," Ramon commented.

"Go tell Mr. Hunter that, Varga," Max grinned.

"Not me! When's the trial?"

"Soon as the judge gets here—day after tomorrow. It won't be a long trial, I reckon. They'll have Holland in the prison at El Paso so quick he won't know what hit him! That's a real rough place, Ramon. Me, I just about as soon stretch rope as do five years hard labor there!"

Lola hurried out of the bar and went to the kitchen to look

over the steaming pots that Barnabas, the new cook, had started. She lifted the lid on one, tasted the contents, nodded at the smallish Mexican who was watching her anxiously. "Very good, Barnabas," she said; then a thought came to her. "What about dinner for the prisoners?"

"Sheriff Marsh said only one today. He let all the drunks out."

Lola's expression changed slightly, and she said, "I'll take it to the jail, Barnabas. I want you to cook the whole noon meal today."

"Sí, Señorita Montez."

Lola put together two lunches of beef and beans on tin plates, adding bread and two generous slices of pie for dessert. She filled a small jug with cool tea, sweetened it, then put everything on a tray and covered it with a towel. It was a little before noon when she left the Paloma, and the streets were filled with mud from heavy rain. She made her way to the jail on a flimsy series of boards that gurgled in the yellow mud as she stepped on them. The jail door stood ajar and she found Sid Marsh seated in his chair behind the battered desk.

"Señor Marsh," she smiled as she entered. "I have brought you a good lunch—and one for the prisoner."

"Why bless your little heart, Lola!" Marsh exclaimed as he looked over the food.

Lola's smile disappeared as she began to set a place for Marsh at his desk. "Oh, Sheriff. . . !" she exclaimed.

"What's wrong, Lola?"

"I had you two bottles of that good beer you like so much—but I left them in the cooler!"

Sheriff Marsh's eyes lit up, for he loved the lager beer that Ramon kept for special occasions. "Why, I'll just step down the street and get them, Lola."

"Tell Barnabas I said to give you three bottles—to make up for your having to go after them."

"Sure will! I'll have to lock you in the building—but it won't take me but two shakes of a duck's tail to get that beer!"

He left hurriedly and Lola at once picked up the tray and walked over to the cell. She watched carefully as the man got up, then stooped and slid the tray under the lower bar. She walked back and filled a mug with cool tea and handed it to him through the bars.

"Thanks." He sat down and began to eat, then looked up, aware she was watching him. His face was gaunt, the beard and hair lank with sweat, and red spots high on his cheeks indicated that he had a fever.

She took a deep breath and almost turned and walked away, but a thought pulled at her, and her lips grew firm. "They're going to send you to prison for five years," she said.

He took a sip of the tea, then turned his eyes on her. "That's what the sheriff tells me." He watched her curiously a moment, for her demeanor puzzled him. She was wearing a modest brown dress instead of the low-cut saloon dress she had worn when he saw her last, and she looked much younger.

She finally spoke softly, "I . . . uh . . . thank you . . . for stopping Hunter."

Mark smiled uncomfortably and looked down at his hands.

A lengthy silence followed before she continued, "I heard you say last night you were on your way to Omaha."

He considered the statement, not understanding what was on her mind. "That's where I *was* headed." He looked down at his hands for a long moment, and when he raised his head his face was bitter. "Looks like I'll be a little bit late. The railroad will be finished by the time I get out of the pen."

"You work for a railroad?"

"Since the war." He regarded her carefully, then added, "I've been in prison down in Mexico. Hired out to build a railroad, but I was working for the wrong side, I guess. The winning railroad company put me in jail." Rash anger brightened his eyes and his fists clenched. "Because of last night, I'm headed back into the same nightmare."

Lola said suddenly, "I can get you out of here—but you'll have to take me with you to Omaha."

He stared at her, then shook his head. "That's crazy. Even if I got out of here, I couldn't get away. They'd have me back in a day!"

She ignored his hopeless response and hurried on, "We've only got a few minutes until Sid gets back." He saw the determined set of her jaw and the intensity in her eyes. "I've got to get away from here myself, but I can't do it alone. If I get you clear of this jail—*and* out of Texas—will you promise to take me to Omaha with you?"

He nodded, dumbfounded, and stammered, "Why do you want to go to Omaha?"

"That's not your business," she said firmly. "Eat your food. Sleep all you can today. Tonight I'll stop in and bring the night man something to drink. It'll put him out, and I'll unlock the cell."

"What then?"

She stared at him and said, "You don't need to know that now. I will arrange something, but I want you to promise me three things before I do." She gripped the bars and said, "First, you'll do what I tell you—no matter how crazy it sounds—until we're clear of Eagle Pass. Second, you'll take me to Omaha. After we get there, you can forget me."

She paused, and he prompted, "You said three things."

She hesitated, then looked him full in the face. "You will not touch me while we are on the way to Omaha." A flush touched her cheeks and she added, "Do you understand?"

He smiled despite her seriousness. "I agree to all three. Do we put it in writing?"

She shook her head, paying no mind to his patronizing tone. "Eat your food. I want to leave as soon as I can. Remember what I've said."

He nodded and ate rapidly. When the sheriff returned Lola smiled politely at him. "I have to go now. Would you send the dishes back with Tomas when he comes in?"

"Sure will!" Sid was already eating when she left, and she deliberately did not look at the prisoner. When she stepped outside, she paused and leaned against the wall. Her hands trembled and her heart beat fast as the near impossibility of successfully carrying out the promise she had just made became clearer to her. Her recent attempt at escape had convinced her that it would take some extraordinary method to get away from Ramon and Eagle Pass, but a fragment of a plan had popped into her mind when she had heard the stranger say he was going to Omaha. She had planned to go to him in his room, but now that he was in jail the whole thing seemed impossible.

There was, however, a stubbornness in Lola Montez, and all morning she had been considering a new plan. She knew that she had to take care of some things before she and Frank Holland could shake off their respective shackles. The thought came to her that Holland might have refused her before—but now that he was locked up he had no choice! He proved he was a strong man in the fight with Boyd Hunter. Whether or not he would keep his word was yet to be seen.

She lifted her head higher in resolve and moved along the street, turning the corner and entering an office with a sign beside the door that read ANTHONY FUENTES—LEGAL COUNSEL in block letters. It was a modest office, but she knew that aside from Faye Hunter, the small man with the big head was probably the most powerful man in Eagle Pass.

"Why, hello, Lola." Fuentes had been sitting at his desk writing, but he got up and moved around to greet her. His large brown eyes watched her as they watched everything else—with a certain amount of cautious suspicion. "What brings you here?"

"I want to do something, Señor Fuentes," she said somewhat reluctantly. "But it will sound very strange to you."

Fuentes smiled reassuringly. "Nothing is strange to a lawyer, Lola." He pulled a chair up close to the desk and waved his hand. "Sit down and tell me."

She still hesitated, for she was unsure of the man's loyalties. He had been her mother's lawyer, and Lola knew that her mother had trusted him as much as she had ever trusted any man— which wasn't a great deal. Now she sat there trying to find a way to say what she wanted, but the words wouldn't come.

"Most people come to see lawyers because they're either in trouble or about to make trouble for someone else," Fuentes smiled again. "Which is it with you, Lola?"

She made her mind up to trust him. "Both!" She took a deep breath, leaned forward and rapidly told the lawyer how Ramon had made life miserable for her. She ended by saying, "I've got to get away, Señor Fuentes! I must!"

He studied her face, and she had the impression that he had already known all that she had revealed. He picked up a letter opener, balanced it carefully, then quietly asked, "And who are you going to make trouble for, then?"

She gave him a direct stare and said bluntly, "You, I am afraid, Señor."

He gave no indication of what he felt, but then a smile touched his thin lips. "You will have to get in line for that, I fear. There are many who do not care for me. But what is the nature of this trouble you are going to give me, Lola?"

"I want you to buy my interest in the Paloma Blanca."

That *did* surprise Fuentes, she saw. His eyebrows lifted and his lips pursed. "And why would that be trouble?"

"Because you would be a partner with Ramon—and he would be troublesome to anyone."

"Oh, I think not. If anything, I would be the one giving Ramon a problem." He stared at her, his large eyes searching her, and she stared back, unflinching. "How much would you want for your half of the property?" he asked finally.

She hesitated, then decided, "I don't know what it's worth, Señor, but I must have $2,000 to get away from here."

Fuentes said at once, "It's worth that—and much more."

"But I want the money right now—in cash."

"You mean today?"

"I mean in one hour!"

He straightened and shook his head. "Lola, in this world, it's dog-eat-dog. I would deceive a man when I felt it necessary, but I wouldn't like to cheat you." He laughed and said, "I didn't realize I still had a conscience! It's worth two thousand just to discover it again!"

Lola shook her head, and he saw the desperation in her eyes. "Will you do it, Señor? I must have the money today—and I'm willing to sign the papers."

He studied her and asked, "Do you want to tell me anything else, Lola? Anything about your plans?"

Lola slowly pulled a single sheet of paper from her pocket and handed it to him. "I found this six months ago. It's from my father."

He quickly glanced over the brief letter.

Dear Delores,

 I have written you five times since coming to Omaha, but have received no answer. I would like to do something for our daughter Lola, as I have said before. Please answer this as soon as you can so I can do so. I have nothing but regrets that you have chosen not to remain married to me, but at least let me help our daughter.

Jude

Fuentes looked up at her. "You intend to find your father?"

"Yes."

"Do you know where he is now?"

She hesitated. "Still in Omaha, I hope."

"It might be hard, Lola. And you might not like the life there."

"Anything is better than here, Señor!" She did not tell him that she had never known her father's last name, and that the only clue she had to his identity was a faded picture. "Please, will you buy my share of the cantina?"

Fuentes considered her carefully. Taking a sheet of paper out of a drawer he began to write. Without looking up he said, "All right. The deal is on." She watched him as he carefully filled the sheet, then he got up and moved swiftly toward the door. "I'll be right back."

Her nerves jumping, she waited until he came back with John Mellon, the banker, and Titus Walker, one of the clerks. "Now, if you'll just sign right here, Miss Montez," he said, pausing until she had completed his instructions, "and if you gentlemen will just sign here as witnesses. . . ." He watched quietly until the two had signed, then nodded his approval. "Thank you, gentlemen," and the men left at once, neither having uttered a word.

Fuentes took the sheet of paper, signed it himself and put it in the drawer, then pulled a sheaf of bills out of his coat pocket. "I got some of the cash in small bills, Lola," he said as he counted it out for her. "I thought that might be easier for you."

"Gracias, Señor Fuentes!" Lola tucked the bills into the pocket of her jacket and turned to leave. "Good-bye, Señor," she said with a satisfying air of finality.

"Vaya con Dios!" he said quietly, and for a long time after she left, he sat at his desk staring into space, wondering at the thing that had just happened. He took the paper out of the drawer, and his thin lips curved in a cynical smile as he thought of Ramon

Varga's response when he walked in and announced their new partnership.

Lola made her way across town, acutely conscious of the sheaf of banknotes in her pocket. *I've got to do it now,* she thought, and a heady excitement surged through her as she passed the edge of town and entered a run-down area of small adobe huts. She passed several women, all of them calling to her by name, and finally stopped before a house that seemed to be surrounded by brown Mexican children of all ages. A harried-looking woman came out to meet her, saying, "Señorita Lola, you come to our house!"

"Hello, Louise. Is Victor here?"

"Sí. I will get him for you. He is taking a siesta."

Lola bent down and picked up a small girl pulling at her skirt, talking amiably with her until a man came outside. She put the child down and said firmly, "Come with me, Victor. I want to talk to you."

He was a strong-looking man of some forty years, with piercing black eyes and visible signs of Indian blood. "Sí, Señorita," he mumbled, and the two of them walked away from the house.

"Victor, I need your help."

"Yes?"

Lola had thought over what she was going to say, and for half an hour the two of them spoke as they walked along aimlessly. Victor's heavy face was not one that revealed a great deal, but as he listened and asked questions, he seemed both amused and startled. Finally she asked, "Will you do it, Victor?"

He nodded at once. "Why, yes, Señorita."

"It will be dangerous, you understand?"

He shrugged and the fatalistic strain of his Indian blood spoke. "It is dangerous to cross Varga, Señorita Lola. But what you wish to do will be a help to my family."

"Very well, let's go over it one more time—and you must explain it very carefully to your family. . . ."

They talked for another fifteen minutes, then she pulled the sheaf of bills from her pocket and counted out some of them. He shoved them inside his shirt, and she left him at once. It was almost three when she returned, and her sister was raging.

"Where have you been?" Maria demanded. "That idiot of a

cook Ramon hired has burned most of supper. Get in and help him with it or we won't make a dime tonight."

"All right," Lola said easily. She put her arm around the other woman in an unexpected gesture and said, "Don't fret, Maria."

"Well enough for you to talk!"

Lola said gently, "Maria, do you ever think of the time when we were little girls?"

Maria stared at her, nonplussed by the unexpected question. "No. I never think of it."

"I do. I was only four, but I remember my father, I think. You must remember him very well."

"He was a religious fanatic!" Maria exclaimed. "Mama and I couldn't stand it—that's why she made him go. You would have hated it, too, if you'd been older! Church all the time—and always talking about Jesus!"

"He was kind though, wasn't he?"

"Oh, he was kind enough—but he drove us crazy with his churchgoing." Maria continued to stare at her half-sister. "Why are you asking about him?"

"Oh, I just think of him sometimes." Lola tried to make her next question seem casual. "I don't think I ever heard Mama mention what his family name was. Do you remember?"

"No. Now get the supper fixed! You can think about him later!"

Lola was disappointed, but she knew better than to ask Maria any more questions. She nodded and went to help the frantic Barnabas remedy the dinner.

She tried to stay in the kitchen as long as possible, but soon Ramon stomped in and barked, "Get dressed and into the bar, Lola. It's already full."

She ran upstairs and changed into the low-cut dress he had bought, and for the next four hours she moved around the bar, singing from time to time and keeping the glasses filled. At exactly ten o'clock, she went to Ramon and said, "I've got to go to bed."

He looked at her suspiciously. "What's the matter?"

"I don't know, but my head is killing me! I nearly passed out just now."

From behind the bar Maria noticed Lola clutching her forehead. "Is something wrong?"

"She's sick, she says."

"It's my head, Maria. It hurts so bad I'm sick to my stomach."

Maria shrugged. "Well, you won't do any good getting sick in here. Go on to bed."

"Can I have some of that laudanum for the pain?"

"It's in our room—on the shelf by the clock," Maria said. "Be careful with it, Lola. It's strong stuff."

"I will. See you in the morning. I'm going to try and sleep this off."

She left and headed straight to the kitchen where she picked up a half-full pint bottle of whiskey from the cabinet. Then she went to Maria and Ramon's room to get the medicine. It was in a brown bottle, and she carefully laced the remainder of the whiskey with several large spoonfuls of the dark liquid. She corked the bottle, then went to her own room.

Moving quickly, she pulled an ancient suitcase from beneath her bed and began to throw her few belongings into it. She had so little that there was plenty of room. She left the gaudy dress on, for it was part of her plan, and finally she made up her bed, using two old blankets to fashion a form that she hoped would pass for someone sleeping. If either Ramon or Maria came close, they would discover her ruse at once, but there was little else she could do.

She opened the door, and seeing nobody in the hall, took the back stair that led to the garden behind the cantina. She walked rapidly down the alley, and the loud music and shouts of the crowd at the bar began to fade as she made her way along the muddy alley.

She reached the end of the alley and glanced out at the dimly lit main street. The window of the jail glowed with an orange light through the darkness, and when she was sure the street was empty, she opened the suitcase and removed the bottle of doped whiskey. Leaving her suitcase in the alley, she set out toward the jail.

Her breath was coming in short puffs and her fingers were trembling, but she forced herself to ignore the nervousness overtaking her. Quickly she walked along the boarded sidewalk, loudly singing a well-known bar song. She hesitated at the door, still singing—then knocked on it, calling out in a slurred voice as though she were drunk: "Hey—Tomas! Tomas! Open the door!"

She continued to call until the door opened slightly. "Lola? Is that you?"

She laughed loudly and pushed at the door. "Course it's me. Who'd you think it was?" She entered the jail, noting at once with relief that one cell was empty. She turned to Tomas, a young man who had long admired her, and said, "Know what? It's my birthday, Tomas!"

He stared at her, for he had never seen her drink before. She threw off the coat and stood there with the whiskey bottle held up. "You just—got to—have a drink," she said in a drunken tone. "To shelabrate—my birthday!"

He took the bottle, but said, "Lola, I'm not supposed to drink when I'm guarding a prisoner."

She moved closer, put her arms around him and pulled him close. He nearly jumped out of his skin at her touch, and she whispered, "Oh, come on! What kind of a man are you? Won't drink with a girl on her birthday?" She ran her fingers through his hair, and whispered, "Please! Just for me?"

Tomas had had many dreams of Lola, more or less like what was happening, but never dared hope they'd actually come true. He turned the bottle up and took a swallow, then tried to hand it back, but she pouted, "Oh, that was such a little drink, Tomas! Is that all you think of Lola?"

He broke out into a sweat, turned the bottle up, and she watched as his adam's apple moved up and down as he swallowed. "There!" he gasped when he lowered the bottle. "Happy birthday!"

She put the bottle to her lips, pretended to drink, then handed it back. "Your turn!"

He gulped nervously, then took another hefty swallow. She took the bottle and put it on the table, then said, "Now, you and me . . . we gotta have a dance, Tomas—for my birthday!"

He seized her and they whirled around the floor as she sang a song in Spanish. Around and around they went, but when he tried to kiss her she laughed merrily, "Not yet—first another drink!" And once again she pretended to drink after he swallowed two big gulps of the potent liquor.

She knew he wouldn't last long, and when she tried to dance with him again, he stumbled and almost fell. "Can't—stand up!" he gasped. Then he shook his head. "Gonna be sick!"

"Here, Tomas," Lola said. "Lie down and be still for a minute. You'll feel better." She guided him to the cot and helped him down. He closed his eyes, and she stood beside him looking down into his face. His breathing was rapid, but gradually it slowed down, and soon his mouth fell open. "Tomas?" she whispered by his ear, but he made no answer.

Swiftly she removed the key from the ring on his gunbelt. Winslow was ready and waiting next to his cell door even before she inserted the key and unlocked the door. "Let's get out of here!" she whispered.

"Right." He moved to the desk and opened a lower drawer, pulling his gunbelt out and buckling it on. "Where to now?"

"This way." She led him to the door, and after a glance outside, said, "Quick, there's nobody on the street." He followed her as she ran lightly down the walk and turned into the alley. She picked up her suitcase, and turned to leave, but he took it from her. "Let me carry it."

"All right, but hurry!"

The night was intensely dark, and they stumbled through the alleys until finally clearing the town. By the dim light of the moon Mark could make out a series of small huts. They all looked alike to him, but she guided him to one and opened the door. He followed her, but stood inside unable to see a thing.

"Shut the door and I'll light the lamp," she whispered. He did as she asked and heard the sharp scratch of a match, then the blue spurt of flame flashed in front of him. The wick of a lamp caught, and the yellow light framed the girl as she stood there holding the chimney. Carefully placing it on the lamp, she turned to face him.

He nodded and said, "You did fine!"

She put a trembling hand to her cheek and said faintly, "I'm beginning to get scared!"

"It always caught me that way," he said. "I always got the shakes after the fight. Sit down and maybe I can find some water."

He found a heavy olla in the corner of the one-room hut and poured some of the water out into a mug for her. "Whose place is this?"

She took a drink of the water and followed it with a deep breath. "It belongs to a man named Victor. He's going to help us get away."

He walked around the room, examining it carefully. "That's going to be quite a trick," he observed. "They'll find out we're gone, and every hole will be stopped up."

"I know."

Her sudden calmness amazed him, and he said impulsively, "No matter what happens from now on—thanks for this much."

She shook her head. "I'm not doing it for you, Holland. I'm doing it for me."

He grinned. "Afraid I'll get too close to you, Lola? Don't be. I made you three promises—and I'll stick with them all. But the fact remains—you got me out of that tin can, and I'm grateful no matter why you did it. By the way, my real name is Mark Winslow."

She nodded and took another sip of the water. "Do you want to hear what we're going to do tomorrow?"

"Sure. Whatever plan you've got, it's probably better than mine." He wiped his sweating face and eased himself down onto the dirt floor.

"Are you sick?" she asked in alarm.

"To tell the truth," he nodded, "I have felt better. But I can make it. Now, what's on for tomorrow?"

She gave him an embarrassed smile and said ruefully, "When I thought of this way of getting out of the country, it made sense, but now it just seems silly, even to me."

He took a drink of water and shrugged. "Let's have it. The good Lord has brought me this far. I don't think He'll let us down now."

Lola's eyes widened in surprise. "You have faith in God?"

He didn't answer at once, but after a long pause he replied, "Well, I guess not—but some of my family does. Maybe a little of their faith will rub off on us. We could use all the help we can get right now."

She regarded him intently for a moment, then said, "They'll

be watching for us. You can bet Faye Hunter will have his men pounding down every trail and checking every stage looking for you."

"You're right there," he nodded. "So what do we do?"

"We give them something different to look at."

He shook his head. "I don't get it."

"People see what they're looking for," she explained. "They're looking for a tall young gringo and a Mexican girl. What we've got to do is become something else."

"Okay," he said unsteadily, feeling his fever rising, "and how do you propose we do that?"

She responded evenly, "I'm going to cut my hair and dress up in men's clothes. You're going to shave your beard and I'll dye your hair white so you'll look like a very old man. Then Victor and about ten of his relatives are going to get on the stage with us. Anybody looking will see a bunch of poor Mexicans, among them a young boy and an old man."

He lowered his head and stared at the floor. He was still for so long that eventually she broke the silence, "You think it's crazy, don't you?"

He lifted his eyes, bright with fever, and smiled slowly.

"It's the only game in town, Lola. And we'll play our stack for all it's worth!"

CHAPTER THREE

ESCAPE FROM EAGLE PASS

★ ★ ★ ★

A small sound broke through Mark's fitful sleep, and he jerked up on the cot with his gun in his hand.

"It's only Victor," Lola reassured him quickly, and he slipped the gun back under the pillow as she opened the door to admit a muscular Mexican who looked across the room at him with a pair of steady black eyes.

"I brought you something to eat, Señorita," he said, placing a covered dish on the floor. He handed her a bundle he'd carried in his other hand, saying, "I got the things you asked for."

Taking the sack from him, Lola asked, "Did you get the tickets for the stage, Victor?"

"Sí. Be ready at ten-thirty. We will all walk to the station together." He looked directly at Mark and said, "Señor, you are a very valuable man. Señor Hunter will pay two thousand dollars to the man who delivers you to him. Everyone in town is out looking for you. The sheriff has wired all the stage stations and train depots as far away as Dallas." A light of humor touched his steady black eyes as he added, "I could retire and live well on that much money."

Winslow gave him a careful look, then a smile touched his own lips. "Hold out for more, Victor. He's got the money."

Victor laughed, then grew serious. "Do exactly as the señorita tells you. All of us are in God's hands, for if you are found out, we will all suffer." He wheeled and left the room without a sound, and Lola moved at once to throw the bolt.

"We must eat now while we still have time," Lola said, and they sat down and chewed the tortillas and beans, washing the sparse breakfast down with water from the olla. As soon as Lola finished, she stood up and moved to her case. She opened it and began to lay items out on the bed. He watched as she propped a mirror on a battered chest, then took a pair of scissors out of the bag. She moved back to the mirror and loosed the pins that held her hair. Mark admired the glossy waves of dark hair that fell to her waist, and something like a shock ran through him as she deliberately lifted the shears and began to cut through her hair in the back. Large tresses fell to the floor as she began to work toward the top, shaping the crown carefully.

"Hate to see that," he remarked, shaking his head. "Doesn't seem right to cut your hair."

"It'll grow back," she answered calmly. She moved the shears with precision, and after making a few more cuts to the front, she put the shears down. Picking up a bottle, she shook some liquid out into her palm and began to work it into her hair, and with that done, she took a comb and brush and brushed it back in the style so admired by many Mexican dandies.

Mark, feeling weak after a feverish night of tossing on the narrow cot, sat and watched as she picked up a dark brown bottle and poured some of the contents onto her palm. As she began to work it into her face and neck, she realized he was watching and stopped. "Please turn your back," she asked.

He lay down on the cot, turning his eyes to the wall, and she at once removed her dress and began to work the liquid into her neck and the top of her chest. When she was satisfied, she gave him a quick glance, then, pulling off the rest of her clothes, put on the things that Victor had brought. They made up the garb of a young Mexican male, and included a pair of dark brown breeches, a white shirt, a short jacket with silver buttons, a pair of half boots with high heels, and a tall sombrero. When she had dressed, she wrapped herself in a gaily colored serape, pulling the borders close over her chest.

"How do I look, Mark?" she asked, turning to face the cot.

He rolled over and sat up, noting her use of his first name. She saw his eyes widen and blink. He got to his feet and stared at her in consternation, for the haircut had altered her beyond recognition. Her face looked more slender and the style made her eyes seem smaller. Though she still had a feminine look, he admitted, "Beats anything I ever saw, Lola!" He shook his head, adding, "Why, it's like magic! A beautiful young woman turns into a Mexican dandy!"

She laughed, the first time he'd heard her do so, and went to admire her work in the mirror. "Just what I wanted—and it'll look better before I'm through. Now it's your turn. A troop of actors came to perform at the cantina last year. I got to be good friends with one of the actresses. She did the make-up for all the others, and I used to watch her. She left this case by mistake. I started to throw it away—now I'm glad I didn't."

"Going to use that stuff on me?"

"Yes. First, you shave." She waited until he had shaved, using cold water from the jug, then she said, "Sit down where I can reach you."

He took a seat in the only chair, and she picked up the shears and began to cut his hair. As she worked, trimming the hair that had only been hacked off roughly two weeks earlier in the Mexican prison, the touch of her fingers made him feel strange. She was absorbed by the task, but when her face was directly in front of his, he was forced to look at her, and could not help admiring the satiny complexion of her face and the smooth curves of her neck.

Finally she stepped back, examined him critically, then nodded. "Now for the dye." She took a bottle out of the case, shook it up, and began to apply it carefully to his hair, working it in toward the scalp. It took fifteen minutes to do the entire thing, and when she had finished, she handed him a cloth, saying, "Cover your eyes—I need to do your eyebrows." He obeyed, and then she said, "Take your shirt off, Mark, so I can tint your skin."

When he stood up and took off his shirt, she stared at his bandage, appalled, exclaiming, "That has to be changed!" She temporarily abandoned her make-up work to change the soiled dressing, wash the wound out carefully, then make a clean dressing from one of her petticoats. "No infection," she announced with a smile, and she reached for the dye and deftly applied it to his face and shoulders. She looked at him, then smiled, "You look funny! All brown down to your chest, then pale as a plucked chicken!" Her eyes crinkled when she smiled, something he had not noticed before. "Put these clothes on, and let's see what you look like," she said as she turned her back to him.

He put on the heavy wool pants and a loosely fitting white shirt, slipped his head through a hole in a serape, and donned a high-crowned sombrero that came down almost to his eyes. All the clothing was old and dirty. "You can look now."

He watched her face when she turned, and her expression told him that the experiment was a success. She smiled and said, "Beautiful!" Then she brought the mirror to him. "Look."

He stared into the mirror held before him, and was even more aghast at the transformation in his own appearance than he'd been at hers! Shaking his head, he said, "Always wondered what I'd look like when I got old. Now I know—just as ugly as ever!"

"No, you look like a fine old Mexican laborer—except for one or two things." She studied him and said, "Bend over—no, more than that, Mark. Put a real stoop in your shoulders." He did his best, and she clapped her hands together. "That's fine! Now, take this walking stick that Victor brought—walk, but remember, you're a *very* old man—move very slowly—Yes! That's it! Good! Sort of a shuffle, and you might even stumble at times for effect!"

She made him practice his walk until she was satisfied, then worked on the details. "Your hands could give you away," she announced, picking up one of his hands and examining it. "They're too big and strong looking for such an old man. We'll have to get some gloves—or better, just wrap them in rags as some poor peons do in winter."

For the next two hours Mark watched as the creative mind of the young woman prepared them for the test that lay ahead of them. She was, he decided, like the director of a play, or like a child making up a game and enjoying it immensely. Constantly in motion, she sometimes walked around the small floor practicing the sort of swagger that a young man might employ, sometimes coached him to speak in a mumble, one time pulling off her hat and putting up her hand to arrange her hair in a feminine gesture. When he said "You do that one time in public and we're busted," she flushed and nodded. "Tell me about things like that, Mark."

Finally her momentum ran down. She packed her things in a blanket in the manner of the Mexicans, and when he moved to put on his gunbelt, she said, "No—let me keep it until we're clear."

As she put it in the center of the bundle, he said, "I feel kind of naked without a gun—but it's your show, Lola." He got up and got a drink of water, then looked out the window. "Weather's getting bad. That sky's got some snow in it, I think."

"Better for us, maybe," she nodded. "I wish a snow storm would hit. They wouldn't be so anxious to be out looking for us." She was sitting on the bed, leaning back with her head against the wall, her eyes closed. He was silent, noting that now that the fit of action was over, she seemed tired.

Suddenly she opened her eyes and looked at him. "Mark, do we have any chance at all?"

He nodded confidently, saying much more strongly than he felt, "Sure we do. I've been in worse spots than this many a time, Lola. Thing to do is take it one step at a time. Most people spend so much time worrying about something that never happens, they can't handle their immediate problems." He stood up and stretched carefully, favoring his wounded side. "Look at me. Last night I was locked up with a five-year stretch in the pen staring me in the face." He gave her a quick grin. "Now, I'm just one step away from getting out of Eagle Pass, and that's all I'm thinking about right now."

He hoped the conviction in his voice would restore her obviously flagging courage. An intense curiosity concerning her had grown in him, but he knew it was no time to try to discover what went on behind that smooth face of hers. Instead, he began to tell her of the great Pacific Railroad that was going to be built, and he was pleased to see her relax as the morning wore on.

After what seemed hours later, they heard voices, and Lola said, "I think it's time, Mark." She rose quickly, wrapped herself in her serape, and picked up the bundle. She paused and gave him an odd look, her eyes looking large in the gloom of the small room. "I wish I believed in God. If I did, I'd ask Him to get us out of town."

He blinked his eyes, then shrugged. "I'm in just about that same shape, Lola. I believe in God, but I'm not sure He believes in me anymore." His shoulders drooped as a wave of memory broke over him, bringing a sadness to his face. Finally he said heavily, "I sure haven't given Him any cause to think well of me the last few years." Then a tap at the door sounded, and his attention reverted to the present. "We'd better go."

He opened the door and they stepped outside to find that tiny flakes of snow were beginning to fall, putting a sheen on the heads and shoulders of the small crowd that stood with Victor looking at them. "This is my family," Victor said quickly. "Some nephews and nieces, and my aunt Elizabeth and my uncle Roberto." Elizabeth was a heavy Mexican woman of forty and Roberto was a slight man, advanced in years, but with a pair of bright black eyes that seemed to miss nothing. In addition to the adults there were four children ranging from about six to ten, as far as Mark could guess. Victor saw him looking at them with caution in his eyes, and he said quickly, "Do not worry, Señor. They will speak no English—in fact they will all chatter like squirrels in Spanish. And they know that it is due to the Señorita Montez that they are being taken to my brother's house." He shrugged and added, "We have tried to get enough pesos to get them there for many weeks, but could not. We are all very grateful to the Señorita. At last, it is time!"

The small group covered the distance to the edge of town slowly, and only once did Lola have to say quietly, "Bend lower, Mark—and shuffle your feet on the ground."

When they moved onto the main street, Mark felt a streak of alarm run through him, for despite the lightly falling snow, the street was busy. More so than usual, he thought, for he saw several punchers riding mounts with a Box M brand, and there were quite a few townspeople visible, most of them talking in small groups. *I can guess what they're talking about*, he thought with irony. *Wouldn't be surprised if Hunter has upped the reward.*

The stage station lay on the far side of the town, and they passed in front of La Paloma Blanca. As they approached the front, Ramon Varga suddenly stepped out and turned to face them.

"Victor," he called out, and Mark involuntarily shot a glance toward Lola. She was on the far side of Victor, but when he stopped, she came around to stand beside Mark.

"What's all this, Victor?" Ramon demanded. He came to stand in front of the party, putting on his hat to shield his head from the falling snow. "Who are all these people?"

Victor's voice was even and unchanged. He shrugged and drew his serape closer around him, saying, "You know I've been trying to get my family up to my brother in Quemado." He thrust his chin toward Ramon and said accusingly, "I asked you often enough to lend me the money, didn't I?"

Varga ignored the question, saying, "Well, you got it without my help."

"Sí," Victor said carelessly. "My brother Felipe, he sent his son, Esteban—this young fellow here—with the money to take them back." He waved in the general direction of Lola.

Ramon gave her a quick look, and for one brief moment Lola thought her heart would stop, for it seemed that he could not *help* but recognize her! However, his eyes moved back to Victor, and he said, "Have you seen Lola?"

"Señorita Lola?" Victor asked in a puzzled tone. "Of course! I saw her yesterday at the cantina."

"No, I mean since then—today."

"No, not today." Victor shrugged his shoulders and said, "It's blowing up a storm. Esteban, get these children to the stage— and help your grandfather, you ungrateful whelp!"

"Sí, Uncle Victor," Lola said huskily, and came to take Mark's arm. "Come along, Grandfather—be careful now—the snow makes the ground slippery!"

Mark allowed himself to be helped down the street, with Lola on one side and one of the women on the other. He heard Ramon say, "Victor, Lola's run off—apparently with that gunman who shot Boyd Hunter."

"Madre de Dios!" Victor breathed. "Is it possible?"

Mark and the group continued on toward the stage depot, so that he could not hear the rest, but Victor caught up with them just as they arrived at the unpainted building that served as the station. The coach was already in front, the horses stamping and puffing in the cold, the ice flakes coating their eyelashes like tiny diamonds.

Jake Deifer, the station agent, came outside as they approached, and spotting the group, gave them a sour look. "Get this bunch on board, Victor. Charlie's worried about the weather."

"So am I," Victor nodded. He looked up at the sky and said, "It ought to be all right as far as Quemado, I think."

"That's what Charlie says," Deifer nodded. "These people all going there?"

"Sí. My brother Felipe will pick them up and take them to his hacienda."

He would have said more, but the sound of horses approaching caused him to look to his left. "I see Señor Hunter is bringing all his men to town," he remarked, careful not to look toward Mark and Lola. "He is after the gunman, I suppose?"

"Been out all night dragging the bushes," Deifer said, then lowered his voice. "I ain't never seen the old man so riled, Victor. Keep your head down if he runs into you. He ain't above puttin' a slug in anybody who crosses him."

"Is his son dead?"

"No, still hanging on—but it's an iffy sort of thing Doc Wright says." He leaned toward Victor and asked, "Did you hear about Lola?"

"Ramon told me," Victor said. "She should not have run off with a killer."

There was a sudden hubbub as the Box M riders pulled up and dismounted, and Mark looked up to see Sheriff Marsh coming down the street. He looked worried, and there was an obvious reluctance in his gait. As soon as he was close enough, Faye Hunter boomed out, "Hurry it up, Marsh!"

Marsh pulled up and said quickly, "I got telegrams out to every town within a hundred miles, Mr. Hunter. And the posters are being printed down at Ed's shop right now. Here's the original."

Hunter scanned the sheet that the sheriff handed him, reading parts of it out loud. "Wanted for attempted murder—Frank Holland. Late twenties. Six feet, 185 pounds. Dark eyes, dark hair. . . ." Hunter grunted in frustration, "Fits half the men in the country!" His marble eyes bored into Marsh's, and he said, "I want you to deputize every man in this town, Marsh. You don't even know he's left town. He could be sitting in a cellar somewhere."

"His horse is still at the stable—and nobody's missing one," the foreman put in. "He could have walked out of town and stole a horse from a rancher, though."

"I'll search every house in town, Mr. Hunter," Marsh said, eager to be away from the angry giant before him.

"See you do," Hunter nodded grimly. He turned and saw Jake Deifer, the station agent and Charlie Roxie, the driver, listening. "Who's on the stage, Jake?"

"A whiskey drummer and a married couple, Mr. Hunter," Deifer informed him, indicating three people who had stepped outside the station. "And a whole passel of Victor's family going up to Quemado."

"Buenos días, Señor Hunter," Victor said at once. "I regret to hear of Señor Boyd's misfortune."

Hunter bored his hard eyes into the Mexican, and then let his eyes sweep over the group clustered behind him. He knew Victor, for the sturdy Mexican was one of the best horse breakers in the country. "These your folks?" he asked.

"Sí. They go to my brother Felipe. You remember him, maybe. He sold you that good gray stallion two years ago."

"Yes," Hunter nodded. "Good horse." He looked toward the group again, then Victor added, "I will be by to break the new colts now that my brother takes the relatives."

The statement distracted Hunter, and he looked back at Victor. "What? Oh, all right." He took a deep breath and turned back to his men. "Max, feed the boys, then throw them around in a bigger circle. Go all the way to the Redstone Bluffs north and down to Moss creek in the east." He gave the stage driver a stern look, and said, "Charlie, he won't be dumb enough to buy a ticket in a town, but he might be smart enough to wait out of town and flag you down. If he does . . ." Hunter paused, then said evenly, "Burn him, Charlie. The reward's good even if he's dead."

"It's your say, Mr. Hunter," the driver shrugged carelessly, "but if we don't get going, we ain't going to make it out of town."

"Get loaded," Deifer called, and the three passengers who had been lingering piled onto the coach. "It's a tight squeeze," he said. "Seven adults and four kids—but it'll have to do," he explained to the middle-aged couple. They agreed, and the whiskey drummer looked disgusted, but nodded wearily.

"Careful, Grandfather," Lola said as Mark groped for the step awkwardly. She took his arm, and he pulled himself in, almost falling into the lap of the whiskey drummer, who shoved him off with a curse under his breath.

The rest of them climbed in and settled as best they could, then Lola, who had squeezed in between Mark and the couple, felt the stage sway as the driver boarded. There was a slight pause, then she heard him shout, "Hup, Babe! Hup, Gyp!" and the stage dipped and the wheels splashed through the muddy streets.

Lola's hand was on his, and he turned to look at her from under the brim of his sombrero. Her eyes were bright, and she looked pleased. Despite everything, he saw her lips form a faint smile.

He echoed her excitement with a squeeze of his hand as the stage, swaying from side to side with its heavy load, cleared the town and headed down the flat, muddy road now fast becoming white with billions of tiny flakes.

CHAPTER FOUR

INTO THE STORM

★ ★ ★ ★

The town of Quemado had no shape; nothing held it together where it sprawled on the prairie. Ten or twelve buildings were flung without thought on the flat surface, and these were flanked by dull adobe houses that clustered together without regard to the formality of streets. It was, Mark thought, more like a random settlement than a town.

He stood inside a small room crowded with Victor's family, staring out of the dirty panes of the small window, feeling about as bad as he'd ever felt in his entire life. The ride had been long and uncomfortable, and his fever had risen again. Victor and his bunch had been met by Felipe in a wagon. Victor had spoken softly in Mark's ear before he left, saying, "There's a man watching us, Señor. I think maybe you better go with us—you and the Señorita." He and Lola had piled on the wagon and made the trip to a small farm five miles out of town. There was no snow, but it lurked somewhere out there, he knew, and now he moved closer to Lola where she sat on a packing box close to the fire.

"We've got to move," he said quietly. "Sooner or later somebody back in Eagle Pass is going to start thinking. If they put it together they'll be down on us."

She looked up at him, noting the red flush that tinged his lean cheeks. "What will we do, Mark?"

He stood there, his head bowed, and thought about the options. Nothing seemed good to him, but finally he said, "We can't go north, Lola. We're bound to hit bad weather, and there's no way on earth we're going to make it through the Indian Nations—especially in the dead of winter." He ran his hand along his cheek, and it gave her spirit a lift to see that he was calm. She knew that now that they were out of town, it was up to Mark Winslow to get them through, and despite the fact that she knew almost nothing about him, there was a steadiness in his face and a deliberate quality in his movements that gave her hope.

Finally he nodded and looked at her, asking bluntly, "Have you got enough money to buy some good horses?"

"Yes." She reached into her inside pocket and gave him an envelope. "There's almost two thousand dollars in there."

He gave her a sharp look of unbelief, then after holding her gaze, he stuck the money inside his shirt, asking dryly, "Your mother never taught you to be careful with strangers, Lola?"

"She taught me not to trust anybody," Lola said, and there was pain in the set of her mouth at the memory. Then her lips curved slightly and she said, "You won't cheat me, Mark."

"How do you know?"

"I've been around men all my life. I just know."

He studied her, wondering why her experience as a dance hall girl had not hardened her more. Even with her hair cut and dressed in the garb of a boy there was a womanliness about her face, the shape of her eyes and the curve of her cheeks that made him wonder how they had gotten away with it. But he said only, "All right." He looked out the window and then said, "We'll get Victor to buy us two horses and a wagon. We'll load the wagon with supplies and take off east. Best hope, I judge, is to get to Galveston quick as we can. We can get some kind of a boat to New Orleans. Once we get there, it'll be easy to get passage on a river boat up to the Missouri and from there to Omaha. May take us a while, but I'll feel better if we get out of Texas."

Lola stood up. "Let's ask Victor about the horses."

The process went smoother than they thought, for Felipe bought and sold horses. Victor did the bargaining, and once Felipe was aware of the situation, he nodded. "Sí. It will not be a problem. You can have them for what money I have put into them." It was late afternoon, too late to leave, so they ate a good supper and slept until dawn.

The next morning all had been done. The horses were saddled and the wagon was loaded with blankets and food, purchased in Quemado by Felipe. Felipe's wife fed them a big breakfast, and finally Mark and Lola stood beside the horses with Victor and Felipe. Felipe kept glancing up at the sky nervously.

"That wind, she's warm now. But me, I think she's like a woman who's hated you all year. Even when she smiles, there's a knife in her hand—just waiting to be used."

"I think that's right," Victor nodded. "Could be a blizzard building up." He shook his head, urging Lola, "Better you stay here and let it blow itself out."

"We've got to go, Victor," Lola said, and she smiled, putting out her hand. "You've been a friend."

She turned and climbed into the wagon, and Felipe said quickly, "Señor, you watch careful. If it hits, pull in at any ranch—they will take you in." He thought carefully and said, "You have the map I make for you last night?"

"Right here, Felipe."

Felipe took it and found a stub of a pencil in his pocket. Making a series of X's on the map, he identified several buildings and old line shacks that would give shelter. Mark listened carefully, studied the map, then took it and put it back in his pocket. "Thanks, Felipe—and you too, Victor."

Mark got into the wagon and spoke to the team. Victor called, "Vaya con Dios, Señorita Lola!" and then they were clear of the small house and on their way down the narrow road.

Lola sat upright in the seat beside him, and when Felipe's ranch was out of sight, she said, "I'm glad we're on our way, Mark."

"Long way to go." He glanced at her and saw that her dark blue eyes were alive with excitement. "You must have had a bad time, Lola, to be so glad to risk your life this way."

She dropped her eyes, then said softly, "I'm glad to be going someplace else." She said no more, and they settled down to the long journey.

They made good time, seeing few wagons or travelers on the road. Mark studied the clouds all morning with a searching attention. He kept the horses at a fast clip, and often pulled out the map Felipe had made to study it.

They stopped to rest the horses every hour, and about noon they pulled off the road and ate a lunch that Felipe's wife had packed. He made a small fire so quickly and efficiently that she remarked on it. Mark grinned and said, "I learned to do that when I was a kid, hunting in Virginia. Learned it again in the army. One of my few accomplishments."

She listened, storing up the small items about him that he let drop, then looked up and said, "The sky looks different, doesn't it?"

"Yes—and it's getting colder. We'll find a place to stay the night pretty soon. Wouldn't want to get caught out in an ice storm." Then he paused and said, "But that might not be so good—staying with people."

"Why not, Mark?"

"Well, this dye in my hair is beginning to run, for one thing. And for another, you don't look enough like a boy to satisfy me."

She flushed and then nodded. "I guess that's so. Isn't there an old barn someplace on that map?"

With Felipe's map, they found the dilapidated old barn quite easily. One end of the structure had collapsed years ago, providing them with wood to build a fire. The wind was beginning to rise, but Lola cooked a good meal of bacon and beans, and they had plenty of fresh bread. When they were finished, they sat close to the fire and drank strong black coffee.

"I like this," Lola murmured, staring into the fire. She looked across at Mark and the firelight glowed in her eyes. "I know it's crazy to say this when we could get caught tomorrow—but it seems so—safe!"

He picked up a chunk of wood and tossed it on the fire. "Know what you mean. Out there it's cold and hard and dangerous—but for right now we're warm and full and the world can't get at us." His broad lips turned up in a smile. "I remember a night like this when I was in the army. It was the night before the fight at Gettysburg. Most of us knew we were going to be in a terrible battle. Reckon most of us were sort of thinking that we'd get killed."

He picked up a sliver of pine, held it in the fire until it ignited, then studied it carefully, as if it had some vital significance. Finally, he looked up and went on softly. "But that night somebody liberated a pig and we cooked it and had a great meal. Somebody else had some whiskey, so we had a toast to General Lee and the Southern Confederacy. It was one of the best evenings I had in the army." Then he tossed the stick into the fire where it caught at once, and added, "But the next day we marched up a hill, along with General Pickett—and most of those fellows who shared that meal didn't come back."

There was, she saw, a sadness in him, and she asked in a small voice, "Do you think something like that will happen to us, Mark?"

"It could. Most happy endings take place in story books, Lola."

She shook her head. "No, I don't want to think that way. I want to think that we'll get up in the morning and head for Galveston—and all the way to New Orleans. I want to think that you'll help build that railroad."

"And what about you, Lola?" Mark inquired suddenly. "What's the end of all this for you?"

She lowered her head and stared into the fire for a long moment, then took a deep breath. "Oh, I honestly don't know." The wind rose suddenly, penetrating the darkness like a dangerous beast. Lola sighed and stared out the open end of the barn before saying, "I'm going to try to sleep."

All night she lay there, and his question came to her over and over: *What's the end of all this for you?* It made her feel insecure, for she realized that unlike Mark, who had a job to go to, she had nothing. The lonely sound of the wind and the ebony darkness that enveloped the old barn brought a chill to her shivering body, but finally she fell into a fitful sleep.

When she sat up and opened her eyes the next morning, the first thing she noticed was that he was not in the barn. Fear raced through her, and she threw the blanket back, jumped up and cried out, "Mark!" as she made for the opening. He appeared at once, and asked sharply, "What's wrong, Lola?"

"Oh—I just didn't know where you were."

Mark gave her a strange look. "We better have a good breakfast. I don't think we'll have a chance to cook on the road."

They cooked a quick meal, and she loaded the blankets and food while he hitched the team. When she got into the wagon and looked at him, she said with concern, "You don't feel well, do you?"

He shook his head, not answering. When they drove away from the shelter of the barn, the cold hit her with a force that took her breath. She got a blanket out and wrapped it around herself, then huddled down in it, staring at the sky. Up north the heighth and breadth of jagged clouds was evidence of a tremendous wind—and behind the clouds was a darkness such as she'd never seen during daylight hours. They said almost nothing that morning, instead keeping their eyes on the clouds to their north as if they were some sort of fierce animal that might leap on them at any moment. At noon they paused and made a cold lunch, and at two o'clock Mark pointed far ahead. "I think that's the old line shack that Felipe marked on the map."

Ten minutes later the house was not to be seen. Day drained out of the sky, and like the echo of a waterfall the distant reverberation of wind ended the stillness. In another ten minutes, Mark pulled the team down to a slow walk, saying quietly, "Here's that snow we've been looking for."

It came much quicker than they had guessed. First large flakes swirled in the wind, then in half an hour, thick clouds of snow hit them and closed around them until they could not see the horses in front of them. The temperature dropped faster than Mark thought possible.

After a few minutes of struggling through the white mass, Mark said through frozen lips, "I'll have to lead the horses. They won't go through this without help. Take this rope and hold on to it."

Mark climbed down slowly. Moving like a drunken man, he chose each step carefully, until he disappeared into the haze of the snow. The high-pitched wind assaulted them like a physical presence, and time after time Lola had to reach up with a handkerchief and wipe the ice crystals from her eyes.

After two hours the snow was deep enough that the wagon could barely move. The horses stopped, and Lola sat there peering into the darkness—finally catching a glimpse of a dim form to her left. Mark appeared and came close enough to say, "We found the cabin!" His voice was barely a whisper above the screaming wind, and she could tell that he was almost ready to fall, but he felt his way to the front of the horses once again and led them to the left.

They moved slowly, and then suddenly the horses stopped. She thought she saw Mark move, and realized that they were right at the cabin. He struggled to it, then came back and said, "Get inside!"

Lola climbed down from the wagon and fell to her knees, for her feet had no feeling in them. He reached down and pulled her up. They staggered across the snow, and she became aware of a darkness that formed an open door. He pulled her inside and shut the door. The sound of the wind was muted so abruptly that it seemed almost quiet in the cabin. She heard the scratch of a match, and a blue spurt of flame illuminated his pale, ice-crusted face. He walked woodenly across the floor and picked up a candle stub, lit it, and a flickering light spread over the interior of the shack. The one room was cluttered with broken furniture, but Lola was relieved to see a battered iron stove with some wood at one end.

"Guess God hasn't forgotten us," Mark said, his voice thin and raspy. "Can you get a fire going while I get the horses into the shed?"

"Yes." She took the matches and he left the room at once. Some old newspaper lay around and she broke up an old packing box to make kindling. Her hands were trembling so violently she could hardly hold them steady enough to light the paper, but it caught, and she carefully fed the small flame with pieces of wood. By the time the larger chunks of wood had caught, Mark had come in stamping his feet.

"Come and get warm," she urged.

"Don't want . . . too much heat . . . too fast," he said, stumbling over his words in sheer exhaustion. There was a cot on the far side of the room, and he moved toward it, collapsing with a finality that frightened her.

"Mark!" She sprang to his side, but when he didn't answer she knew he was unconscious. Fear overtook her, and she knelt there helplessly. It was almost as if he had been shot in the heart, and she knew that the sickness and fever had so weakened him that the herculean effort of leading the horses through the storm had been too much. His breathing was so shallow that for one frightening instant she thought he was dead, but when she put her ear on his chest, she could hear his heart beating.

The storm howled outside and made the tiny candle flame seem precariously fragile to Lola, a glimmer of light that threatened to go out at any moment. The tiny fire crackled, but the tongues of yellow flame hadn't yet touched the paralyzing cold. The feeling of security that had come to her the previous night had disappeared with the blizzard. She was alone now—Mark had reached the end of his strength.

An urge to give way to fear, to scream and cry and beat her fists against the cold wall rose up in her—but she fought it down. Slowly she got up and went to the fire. She put two larger pieces of firewood inside the stove, shut the door, then stepped back. She was still cold, but it was not the paralyzing, killing cold she had known on the road. She whispered through tight lips, "It's up to me now. Mark is sick—and I got him into this."

She paced the floor, waiting for the room to warm up. Gradually the feeling returned to her feet, and she began to think more calmly. Just when her feet and hands were beginning to tingle, she pulled on her coat and gloves and went outside. The force of the wind and the iron grip of the cold lashed at her body, but she moved around the cabin holding on to the wall until she came to where the horses were sheltered by the shed roof. Three sides of the shed were walled, offering some protection. She found a bucket and fed them, holding the bucket as they ate one at a time. Then she hauled the supplies into the cabin, making several trips, and filled a bucket up with snow and put it on the stove. It took her a long time to melt enough snow to water the horses, and by the time she had done all this, her legs were trembling with fatigue.

She moved across to where Mark lay and began to remove his coat. He was heavy, but she managed to get it off and put a blanket over him. It was still cold in the cabin, but she knew the wood had to last, so she kept the fire small. Mark lay on the only cot, so she made a pallet in front of the stove and lay down.

She had worked herself hard, but before letting herself fall into an exhausted sleep, Lola whispered urgently, "Oh, God!

Don't let us die in this place! Please, God! Don't let us die!"

But her only answer was the wind scratching at the cabin door and beating against the flimsy boards of the shack with ghostly fists.

CHAPTER FIVE

Friends and Enemies

★ ★ ★ ★

For two days the storm raged, prowling around the cabin like a wild beast. At times the wind screamed like a lost soul in pain; at other times the sound changed to a mournful mutter. Lola slept fitfully, awakening with a start as the cold fingers of the wind groped at the flimsy boards of the shack, rattling the windows in a sinister fashion.

Not knowing how long they would be trapped, Lola rationed the firewood like a miser, keeping a precarious balance between bone-aching cold and mere discomfort. The horses would have died, she knew, if she had not propped up old boards—too damp to burn—over the open end of the shed to cut off the cold wind that sliced like a knife. Melting snow to water the horses was a never-ending chore, and since she had few vessels, it was necessary for her to make many trips.

But it was not the terrible cold or the howling wind that frightened her so much as Mark. A raging fever had taken him, and for two days she battled to keep it down with every resource at her command. She knew that if the fever went too high, he would die, and that fear paralyzed her at times.

Sometimes he was so hot his flesh seemed to burn her hand. The first time that happened, she knew she had to bring his temperature down. She had stripped his shirt off and applied snow-water to his face and upper body until after what seemed like an eternity, the crimson color left his face. She had lain down beside the bunk, only to be awakened some time later by his chattering teeth. The entire bed shook from the chill racking his body. She piled blankets over him, careful to make sure he didn't throw them off in his delirium.

On the second day his face was almost skull-like in the flickering light of the candle—the cheeks hollow and his eyes sunk back into his head. "You've got to eat!" she said determinedly, and she would ladle a thick broth down his throat a spoonful at a time. He resisted her, and in his efforts to avoid the food, he flung up an arm, his hand striking her across the mouth. She tasted warm blood where her lips had been cut by her teeth, but blinking back the tears, she picked up the spoon and forced him to swallow more of the broth.

By the end of that day Lola was exhausted. Life had become a cycle—feed and water the horses, keep the fire going, melt snow for water, keep Mark's temperature from going too high, feed him small portions whenever he seemed awake, keep the covers on him when the chills shook him, try to sleep on the cold floor whenever she could find a few minutes. The cold sapped her strength and drew her down, so that she grew to dread the task of caring for the horses. She was weak, both physically and mentally, and the strain of isolation sucked at her emotions so that she had to consciously struggle against fear, and this became harder with every hour.

The third morning she awoke shaking from the heavy blanket of cold that filled the small shack. She had let the fire go down so low that barely a glimmer of light shown from the charred wood. It took all the will she had to roll out of her blankets and force herself to feed the tiny stove until the fresh wood caught. Her whole body trembled violently from the cold. She built up a good fire and fried four pieces of thick bacon, made a sandwich, then washed it down with black coffee.

When she finished she saw that Mark was having another chill, so she moved the chair close to his bed and sat down, holding his arms down as he tried to throw the covers off. He was too weak to resist, so she relaxed her grip. The food and the warmth of the room soon brought a drowsiness that pulled her eyelids down. She fought against it, but finally leaned forward and rested on his chest, pinning his arms down to keep him from throwing the covers off, thinking she would rest only until his chill passed away. After struggling to stay awake, she closed her eyes and was asleep at once.

"Lola?"

The sound of his voice startled her, and she came up from where she lay against him, disoriented and frightened. The sudden move made her dizzy and she put her hands up before her in a defensive gesture, unable to focus on anything.

"Easy, now!"

She gasped when she felt his hands on her wrists, then her vision cleared and she saw his face by the dim yellow light from the stove. He looked haggard and worn, but his eyes were clear, and when he spoke with a husky voice, she opened her eyes wider, exclaiming, "The fever's broken!"

"I reckon so." He released his grip and pulled himself up to a sitting position, but the effort made him so dizzy that he swayed and closed his eyes. She reached out and steadied him, pulling his sweat-soaked pillow up so that he could lean against it. He tried to speak, then paused to lick his cracked lips. She jumped up and got him a much-needed cup of water.

"How do you feel, Mark?"

He looked up at her after thirstily drinking the cool water, noting the lines of exhaustion on her face, and mumbled, "Hungry."

She laughed and the sound seemed to lighten the heaviness in the air. "That's just like a man—thinking of his stomach first." Feeling his forehead, she said with a relieved smile, "Fever's all gone." After pulling the covers up around him, she turned to busy herself fixing him a meal.

The smell of food soon wafted through the air, arousing his hunger pangs. Mark began to struggle to get out of bed, but Lola wouldn't hear of it. "Mark Winslow—if you put one foot on the floor, I'll hit you over the head with this skillet!"

"Yes, ma'am," he grinned weakly, and lay there watching her as she prepared the food. Running his hand over his face, he felt the bristles and asked, "How long have I been sick?"

She ladled some broth into a bowl, picked up a piece of bread and brought it over to him. "Three days," she said, giving him the food. "This is Sunday."

He dipped the bread into the hot broth before shoveling it into his mouth so fast she cried out, "Don't choke yourself!" Laughing again, Lola got his coffee and came back to sit down with it, watching as he ate. When he handed her the plate, she gave him the coffee, saying, "Better wait for a little while—then you can have some bacon."

He took the coffee, sipped it and closed his eyes with pleasure. "Never knew anything could taste so good!" he murmured. He gave her a quick glance and the corners of his mouth turned up in a smile. "Once in the trenches at Petersburg we ate one of our ammunition mules—but this is even better than that."

She leaned back and was amazed at how light and happy she felt. The burden of fear had been heavier than she had thought. "I'm glad you're better," she said. Her short hair framed her pale face, and he saw the relief in her dark blue eyes. "I was so afraid."

He studied her closely, then nodded. "Been worse on you than on me." Several moments passed before he spoke again. "Thanks, Lola. Seems like you've made a habit of getting me out of jams."

"Well . . ." Flustered by the steadiness of his smoky gray eyes, Lola reached out to take his cup to cover her confusion. "You're out of coffee."

She had, he saw, built up a wall around herself. *Trespassers keep out*, he thought suddenly, and remembered how adamant she had been about the third condition—that he keep his distance. He took the cup and said easily, "Well, I reckon it's hard to be hit with a lot of gratitude all at once. . . ." He paused to sip the coffee, then smiled and added, "So I owe you a couple of thank-yous, okay?" He saw her relief, and began to question her about the horses and the supplies. The change of subject put her at ease, and soon they were talking in a relaxed manner. *Just got to remember to keep my distance*, Mark resolved.

Aloud he said, "One good thing about all this—no danger of anyone coming out to look for us in a storm like this."

"But as soon as it stops, they might."

"Sure enough—but we'll be on our way by then."

She gave him a stern look, saying, "You're weak, Mark. I

don't think you should travel for a while."

"Just wait 'til that storm lets up, and you'll see how fast I can move!"

He slept peacefully that night, woke up as hungry as a wolf, and for two days did little but eat and sleep. On Wednesday he clambered out of bed, saying, "I'm sick of being an invalid, Lola," and proceeded to take over the chores outside. The next day the wind suddenly died down, bringing an eerie silence to the white world around them. Mark said that night as they ate their simple supper of beans, "If what I've heard about these blizzards is right, this one's about played out. Temperature's rising fast and the wind's stopped."

"Thank God for that!" she exclaimed, then flushed as he gave her an odd smile. "I'm no believer—but it seems like a miracle that we found this place."

"Reckon that's right, Lola," he mused. "Just ten more feet— and we'd have missed this shack. They'd be coming along in a few days, and we'd be ready for the undertaker." He was cleaning his Colt, looking out the window at the pale sun beginning to break through the ragged clouds. "Had many a minie ball come so close I could hear 'em whistle during the war. Just an inch to the right or to the left, and I'd have been one of those boys we had to bury." He looked down at the revolver, not really seeing it, then gave her a direct glance. "Why was it me and not them that lived? And why did we find this place instead of missing it?"

"Maybe just luck."

He shook his head firmly. "No, I can't believe that. A man is born into this world. He's got a brain and a heart. He can look up at the stars and see them marching across the skies in perfect order just like a drill team—and he knows something's made them to do that! Then he sees a woman and she sees him. They touch—and there's something more than chance in that."

"You believe love is like that?" she asked softly, then shook her head. "I don't. I've seen too many ugly and grasping people. Men take what they want—and then leave the woman to get by as best she can!"

The bitterness of her words drew his gaze, and he considered what she had said. It had been the most revealing clue that she'd let slip, and he thought it might be a common enough philosophy for a saloon girl. Nevertheless, he shook his head in denial. "No, there's more than that to love, Lola. I've seen the men you're talking about—and some women are just about as greedy. But every now and then I see someone who's *not* like that—like my parents." He rolled the cylinder of the Colt, slipped it into the holster and laid it down on the table.

She was staring at him with a faint wonder in her eyes. They were so blue they looked almost black, and her lips were parted in an unconscious look of awe. "Maybe a few people love," she admitted finally, then shook her head in a gesture of doubt, "but most do not."

"If one man and one woman can love," Mark said, "it's possible." She was, he saw, tremendously interested in what he had said, but he did not push his sentiments. Instead he said, "I think we can get out of here by Friday."

"Good. I don't feel safe this close to Eagle Pass."

The temperature rose steadily and the clouds changed from sullen gray to azure the next day. The snow began to melt and Mark took the horses out for exercise, riding one and leading the other. When he returned he said, "It'll be rough going, Lola, but we'll pull out in the morning. Let's get everything packed up."

They left around nine the next morning, and as the horses plodded through the melting snow, they both turned around for a final glance at the cabin.

"Fort Salvation," Mark murmured.

"Yes." Lola felt a strange sensation as she gazed at the dilapidated shack, and added, "I feel like we're leaving home somehow, Mark." She thought of the shelter it had provided as the storm had howled outside. "I'll never forget this little place."

He nodded, then said soberly, "Neither will I, Lola. Lots of places I'd like to forget, but like I said, this little cabin saved our lives." He spoke to the horses sharply, and soon they had passed over a hill and into a valley, leaving the line shack behind.

All day long they traveled through the melting snowdrifts, the horses as happy to be out of the confinement of the past days as Mark and Lola were.

At noon Mark stopped to make coffee, and just before dark they made camp inside an abandoned barn. Most of the roof was off, but they found enough loose timber to make a place for beds free from snowdrifts, and after cooking a quick meal, they rolled into their blankets. "You're pushing yourself too hard, Mark," Lola said as he lay down wearily.

"Won't kill me," he muttered sleepily. "I want to get to Galveston as soon as we can. Won't feel safe as long as we're in Texas."

Both of them slept soundly, rising before dawn to eat a hurried breakfast. The snow melted rapidly, so that two days later the horses' hooves were churning up brown mud instead of snow. They stopped once at a run-down hotel in a little town called Unity, dividing one room for them both, then turned south the following morning. Two days later they passed into Galveston at dusk.

"Warmer here, isn't it?" Lola remarked.

"It's the Gulf, I guess," Mark nodded. "Smell that air? That's salt water." He drove into what seemed to be the center of town, pulled up at a cafe called The Blue Goose, and got out of the wagon. "Come on. Let's eat somebody else's cooking."

He reached out his hand, and when she took it and stepped to the ground, he laughed.

"What's so funny?" she asked.

"We are," he grinned. "This dye in my hair is half in and half out, for one thing. And it looks pretty suspicious for one man to be handing another down out of a wagon."

Lola's face burned, for she had completely forgotten her role as a boy. Looking down at herself she said, "I can't go in like this."

He gave her a skeptical look, then shook his head. "I reckon not. You've got to either be a boy or a girl. You're not going to fool anybody very long."

"I—I'll stay in the wagon and you can bring me something to eat."

"You can't stay in the wagon all the way to Omaha," he said practically. His eye roamed down the mud-filled street. "There's a hotel," he signalled. "It's not much, but it'll do for one night." They moved along the street until he pulled them up in front of the Palace Hotel. "I'll go get a room, then you can sort of sneak in and change back to what the good Lord made you," he grinned.

Mark entered the hotel, and in less than five minutes came back out. "Come on," he said. She jumped out of the wagon. "You take your case and I'll get the bedroll," he said. They entered the hotel and the elderly clerk did not so much as glance in their direction as Mark led her through the small lobby and up a set of flimsy steps that groaned under their weight. The hallway was dim, and he had to peer carefully to discern the faint number on the door. Shoving it open he entered, and she followed him into the small room. He lit a lantern mounted on the wall, and took a quick look around. It was a rough, unlovely room with a single bed, a four-poster made of solid mahogany, the only touch of elegance in the coarse room. The floor had once been covered with a lead-colored paint, but this had chipped away until it was a kind of leprous gray and brown.

"If you don't want to go out, I can bring you something to eat," he said.

She gave him a quick look and understood that he was aware that she felt awkward. It gave her a warm feeling, and she shook her head. "No, just give me a few minutes."

He smiled and left the room, going downstairs to wait in the lobby. Picking up a March 16, 1867, newspaper, he scanned it casually until he ran across a small article on the third page, entitled PACIFIC RAILROAD READY FOR SPRING. The first line told him what he needed to know: "General Grenville Dodge, Chief Engineer of the Union Pacific Railway, announced today that he intends to push the railroad as far as Cheyenne this year. Speaking from his winter headquarters at North Platte, Dodge issued a challenge to the Central Pacific Railroad which is building north from Sacramento, California, stating flatly, "Mr. Leland Stanford and the C.P. will never beat the Union to Salt Lake City."

"So Dodge has got to get there first," Mark said with a smile. It made him feel lighter in spirit, for he knew that his services would be needed—something he had not been certain of previously. He read the article several times and was caught off-guard when a voice said, "I'm ready now."

He lowered the newspaper and his eyes reflected the shock that ran through him as he looked at Lola. "Why. . . !" He got to his feet, pulled his hat off, and then caught himself when he saw the old clerk watching them. "All right," he murmured, casually tossing the newspaper down. Taking her arm, he gently directed her toward the door.

"You shouldn't surprise a man that way, Lola," he said when they turned down the walk toward the cafe. He had seen her in the revealing dress of a dance hall girl, then in the masculine attire of a young Mexican, but he would not have recognized her as she now looked. She wore a simple blue wool dress, fitted around the bodice with a full skirt that swirled when she moved. A hat of a lighter blue was tilted on her head. It was not an expensive dress, but it lent her a touch of elegance.

"It's just an old dress," she said quickly, but her cheeks grew warm at the admiration that showed in his face. She walked beside him to the cafe and they enjoyed a good meal of pork chops and baked potatoes with apple pie for dessert. Afterward they sat there talking quietly, watching the customers, mostly roughly-dressed working men and their wives.

Mark took one last sip of his coffee and said, "Tomorrow I'll sell the horses and wagon. Got to be some kind of a ship going to New Orleans." Then he stood up to leave and stretched. "I'll take you back to the hotel."

He paid the bill and they left the cafe to walk along the wooden sidewalk. "I don't like using your money, Lola," he acknowledged as they reached the hotel. "Makes me feel like—" He paused and shook his head.

"It's something we have to do, Mark," she assured him. "Don't think of it."

Leaving her at the door he said, "I'm going to go out to see if I can't find out about a ship tonight. Lock the door and keep it locked until I come back." He slipped his Colt out of his holster and gave it to her. "If you have any visitors, put a shot in the door."

"You might need it," she said quickly.

"No. I'm a tame cat tonight." He turned and left, and she shut the door and bolted it. She put the gun on the table, then washed her face and got ready for bed. For a long time she sat in the chair looking out at the street, but finally grew sleepy and went to bed.

A slight knock awakened her, and she was off the bed in one motion. "Who is it?"

"Winslow, Lola. Open the door."

"Just a minute." She quickly lit the lamp, slipped on a robe and unbolted the door. As Mark entered the room, she saw by the look on his face that he was pleased. "What is it?"

He took off his hat and tossed it on the floor, then turned to her. "There's a banana boat pulling out at eight tomorrow morning. It'll stop at New Orleans. I got us two places. Sold the horses and wagon, too. Had to give a bargain—but I got most of the money back. They sure earned their keep!"

She smiled up at him. "You certainly accomplished a lot tonight!"

He looked down at her, aware for the first time that she was only wearing a robe over her nightgown. He had had several drinks, and though he was not drunk, his natural impulses were not under his usual tight constraint. Now that he was a free man again, he realized that the long months of isolation in prison had been harder on him than he had thought at the time. The past days spent lying helpless in a cot with the constant threat of being hauled back to prison hanging over him had ground his nerves to a razor-sharp edge. All of this, combined with the admiration he had gained for Lola, caught him off-guard.

Her beauty struck him with a raw force, and he reached forward without thinking. There was no conscious decision to do so, and the suddenness of his action caught both of them by surprise. Her soft body came against him, stirring old hungers, and again without thought, he lowered his head and kissed her. At that moment, she was for him like cool water to a thirsty man, and the touch of her lips under his awakened the longing he had kept penned up for so long.

As for Lola, she surrendered to his sudden embrace, not out of a single impulse, but for several reasons. She had yearned for a man she could trust, and in this tall Virginian it seemed that she had found him. Like Mark, she had kept herself apart, a prisoner no less than he. The years of constant vigilance, the eternal necessity of fighting off Ramon and a hundred others like him had forced her to erect a wall—and it was just as firm as the steel bars of the Mexican prison that had held Mark captive.

She was a woman of strong emotions, but her hard life had forced her to bury them. They lay under her outer stillness like a bomb ready to explode. But as he kissed her, she too had a moment of weakness. Nothing had touched her spirit, and even after all her hard experiences, she craved something to believe in and to love.

If he had released her at that moment, as he was about to do, things would have been vastly different. It might have been a moment for her to treasure, for she thought she sensed in his caress something different from the crude advances of the men she had spent a lifetime avoiding.

But her long habit of self-defense caused her to shove him away. "Leave me alone!" she breathed quickly. His reaction came slowly, and a fear touched her nerves. She was, after all, alone with him and in his power—just the sort of situation she had learned to stay clear of at all cost.

"Lola. . . !" he started to respond, but she misread the look in his eyes. With a quick angry motion she struck at him, hitting him in the chest. Her eyes were filled with a mixture of fear and loathing, and he saw at once how badly he had hurt her.

He tried to hold her, to explain, but she was beyond that. She frantically jerked herself free and backed against the wall, her eyes fixed on him. "You're no different from all the rest, Mark Winslow."

He stood there, a tall shape framed by the yellow light of the lantern, looking down at her. He was a hard man, hammered by the blows of war and the demanding forces of the West. In the silence, broken only by the sound of her quick breathing, he sought to find a way to explain his action. But that softness which had been his in a youthful day was now less malleable.

He tried anyway. "Lola, it was just a kiss. Nothing more."

"I've heard that before," she announced in a flat voice. She crossed her arms over her breasts in a defensive gesture and shook her head. "I won't sleep in this room."

He stared at her, realizing that his rash gesture had thrown up a wall in her spirit he would never break through, and in a manner of self-defense, let his voice grow hard. "You get in bed. I'll make myself a pallet on the floor," he commanded.

She saw the determined look in his face as he turned and left the room. Still frightened, she climbed into the bed. Lying there, she listened as he made up a bed with the blankets he had brought up, then she heard his boots hit the floor. Eventually he was still, though she could hear his breathing plainly. She opened her lips to say something, for it occurred to her that she might have misjudged him—instead she paused, abruptly rolled over and lay there quietly until she heard his breathing deepen. For a long time she thought about the past few days, a tragic sense of vulnerability came to her. She longed to cry out to him— but the old defenses were too strong. *He's just like the others*, she reminded herself. For hours she lay there, filled with the sense that she'd made some sort of wrong decision. The darkness seemed cold and the future lay before her like a black tunnel whose end she could not see.

Finally she did sleep, though not soundly. She came awake with a jerk, her eyes going at once to the blanket roll beside the bed. It was empty, and it frightened her that he had risen and left so silently that she had not even sensed it. Quickly she rose and dressed, the thought plaguing her mind that he might never come back.

He did return, however, just as she was pinning a bow into her short hair. She went to the door at a quick knock, and after hearing a stern voice announce, "It's Winslow," she opened it and started to speak. The unfriendly expression on his face silenced her, so she merely stepped aside as he came into the room.

"We won't have time for breakfast," he said evenly. "If you're ready, we'll go to the ship. Maybe we can get something to eat there."

"No matter," she said. "I'm not hungry."

They gathered their things, then Lola followed Mark out of the hotel and along the street. The vendors were already out, hawking their cheap wares and vegetables. The smell of the Gulf was strong as he led her to the dock, then stepped aside at the gangplank that led up to a tired-looking packet boat. "Watch your step," he said. "That gangplank's not too secure."

He followed her up the swaying plank and then turned left. "Room is down this way," he said briefly. He led her along the narrow deck to a door, and after putting the luggage down, pulled out a key and opened it. She stepped inside and he brought the bags in. It was a tiny room, no more than eight feet long and six feet wide. Two narrow bunks, an upper and a lower, were fastened to the inside wall. The only other piece of furniture was a small pine chest with three drawers. She moved to look out the porthole, then turned to face him. The encounter last night had shaken her, and she didn't want to let the situation haunt them.

"I'm sorry I spoke to you so sharply last night, Mark," she said evenly.

He nodded. "The fault was mine. It won't happen again."

It was a brief apology, unsatisfactory to her, but there was nothing else to do. She said, "I'll take the top. That bunk doesn't look strong enough to hold you."

"Take the lower," he said with a shrug. "I was able to get another room." He looked at her, and for one moment the silence seemed to hang in the air between them. They were both proud, independent people, and had little experience making apologies. He would have done better if she had been a man. But as that was not the case, he changed the subject. "Come along and we'll find some breakfast."

The dining room was small and foul-smelling, but the eggs and bacon were decently cooked. For a time they ate silently, the room filled with the conversation of four other passengers. After the others left, Mark observed, "Well, we've got a long way to go, Lola."

"How far?"

"To Omaha? About a thousand miles." He shrugged and traced the journey for her. "We'll take a riverboat from New Orleans up the Mississippi as far as St. Louis. From there we'll take another boat up the Missouri to Omaha. Won't be hard to get to the end of track from there."

"Do you have a job there, Mark?"

"No. But they'll need men." He rose and she followed him out onto the deck. They leaned on the rail and watched a pair of late passengers scurry up to the deck. The first mate yelled for the gangplank to be raised, and almost at once they felt the ancient boat shake beneath their feet as the engine took hold. "What will you do, Lola?"

She looked up at him and saw that the old camaraderie was gone. Formal politeness lay in his eyes, and she felt isolated. "I'll make out all right, Mark."

He asked no more questions, either then or during the long days that followed. Every day they ate together, and he pointed out the features of the banks as the country flowed by. She was delighted by the trip, never having been on a boat of any kind, and he took pleasure in her excitement. They went ashore at riverports several times in order to feel solid ground under their feet. At night, however, he left her alone. Most of the time he spent in the saloon, watching the other passengers play poker. Once or twice he walked with her around the narrow deck before bedtime, always saying in a strained voice when he brought her to her cabin, "Good night, Lola."

So the journey went, with both of them under an awkwardness that had been birthed in one moment—one which both of them regretted. They ate together and talked for long periods, but it was artificial. Lola regretted the loss, but did not say so, nor did Mark.

Weeks later, they made the final trip up the Missouri, and when they got off the boat at Omaha, the din and ferocious activity of the place stunned Lola. Omaha was alive with men, all of them, it seemed, shouting at the top of their lungs. Everywhere she looked, mountains of materials were stacked high—rails, ties, boxes—scattered all over the streets. Ferries were working overtime, moving the freight across the river to Council Bluffs. From there, he told her, it would go to the end of track.

He took her to a hotel named The Royal, and after she had registered, stood before her, his hat off. "I'll be looking for a job," he said. "But I'll be around."

She gave him an odd look, then shook her head. "No, you've done enough for me, Mark," she said firmly. She put out her hand and he took it with a confused look on his face. "Let's say good-bye here. We may meet again—but you won't have me on your hands anymore."

He stood there silently, weighing her words. Something about them seemed like a judgment on him, though he could not say why. He protested, "This is a rough place, Lola—especially for a woman."

She shrugged. "I've never known anything but rough places." Then she smiled at him. "Thank you . . . for being good to me."

He was not happy with her decision. "No, it's you who've been good to me, Lola. If it hadn't been for you, I'd still be stuck in a Texas prison."

"Then . . . we've helped each other," she said, and smiled again briefly. "Not many people can say that, can they?" She turned quickly, going up the stairs and disappearing down a hallway, leaving him standing alone in the lobby.

He moved away slowly, greatly dissatisfied. He wanted to go up the stairs, to argue with her, but then thought, *I've had a thousand miles to talk to her. What would I say now?* He left the hotel and moved down the bustling streets of Omaha, trying to put her out of his mind—but he knew that would be virtually impossible. He shook his head sadly, filing his memories of her away with others he tried not to think of too often, and directed his steps to the sound of the steam whistle that screamed loudly from its place at the terminal.

CHAPTER SIX

A NEW KIND OF DEALER

★ ★ ★ ★

For over a week Lola remained at The Royal. Her second-floor room was directly over the bar and the late night raucous din disturbed her sleep. During the days she walked the plank sidewalks that practically floated in a sea of mud created by the April rains. Women were scarce, and the annoying, coarse cat-calls from the men grew tiresome. She soon formed the habit of going to her room after supper in order to avoid the male-dominated crowds. The rough voices of men and the shrill laughter of women from the saloon below were much like the world she had come from, as was the tinny piano music and smell of cigarette smoke and whiskey that permeated The Royal, and by the end of the week she was growing desperate.

She showed the manager of the hotel the faded photograph of her father, asking if he'd ever seen him. "Never did. What's he do?"

"I think he works for the railroad."

"Doing what?"

She hesitated, not knowing how to answer. "I don't know."

He shrugged and suggested, "Guess you might ask over at the construction headquarters," before returning to his work.

The morning sun was high in the sky as she stepped out of The Royal and walked east along Front Street. Wagons jostled one another, piled high with freight and timbers, and the rough voices of the mule-skinners rose above the sounds of the street. She had to cross several precarious bridges made of planks that spanned the muddy intersections, but soon found it impossible to keep the red mud from staining her skirts.

The river ran parallel to Pine Street, she had discovered, and the closer she got to it the heavier the traffic became. Ferries constantly plied back and forth across the swift-flowing current, and she stopped to watch one of the cargo boats docking. It was piled high with timbers, ropes, steel rails, barrels, and a hundred other items, all looking thrown together in a confused state. But the men who unloaded the material knew how to sort it out, for it flowed off the deck onto the flat cars that waited on the side track. Even as she watched, a long trainload of materials moved off, drawn by a puffing steam engine.

One of the buildings had a sign in front, UNION PACIFIC, and she entered it. It was as busy inside as on the loading docks outside, filled with desks and men who talked loudly to one another as they hunched over paperwork. She stood there hesitantly, not knowing what to do. A man with a young face but gray hair walked out of the inner office at once and asked, "Can I help you?"

"I'm trying to locate someone who works for the railroad," she said.

"Why don't you come into my office," he nodded. "It's a little noisy out here." She followed him across the large room into a small office. Most of the space was taken up by a large draftsman's table, but he hastily cleared one of the two chairs. "My name is Lowell Taylor," he said as she sat down.

"I'm . . . Lola Montez." She paused slightly when she gave her name, a hesitation not lost on Taylor. "I'm looking for a relative."

"He works for the UP?" Taylor asked.

"I—I think so," Lola said. She felt awkward, and for one moment was tempted to tell the man she was looking for her father, but a lifetime of keeping her own counsel stilted the impulse. "He's a relative and I'd like very much to find him." She felt like a fool as she pulled the picture from her purse, saying, "This is an old picture of him. I only know his first name—Jude." Feeling the weight of his steady gray eyes on her, she added hurriedly, "I haven't seen him for years, Mr. Taylor, and I don't know what he does—or even if he still works for the railroad."

Her words sounded feeble to her own ears, but Taylor did nothing to indicate he found her request unusual. He rose to his feet. "If you'll wait here for a few minutes, I'll check with our payroll department. Maybe one of them has seen him."

"Thank you."

Taylor walked out of the room with the picture, and Lola sat in the chair, aware that her hands were clenched tightly in her lap. She had no other plan, and suddenly she realized how important it was for her to find her father. For weeks she had thought of him, and now her mind was cloudy with a sharp fear that she would never find him—or if she did, that he would have nothing to do with her. All of her information about him came from her mother, who had said little of her marriage. Now the door was shut on her past and the future was obscure, and she had to fight down the fear that rose sharply as she waited.

He was back in five minutes, a smile on his face. "Well, Miss Montez, one of our men thinks he remembers this man—but he can't remember the name. He did remember that he was with one of the track crews. So he would not be here."

"Not in Omaha?" she asked. "Where is he?"

He looked at a slip of paper in his hand, then back at her. "He's working at the end of track."

"The end of track? What is that, Mr. Taylor?"

"Why, that's the spot where the railroad has reached. Right now it's in a place called North Platte."

She smiled and her dark eyes were more peaceful than when she had come in. Taylor was curious about her. Not many beautiful young women came into Omaha, and he realized from her accent that she was from Mexico. Her dark green dress was of good quality, and he noted that her hands were well cared for, not roughened by hard labor. There was no wedding ring on her finger, and she had not introduced herself as a married woman, so he assumed she was single.

"Can I get a train to North Platte?" she asked.

He rubbed his chin and gave her a doubtful look. "Well—to tell the truth, Miss Montez, there's not really a town there—at least not what you'd call a town. It's just a bunch of shacks thrown together out on the prairie—that and some tents. There wouldn't be any place for a lady to stay."

Lola shook her head. "I'm not afraid of roughing it, Mr. Taylor."

Lowell Taylor was intrigued. "Well, I can get you a place on the work train, that's no problem." He hesitated, then added, "Omaha is pretty rough with all the saloons and bars, but believe me, North Platte is even worse, I'm afraid. These end of track camp towns are a lot worse. No respectable women there, you understand? Right now," he added dryly, "there are twenty-two saloons in North Platte—and all of them pretty rough."

"I understand, Mr. Taylor," she smiled, and her face seemed to him very fresh and unspoiled. "But I must find this man. Will you get me a ticket?"

He bit his lip, not wanting to do anything improper, but seeing that her mind was made up, offered, "You'll be a guest of the Union Pacific, Miss Montez, no charge. When would you like to leave?"

"Today," she said at once.

"Well, I'll give you a note and speak to the conductor. And I'll give you another one for Jack Casement. He's in charge of construction and should know the man you're looking for." He went to his desk, scribbled out the messages, then gave them to her. "The train leaves at one-thirty."

She took the note and then put her hand out. It was warm and soft in his, but with a firm grip, and her smile was not only on her lips but in her fine dark eyes. "Thank you so much, Mr. Taylor."

He hesitated, then made one more effort. "It's a rough world at North Platte. Many people refer to railroad towns as hell on wheels. I'm afraid that's pretty close to what they are."

An enigmatic light touched her eyes, and she said evenly, "Thank you for the warning. I'll be all right, Mr. Taylor." She rose to her feet and gave him a final smile. "You've been very kind."

He walked over and opened the door for her. "I'll be in North Platte in two weeks," he said, walking with her through the office. "If you're still there, perhaps I'll see you."

"Perhaps." She paused and turned to face him at the outer door, conscious that most of the men in the office were staring at them. She had met very few men like this one. He was not one of the roughs, she saw. His clothing was better than most, and there was something about his manners that revealed he was used to a better class than she knew. He had been kind and gracious to her, and such treatment from a man was a rare thing for Lola Montez.

"Thank you again, Mr. Taylor," she said, offering her hand once more.

She turned and left the office, and at once L.C. Dance, the assistant manager, came to say, "Where've you been keeping that one hidden, Lowell?" He was a bright-eyed young man of twenty-five, tall and thin. "You might have introduced me, old man!"

Lowell shook his head, not answering. He was thinking already of North Platte and what it would do to a woman like Lola Montez. *Maybe I can get this paperwork done and get away from Omaha in a little less than two weeks.* He turned and walked rapidly back to his office, attacking the pile of papers on his desk with a new energy.

★ ★ ★ ★

Taylor had not underestimated the raw quality of North Platte, and Lola discovered this at once. She had gotten her single suitcase from The Royal and been on the work train when it pulled out of Omaha. It had been a rough trip, but the middle-aged conductor, a thick-set man with hard brown hands and a pair of bright black eyes, had made things more comfortable by creating a place for her near his seat at the front of the train. He had told her of his family and refrained from any personal questions, but she knew that he was curious. *I'll have to get used to that*, she thought. *A single woman out here is going to be an oddity.*

She got off the train and the conductor said dubiously, "You might ask General Jack about a place to stay, Miss Montez. There's not much choice. Good luck to you."

She thanked him and walked down the wide street in the falling darkness. Both sides of the street were lined with flimsy buildings and tents, all ready for the nightly blast of activity. The railroad workers, she saw at once, were milling around, shouting and punching at each other, the sound of their varied accents rich in the cool afternoon air. She made her way through the throngs of track hands—Mexicans, Indians, and dozens of Irish laborers—but had not gone a block before she realized the peril of her situation.

A dozen times in that space she had been approached by men, and not all of them were gentle. One of them, a huge man with a pistol at his side, took her arm with a force that shook her, and the whiskey on his breath was raw as he said, "Aw, c'mon, honey. Let's you and me have a drink!"

She had pulled away from him in something close to panic, making her escape in the crowd. But there were others, and for one frightening moment her mind was blank with fear. She had never felt so alone, so vulnerable, and her eyes darted around wildly as she sought some sort of refuge. She still held the note for General Jack Casement, so she entered a supply store and asked the man behind the counter, only to hear, "General Jack? Why he went out two days ago with a survey team, Miss. Won't be back for a week at least."

She thought for a moment, then asked, "Is there a hotel in town?"

The store owner, an older man with a full set of whiskers, gave them a thorough scratching before answering. "Well, not what you'd call a hotel. Woman named Langley keeps a boarding house. Don't know if she's got any room, though."

"Can you tell me how to get there?" she asked. The fatigue of the long trip and the pressure of the search had begun to wear her down. "I've got to find someplace to stay."

The owner studied her carefully. He had thought at first that she was a saloon girl, but now a more direct examination gave him some doubt. She had none of the hardened look of that breed, nor was she dressed like one of the shrill-voiced women who prowled the streets of North Platte like predators. He rubbed his beard, thinking hard, then seemed to come to some sort of decision. "I'll have to take you there," he said finally. "Too dangerous for you alone." He called out, "Larry, I'll be back in a few minutes. Keep an eye on the store."

"I'm very grateful. My name is Lola Montez," Lola said quickly as the tall man pulled off his apron.

"I'm Austin Carroway." He offered his name as he reached up and pulled down a gunbelt from a peg. She watched as he strapped it on, clapped a brown hat on his head, then followed her out on the street. She knew at once that without him, she would never have made it, for the eyes of all the men they passed were drawn to her. Seeing Carroway holding her arm tightly, though, the men refrained from the usual crude invitations.

The house Carroway led her to was tucked away in a grove of scrubby trees. It was a single-story house with a porch wrapping around three sides. As Carroway's boots echoed on the porch, a woman opened the screen door. "Come in, Austin," she said, then peered into the fading sunlight. "Who's that with you?"

"This here is Miss Lola Montez, and this is Hattie Langley," Carroway said, gesturing to the two women. "She just got off the train from Omaha and needs a room. You got one left?"

The woman, Lola saw, was instantly suspicious, but she said slowly, "Just one. How long will you be staying?" She was an older lady, but traces of beauty still remained on her oval face and in her trim figure. She had light blue eyes and blonde hair, and would have been pretty except for the cynical attitude that hardened her lips and narrowed her eyes.

"I'm looking for a relative of mine," Lola said. "I don't know if I'll stay very long—but I can pay in advance for a week."

The woman hesitated, but Carroway said quickly, "Guess that's all right, isn't it, Hattie?" He waited for her slow nod, then turned to Lola. "Got to get back to the store. Hope you find your relative."

Lola put out her hand, which took him off guard, but he took it. "Thank you for helping me. You've been very kind."

Carroway nodded sharply. "Let me know if I can be of any more help."

"I'll show you the room," Hattie said as soon as Carroway left. She picked up a lamp from the mantel and led Lola through a parlor and down a short hall that veered off to the left. She opened a door, and stepping inside, placed the lamp on a cherry-stained wash stand. "Sheets are fresh. Breakfast is at six." She gave Lola a hard look and warned, "I run a decent place, Miss Montez. No men in your room."

"No," Lola agreed quickly. She had an urge to break through the obvious suspicion on the woman's face, and said, "I was in a pretty bad way. Mr. Taylor told me in Omaha that North Platte was rough, but I didn't pay enough attention."

Hattie asked at once, "You know Lowell?"

"Well, not really. He was very helpful to me in Omaha." She saw that the mention of Taylor's name had modified the stern look on Hattie's face, and added, "It will be nice to stay with you. From what I hear there's no other place in town where a single woman would be safe."

Hattie studied the beautiful face of the girl, her thoughts hidden, but she said, "Freshen up a bit, Miss Montez. There's some fresh bread, and I'll fix some bacon and eggs."

"That would be nice—and please call me Lola."

Hattie left and Lola removed her travel-stained dress, washing her face in the lukewarm water from the pitcher. She put on a clean beige cotton dress with a high neck, brushed her hair, then left the room.

Hattie was in the kitchen shelling peas. "I'll fix your meal in a minute," she said.

"Please let me shell the peas," Lola offered readily. "I'm not a very accomplished cook, but I'd like to help." She sat down and began to shell the peas, and for a time neither of them spoke. Hattie Langley was not a talkative woman, Lola sensed, and she herself was too tired to carry on more than a casual conversation. When the meal was ready, she sat down and ate hungrily. Hattie hesitated, then sat down across from Lola and drank a cup of coffee.

They talked for a time, and Lola understood that Hattie was puzzled by her coming. She had an impulse to tell her story, but she didn't know the woman well and was very tired. She insisted on washing her dishes, then said, "I don't mean to be rude, but the trip from Omaha was longer than I expected, Mrs. Langley, and I'm very tired."

"I'm not married," Hattie said with a sharp edge to her voice, as though she were angry or defensive about the fact. When Lola didn't respond, Hattie Langley spoke again quickly, "Breakfast is at six." When the girl had left, she stood there staring at the door, her lips tightened in a frown. "Too pretty for this town," she muttered, turning to leave the kitchen through another door.

For the next three days Lola kept close to the house in the evenings. The town was a beehive of activity, work by day and drink by night. She got somewhat closer to Hattie Langley, but understood thoroughly that the woman would not give her any solid trust until she was somehow able to prove herself.

For large parts of the days, and most of the nights, Lola puzzled over just how to accomplish that. A sense of desperation began to grow in her, for it was obvious that she could not continue living as she was for long. Her money was draining away, so that she would soon have to work. She considered going back to Omaha more than once, even back to the border, to a world that was more familiar to her, but that choice repelled her more than remaining in North Platte.

Her one great hope was to locate her father, but even that seemed beyond her grasp. "How can I find him among all these men?" she pondered late one night. Her window was open and the sounds of the rowdy men floated across to her ears, muted by distance. She was sitting in the single chair, looking at the yellow glow in the dark sky that rose from the lanterns of the saloons and dance halls. She had counted her store of cash before dressing for bed, and was frightened by the sum. "I've got to do something," she whispered, "and very soon."

Lola sat there quietly, but inside, her mind was beating almost frantically. She thought once of Mark, and the memory stirred her. He had been kind to her—but that door was closed. She wondered if they would meet again, then hoped that they would not. They could not go back to what they had been, and there was no use trying.

Finally a thought came to her—a thought that she rejected at once. But it came back several times, and she forced herself to consider it. For over two hours she sat in the chair, struggling with her sparse choices. Finally she said aloud, "It's the only way left for me." Her lips tightened, and she went to bed at once. For a long time she lay rigidly in the bed, considering the next day, and finally said again, "It's the only way. I've got to do it."

★ ★ ★ ★

Cherry Valance, owner of the Wagonwheel, the biggest bar in North Platte, saw the girl as soon as she came through the entrance. It was almost ten o'clock in the morning and he was seated at a small table eating breakfast. The swampers were cleaning up and one bartender stood behind the long bar idly polishing glasses.

The girl was a beauty, Cherry noticed, as she went over to Shep Yancy, the best bouncer in North Platte, and spoke to him. Yancy was sitting in a chair that was tilted back against the wall, half asleep. He pushed his hat back, allowed his chair to settle, then said something to the girl and gestured toward where Valance was sitting.

As the woman came up to his table, Cherry took in the strange combination of dark blue eyes and olive complexion. He would not have imagined that mixture to be attractive, but admiration came to him as she stopped in front of him and asked, "Mr. Valance? I'm Lola Montez. I wonder if I could talk to you for a few minutes."

"Sure." Cherry rose and pulled a chair around saying, "Sit down. Care for some breakfast?"

"No, thank you."

Not a talker, Cherry thought, *but she's a real looker!* He bit into his bread, waiting for her to continue. Valance was twenty-eight, a trim, well-built man with crisp dark hair and heavy black eyebrows. He was finely dressed, as always, with a fawn-colored suit and a snowy-white ruffled shirt. Yet for all his fancy clothes, he was a hard man, handy with gun, knife or fists. A Cajun from New Orleans, he had built a fortune by pandering to the raw desires of the wild railroad laborers who spent their hard-earned cash at his gambling tables and bar.

"I need a job, Mr. Valance."

Cherry was surprised, for Lola Montez didn't have the air of a saloon girl—the only job he had to offer. He said as much at once. "Lola, there's only one job for a woman in this place. And I can see you don't want that."

She allowed a smile to lift the corners of her lips. "I want to deal blackjack for you," she said.

Her statement achieved what she had hoped—and expected. She had picked up enough information about Valance from Hattie to know what his reaction would be. She knew by looking at him that he was a man who used women—and she had heard that he prided himself on his skill with cards.

Valance gave her a sharp look, then shook his head. "A

woman can't deal blackjack. She'd lose her shirt—" He laughed, and amended his words. "Better say, she'd lose *my* shirt!"

Lola had planned what she would do, and he had given her an opportunity. "That's what you think now, Cherry," she smiled. "But suppose I beat you at the game?"

His pride was aroused, and he said immediately, "Can't happen!"

"Then you're not afraid to play against me?"

Cherry laughed quickly, but his cheeks reddened. "Afraid? Lady, I never heard the word!" He called out suddenly, "Nick, bring us a fresh deck."

While the barkeep was bringing the cards, he studied Lola. It pleased him that she was there, and the thought of losing to her never entered his head. He'd had a lifetime of practice and knew himself capable of handling cards with anyone. Still, there was something rich and strange in the encounter, and he was a man who enjoyed new experiences. As he took the deck, he asked, "How about the stakes for this little game?"

She said, "I don't have much money. If I did, I wouldn't be asking for a job, would I?"

"I guess not," he admitted.

"But I'll risk all I've got, Mr. Valance." She took the bills out of her purse and put them on the table. "You win that and I'm broke. But if I'm ahead in an hour, you'll think about the job?"

"Fair enough, Lola."

She took the deck from him, laid the cards down, and he said, "Hit me." When she laid the next card down, he laughed and said, "You win first blood, Lola."

The game began slowly, and within twenty minutes the stack of bills in front of Lola was almost gone. But she knew her man, and forty minutes later she had won three times her original stake. "Want to stop?" she asked.

"You said an hour," Valance said. His lips were thin, and he looked angry. "Deal the cards."

An hour later he had won back a portion of the cash when she pointed out, "The hour is up, Mr. Valance."

"Let's play thirty more minutes," he urged. "I can take you now."

"That wasn't the bet."

He stared at her, then taunted her. "Afraid to take a chance?"

Lola put the remaining bills into her purse, then sat there, her eyes suddenly bright. "I did take a chance. The only question now is—are you going to give me the job I won—or are you going to be a welcher?"

Valance flushed and said instantly, "I never welched on a bet in my life."

"Glad to hear it," Lola said. "Now, let's talk terms. We won't argue over money, but one of my terms is very clear. I deal blackjack in your place. And that's *all* I do."

Cherry Valance figured himself for a pretty tough character—but he also had a romantic streak. A thorough cynic in most things, from time to time he would see a situation that caught his imagination. This beautiful woman who had walked into his place, beating him in a way he would never have dreamed possible, suddenly became an appealing challenge to him.

"Why, sure, Lola," he said smoothly. "That's fair enough." He gave her a smile and added, "If you want to change the rules later, why, I'll be happy about it."

"All I want is a job, Mr. Valance," Lola stressed quietly, a direct look in her eyes.

"Be mighty fine, Lola," Cherry said at once. "Now, let me tell you a little bit about how our operation works. . . ."

Thirty minutes later, Lola rose, saying, "I'll be back at six."

Shep Yancy came over and stood looking down at his boss. "Who was that, Cherry?"

Valance gave him a crooked smile. "Why, that's my new blackjack dealer, Shep." He watched the face of the huge man change from curious to astonished, and added, "May be trouble for you. I figure the boys will be anxious to get their hands on a pretty thing like that. See that they mind their manners, Shep."

"Can she deal?" Shep asked, still incredulous.

Cherry pulled a thin cigar from his breast pocket, bit off the end and lit it. The fragrant smoke rose, and he said slowly, "Yes—but even if she lost, I figure she'll make me a whole pile of money. Way I see it, every man in camp will want to sit down and try his luck with that lady. If they win from her, we'll win it back from them."

That was exactly the way it worked out. Lola came back at six wearing a black dress with blue sequins that matched her eyes. Her shoulders were bare, and she no sooner sat down than a line formed waiting to play at her table. Some of the remarks were coarse, and most of the men laughed at the idea of a female blackjack dealer, but they soon discovered that she was almost impossible to beat.

After a couple of hours, Cherry said, "Shep, she's winning, and she's making them *like* it. Now, that's talent for you."

Shep started to answer, but a movement caught his eye. A short, chunky man had reached out and grabbed Lola's arm, saying, "Honey, you and me need to take a little walk."

Shep Yancy was six four and weighed two hundred and twenty pounds, but he moved like a cat across the room. His huge hand closed on the back of the track-layer's neck, and the surprised Irishman found himself lifted up on his toes. "Now, Paddy," Shep said, "you can't touch the lady. Either play cards with her, or move along."

The Irishman took a wild swing at the huge bouncer, who avoided the blow easily and walked the man out the front door. When he came back he smiled and said, "Sorry about that, Lola."

"Thanks, Shep," she nodded. "It's nice to know you're here."

When Shep returned to stand beside Cherry Valance, he said, "She's a pretty little thing—but I figure she's right tough, Cherry."

The owner of the Wagonwheel agreed. He had been doubtful about the experiment, but looking across the room at the smooth profile of Lola Montez, he felt a streak of admiration.

"She's that, all right." He lit a cigar, and a thought brought an amused light into his dark eyes. "She's made out of iron—or so she thinks now, Shep." The thought grew in him, and he laughed softly. "I guess she'll stick with the Union Pacific all the way to Utah. She's so much a part of this railroad we could call her the Union Belle!"

Shep stared at Valance, then turned to look back at Lola. "She don't look like no Union belle to me, Boss."

But the name got around. Perhaps Shep mentioned it, or Valance. But however it happened, within a week, every man in the camp knew that there was a new dealer in the Wagonwheel—a beautiful woman who distanced herself from men. She took their money at cards, but remained aloof.

And so they called her the Union Belle.

PART TWO

FURY AT JULESBURG

★ ★ ★ ★

CHAPTER SEVEN

AN OLD ACQUAINTANCE

★ ★ ★ ★

Ray Hayden leaned back in his chair and let his eyes run around the table with an air of satisfaction. He was a man who loved the finer things in life, and few things were finer, materially at least, than the luxury coach that had been built to order for Sherman Ames. All of the plush chairs were a deep crimson, and the delicate lace curtains that were drawn back from the windows were snowy white. The table glittered with the sheen of heavy silver bowls, tureens, and only the best silverware available. Polished rosewood paneling lined the walls, and the cut-glass chandeliers—three of them—illuminated the car with a shimmering light.

Hayden picked up his Dutch crystal goblet, tasted the wine, and thought, *This is the way a man should live*. He knew that he fit the surroundings, for he had developed the air of a man accustomed to fine things. He was a handsome man, with wavy blond hair, fair skin, and a pair of quick blue eyes. There was something almost feline in his features, but his quick smile and gracious manners drew attention away from that. He wore an impeccably tailored brown suit and low-cut brown shoes. A brilliant diamond gave off its blue fire from where it rested on his left hand, and another matched it in his tasteful cravat.

"You're looking like a contented cat, Ray," Moira Ames said.

There was a light tone of mockery in her voice, and she was amused to see that the remark flustered the man beside her. "I expect you'll start purring any second."

Hayden gave her a quick, embarrassed smile, but laughed off the remark. "I was just regretting that this will be the last time I'll be dining like this for a long while." He moved his hand across the Irish linen tablecloth, feeling its crisp softness. "For the next few months I'll be eating half-cooked buffalo steaks and hard beans," he muttered dolefully.

Moira turned slightly to get a clearer look at Hayden. She had deep-set green eyes, and now a light of speculation glinted faintly in them. "You could have stayed in Boston, Ray," she offered. "Dad didn't insist on your working on the line." Then she smiled, for she knew him well. "But you've got bigger things on your mind than just a job in a shovel factory."

Once again she had touched a nerve, and his fair skin flushed. "I am ambitious, Moira. You've always had money, so you don't know what it's like to stand around with your hat in your hand waiting for someone to give you a tip."

"Is that why you keep asking me to marry you?" Moira raised her eyebrows in mock horror, then shook her head. "Marrying the boss's daughter is the quickest way to the top, I suppose."

"Moira! You know better than that!" Hayden lifted his voice in protest, which drew the attention of Moira's father, Sherman Ames, who sat next to General Dodge at the end of the table. Lowering his voice he murmured, "You must know I love you, Moira. And I can't expect you to marry a poor man, so that's why I'm ambitious." A rash smile creased his full lips, and he shook his head. "If I didn't love you so much, do you think I'd leave the comforts of Boston—and you—for a raw frontier?"

Moira Ames studied Hayden, her head cocked to one side. She was a striking woman of twenty-two, tall and well-formed. Her straight blonde hair framed an oval face, and the hand she lifted to touch her cheek in a meditative motion was rounded and smooth, never having done a day's hard work. She had had many offers of marriage, but none of them had suited her. Her father had cried out once with a rare impatience, "Moira, you try out men like you're picking out a new dress!" And she had not disagreed with him, for her wealth and position had spoiled her terribly. She would often remark that her only redeeming feature was that she knew she was spoiled—and planned to continue exactly in that way.

Ray Hayden had come to work for her father at Ames Shovel Company two years earlier. He had impressed Sherman Ames, who had promoted him rapidly and, as a matter of course, admitted the young man into his inner circle, which included his family. He had been witty, charming and deemed a suitable escort for Moira, and within a year he had become an ardent suitor.

Now as she looked at Ray, Moira wondered exactly how she did feel about him. He had come into her life at a time when she was bored, and when she had just handed Jeffrey Sloan a refusal of marriage. Life had been dull—but Ray had been there. She had kept him dangling, which did not bother her, and which he didn't seem to mind, but now she was suddenly dissatisfied with the relationship. It must have been a feeling that had lain dormant, but now it rose to her mind, and she said carefully, "This will be good for you, Ray. You're smart and charming, but so are lots of other men. You're smart enough to see that the building of this transcontinental railroad is going to make a few men rich. And you're sitting in the car with most of those men."

Ray glanced around the table at her words. Grenville Dodge, Chief Engineer of the Union Pacific sat at the head of the table. He had been a commander under Grant during the war, and it had been Grant who had given him a leave of absence from the Army to serve in that capacity. He was an unimpressive man in his mid-thirties, with a short black beard and a set of careful black eyes. His word was law on the Union Pacific, and that word usually was soft spoken.

To his left was Sam Reed, Superintendent of Construction. He was a small man with a rather gentle face set off by a brown beard. It was his job to get the actual rails laid, and since Dodge was usually off to Washington or in an advance survey party, he often had to make the big decisions.

General Jack Casement sat across from Reed. He was the smallest man in the room, not over five feet five. He had served under Grant, and it was his job, along with his brother Dan, to control the actual construction. He was a feisty man, always ready to take up fists or guns with any of the thousands of workers on the line.

To his left sat Sherman Ames, his 220 pounds spilling over his chair. He had graying hair and beard, but no moustache, and his blunt features gave plain warning of the stubbornness that lay underneath. He was very wealthy, and had come to be one of the prime movers in the financing of the Union Pacific. He was talking now to the last member of the party, and his voice was gruff and displeased.

"We've got to keep the cost down, Durant," he said bluntly to the rather flamboyant man who sat somewhat apart from the others. "Some of the lines you want will run the UP over the country like a snake!"

Doctor Thomas C. Durant studied the table, not answering at once. He was isolated not only by the fact that he sat apart from the others at the table, but also by every other measurement. He was a small man, with thin fingers and a Vandyke beard that he often stroked, and there was a shrewdness in his eyes as he looked up and measured the other men in the car. He had studied medicine at Albany College, and had later taught there. His mind was too quick and active to be satisfied with a medical practice, so he had leaped into railroad construction and promotion. This change in vocation had proved tremendously successful, and he now owned more UP stock than any other individual. He was also known to squeeze as much profit from construction as the traffic would bear.

"Of course, Ames, we all want that," Durant shrugged. "But you have to remember that we can't afford to economize. Don't you know that the Big Four have already boasted that they'll beat us to Utah?"

"Durant is right," General Dodge nodded. He stroked his beard and added, "It's going to be a war, this railroad. And the Big Four are formidable."

The Big Four were the men who controlled the Central Pacific: Leland Stanford, a slow-spoken wholesale grocer with political ambitions, Charles Crocker, Mark Hopkins, and Collis P. Huntington. They had combined their wealth and were determined to cut the Union Pacific out of the big government money.

Reed gave General Dodge a curious glance. "They'll cut our throats if they can, General. There's not an ounce of mercy in the four of them!"

"Exactly!" Durant said quickly. "We've all got to realize that this is no time for niceties. For example, I wish that we could put down good oak ties all the way from end of track into Ogden. But if we wait until those ties catch up, the Central will forge ahead of us and beat us to Utah."

"We have to have ties," Jack Casement protested.

"Of course, but we can't wait for the oak. They have to be cut and shaped in Michigan or Wisconsin and cost as much as $4.50 apiece delivered. We'll have to use cottonwood. There's plenty of that available."

"Cottonwood won't stand up, Durant," Sherman Ames said at once.

"It'll last long enough for us to get this railroad built," Durant shot back.

"So you would have us throw down a road that'll crumble— anything for a dollar!" Ames was a ponderous man, and his anger came slowly, but it was obvious that he disliked Durant. They had clashed already several times, and it was said that Dodge had asked Ames to come in to keep Durant from running wild with finances. "We can't do it—we won't do it!"

Dodge broke in, heading off the argument. "I agree with you, Ames, but at the same time, Durant may have a point. We'll have to consider it, much as I hate poor building."

"General Dodge, may I put in a word?"

They all looked with surprise at Ray Hayden. None of them expected him to speak; all of them considered his role to be limited to courting Ames's daughter. Dodge, ever courteous, said, "Certainly."

Hayden was nervous, but it did not show in his face. With a quiet confidence, he said, "You gentlemen have all probably heard of it, but perhaps you have forgotten the Burnettizer."

Reed asked at once, "The Burnettizer? What's that, Hayden?"

"It's a new method of treating soft wood that makes it suitable for ties. I've been thinking about this problem for some time, and I wrote off for information."

"I didn't know you were doing that, Ray," Ames said in a pleased voice. "What did you find out?"

"It seems to work very well from all reports," Hayden said. It gave him a heady sense of power to have these giants listening carefully to him, and he made the most of it. "It's a huge steel cylinder, and as many as 250 cottonwood ties can be crammed into it. The air is pumped out, which drains the pores of the timber, then a zinc solution is administered under high pressure. After the ties are heated and dried you have a piece of wood that looks metallic and weighs almost as much."

Durant said, "I've heard of this, young man. As a matter of fact, it's been my thought that this might be our answer, but I haven't had time to move on it." He added suavely, "I think Mr. Hayden has given us a real possibility. If you gentlemen approve, I'll wire Omaha at once and have my manager move on getting a Burnettizer."

Dodge knew that the storm between Durant and Ames was only postponed, but he was wise enough to know that corners would have to be cut. This seemed like a good place to begin, so he nodded. "I think it will be an excellent option. We're in your debt, Mr. Hayden." He took a few rapid puffs on his cigar, then gave an unexpected smile. "You may have to keep Mr. Hayden around, Ames. He's the first man I've met who can make Durant and yourself come to any sort of agreement."

A thrill went along Hayden's nerves, and he felt Moira's knee press against his. "I'll be glad to serve in that capacity, General— at no extra charge."

A uniformed conductor entered the car and announced, "Five minutes to North Platte, General."

They all rose and went to their sleeping cars, but Moira lingered long enough to lean against Ray and murmur, "Wonderful! You've made your mark with General Dodge—and the others, too. I was so proud of you, Ray!" She reached up and pulled his head down for a quick kiss, then whirled and ran down the aisle, asking, "What does one wear in a wild west town, Ray?"

He stood staring after her, and the giddy sense of success seemed to lighten his brain. "By Harry! It's a beginning!" he breathed, and being an imaginative man, he moved toward his compartment, his brain swarming with exotic possibilities.

★ ★ ★ ★

The wind tore at Moira's hair as she and Ray followed General Dodge and Jack Casement toward the end of track. It had been three days since the dinner party in the private car, and her father had been called back to Boston. He had argued that she should return with him, but she had laughed and said, "I want to see some of the wild west, Dad. Ray will look after me for a few days."

It had been fun, she thought as she clung to Ray's arm. They had prowled the sinful streets of the hell-on-wheels, shocked by the violence and raw sin that erupted at sundown. Ray had protested that it was too dangerous, but General Jack had sent two of his roughest men with pistols in their belts, and there had been no trouble.

"You like all this, don't you, Moira?" Ray asked. "Is it the fact that you're the only woman among thousands of men?"

"That's it," she said at once, squeezing his arm. She had been, he had noticed, much more affectionate since the dinner party. "What are those huge cars?" she asked.

"Work cars," he answered. They were indeed huge, over eighty-five feet long, ten feet wide and eight feet from floor to ceiling. They were so long, he pointed out to her, that they were swaybacked. One of them served as the Casements' office, a twenty-foot kitchen, and a forty-seven foot dining room. Another was a bunkhouse with three tiers of bunks along each wall. There were still others with blacksmithing equipment and tools of all sorts.

"And there are rifle racks in every car, over a thousand of them."

"What in the world for?"

"For Indians, Moira," he said. "We'll be pushing into their lands soon, and the tracklayers will have to be ready to throw down their shovels and pick up their guns to fight the Sioux."

She stared at the workers carefully. "They're very rough, aren't they?"

"Most of them are ex-soldiers from Grant's army. Yes, they're pretty tough, but it takes a tough bunch to face what's coming up." They reached the end of the work cars and he said, "Now you can watch a minor miracle. The Casements claim they're going to lay a mile of track a day—and that's never been done. Let's stand over here where you can see the show."

They moved to a slight crest and watched the tracklaying

operation. Steel rails and ties were piled beside the track, and these were loaded onto four-wheel lorry cars. A horse was hitched to it with a long rope, and a small wiry boy was perched on its neck. He yelled and thumped the horse, and off it went at a gallop. At the end of track men jumped in and stopped the car. The horse was unhitched, and men seized the ties and spaced them out on the grade ahead.

The two-rail gangs moved in from right and left. The first pair of men laid hold of a rail's end and drew it out over a greased roller on the lorry's front. Other gang members took hold, two by two, as the rails' twenty-eight-foot lengths came clear. Each pair of rails was carried forward, fitted and gauged. Then the spikes were driven and the fishplates set. The lorry was shoved ahead over the new rails, and the operation was repeated.

"Why, they're laying track almost as fast as a man can walk!" Moira exclaimed.

"Yes," Hayden nodded, "but it takes much longer in the mountains or in the dead of winter."

They walked along slowly, watching the tracklayers at work, and Moira asked more questions than Ray could answer. They caught up with General Dodge and Casement who were standing beside the roadbed discussing the grade. Dodge was saying, "I've got to get the survey work done up ahead, Casement— especially that 275-mile stretch west of the Green River. That's where we'll jump off with construction next year, and we can't wait until then to set our stakes."

"Indians will be thick out there, General," Casement said.

Dodge nodded. Seeing Ray and Moira, he turned and asked, "What do you think of the tracklaying, Miss Ames?"

"It's spectacular, General Dodge," she said with a smile. "I never saw men work so well!"

"Yes, it's the best organized, best equipped and best disciplined work force I've ever seen." He frowned and said, "The workmen are fine, but we're short of engineers."

Ray had been listening as he watched the tracklayers. Suddenly he exclaimed, "By Harry!" and without a word broke into a run toward the tracklayers.

"What in the world is he doing?" Moira asked in surprise.

"Looks like he's found an old friend," Dodge said. And so it was, for Hayden called a name and a tall, sunburned man had turned quickly from where he was bossing the tracklaying crew. It surprised Moira to see Ray throw one arm around the shoulders of the man, for he was not an overly friendly man when it came to other men.

"That's my foreman, Mark Winslow," Casement volunteered. "He's a good one, too." He saw that Hayden was pulling at the foreman's arm, and called out, "Come up here, Winslow. Let Lemmons take over."

The two men approached, and Ray's eyes were bright as he said, "Like to introduce an old friend, General Dodge. This is Captain Mark Winslow. We were at West Point together before the war."

"Glad to know you. What was your unit, Captain?" Dodge asked.

Mark Winslow smiled and said, "The Stonewall Brigade, General."

Dodge's eyes opened wide, for he had assumed that Winslow had been in the Union Army as most of the other men had been. Then the humor of the thing gripped him, and he smiled. "That particular brigade gave me more trouble personally than the rest of the rebel army. I could usually figure out what other generals would do, but Old Stonewall just wouldn't do what I expected." He paused and said pensively, "He was a great soldier—sometimes I think even greater than Lee."

Mark swallowed, for to hear such a tribute from a former enemy was unexpected. He said at once, "I remember once when a runner came and said, 'General Jackson, they've replaced General Wash with General Dodge.' The General got mad—one of the few times I ever saw that happen. He was sucking a lemon, as he usually was, and he threw it to the ground and said, 'Oh, blazes! I always know what Wash is thinking—but that fellow Dodge—he's apt to surprise a man.' "

Dodge liked the story. His eyes gleamed and he said, "There were giants in the earth in those days." Then he said, "I suppose you went south with General Lee when the war came."

"Yes, sir. I'm from Virginia." That seemed to say it all, and Mark thought of the days that had drifted by since that time he had ridden back to his home. He had no bitterness, even though the war had torn up his world and left him an alien. But at least he was alive and whole.

"Sir, you just said you needed engineers," Ray spoke up. "Well, you're looking at one of Lee's finest. Close to the top in his class at the Point, too. And I was darned near last."

Casement said in astonishment, "You never told me you were an engineer, Winslow!"

"I needed a job, and a foreman position was what you offered, General Jack."

"And he had to lick the bully boy of the crew to hold it," Casement nodded.

Dodge was staring at Mark, and remarked abruptly, "Casement, you'll have to get another foreman. I need a man to go with Peter Brown to Green River. That is, if you want the job, Winslow."

Mark stared at him in disbelief. He had had nothing much come his way since the war but disappointment, and now to be sought by General Dodge! He nodded, "I'd like nothing better, General."

"Well, then that's settled." Dodge liked the way Winslow made no promises. "Get your things together. Come back to North Platte and we'll meet with Brown. You two can go over the preliminary survey tonight. He's leaving day after tomorrow."

He turned to go, and as he did, Moira said, "I'm Moira Ames, Mr. Winslow. I think Ray must be ashamed of one of us, since he refused to introduce us."

"Oh—Moira, I'm sorry!" Ray exclaimed. "I was so excited I forgot. . . ."

He broke off, and Moira said pettishly, "Go on and admit it, you forgot me."

"That must be a new experience for you, Miss Ames," Winslow nodded. A whimsical look touched his eyes and he said with a straight face, "Ray was known at the Point for his forgetfulness. Especially about women."

"Why you slab-sided rebel!" Hayden broke out angrily, "You know that's a lie. I never forgot a woman in my life!"

Mark nodded. "What about that redhead Tom Jenkins was courting?"

Hayden flushed, but then laughed. "Blast your hide, Mark Winslow! Here I get you the best job you ever had, and you start right in showing up my weak character to my girl."

Mark suddenly sobered. He reached out and put his hand on Ray's shoulder and said, "It's good to see you, Ray, real good." He hesitated before adding, "I lost so much in that war—and I thought you were gone, too."

The real affection in Winslow's expression moved Hayden, and he nodded, "I've missed you. Those were fine days, Mark."

"Come along!" Casement yelled. "Train's going back!"

The three of them hurried back along the track, and Mark left to go to the crew train for his belongings.

"You never told me about him, Ray," Moira said.

"No, I never did. We had a big row when he left to fight for the South. But afterwards I saw it was the only way a fellow like Mark could fight in the war. I've always hoped we'd meet up again." He watched as Mark came out of the car and broke into a run toward the huffing engine. "Let's have him to the party tonight."

"If you like, Ray," Moira said. "It might be fun."

★ ★ ★ ★

North Platte was not equipped to handle genteel affairs. It catered to the Casements' rough-handed tracklayers, and as Ray led Moira down the wooden sidewalk, he commented, "This won't be much like your Boston parties, Moira. I doubt if we'll be served cucumber sandwiches."

She laughed and clung to his arm. "It's fun, Ray. Besides, I never liked cucumber sandwiches anyway." She tried to hold her dress high enough to keep the red mud from soiling it, but had little success. "Where will this party be?"

"At a saloon," he grinned. "The owner was shot two days ago, and Dodge commandeered it for the event. I think that's the place over there." He led her to an unpainted frame building with a crudely painted sign over the door: THE EAGLE SALOON AND BAR. There was a picture over the sign, and Moira said, "Is that supposed to be an eagle? It looks more like a buzzard."

"Art critics aren't too plentiful in North Platte, I guess." Ray looked inside and said, "Come on, this is the place." He let her go inside, and Sam Reed moved away from the bar to meet them.

"Welcome to the Eagle Bar, Miss Ames." He turned to the two men beside him with a wave. "You've met Mr. Winslow. Peter Brown, may I present Miss Moira Ames."

"Happy to meet you," Brown said. He was a very tall man with a homely face and a wild growth of ginger-colored hair.

"These two will be leaving for Indian territory tomorrow, so they may want to turn their wolf loose," Reed smiled.

"Well, this is the town to do it in," Brown nodded. He grinned crookedly, adding, "I'm not afraid of the Indians, but this town scares me. It kills an average of a man and a half a day."

Moira commented with a smile, "Then there must be many half men in the place, Mr. Brown. Come along, you and Mr. Winslow. I want to hear all about the red Indians."

She led them away promptly to a table along one wall that was loaded with sandwiches and sweets. As she held them there, Reed said, "That's a vibrant young woman, Ray. North Platte doesn't know what to make of her."

"Who does?" Hayden asked gloomily. "She's kept me on my ear for two years now."

Reed asked tentatively, "Are you two engaged?"

"No. But we will be." A stubborn look pulled the edges of Hayden's lips down, and he added, "She's almost as ambitious as I am."

Reed nodded. "I can see that. Well, the man who marries her won't be bored, will he?"

"Not likely." He watched the three figures at the table moodily, then turned to the bar and got a drink from one of the full bottles. "Will they be gone long on this survey?"

"A month or so. Depends on the weather and the Indians."

Moira was asking the two men the same question. "How long will it take, this survey?"

"Too long," Brown shook his head. "I said back there I wasn't afraid of the Indians, but that's not really true."

"How dangerous is it?" Moira asked. "Hasn't the Government already paid the Indians for the land?"

"That's a lot of hot air." Brown opened his large mouth, took an enormous bite of a sandwich and swallowed it apparently without chewing, then took another bite. "We've broken every treaty we ever made with the Indians, and they know we'll never keep one. Someone from the Department of Indian Affairs goes out, gives some chief a few dollars, and that settles it in Washington. But the Indians don't see it like that. They look on that money as rent, not a sale. They can't understand owning the land. They're backed up now and ready for a fight."

"What about Federal troops?" Mark asked. "The papers say that Custer's left Fort Hays to sweep the plains clean of hostiles."

"Might as well try to clean it of bees!" Brown grumbled. "The Indians just melt away before any significant force arrives, then come back together. They're hitting at our survey teams all the time. A Sioux war party jumped L.L. Hillis two weeks ago. Killed him and scattered his party." Brown took a bite of cake, but not to taste it. "He was a good friend of mine, Hillis was."

Moira nodded sympathetically, but could not picture the horror of a Sioux raid; it was too foreign to her experience. She tactfully changed the subject, and soon had both men smiling.

The party was uneventful. Dodge had invited only a dozen people, and all of them were caught up almost at once in talk about the problems of the coming spring. After an hour of this, Moira was bored. She whispered to Ray, "Come on. Let's wander around town."

"Better not," Ray said. "Or if you must go, let me get Casement to lend us a pair of bodyguards."

"I've got two bodyguards," Moira smiled. She took Ray's arm with one hand and Mark's with the other. "You two look capable to me."

She pulled them with her, and they walked along the sidewalk. As they made their way along, she read the signs that identified the special drinks of the saloons—"Red Dog," "Blue Run," "Red Cloud," and "Pop Skull" were a few of them. Across the gulf of mud she saw the glitter of the saloons and dance halls and business houses stretching away into the night. Over on the corner, the vast shape of a huge tent loomed. "What's that?" she asked.

"That's the Wagonwheel," Ray said. "Biggest saloon in North Platte. Run by a tough man by the name of Cherry Valance."

"How do you know?"

Ray grinned at her. "I sneaked off last night and had a look. It's quite a place."

Moira's spirit rose. "Let's go inside."

"Moira! You can't do that!"

"Why not?"

"Well, for one thing, it's a rough place. For another, your father would fire me if I took you to a place like that."

"You can blame it on me," she said. Excitement gleamed in her eyes, and she pulled at the two men. "Come on, bodyguards. Do your duty."

"Mark, tell her about this place."

Mark grinned at his friend, enjoying his discomfort. "She's your woman, Ray. You do the telling. Besides, I've never been in this one."

"Oh, don't be such a pair of deacons!" Moira said. She let go of their arms and marched toward the Wagonwheel.

"Come on, Mark," Ray said in alarm. "She's got her mind made up, and nothing will stop her."

As the three entered the tent, their ears were struck by the enormous clatter of a band, and their eyes by a solid gush of light. All the games were in full blast, and the flash of light on the fifty-foot mirror covering the saloon's back bar lit the tent like a house on fire. Over on the dance floor the white faces of women and the color of their evening dresses went around and around in a blur. There was no calm, only a surge that swelled more and more vibrantly against the canvas ceiling of the tent.

Mark moved in front of the pair, shouldering the crowd aside. He paused beside a small table and waited until Moira and Ray were seated before taking the other chair. A highly painted woman came and looked hard at Moira, asking, "What'll it be?"

"What wine are you serving?" Moira asked.

The woman stared at her in disbelief. "Red," she said derisively. "You want the whole bottle?"

"Yes, bring the bottle," Ray said quickly. When the woman left, he said, "I hope you get enough of this in a hurry." His eyes swept the room with a worried look.

Mark saw that Moira was enjoying Ray's anxiety. He sat there, his elbows resting on the table, considering her as she watched the wild dancers. She was the most beautiful woman he'd seen, or close to it. She was definitely going to be a handful for the man who married her. His glance shifted to Ray, and he felt the same surge of affection that had come earlier at end of track. The memories of their days at West Point were rich and sharp, romanticized, he realized, by the passage of time. He had made no friend so close since then. At least, no friend who had survived the war.

He was thinking of those days when the woman returned with the bottle of wine and three dingy glasses. Ray poured the wine, laughing at the cheap quality. "We'll probably taste the feet of the women who stomped the grapes!" he grinned. Then he lifted his glass and said, "Here's to old friends. And the beginning of good days."

Mark lifted his glass, but as he did, someone bumped into his chair, causing the wine to spill over the table. He turned and saw a thick-set man of thirty grinning at him. "Sorry about that," he said thickly. He had tight curly hair, a square face, and was so muscular that his arms stood out from his body. His small eyes ran over Moira, and he said, "Guess you're new in town. Maybe I can give you some pointers."

He moved around to the fourth chair, and Ray got up at once. His face was pale, but he said evenly, "Move along, fellow."

"Fellow? My name's not 'fellow.' It's Dent Conroy." He stared at them as if he expected them to recognize it. Then he said, "Let's just have a friendly drink."

Ray said, "I told you to leave us alone."

Conroy's hand shot out and struck Ray in the chest, sending him reeling back into the chair where he collapsed. He was struggling to get up when Mark rose and moved smoothly around to stand between Conroy and Moira. He said nothing, but something in Conroy's face changed. A quiet had settled on that part of the saloon, and Mark saw a huge man coming across the room. The bouncer, he figured. "Conroy, move out."

The words set off a reaction in the muscular man, and he drew his massive hand back to strike. With one smooth motion, Mark picked up the bottle of wine by the neck. He avoided Conroy's blow, and aiming the bottle at the man's round head, he brought it down, lifting on his toes to get more force into the blow. The bottle struck Conroy slantingly above the ear, broke, and the ragged remnant scraped down the side of his face, leaving a deep red track of bloody wine.

Conroy collapsed bonelessly to the floor, and Mark turned at once to face the big man who had come to stand in front of him. He thought he had another fight on his hands, but a slight smile touched the big man's lips. "Dent never had any sense," he commented. Then he turned and said, "Another bottle of wine for these folks." He bent and picked up the limp form of the bully with no apparent effort and gave Mark a curious look. "Be careful. He'll be after you when he wakes up."

Mark turned and saw that Moira's face was, for once, enormously sober. Her hands were twisting a handkerchief, and there was a slight tremor in her lips.

"Sorry about that, Moira," he shrugged. "It goes with a place like this."

"Are you about ready to go?" Ray demanded.

"Yes," she murmured, getting to her feet. She had been shocked by the explosion of violence, and stole a quick glance at Mark Winslow. He was calm, as though nothing had happened, and she realized that in his world such fights were not unusual.

Ray said, "Thanks, Mark. I couldn't get untangled from that blasted chair."

"Sure."

They were moving through the crowd when a voice came, a woman's voice.

"Hello, Mark."

Both Ray and Moira halted, for Mark had stopped abruptly. He was facing a woman who was standing beside a gaming table, and now Moira saw that Winslow was not impervious to shock. His face was toward the woman, but Moira saw his jaw tighten and there was a hesitation in his manner that she instinctively knew was not his way.

"Hello, Lola," he said quietly. He went over to her side, and Ray said, "Come on, Moira. Let's get out of here."

She wanted to resist, her curiosity once more overcoming her better judgment, but Ray's hand was firm. When they were outside, she asked, "Who was that woman?"

"I don't know. One of the saloon girls, I suppose."

They walked slowly down the sidewalk, each of them wondering about the meeting. Finally she said, "I wouldn't have taken him for a man who was attracted by a saloon woman."

Ray defended Mark at once. "He's had a rough life, Moira. You can't know how a man feels." He was silent, then said, "We used to fight over girls all the time at the Point. Oh, not really fight, but we were competitive where women were concerned. And not all of them were in the social register."

Moira looked at him with interest. "Who won?"

He grinned. "Me. I was far more clever than Mark. He was so blasted noble in those days, it was easy for me to work him. But I expect the war knocked those romantic notions out of his head." A thought struck him, and he said, "Moira, don't get attracted to Mark. He's not for you."

"Oh, don't be silly, Ray," she said with a flash of irritation. "I've only known the man two days. He's off to fight the wild Indians tomorrow—and he's taken with that black-haired saloon girl."

He took her home, but when he tried to kiss her, she turned her head, saying, "Good night, Ray."

He stared at her, then shook his head. "I'll never understand you, Moira. But you're going to marry me, anyway. And it's not because you're the boss's daughter!"

CHAPTER EIGHT

SIOUX RAIDERS

★ ★ ★ ★

At the battle of Chancellorsville, Mark had rounded a grove of trees while on a scouting mission and found himself face-to-face with a Union officer, no doubt on the same errand. Mark never forgot the shock that ran along his nerves as the two of them frantically grabbed for their pistols—only a fraction of a second's difference left Mark alive and the Union lieutenant dead.

Something of that same shock hit him as he looked across the smoke-filled room of the Wagonwheel and saw Lola standing beside a table. He had thought of her every day since their parting, and never ceased to reproach himself for the way he had let his desires close the door on their friendship. More than once the impulse to go back and look for her came to him, but that seemed impractical—he didn't know what to say to her. He never forgot the hurt look in her eyes when he kissed her, and regretted that one action more than any other in his life.

He moved toward her, taking in the black sequinned dress, not low cut as most dance hall girls wore, but exposing her honey toned shoulders. She wore little make-up, he noted, and only a single pearl at each ear lobe. Her hair was swept back, and he marveled that she had that same look of innocence he had admired back in Texas.

"Hello, Lola," he said, coming to stand beside her. He removed his hat and looked down at her thoughtfully. A faint scent of lilac came to him, even over the raw stench of cigarette smoke and alcohol. "I'm glad to see you again."

She gave a quick look around the saloon and asked, "How have you been, Mark?"

"All right." He hesitated, not knowing how to speak to her. Mark realized that he should not feel so surprised to find her working in a saloon; she had grown up in one. Yet the days they had spent together had caused that part of her life to fade in his memory. His mind had formed some sort of picture of her that the Wagonwheel didn't fit into, and he had to make an effort to adjust his ideas. "I'm working for the UP," he said, searching for words. Then he said idly, as if it were not important, "This is where you work, I see."

"Yes." She made no excuse, but stood looking up at him with her eyes fixed on his face. "I deal blackjack," she shrugged.

He was uncomfortable and showed it, but he came up with a smile of sorts. "I've thought about you often," he admitted.

"And I have thought of you." She would have said more, but a man had come to stand beside her. She gave him a look and said, "Mark, this is Cherry Valance. Mark Winslow."

Valance shook Mark's hand and commented in an amiable tone, marked with his Cajun accent, "Sorry about the trouble, Winslow. I'll have a word with Conroy. But make sure you don't turn your back on him."

"I'll remember that," Mark said evenly. "But I'm leaving in the morning. By the time I get back he'll have forgotten it."

"Not Conroy," Cherry said. "The only thing he's good at is carrying a grudge. I'll keep my eye on him for you."

Mark nodded his thanks, then said, "Nice to meet you, Valance." He turned his attention back to Lola. "I'll be gone tomorrow, but it's sure been good to see you again, Lola."

"Good-bye," she said, and fought down an impulse to ask him to come back. That part of her life was over.

"An old friend?" Cherry asked, coming to stand beside her as she seated herself at the table.

"I haven't known him long," she murmured. She took the deck of cards and riffled it, adding, "He did me a good turn, and we could have become closer friends—but things didn't work out."

Cherry studied her thoughtfully. "They usually don't," he said quietly, then turned and walked away.

★　★　★

Mark rode along the sun-baked earth, sitting loose in the saddle, his eyes moving restlessly along the line of cottonwoods that marked the serpentine course of a small creek. *Big enough to hide a Sioux war party,* he observed. But when he edged over and took a look, he saw no sign of Indians. The sun's heat had narrowed the creek to a mere trickle, but it would provide enough water for the horses and men of the engineering party.

Slipping from the saddle, he knelt by the stream and lowered his head down to the water to drink deeply, then splashed his face and wiped it with his neckerchief. After watering his horses, he went back to a tree and sat down to wait for the rest of the party to catch up. It was relatively cool in the shade, and the trickling sound of the brook made him drowsy.

A sense of well-being suffused him, a strange sensation considering the constant threat of a Sioux raid, but the six weeks with the survey party had been the most peaceful time he'd known since before the war. Taking out his pipe, he lit it and considered the trip, thinking of how fortunate they'd been up until now. The party consisted of Brown and himself as engineers, and a full crew of rodmen, chainmen, axmen, flagmen and teamsters to handle the considerable train of wagons and pack animals. Brown had argued for a professional hunter, the usual practice in regions like this, but there had not been one available. Mark had proven his worth at once to Brown, for he had had no trouble bringing in plenty of game.

"You're as good as a professional hunter," Brown had remarked. "Where'd you learn to hunt like that?"

"My grandfather was a mountain man," Mark explained. "And my father's half Indian. I learned a lot from them."

Brown stared at him. "Your grandfather—would that be Christmas Winslow?"

"Yes."

"I've heard plenty about him," Brown said, and looked at his assistant with new respect. "And if you're part Indian, I hope that means you know a little bit about these Sioux."

Mark had shrugged. "Not as much as my father. He always knew what to do."

But no trouble had come, which worried Mark. He said as much to Brown later that night when the main party pulled up. Mark had dressed the antelope he had shot, and soon the delicious smell of fresh cooked meat filled the air. Mark sat down with Peter Brown and the two of them ate slowly.

"Any sign of Indians, Mark?" Brown asked.

"Not that I've seen—but I've got a feeling they're out there. My hair won't lie down on the back of my neck. I feel just like I did the night before I went up the hill with General Pickett."

They had come over a hundred and fifty miles across the Laramie Plains, a lush and rolling grassland where great herds of buffalo and antelope grazed—an age-old hunting ground that the Sioux would surely defend with jealous fury. In the spring of the year the tribes' supplies of winter meat were depleted and their hunting parties usually ranged far and wide, so it troubled Mark that they had seen none.

He and Brown had to proceed well out in front of the rest of the expedition—the most vulnerable position of all. It was Brown's responsibility to determine the over-all line to be followed, working from rough maps prepared by earlier reconnaissances, and to designate reference points in the terrain for the surveyors who followed. He had quickly learned to trust Mark's judgment, and it was a relief to have someone to share the responsibility. A half mile or more separated the front and rear flagmen, with the rodmen and chainmen strung out between. These middlemen laid down the actual right of way, recording distances, compass directions and elevations, and putting down stakes to guide the final location crews that would come later, just ahead of the graders. The pack train plodded in the wake of the rear flagman, and the axmen worked along the line as needed, clearing away trees, brush and other obstructions to give a clear line of sight for the transits.

Mark said suddenly, "You know, Pete, the way we're strung out—it's the worst formation possible. I can't understand why the Sioux haven't picked some of us off by this time."

"Maybe they're going to be peaceful this summer."

"You're the only one who believes that." Mark sipped his scalding black coffee and mused, "They'll run out of meat next winter and come into the forts promising to be good. But right now they're mean and full of meat. Just like I'd be if somebody'd come to take my land."

"A funny way for a railroad man to think," Brown said soberly. "You understand that this railroad means the end of the Indian way of life?"

"It's gone already," Mark said, and if he had any grief, none of it showed on his face. "Someday there won't be any signal fires on the horizon, Pete. All this will be little farms and villages."

Peter Brown shrugged, "Well, just let me get this survey done and I'll thank the good Lord for it. My big ambition is to get back to St. Louis and marry Molly." He took an envelope out of his pocket and asked, "Did I ever show you a picture of the girl I'm gonna marry, Mark?"

"Not today." Mark took the tintype and peered at it by the light of the flickering lantern. Molly Penrose was no beauty in anyone's sight, but the young engineer spent long hours gazing at her picture, and Mark had heard every detail of her virtues many times over. "Wish I could be at the wedding," he commented, then an owl hooted and he swung about abruptly, listening hard. Brown leaped up and peered out into the darkness. "Blast you, Mark Winslow!" he exclaimed. "You give me the willies—got me seeing Indians behind every bush!"

The next day at dusk, however, Mark's fears proved well-founded. Sioux raiders cut off a wood detail at dawn. The first Mark or Brown knew of it was when the detail got back, breathless and scared witless.

"I was standing beside John Clair," a young axman named Stevens said, "and I heard something go thunk. When I looked around, there was John pulling at this arrow that went clear through his chest!" He licked his lips and whispered. "I—I tried to pull it out, but he died right off. We had to fight our way back with 'em shootin' at us all the way, and I couldn't even see 'em!"

Mark decided quickly, "We'll have to throw a ring around the camp. Every man get his rifle."

"Ain't you going out to get them Indians?" Stevens demanded.

Mark looked at him in disbelief. "You can go hunting a Sioux war party in the dark if you want to. I'll wait for dawn."

Brown said, "I heard that Indians won't attack at night."

"Some won't, these Sioux will try it anytime," Mark said. "Half of us will stand guard till midnight, the others will take over then." With his military background, it seemed natural for him to assume command, and Brown felt better with the ex-officer giving orders.

All night the men lay with their rifles ready, keeping an uneasy watch. At the first gray of dawn the enemy struck with a flurried drumming of hoofs in the half-dark. Mark heard it first, and yelled, "Here they come! Wait till you get something in your sights to shoot!" There was a quick yelp of war whoops, then a spatter of rifle fire and the hissing whisper of arrows. Mark moved up and down the line, giving advice and calming the men.

A yell down the line caught his attention and he whirled and raced toward it. A group of ten or fifteen Indian ponies had broken through. "Hold the line!" he yelled. "Don't break the line!" He joined the fray, pausing to put two Indians on the ground with as many shots from his Spencer. His Spencer bullets expended, he yanked out his pistol and advanced, firing as he went. The Indians had seen him, and a pair of them, still mounted, turned their horses and came at him screaming. He knocked the first one off, but his second shot missed and the pony crashed into him, throwing him to the ground. Revolverless, he looked up to see the muzzle of the Indian's rifle centered squarely on him. A moment later, the warrior fell over backward, fatally struck by a bullet. Mark rolled over to see Brown, who had shot the Indian, coming at him. "We've got to hold 'em off, Mark!" he yelled.

The men continued to fire at the Indians who had broken into the camp, advancing as they shot, until the warriors left in a rush, hunching low on their horses. The firing went on spasmodically over to Mark's left, but he said, "I think that's it. They'll probably pull back now."

He was right, and five minutes later a calm came over the

camp. "Let's see how much damage they've done to us," Brown said with a pale face.

"Pete—thanks," Mark said. "You saved my life."

"I was scared spitless," Brown admitted. "Still am."

"No matter. You stuck to your guns. That's what counts."

"Never been in a fight," Brown said in a voice of shaky wonder. "Always wondered if I'd have the grit to face up to it."

"I wouldn't have guessed you'd never seen action before. You did fine, Pete!"

They had lost four men, with five more wounded. Six Sioux lay where they had fallen. Brown looked toward Mark. "We'll have to bury the dead right away."

A grave digging detail was set to work, and by ten that morning the company stood at the common grave for a brief service. Brown read from a New Testament and said a halting remark or two, then turned away saying, "Get the burying over with."

"It's so hard, Mark!" he said bitterly. "Take young Clark. He was engaged, just like me. This morning he had the world—now it's all over for him." He gave Mark a queer glance. "I guess you're used to this, being in the army and all."

"You never get used to it," Mark said in a clipped tone. "At least I never do." Then he shook his shoulders as though throwing off the gloom. "We've got to get moving. The men are plenty spooked."

"Think they'll hit us again?"

"Probably. They can live on almost nothing, and we've got to haul all our supplies. They'll wait until we get careless, then take another try."

"Maybe we ought to go back and get some troops."

"Up to you, Pete. You're the man in charge."

He watched Brown struggle with the decision, remembering well his own struggles over such things. It was a thing some men could not do, and he was not sure about Peter Brown. It took something special to lead men into situations where they might be killed. General McClelland, for all his other good qualities, could never do it. Robert E. Lee and Stonewall Jackson could. Because of them, the South lasted as long as it did in the unequal struggle.

"We'll go on," Brown said. "But we've got to send word to

General Dodge about this. Might mean trouble for the UP. Clark was the nephew of Thurlow Weed, an influential newspaperman from New York."

A messenger pulled out at once, and the rest of the party continued on. They forded the North Platte River and headed into the Red Desert beyond. This was rough country, a region of bleak rust sandstone, wind-tortured mesas, and arid earth clumped sparsely with the dull gray-green of sagebrush and crusted with bitter alkali deposits. The land seemed devoid of life. But the Overland Stage ran along its southern edge, and Sioux war parties had long been accustomed to riding across it to and from their raids southward.

The men grew surly, wanting to turn back, and the maps were inaccurate and misleading. Several times they missed the scanty watercourses, and by the end of the month, a hundred miles out in the wasteland, they were in poor shape.

At supper, Brown remarked, "I can't shake this feeling that trouble's coming, Mark. Guess I'm superstitious."

They were sitting down, drinking coffee, and Mark looked out into the darkness. "Sometimes it's more than superstition that makes you sense something's out to get you. Had that feeling a lot during the war. I've got it right now."

"Think we ought to turn back?"

Mark studied the fire, then said, "Maybe so, Pete. The men are about played out. We need a big show of force here."

"I was hoping you'd say that!" Pete grinned. "Didn't want to suggest it, but it sounds good to me. We'll turn back first thing in the morning."

They got an early start, breaking camp while the stars still glittered in the blackness of the sky. Mark cautioned the men to keep as quiet as possible, but as the pack train clattered along the hard-baked floor of the desert he knew that subterfuge was impossible. "Let's make a quick trip, Pete," he said as dawn fired the tops of the buttes to their left. "They know where we are anyway. Maybe we can get close enough to Fort Sanders by afternoon to send for an escort."

Brown nodded, and they moved along the line to spread the word to the men. Noon came, and they stopped long enough to eat a hurried dinner, then forged ahead.

It was after three when they came to a small canyon, framed by rising cliffs of red sandstone on each side. Mark had gone back to ride at the rear of the column, and Brown, unaware of the Sioux habit of using such terrain for an ambush, led the party into it. They were almost half way through when a shot rang out, and a man pitched to the ground.

At once a fusillade of shots followed, and Mark moved toward the front at a dead gallop. The men were trying to return the fire, but firing up at the shadowy targets was utterly ineffective. "Pete!" Mark yelled. "Get moving! We've got to get out of this canyon!"

Brown shouted, "Men! Come on!" and wheeled his big bay. He had not gone twenty feet when a slug struck him in the body, knocking him to the ground. The terrified men galloped past him, seeking cover from the deadly fire, but Mark stopped and lifted him up. He spared no words, but shoved Brown across the saddle, swung up behind him, and spurred his horse into a dead run. Lead whizzed past his ears, kicking up small geysers of dust, but miraculously Mark emerged from the canyon unhurt.

"Make for that hill!" he yelled, and the others, seeing him driving his horse to a rise of ground spotted with large broken rocks, followed. Even as the last of them reached the crest and threw themselves off their exhausted mounts, a file of mounted warriors erupted from a hidden ravine and Mark yelled, "Patterson, take five men and get the horses back out of the line of fire! Stay with them—we're dead men without them! The rest of you, take shelter and hold your fire until I give the order! We're not going to make it if we don't stop this charge!"

They all waited as the screaming warriors drove their mounts up the hill, and it was not until they were twenty feet away that Mark yelled, "Fire!" The volley that followed emptied at least a dozen horses, and knocked down at least that many of the Indian ponies. It broke the charge, and the Sioux raiders faded like ghosts.

"They'll be back," Mark said. "Get your rifles loaded. Mallon, look after the canteens. We're going to need that water!" He wheeled and ran to where he had put Brown in the shadow of a huge rock. The engineer was lying on his back, clutching his stomach, the crimson blood staining his hands.

"Let me take a look, Pete," Mark said. He pulled the man's hands away and saw what he had feared. The bullet had taken Brown squarely in the stomach. He'd seen enough of such injuries in the war to know that the young man would have been better off if the bullet had hit him in the brain. There was, Winslow realized grimly, nothing but a horrible death ahead for Brown.

"It's—bad, isn't it, Mark?"

Winslow made himself smile. "We'll take care of you, Pete. Let me get a bandage on that wound." He removed shreds of clothing from the area, talking to Brown steadily, calling for Roger Mallon to bring the medical kit. He dressed the wound and gave Brown a huge dose of laudanum, hoping that it would put him out, which it did.

Mallon stayed close, and when he got Winslow alone, he whispered, "He's bought it, ain't he, sir?"

Mark shook his head, but said only, "I want you to stay with him, Roger. I'll be close, but I've got to organize the defense. All of us are going to be dead if we don't watch it."

All that late afternoon the Sioux kept up a steady fire, and Mark had to keep warning the men to save their ammunition. He called the three men who were leaders of the party to him and told them, "We're not out of this thing yet. They've got us pinned down, and they know we haven't got any help coming."

"How about sending someone to Fort Sanders for soldiers?" one of them asked.

"No single man would ever get through," Mark said. "What we're going to have to do is fight an orderly retreat. In the morning we'll all move out together. We'll take it slow, with an advance guard to clean out anything that's in front of us. A rear guard will cover the party. The land is flat and the Indians are poor shots as a rule. We'll put our best marksmen in front and in the rear, and we'll move slowly. They'll try to scatter us, and if we let them do it, we're goners. But if we stay close and don't panic, they'll have to give up."

He spoke firmly, but he knew more than anyone else how slim their chances were. It was suddenly as though he were pulled back in time, to one of Stonewall's expeditions, when they had been cut off from help and surrounded by large Union forces. *We got out of that, so even if I'm not Stonewall Jackson, I guess we've got a chance.*

All night long he sat beside Peter Brown. He offered him more laudanum, but Brown stared at him and said, "No. If I'm dying, Mark, I want to stay awake." The pain came and went, and he talked about the men, how he wanted them to make it. He slipped into a half-conscious state until about three in the morning, when he called suddenly, "Mark—you there?"

"Right here, Pete."

The dying man reached out his hand, and Winslow took it. "Are you a Christian, Mark?"

"No. My folks are all Christians—but I've been a black sheep."

Brown thought about that, then said, "I've been a Christian since I was seventeen years old. Got saved at a revival in St. Joe." He took a deep breath as the pain hit him, his grip tightening on Mark's hand. He looked up and despite the pain in his eyes, he was not afraid. "Sure am glad about that, Mark. I'd hate to go out without knowing things were all right."

"I'm . . . glad for you, Pete." Winslow's voice was unsteady. "Can I take any messages for you?"

Brown's eyes fluttered and his chest moved rapidly. He tried to speak, and Mark had to lean forward to hear. "Tell—Molly—tell her I loved her best of all." His back arched, and he gave a rasping sigh. Mark thought he was gone, but his eyelids fluttered, and Peter continued, "And . . . tell my folks . . . I died believing in Jesus . . . and Mark . . ." Blood flooded his mouth as he fought to speak. "Mark . . . I . . . want you . . . to believe . . . too!"

Peter slumped back and Mark knew he was dead. He held the still hand for a long time, his eyes moist. Finally Roger came and said, "How is he, sir?"

"Gone, Roger." Winslow put Peter's hand on his chest. "Get a detail. We'll bury him here where we can roll some big rocks over the spot so the Indians won't find him."

He rose to his feet, looked up at the stars doing their great dance in the sky. He clenched his jaw, then turned to go to the men. Morning would come soon, and he knew that he might be as dead as Peter Brown—so might they all. He knew that he could go to death with courage—but not with the faith that Peter Brown had shown. He wished now that he had that kind of faith in God, but he said nothing to the others, for he didn't know himself what brought a man to that kind of belief.

★   ★   ★   ★

Lola saw Ray Hayden come in the Wagonwheel, and immediately closed her table. She went over to where he stood at the bar waiting for a drink, and said, "Please, may I speak with you?"

Hayden turned, surprise rising in his eyes, but he nodded. "Of course."

"Come with me." She led him to one of the small rooms where big poker games took place, and as soon as the flap was closed behind her, she turned to him. "Is it true about the survey party—the one Mark Winslow was with?"

Hayden nodded, "I don't know what you heard, but the party was attacked by the Sioux. General Dodge is taking a relief force out right away. As a matter of fact, I'm going with them."

She moistened her lips, then asked, "Is—does anyone know who was killed?"

"Mark's all right as far as I know. But they're in bad trouble." He waited for her to speak, but she was silent, her dark eyes cloudy with some emotion he couldn't identify. "Are you and Mark—close friends?" he asked delicately.

"We were once—very close." His meaning dawned more fully on her, and she continued bluntly, "We were never lovers."

He had the grace to show embarrassment. "Sorry. You never know how it is with a man and a woman." He studied her, then said, "He's a good friend of mine. I've felt miserable ever since word about the attack came."

"If you see him . . ." she began, then bit her lip. He saw that she was not going to finish her statement.

"Shall I tell him you've asked about him?"

"No, don't do that." She shook her head, and he could see that she grieved for Mark. "I hope he's all right. But don't tell him I asked."

"All right." Hayden was taken with her beauty. "Look," he said, assuming that like other saloon women she would be easy to know, "I've got to have something to eat. I haven't spoken to a soul since this happened. Have supper with me. I want to talk about Mark."

She gave him a steady look, then nodded. "I would like to hear about him." Then she added, not taking her gaze from his eyes, "Just supper. You understand?"

"Why—of course!" he said at once. He led her away, and they had supper at one of the better restaurants. He did most of the talking, and if he had intended to find out something about Lola Montez, he failed. But he was a patient man, and when he left her and went to his office for a few hours sleep, he smiled and told himself, "A lovely woman. For all her rumored toughness, I think I see a little soft spot!" He laughed and went to sleep thinking of her.

The column left at dawn, and Dodge drove them at a killing pace. It was a strong expedition, made up of a large force of cavalry, well-trained and hardened.

The journey was difficult for Hayden, but he didn't complain. He had a genuine concern for Winslow, but he also wanted to impress General Dodge with his ability to take the field.

It was on the third day that they came upon the survey crew. A scout came back at a dead gallop around two in the afternoon. He pulled his horse up, and said excitedly, "General, they're up ahead—no more than two miles!"

"Any hostiles?" Dodge demanded.

"The Indians had the party surrounded, sir, but when they saw us, they ran for it."

"Column forward!" Dodge shouted, and the dust rolled upward as the command moved across the desert at a fast trot. Dodge was in the front, and he called out, "That's them, Lieutenant!"

He pulled the column up and saw that the survey party was drawn up in a tight body, with scouts in the rear. Dismounting his horse at once, he walked across to meet the tall, sunburned man who stood waiting. "Winslow, you're all right?"

Mark almost saluted, but nodded instead. "Yes, sir. We lost some men."

Hayden was there almost immediately, and his eyes were glad as he reached out for Mark's hand. "Thank God you made it!"

Dodge didn't miss the fatigue that scored Winslow's face, nor the gaunt look of the men and horses. "Tell me about it."

Mark gave a simple report, leaving himself mostly out of it, but Dodge kept probing. He gave the lieutenant a glance once, for both of them realized that if it had not been for Mark Winslow's leadership, the entire crew would have perished.

Finally Mark said slowly, "We lost Peter Brown, sir."

Dodge said in a sad voice, "Too bad! Too bad! He was a fine young man." Then he said, "I'm in debt for your help, Winslow."

"I was saving my own neck, too, General."

"Well, I know about that, Mark." The general's use of his first name came as a shock to Winslow, but he was so tired he could only smile with cracked lips. Dodge studied him, then seemed to make up his mind. "I want you to work for Reed. You'll be Assistant Superintendent of Construction." He took out a cigar, bit off the end and made quite a business of getting it lighted. He was a man who had learned to judge the quality of a man's spirit, and he saw something in Mark Winslow that he had seen before.

"You'll work with Reed—and your job will be to fix up any kind of trouble. You want the job, Mark?"

"Yes, sir."

"Good!" Dodge felt a lightness that always came when he felt he had made a good decision. He knew that the fight to build the Union Pacific was going to be longer and meaner than anyone dreamed—and it would be men like Mark Winslow who would be tough enough to get the thing done.

As the troop turned to start back, Ray rode beside Mark. "It was a close thing, I take it?"

Mark gave him a tight smile. "Very close, Ray. I feel like I used to after a battle—surprised to be one of the survivors."

Ray said impulsively, "Lola asked about you." He had not intended to tell Mark about his conversation, but when he made his remark, he saw a change in Mark's spirit. He added, "She was worried about you. The way a woman is about a man she likes."

Mark shook his head. "You're no smarter about women than you were back in the old days, Ray. Lola was just being polite.

Of all the men in the world, I'd be the last she'd be interested in."

"So? That's never stopped you before," said Hayden, slyly glancing at his friend.

CHAPTER NINE

CLEAN UP JULESBURG!

★ ★ ★ ★

Julesburg lay on the Colorado-Nebraska border on the banks of the South Platte, a shallow, yellow and muddy river. Before the rails had heaved into sight, it boasted only a score of rude huts, but by April over three thousand people had crowded its tents and knock-downs, and business went on around the clock.

The town was a sinner's nirvana, for here by sheer numbers, the roughs, gamblers, and outlaws dominated a small nucleus of respectable citizens. Whole battalions of prostitutes and gamblers descended upon dusty Julesburg to ply their nefarious trades, and by late May, with the Union Pacific using the town as a major base camp, some four thousand people had crowded into the newest hell-on-wheels.

As Mark stepped off the train onto the station platform at dusk, he was taken aback by the bustling throngs. He had just returned from a week in Omaha where he had met with Reed and Dodge after finishing the survey line to the Wasatch Range. Now as he stepped clear of the coach, holding on to his bag, it was like moving out of a quiet room into a tornado.

"Not ten shacks here three months ago—now look at it," Mark said to Jeff Driver and Lowell Taylor, both of whom had been assigned to work for him.

Driver looked across the eight-inch-thick dust that composed the main street of Julesburg with a cynical eye. "Four thousand citizens," he observed in his customary soft voice. "Steeped in sin and proud of it." He was no more than five foot ten, but the one hundred seventy pounds he carried was muscular and compact. Dark hair escaped his low-crowned wide-brimmed hat, and the silver dollars that made up the band flickered faintly. He wore dark clothing, and the gun at his right side was tied to his leg with a rawhide thong. He lifted his tanned face, dominated by black eyes and sharp features, to his companion. "That's your baby, Mark."

Taylor added, "It's not going to be a Sunday school picnic."

Winslow nodded, mentally replaying the last conversation he'd had with Dodge. It had been a brief meeting, and only Sam Reed had been present. Dodge had said, "Mark, I don't want you to do any more office work this year. From now on your job is to handle any trouble along the right of way. We've got some agitators in our construction gangs, and we all know that the Central's paying them—you'll have to stop that." He had paused and a frown creased his cheeks. "The government expects the railroad to keep order in the end-of-track towns, and I propose to do it. We know that the gamblers have already taken over Julesburg, and they plan to take the other towns as the track goes west. Cherry Valance is the ringleader. He's already served notice that they do not propose to observe the authority of any mayor or town marshal we may appoint."

Dodge had seemed to be finished, so Mark had asked, "How far do you want me to go, General?"

"How far?" An angry light had flared in Dodge's eyes. "Hang them from the nearest tree, Mark!"

"No trees in Julesburg, sir," Reed had commented with a droll smile.

Dodge had responded with a quick answer. "Use a telegraph pole, then. Reed has enough to do as it is, Mark, so it's up to you to see that Julesburg behaves itself."

As Mark walked along the dusty street, he thought of that meeting, understanding that Dodge meant exactly what he said. He lifted his eyes across the bustling crowds and saw the string of dance halls, saloons and business houses stretching away to the flat prairie. Whether canvas or log-framed or pine-boarded, all of them boomed with the traffic and trade of the newly opened construction year. Over on the corner the vast shape of Valance's Wagonwheel saloon, a circus tent fifty feet wide and a hundred feet long, emitted its constant gush of light and sound.

The three men turned into the Crescent Hotel, and Billy Carter, the clerk, shoved the register across the desk. "Been a fellow looking for you, Mr. Winslow," he commented as Mark signed his name. "He wouldn't say his name, and I never saw him before."

Mark shrugged and said, "I guess he'll find me if he wants to bad enough." He led the way up the steep stairs and unlocked the door of the second room on the left. Once inside, Driver and Taylor dropped their bags and sat down while Mark poured a basin full of water. Standing in front of a dresser mirror, he lathered his face.

"I'm glad to be out of Omaha," he said, pulling the razor down over one cheek. "Too much book work."

Driver gave him a cheerless glance. "May be wishing for a little more of that before we're through here," he said. "This town is like nothing I've ever seen."

Mark started to answer, but a knock broke in. "Come on in," he called.

The door opened to admit a colorful-looking character. His wiry frame was not over five feet eight inches, and a tremendous droopy walrus moustache seemed to pull his head forward with its weight. He seemed not to notice Driver and Taylor and said in a loud voice, "Hidee, Captain!"

Mark whirled around, his lathered face suddenly filled with pleasure. "Well, deliver me!" he laughed, crossing the room to grab the little tow-headed man's hand. "Dooley Young! What in the world are you doing in this part of the world?"

"Aw, Captain, yore ma's been after me to come out and see you don't git in no trouble," Young answered. He reached inside his inner coat pocket, retrieved a small bundle of envelopes tied with a string, and handed them to Winslow. "Here's the mail I brung you."

Mark took the letters, broke the string, and scanned the names. "Looks like I'll be answering letters for a week, Dooley." He put the letters on the washstand and introduced his friend to the others. "This is Dooley Young. He was in my company all the way through to Appomattox. Dooley, meet Jeff Driver and Lowell Taylor."

Driver's serious face broke into a broad smile, revealing even, white teeth. "Well, I thought it was *my* job to watch Mark, Dooley—but I guess I'm not up to it."

Dooley gave Driver a bland look. "Mebbe you can be my helper."

Mark quickly finished shaving, a delighted smile on his face. "Come on, we can get something to eat and you can bring me up to date on everyone back home."

The four men went downstairs, and as they ate Dooley talked constantly. The way he could down immense amounts of food without missing a word amused the three men. Mark forgot to eat, his eyes hungry as Dooley rambled on about his home.

"Wal, that Pet and Thad are out to do what the Good Book says, Captain," he grinned. "Two young'uns an' one in the chute. Gonna name this one after you if it's a boy, Thad says. And lemme tell you that Thad Novak is about the best farmer in the state of Virginia! Never thought the first time I seed that boy he'd be the hairpin who'd jest about save the hull Winslow tribe—but that's 'bout whut he's gone and did!"

"Things have been pretty bad at Belle Maison, I guess."

"Most of the big planters lost everything, Captain," Dooley said. "And like you know, most of them's too poor to paint and too proud to whitewash!"

"I haven't been much help," Mark said soberly. "Maybe I should have stayed and tried to put the place back on its feet." He toyed with his fork, his gray eyes unhappy. Then he shrugged and tried to smile. "But you say Thad's held things together?"

"Shore has!" Dooley nodded. Then his face grew angry. "In spite of them pettifoggin' carpetbaggers! They'd steal flies from a blind spider."

"What about my folks? How are they?"

"Why, yore ma's pert as ever, Captain. Mister Sky, he's been ailin' a leetle bit. Me and Doc Lindsey been treatin' him," the little man nodded confidentially. "Doc knows all the fancy terms, but he had to come out and admit that my medicine was better'n any he could come up with."

"What'd you give him?" Mark asked curiously.

"Wal, I give him some wintergreen tea—good for the heart, you know? Then I figured a little wild plum bark ort to take care of that asthma he's been plagued with. An 'course I give him some of my special slippery elm compound for his stomach."

Driver grinned at the feisty little man. "Sounds like you got Mark's dad all fixed up," he said. "I'll know who to come to if I get sick."

Dooley rambled on, describing Tom's life at home and telling about Dan, Mark's youngest brother, who had gone to Texas. "Belle and that Yankee husband of hers live in Washington," he concluded, "but they come home two or three times a year."

"How long you here for, Dooley?" Mark finally asked.

"Why, like I said, Captain, yore ma says for me to watch out for you." He shrugged and added seriously, "No way for a man to make much of a livin' right now in Virginia. Thought maybe you might need a hand with this here railroad you're building."

Mark said at once, "You're on the payroll. It's going to be a little rough, though."

"Won't be quite as easy as you had it in the war," Driver said with a wink at Winslow.

"What outfit was you with in the war?" Dooley spoke up, and the light of anger brightened his blue eyes.

"Why, 14th. New York."

"Oh, that outfit," Dooley said with an air of disdain. "You must not of been there when we give that particular outfit a lickin' at Pittsburg Landing."

Driver stared at him. "I was there—right in the middle of the hornet's nest."

Mark looked over at Driver. "I never knew that, Jeff. That was a rough spot—maybe the worst in the whole war."

The three of them remembered the battle all too well. There had been a small pond in that area, and the blood of the Union men who were cut down by the merciless fire of the Confederates had stained it so red it was known afterwards as the Bloody Pond.

"I was there, all right," Driver said. "And I was there at Lookout Mountain when we ran you jaybird rebels backwards so fast we only got a glimpse of your backsides."

"War's over," Mark said, heading off the argument. "We got enough trouble with the roughs in this town without raking up old wars—and most of the trouble answers to Cherry Valance."

"Yep, I done heard about him," Dooley nodded. "He's a fancy man who uses toilet water," Dooley said in a deprecating tone, "but he's meaner'n a yard dog, and he'd steal a chaw of tobacco out of your mouth if you yawned! He's got him a helper who's got the hull town buffaloed. Goes by the name of Lou Goldman."

"Goldman?" Driver lifted his head suddenly. "He's bad medicine. Comes from Texas. He's smelled lots of gunpowder."

Taylor broke his silence. "He's wanted on a dozen charges, I hear."

"Aw, I'll take care of that hairpin," Dooley snorted. "But 'fore I punch his ticket, I gotta find me some violets to fix it."

"Violets?" Driver asked. "You gonna put them on his grave?"

"No. I sprained my wrist and I gotta have some violets." He stared at the two men, then shrugged. "I swear, I thought everybody knowed that the juice of violets was a shore enough cure for a sprained right wrist!"

"I never knew that, Dooley," Mark said. "What's the cure for a bad left wrist?"

Dooley slipped his Bowie into the sheath at his side and said in a condescending tone, "I don't aim to put no pearls before swine!" Then he sobered and shook his head, "Captain, it's shore a hummer of a place! Miz Winslow said for me to watch you, and that's what I aim to do."

"If you can use that cannon you're packing," Driver smiled, "you'll be useful."

Lowell gave Mark a curious look. "What's the first step?"

"A visit to the opposition," Mark said. He straightened his gun on his hip and said, "We wait until Valance steps over the line—then we sit down on him."

A wicked gleam in his eye, Dooley said, "Boss, ain't you heard? One of Cherry Valance's house dealers put a slug in one of Casement's best track foremen."

"Killed him?"

"Yep. Paddy Ryan done set his bucket down," Dooley said. "And he was a good feller, too. The General said it might be a good way to make your intentions clear if you was to yank that dealer out and decorate a telephone pole with him." He added drolly, "That would give Cherry to understand that you are serious."

Mark gave the two men a quick glance. "Let's make our call, boys."

"Give me a gun," Lowell demanded quickly.

Mark and Driver exchanged glances. "This isn't your cup of tea, Lowell. Better wait here."

Lowell's youthful face stiffened. He said roughly, "I know it isn't. But if you think I'm going to stay here while you do the dirty work, you've got another thing coming. Besides, General Dodge said I was to help you any way I could."

"He meant engineer work, Lowell," Mark argued.

"Give me a gun—or I'll go buy one!"

Mark sighed, and Dooley pulled an old .38 from under his coat, checked the loads, then handed it to Lowell. "I always carry a spare," he grinned.

"Try to stay out of trouble," said Mark grimly.

The four of them shouldered their way down the street until they came to the Wagonwheel. They passed by spielers crying out, "Come on you rondo-coolo sports—come on in and give us a bet!"

As soon as they were inside, Dooley said behind his hand, "That's the hairpin who done Ryan in, Boss. The one in the striped shirt dealing faro—Hugh Gardner, he calls hisself."

"Watch out for yourself, Mark. The white-haired man sitting with Valance is Goldman," Driver softly pointed out. "They've got us spotted."

Mark got a quick glimpse of the two men. Valance was looking down at his hands, but Goldman had his hazel eyes fixed on them. His white hair and rail thin build made him look older than his thirty-four years. Mark noted that the big bouncer was also watching him, but he walked across the crowded room and came to stand behind one of the men at Gardner's table.

The dealer looked up, started to say something, but seemed to change his mind. "Game's full, gentlemen," he said. He gave a quick look to his left and seemed reassured. "Try me later."

"Get up, Gardner," Mark said in a loud voice. "I'm taking you in for killing Paddy Ryan."

His voice carried over the room, and the music immediately died to nothing. The men at Gardner's table turned, got one look at Winslow's face, then scrambled out of their chairs and moved to one side, alarmed. Mark heard the men behind him moving to the sides of the tent as well, and he noted that Dooley and Taylor had arranged themselves well back so that he did not have to think about what was behind him, but Driver was nowhere to be seen.

Gardner was a cool one. He carefully laid his cards down, then got to his feet, keeping his hands away from his body. He had a gun, Mark knew, but it was underneath his coat, probably in a shoulder holster. His pale eyes remained carefully fixed on Winslow. "Ryan was drunk," he said. "It was self-defense—ask anybody here."

"You'll have a chance to prove that in court," Mark said. "Come along."

Gardner shook his head slightly, saying, "You're not going to railroad me."

Valance rose up from his chair to stand about six feet to Gardner's left—Goldman moving in behind him and still farther to Mark's right. "You've got a bum steer, Winslow," Cherry said easily. There was a watchful look on his face and Mark noticed that, like Gardner, he wore his gun in a shoulder holster. "Send the town marshal by if you've got a complaint."

Winslow turned to face Valance. In doing so he had to glance away from Gardner, but he noted that Taylor was facing him, his hand on the gun in his waistband. The saloon was still, and Mark's voice sounded loud as he said, "You've been having your own way, Valance, but that's over now. There's been a man a day killed in your joint or one like it. The Union's going to clamp the lid down. I propose to take Gardner in. If you interfere, I'll stop your clock."

The harsh words struck against the smooth demeanor of the saloon owner, ruffling his temper. He yelled out, "You'll be a dead man if you try to take Hugh, Winslow."

"Don't move your hand unless you mean to pull iron," Mark barked. His warning froze Valance's hand where it reached under his coat. He gave a quick glance at Goldman and the thin gunman let the palms of his hands brush the handles of the twin Colts he wore.

"You're taking nobody, Winslow," Goldman said. He smiled as if he were enjoying the tension, and added, "Don't worry, Hugh. This big wind is out of steam."

Valance studied the situation and found it to his liking. "All right, get out of here, Winslow, and don't meddle with my operation again."

Mark said, "I'm moving around to get this man, Cherry. Don't try to stop me."

He was hipped and in a bad position, for he could not keep his eyes on Goldman and Valance and at the same time watch Gardner. Even though both Dooley and Taylor faced Valance, Mark was uncertain about how much help the inexperienced Taylor was capable of providing. He didn't miss the sudden nod that Valance gave Goldman.

The thin, white-haired gunman kinked his arms, his hands poised like claws over his guns—but a voice broke the tense silence: "You scratch for it, Goldman."

Goldman swiveled his head to find Jeff Driver behind him to his right, his gun drawn. Goldman was a reckless man, but he could not ignore the yawning muzzle of Driver's gun. He froze where he was, and Mark, knowing that the gunman was out of it, turned and started around the table. He kept his eyes on Valance, but the saloon owner made no move.

Suddenly a flash of movement caught his eye, and Mark knew that Gardner was going for his hide-out gun. Mark made a smooth draw, lifted the gun and fired two shots just as Gardner's gun cleared his coat. The bullets took the gambler in the chest and he fell to the floor, dead before he landed. Mark immediately shifted his gun, aiming it right at the owner of the club. "What about it, Cherry?"

Valance did not move. He had been around the hard fringes of the West most of his life, and he had never seen anything like the speed with which Mark Winslow had just drawn and fired. He held his hands carefully away from his body, saying in a clipped voice, "I guess you got the best of the argument, Winslow."

Mark said, "If I have to come back, Cherry, it'll be to tear your joint down." He turned and walked toward the entrance, not giving Lola a glance, but aware that she was sitting behind the blackjack table. Driver slipped Goldman's guns from their holsters, saying, "You can pick these up outside, Lou. I wouldn't put it past you to shoot a man in the back."

Goldman's face was pale, but he whispered, "Have your fun. There'll be other days."

After the four were gone, Lou turned to the swamper and ordered, "Mack, get my guns." Mack brought the guns back inside, handing them gingerly to Goldman who had gone to the bar and asked for whiskey.

Cherry shouted, "Well, that's over. Drinks on the house!" Then he said to Shep, "Get Hugh out of here, Shep."

Yancy shook his head. "Nope." He caught the rough glance which Valance threw at him, but he was too tough to budge. "That's not my job," he commented, then walked away.

Cherry glared at him, then said, "Mack, Perry, take Hugh out of here."

"Well, we're the suckers, Cherry," Goldman said as the men dragged the dead dealer out of the saloon.

Valance was boiling with rage. "Winslow'll pay for that! I protect my men!"

"You'll play hob protecting Hugh," Goldman said callously. "He's dead meat."

Cherry considered the night's events for a moment, and a way of dealing with Mark's unwelcome presence came to him. "Drift around town, Lou. Get the word to all the owners that there'll be a meeting tonight after closing. He's only one man, this Winslow."

"Only one," Goldman said calmly, "but he pulls fast, don't he?"

"You scared of him, Lou?"

Goldman laughed recklessly. "I pull faster, Cherry. Let me get him in front of me without a gun in my back, and you'll see the end of Winslow!"

Lola had not moved from her table, but she'd noticed Lowell Taylor as soon as he came in with Mark and the other two men. He recognized her at once, and an hour later, after the crowd was back to its normal condition, he appeared before her. "Mind if I play?" he asked quietly. He was wearing a different suit, and had a black hat pulled low over his face.

"Mr. Taylor, please leave!" Lola said through clenched teeth. "Cherry or Goldman would kill you in a second!"

"But I'm wearing a disguise," he smiled. He looked down and said, "I'll take a card." She put a card face up, and he said, "Busted! Let's try again."

She shook her head. "You were very kind to me in Omaha, Mr. Taylor—but you're a fool for being here."

"Will you have lunch with me tomorrow?"

"Yes—if you leave now!"

"All right. What place?"

"Adams' Cafe."

"I'll see you there at noon." He left at once and she saw that her hands were trembling. He had appeared like a ghost from her past, and she dreaded seeing him the next day. But at least saying yes meant she could keep him safe for the moment!

★   ★   ★   ★

Lola had seen much violence in her life, but she was shaken by the scene that had exploded in the Wagonwheel. She dealt the cards mechanically until nine o'clock, then said, "Shep, tell Cherry I'm leaving early, will you?"

"Sure, Lola." The big bouncer asked idly, "You going to get something to eat?"

"I guess so." She was not hungry, but the thought of sitting in her small room depressed her.

"You don't need to be walking the streets alone this late," he commented. He added, "I'm kind of hungry myself. Mind if I tag along?"

"Not at all, Shep." The two of them made a strange enough pair—the dainty beauty and the gruff giant. But over the days she had learned that Shep was safe. He often stopped to talk to her, never about anything personal, and never with a hint of any baser motive. As he shouldered men aside for her, and then opened the door, she realized that he was the only person in Julesburg she could trust.

She took his arm as they cleared the entrance, which made him give her a sudden look of wonder. He was a simple man, steeped in the sin of his trade. Many things he'd done had left their mark on his spirit—but somehow the fragile beauty of Lola drew him. He had appointed himself her protector, and she knew the threat of Yancy's murderous fists had provided her with safety. He had beaten one man who had tried to force himself on Lola, and word got around, "Don't fool with the Union Belle—Yancy will beat your ears off!"

They made their way to a small cafe run by a short, one-legged man named Caleb Adams. It was fairly empty, and the owner came forward with a smile, his peg-leg rapping on the wooden floor. "Why, hello, Miss Lola—Yancy. Got some fresh pork chops tonight. I saved the choice ones just for you. And we got some new potatoes." Lola ate most of her meals here, and he had quickly learned her favorites.

"That sounds good, Caleb," Lola smiled appreciatively. "And if you happen to have some hot tea, I'd welcome a cup."

"Sure have! Be right out with it! What'll you have, Shep?"

"T-bone and coffee. Pie if you've got any."

They leaned back in their chairs, and soon Lola was sipping the China tea that only Caleb Adams could provide, while Yancy poured cup after cup of steaming black coffee down his throat. Only two other tables were occupied, so they sat there soaking up the peace of the small cafe, a dire contrast to the raucous noise of the Wagonwheel. Shep did most of the talking, speaking idly of the small events of the day—unimportant things. He had a soft voice for such a rough man, and soon Lola was leaning forward, a relaxed smile on her face—a look which pleased him.

The food came, and it was very good. They ate slowly, and Adams kept their mugs filled with fresh coffee and tea. An hour later they were still there, basking in the feeling of comfort that comes after a good meal. Without meaning to, Lola was led to talk about herself. Shep didn't look at her, but kept his eyes on the cup of coffee in front of him. He knew that she was off her guard, and was afraid to move lest she suddenly hide herself behind the wall she kept between herself and the rest of the world.

"I never knew anything but a saloon," she was saying quietly. "I guess it could have been much worse. At least I had a place."

"How'd you wind up in Julesburg?" Shep asked casually.

She looked at him suspiciously, but his expression showed a genuinely friendly interest. "I came here to find someone," she said, then added before thinking, "I heard that my father worked for the railroad."

"That so?" Shep murmured. "What's his name?"

She laughed shortly. "My mother never told me—but I discovered his first name is Jude. I have an old picture of him—but I'm afraid he can't look much like it anymore."

"Can I see it?"

She took the picture out of her purse and handed it over to him. It was very small in his large hand, and he studied it carefully. She felt a shock when he remarked calmly, "I seen him somewhere, Lola."

"You have!" she exclaimed, clutching his arm. "Where did you see him? Are you sure?"

"I'm sure about seein' him somewhere—I can't think where. You know how it is, Lola. I see hundreds of men every night. Hard to keep them separated. They all kind of swim together after a while."

Lola was disappointed. "Oh," she said faintly. "I . . . I was hoping—"

"Hey, I got a good memory, Lola," Shep said quickly. "Let me think about it, all right? If I try to force it, it won't come. But if I just kind of nibble at it, why, it'll come to me sure enough."

"Thank you, Shep," Lola said. She smiled at him and added, "You're a good friend."

Yancy's face reddened, and he cleared his throat to say something—but a man walked through the front door, and he said quickly, "Well, here's company."

Lola turned to see that Mark had entered. Tension filled the room as he noticed her seated across from Yancy. She felt that he wanted to turn and walk out, but after a moment's hesitation he came to stand beside them. "Hello, Lola," he said, then added, "How are you, Yancy?"

Shep grinned at him. "You're not really interested, are you, Winslow? I guess you made it pretty clear tonight that all of us sinners are in for a housecleaning."

Winslow studied him, sensing that there was no real malice in the big man. "Just tell your boss to keep it quiet in there and I won't have to come back."

"Mark, sit down," Lola begged, hoping to direct his attention back to her. He hesitated, but she insisted. "Please, I want to talk to you."

Shep got up, saying, "Winslow, you see Lola home, will you?"

"Why—all right."

Yancy pulled some bills from his pocket and tossed them on the table. "You won't be as safe as you'd be with me, Lola." He gave Winslow a careful glance. "Don't walk by any dark alleys when Lola's with you. I don't want her to take a shot that's meant for you." He turned and walked away with a devilish grin.

"Sit down, Mark." Lola waited until he took Yancy's chair, and Adams hobbled out to take Mark's order.

After Adams had left to fix a steak, Mark leaned his elbows on the table and waited for her to speak. She looked tired, he thought, but the fatigue lent some sort of special fragility to her beauty. "Mark, did you know that Lowell Taylor came back into the Wagonwheel after you left?"

"No. What for?"

"To see me." She lifted her chin and added, "When I was in Omaha I persuaded Lowell to help me get out here. You've got to tell him to stay out of the Wagonwheel."

"I'll tell him," Mark nodded. "But he's his own man. I found that out tonight." He gave her a peculiar look. "Shep may be right," he murmured. "May not be too safe walking with me."

"Mark, do you know how dangerous it is—what you're doing?" she said urgently. "I've been listening to the talk. The owners won't let you tell them what to do." She leaned forward and lowered her voice, though there was no one to hear except him. "They're having a meeting tonight—Cherry and the rest of them. They'll be finding a way to stop you."

"Probably so," he said, speaking as if he had no particular interest. "They've got to be made to mind, Lola. My job is to get the railroad built, and with so many of our workers getting robbed and killed in joints like the Wagonwheel, railroad construction's bound to suffer. General Dodge wants the town tamed, and I aim to do it."

She shook her head vigorously. "Men will always gamble, that's just the way they are."

Lola was a woman a man couldn't easily forget, and Mark

wished it were not so. He said softly, "Back when you were helping me get away, you knew I was a man. And you knew I had weaknesses, like all men. Why did you get so angry when one of those weaknesses showed through?"

She grew very still, for she knew he was asking her why she had withdrawn from him after his kiss. She wished desperately that she could explain, but somehow the words to describe what she felt were not there. Even as she looked at him, she remembered how she had held his hand when he had lain sick and helpless. It came to her how her heart had softened and how she had lavished such care on him that it was almost close to love. But he was not a helpless man, she knew, and he had the full appetites and hungers that all men have—and it was these hungers that she did not know how to handle. She wanted to cry out, *Mark, be patient with me. Be my friend, but don't ask for more!*

But all the men she had known asked for more—more than she was willing to give. So now she sat there struggling with the attraction she had felt for him almost from the first time she'd seen him—afraid that he would trample on her vulnerability if she let down her defenses.

"I don't know, Mark," she said wearily. "Don't ask me to explain—and don't try to understand me." She lifted her eyes and said intensely, "You should be thinking of things other than a woman right now."

"Why, what else would a man think of, Lola?" he asked, a glimmer of gentle humor in his eyes. "It's a woman that makes a man whole. Alone he's a pale stick of a thing. And when a man sees that beauty—as I see it in you, why, that's what makes him alive."

Lola sat still, swayed by his words. They had set off a rich riot in her own imagination. She had never heard a man speak so, had not even known that any man had such thoughts in him. These were things she had often thought and felt in her own solitary spirit—but had never expected to find in another.

As for Mark, he was astonished that he had spoken in such a way. He had not even realized that those thoughts were in him, and he gave her a guarded look, half expecting her to rise and walk away as she had done once before. But she was watching him with a softness that reminded him of the days they had spent together in Texas. That softness made him add, "It's tough on me with the way things are between us, Lola, but I see that kind of beauty in you more than I've ever seen it in any woman."

What would have happened if they had been left alone was a question that haunted him later—but at that moment, the door burst open, admitting Driver and Dooley. They spotted Winslow and came to the table.

Driver gave Lola a curious glance, but said only, "Mark, we've just got a message from the construction camp. Some kind of trouble. Reed wants you to see to it."

Winslow got up immediately and quickly introduced the two to her, "Lola, this is Jeff Driver and Dooley Young. If you ever need help, go to them. I'll have to take you to your room now."

"I'll be all right, I'll have Caleb go fetch Shep," she said. But as he turned to go, she added impulsively, "Be careful, Mark! Oh, be careful!"

Outside as the three marched toward the hotel, Driver said, "You know she's Valance's girl, don't you, Mark?"

He got as withering a glance from Winslow as he had ever received from any man. "That's town talk, Driver! Don't repeat it to me ever again."

"Wal, you shore plowed up a snake that time, Jeff," Dooley remarked as Winslow stalked away, anger in every line of his body. "And if whut I hear is right, Lola's nobody's gal. She's the Union Belle, so they say."

Driver looked at the smaller man with irritation. "You're a pest, Young."

Dooley grinned at him. "Why, anytime you need somebody to push you in the creek, Jeff, just call on me."

Driver shook his head. "Mark better get his thinking straight about this thing. He's out to wreck Cherry, but he's cuddling up to the woman who works for the man. Nothing but trouble can come of that! This thing's going to blow wide open some day, and the last thing he needs is a woman to complicate matters."

CHAPTER TEN

DEATH AT THE SILVER DOLLAR

★ ★ ★ ★

By the middle of July some sort of fine balance had been struck between the saloon owners and those who stood for or-der—which primarily meant Mark Winslow. After a few harsh clashes, Valance and the other owners had sullenly put some sort of limits on the rough stuff. "Just until we can take care of Winslow," Cherry murmured. "And that won't be long."

As the hot summer dragged on, Mark was busy, not only in Julesburg but at the construction camps, and from time to time he initiated peace-keeping efforts with the Indians. Lowell Taylor stuck close to him, and Mark grew very attached to the engineer. Taylor said little, but he was straight as an arrow. A better en-gineer than Mark, Taylor often kept Winslow from making a mistake. Mark had little time left for a social life, but twice he met Lola for a meal, and he spent what time he could with Ray.

Hayden, Mark realized, was not happy. He traveled back to Omaha twice to do some business for Sherman Ames, but he seemed out of sorts. Mark tried to find out what his problem was, but Ray was surly and would say little. On the twenty-third of July, Mark went to speak to him at the office and found him sitting at his desk, staring off into space.

"Got to make a trip to Fort Sanders," Mark said. "Some of the big Sioux chiefs are gathering for a meeting." He saw the boredom on Hayden's face and suggested, "Why don't you come along, Ray. Be a change for you."

"I can't," Ray protested. "Too much book work here." That was not so, but he saw no point in making a trip just to watch a few Indians sit around and grunt.

"Well, when I get back, let's go on over to the South Hills for a hunt. Might be that the sight of a charging grizzly would perk you up." He smiled and clapped Hayden on the shoulder. "See you in three or four days."

When Mark left, Hayden got up and walked out of the office. The grim ugliness of Julesburg always depressed him, but this time an urgent dissatisfaction rose up, almost choking him. He swore quietly, and walked rapidly down the street. It was after one o'clock, but he had had no breakfast. When he turned into Adams', he found Lola at a table by herself.

She looked up with a smile. "Hello, Ray. Like to join me?"

He sat down at once, his eyes brightening at the invitation. He ordered his meal and as soon as Adams left to get it, she asked, "What's been wrong with you lately, Ray?"

He lifted his head and asked defensively, "What do you mean by that, Lola?"

"Why, you've been acting like a greenhorn fresh from the East," she said. "How much have you lost at cards lately?"

Hayden flushed and moved uncomfortably in his seat. She had touched a nerve, for Julesburg was driving him to gamble more than he felt he should. But he said, "Oh, not much, Lola. A man's got to do something to keep from getting bored."

Lola smiled in amusement. "If you're going to play poker every time you get bored, Ray, you'll never leave the table."

He grinned sheepishly at her. He had long been drawn to her wit, even when it was used on him. "Well, that's true enough. I ought to know better, but I thought I could win."

"Against Del Longstreet?" she asked, her eyes opening wide. "You're more naive than I thought, Ray. Longstreet could deal himself pat with one hand tied behind him. I thought you knew that."

Hayden shook his head stubbornly. "Don't you ever get bored and frustrated with life, Lola? Nothing seems to touch you."

Lola dropped her eyes, thinking of how she had longed to leave Julesburg a hundred times, of how she'd had to clamp down on her impatience and frustration with an iron will. But she knew Hayden would never understand that. He was, she had learned, basically a selfish man, interested only in his own needs. The smooth manners and the warmth that sometimes came out of him were superficial. She merely replied, "We all have our bad times, Ray. I'm no different."

He leaned back in his chair, trying to understand her. He was a man who had had considerable experience with women, and had fully expected after a time to succeed with Lola, but it had not happened. He had tried every method that had worked for him in the past, but whatever he did, she maintained the space between them, her dark eyes continually weighing him. Once she had asked him, "You're engaged to the Ames woman, I hear. Young, beautiful and all the money in the world. Why can't you be satisfied with her, Ray? Why do you have to keep after me?" He had been speechless that she should have understood him so well, and she had said gently, "Let me be your friend, Ray. That would be worth something to you—and to me as well."

He had thought of that often, knowing that she saw his weaknesses better than Mark or Moira would ever see them, though how she'd learned such things about him he couldn't fathom.

He changed the subject and they talked for nearly an hour. He was about to get up when the door opened and Moira and her father walked in. Dismayed, he jumped to his feet, his first impulse being to walk away from Lola, pretending he didn't know her. But he saw from the look in Moira's eyes that would not do. He had an agile mind, and moved toward her with a smile on his face.

"Moira! Mr. Ames—what in the world brings you here?" He took Moira's hand and leaned forward to kiss her cheek. She received it coolly, and he shook Ames's hand firmly. "Come over and meet a friend of mine."

Ames said dryly, "Glad to, Ray."

Lola had been amused by the quandary Ray had found himself in, and she was more amused at how he extricated himself. "Lola, this is Moira Ames and her father. You've heard me speak of them often. And this is Lola Montez—a very close friend of Mark Winslow's," he added.

Lola inwardly smiled at his subterfuge, but simply nodded, "How are you Miss Ames—Mr. Ames." Then to give Ray a little help she added, "Mr. Hayden was just giving me the news that Mark has gone to Fort Sanders."

Ames took her words at face value. "Very nice to meet you, Miss Montez." He had no idea who she was, which only added to Lola's amusement.

But Moira, she saw, was not fooled for one second. *She knows her man, all right,* Lola thought, noting the tightening of the wide mouth and the glint in the greenish eyes. Lola fully expected the spoiled woman to pull Ray up short, and she didn't have to wait long.

"Why, yes, Miss Montez, I saw you in the—what was the name of the saloon?"

"The Wagonwheel," Lola said. She saw Sherman Ames take a startled look at her, then proceeded to spike Moira's guns. "I deal blackjack there. But I expect Ray's told you all about that?"

"No, he hasn't mentioned you," Moira said briefly.

Lola knew that Ray was in for a hard time, so she rose and said, "Very nice to meet you, Miss Ames—and you, Mr. Ames. Come down to the Wagonwheel if you want a little action at the blackjack table." She smiled sweetly, left some money for her bill, picked up her purse and added, "Thank you for the information about Mark, Mr. Hayden," before sweeping out of the restaurant. Once outside, she laughed out loud, "*That* certainly took the wind out of her sails!" As she walked slowly down the sidewalk she thought about Moira Ames. "She's the most attractive woman I've ever seen," she mused. "But Ray's going to have his hands full!"

Her thought was prophetic, for Hayden saw at once that Moira was angry, though she merely said, "I'm tired. It was a boring trip. Father, if you don't mind, I'll skip lunch and go to the hotel."

"But I'm starved!"

"You go ahead and eat, sir," Ray said quickly. "I'll see Moira to the hotel."

"All right, but come back soon. I've got some work for you to do."

As soon as they were outside, Ray said, "I didn't expect you to come to this terrible town in the heat of summer, Moira."

"No," she said evenly, "I noticed you didn't expect me."

He laughed and said, "You're jealous of Lola Montez! That's the most encouraging sign I've ever gotten out of you, Moira."

"You're a clever man, Ray, but I know what I saw."

He walked along beside her, silent and thoughtful. He was in love with Moira, or as close to it as a man like him could get. He had tried to be honest with himself, but could never decide if it was her cool beauty or the fact that she was Sherman Ames's daughter that made him pursue her. In either case, he would not give her up. He waited until they were at the hotel, then after she signed the register, he said, "We've got to talk, Moira. Let me come up to your room."

"A man in my hotel room?" she asked in mock horror. The anger had left her, and the cynical humor that lay in her nature began to assert itself. She had been amazed that she could feel jealousy over any woman where Ray was concerned, especially over a saloon girl. Upon reflection, however, she realized that a girl like Lola was exactly the kind that Ray would be drawn to. Moira had enough confidence in her own powers to believe that he would never entertain a serious thought about another woman—but she also realized that he was a ladies' man. "Well, I suppose you're trustworthy. Come along."

He followed her to the second floor and unlocked the door for her. They stepped in and she took off her hat. "What a room!" she exclaimed, looking around at the cheap furniture and warped green lumber walls. She went to the window and looked down on the unlovely street below, then sighed and turned to face Hayden. "Now, tell me about Lola." A smile crossed her lips, and she said thoughtfully, "She's very clever, isn't she?"

"I don't know, Moira," Ray shrugged. "I suppose so. She's had a pretty rough life."

"All saloon girls have, haven't they?"

"She's not really a saloon girl, though she works in one. Actually, nobody knows exactly what she is. The name everyone calls her, the Union Belle, fits her better than any other description I can think of." He walked over and stood closer to her. "You don't have to be jealous of her. She's not interested in men."

"Not even in Mark Winslow?"

Hayden paused, his handsome, florid face thoughtful as he considered her question. "I thought so once—now I'm not so sure. They knew each other sometime back, but they never talk about it—at least not to me."

"They'd make a handsome couple," Moira mused. Then she laughed and lifted her arms to him. "Oh, Ray, you looked like a criminal when Father and I walked in on you!"

He grinned and put his arms around her, glad to be let off so easily. Pulling her close, he kissed her on the lips. But after a moment she pulled away.

"What have you been doing?" she asked, reaching up to straighten her hair.

"Nothing much."

The flat answer drew a quick glance from her, and she asked, "You don't sound happy, Ray. What's wrong?"

"Oh, Moira, I'm caught in a backwater here!" he exclaimed. "There's nothing big happening in Julesburg."

"Father says you're doing a fine job!"

"But it's so . . . so small!" he moaned. He walked over and looked down at the street, then turned back, his face tense. "When I was with Dodge and Reed and the others at that dinner party, I felt more alive than I'd ever felt in my life, Moira!"

"Of course—and they were all taken with you, Ray. I could see it."

"But nothing's happened!" he exclaimed bitterly. "Day after day I sit here doing paper work—and it means nothing!"

She was astonished by the intensity of his feeling. He was not a man who expressed much emotion, and for the first time she began to think that there was more beneath his smooth manner than she had thought. Perhaps it was only because she had seen too many fine manners, but Hayden's burst of raw emotion drew her to him.

"Why, Ray, I didn't know you felt that strongly," she admitted.

"Just because I don't shout it from the rooftops doesn't mean I don't feel things," he said sharply. "And while we're talking about strong feelings, Moira, I guess it's only fair to tell you that if you don't care any more about me after two years than I sensed a moment ago, it's time to call it off!"

He half expected her to order him out of the room, but he saw that his forceful words had pleased her. He took advantage of it, pulling her in his arms and kissing her hard, and this time she kissed him back with a fierceness that amazed him. When he stepped back, she said, "Maybe it's a good thing I went away, Ray. You've changed."

"No, I'm the same," he said. "But I've got to do something. This job is a dead end."

"Tell me what's going on," she said, pulling him down to one of the chairs along the wall, then sitting down in the other. She held his hand, and he told her about the titanic struggle the Union was putting up to get the track laid, despite weather, Indians, and the troubles of construction.

He said finally, "This town is a powderkeg, Moira. Mark walks such a fine line! But sooner or later, the roughs will go too far—and there'll be a war!"

"Will you be involved in that?" she asked.

"No," he smiled grimly. "That's for fellows like Mark. Let them wallow around in the mud and do the killing. After he's tamed the town, that'll be the time to make a move."

She found that odd. "But—it'll be Mark that makes it work, won't it, Ray?"

"Oh, he's necessary—but so are the track hands. I don't want either job, Moira," he said, and his face was as intense as she'd ever seen it. "I want to be a success. Not just for me—but for us!"

She leaned forward and kissed him, whispering, "You will be, Ray!"

★　★　★　★

When Mark came back from Fort Sanders, Ray met him at the station. "Things are worsening, Mark. Ames is here with bad news, and that's only part of it."

"What's the rest of it?"

"Ever since you've been gone, the town's been terrorized. I think they waited for you to leave—and now they're daring you to do something about it."

"Let's talk to Ames first, and we'll see what he has to say."

Ames was glum when they met with him. "Durant has gone

crazy!" he declared bluntly. "He's challenging every decision I make, and he's got the finances tied up so tight I don't know where we're going to get the money to buy rails and ties."

"What does General Dodge say?" Mark asked quickly.

"Dodge is fighting twenty-four hours a day with the law-makers," Ames sighed. "It's my job to see to the money." His face was filled with apprehension. "I've mortgaged my business to the hilt, but it's not nearly enough."

"So what comes next, sir?" Ray asked.

"I'll talk to Reed. He may have to go to Washington and help Dodge. If that happens, you two will be responsible to keep things going."

A thrill of exultation ran through Hayden, but he kept a serious face. "We'll take care of this end, Mr. Ames."

They talked about the railroad for two hours, then left Ames's room. The sound of gunfire broke the night, and a group of horsemen rode down the street, screeching like banshees.

"Maybe it's time I paid Cherry another visit," Mark said grimly.

"That's just what they want," Ray argued. "Let's get the army to put the town under martial law."

"No, this is the Union's job, and I'm the man the Union has chosen to do it." He thought hard, then said, "I'm going to the Wagonwheel. Will you go find Driver and Young and tell them to meet me there?"

"Get them first," Ray insisted.

"No, just tell them to be quick." Mark walked off before Hayden could argue anymore.

He ignored the looks he got on the way down the crowded street. The Wagonwheel was in full swing, but Mark moved easily across the room, taking a seat at one of the few empty tables. He looked around for Valance, but didn't see him, nor did he see Goldman. A nondescript man came out of the crowd and asked, "You looking for Lowell Taylor?"

"No," Winslow said.

"Well, he's up at the Silver Dollar Saloon, in trouble." The man faded away at once. Mark got to his feet and left the saloon at a fast walk. The Silver Dollar was a poker club on the second floor over a hardware store. He made his way through the crowd, turned off on the side street, and noted that no lights burned on the second floor. A stairway led along the outside wall, and he climbed it slowly, pulling his gun as he reached the landing. He put his hand to the knob of the door and stepped into a hall illuminated by one small lamp bracketed against the boards. A little ahead of him a door stood ajar, and he moved cautiously toward it. A slice of light crept out of the crack, and Mark took a quick step into the room, pistol raised and ready for an ambush. But what he saw hit him harder than a bullet.

By the dim light of a lamp, he saw Lowell Taylor sprawled out on his chest, his head twisted to one side. A pool of blood spread out from the still body, and when Mark felt for a pulse, he felt nothing.

Suddenly a board squeaked behind him, and he immediately fell flat on the floor beside the still body. An explosion rocked the room, and Mark rolled over, laying a raking fire on the open doorway. He rose and plunged into the hall, just in time to see a figure disappear through the door that led to the stairway. He dashed down the hall, flung the door open and stepped outside. A figure at the foot of the stairs turned, and he saw the flash of a gun even as the breath of a bullet licked across his face. He laid his gun on the man, but the hammer clicked on an empty cylinder, and before he reached the foot of the stairs, the gunman had vanished into the darkness.

He returned to stand beside Taylor's body, a great sadness filling him. He had grown fond of this man—and he knew for a certainty that Taylor had died because of his connection with him. A seething rage began to rise in him, and he slowly replaced the loads in his gun, then walked out of the door and down the stairs.

He met Young and Driver rushing down the street.

"Mark?" Driver asked. "What's up? You all right?"

"They got Lowell," Mark said evenly, and both men saw the anger in his gray eyes. "Come on." He strode down the street looking from side to side, and then seeing a short, chunky Irishman, he stopped. "Terry!" he shouted out, and the short man swiveled his head, then came at once to wait for orders.

"Terry, it's time to give Mr. Cherry Valance a little lesson in manners. Go get some good men, and pick up some axes. Meet me in front of Cherry's place."

"Sure, it'll be no trouble at all, Mr. Winslow." Terry McGivern grinned. He left at once to round up those men he knew would be willing. By the time Mark and his two friends arrived at the big tent, McGivern and about forty or fifty track hands were there, all of them carrying double-bitted axes and most of them smelling like the whiskey they were full of.

"Terry," Mark said, "that building over there belongs to Cherry. Tear it down."

A yell broke out and the men began hacking at the frame building, a house of prostitution owned by Valance. They hit the building straight on, and the axes bit into the cheap lumber with deadly blows. Almost at once women came rushing out, cursing and yelling, but the axmen only laughed. Some of them scrambled to the roof and peeled it off, shingles flying through the air wildly. They tore at the walls, and soon the roof fell in on the second floor. McGivern encouraged them. "Now, just a little push, boys—and down she comes!"

The mob moved to one side and gave a mighty heave, the skeleton collapsing with a crash. The Irishmen gave a cheer, and McGivern said, "How about another building, Mr. Winslow?"

"Let's go ask Mr. Valance about it, Terry." Mark led the wild mob straight into the Wagonwheel where Valance and all his housemen were lined up behind the bar, waiting. There were no customers, and Lou Goldman stood to the left of Valance, waiting.

"Cherry, we've pulled one of your buildings down. Got any more you want down?"

Valance shook his head. "You'll never get by with this, Winslow."

"Maybe we ought to pull this tent down, Mark," Driver observed. "Wouldn't be too hard, now would it?"

All Winslow had to do was speak one word, and the tent would be afire, but instead he said, "No, we're going to give Mr. Valance twenty-four hours to move his little tent out. If it's still here, Cherry, we'll burn the tent—and maybe you with it."

Valance stood there, his face pale, but there was no fear in his eyes. "It's your day, Winslow," he said.

"Twenty-four hours—and you go with the tent, Goldman," Mark said. "If you're here after that, you'll hang."

Goldman stared at him, licked his lips, but nodded. "Like Cherry says, it's your day."

Mark turned and walked out of the tent, then called the men together. They gathered around him like a pack of wild wolves, and he knew exactly how to handle them. "We're going to make a few calls. Go to the work train and get your rifles and plenty of ammunition. Be back here as quick as you can. We've got quite a few visits to make tonight, and maybe a few more buildings to pull down."

They let out a wild yell and left running. When they were gone, Young said, "Well, you shore played thunder, Boss. But that bunch ain't whipped. We run 'em out of Julesburg, and they'll just set up again down the road."

"But they won't have the upper hand there, Dooley," Mark said wearily. "Come on. Let's go take care of Lowell."

That night was never forgotten. Not all the roughs went as easily as Cherry did. There was a virtual battle in the streets, and five more men died before the night was over. The next day, Mark wired General Dodge to state only that "Julesburg is quiet enough for you now."

The railroad men called Winslow the man who tamed Julesburg. But Mark thought more about Lowell Taylor than his victory over the roughs. And he was sure that Lowell would not be the only man to die before the rails reached Utah.

CHAPTER ELEVEN

SHEP'S NEW PLAN

★ ★ ★ ★

The shock of Winslow's attack on the roughs paralyzed Julesburg, or so it seemed. There were still enough saloons and gambling houses to syphon off the earnings of the UP hands, but the cemetery no longer got its man each day, and Mark spent most of his time helping Reed get precious cottonwood ties for the seemingly endless miles that stretched out toward the west.

He had come back from one of these expeditions late one Tuesday afternoon to find Ray and Moira walking along the main street. Getting off his horse, he took off his hat and beat it against his thigh, sending the powdery dust flying. "Been a hot one," he said. He licked his dry lips, asking, "How've things been in town?"

"Quiet," Ray said. "The saloon keepers are afraid to spit since you ran Valance and his crowd out of town. The ones who stayed are pretty tame cats." He looked down the street and nodded at the gaping space where the Wagonwheel had stood. "Makes quite a hole in the landscape, doesn't it?"

"I suppose, but Cherry's already set up down the line, along with most of the other gamblers." Mark was tired and stained with the fine dust of the trail. He was, they both saw, not as easy in his ways as he had been before the cleanup. There was a hardness in his expression that hadn't been there before, and

Hayden assumed Mark still grieved over Taylor's death.

Moira said quickly, "Go get cleaned up. You're having supper with us at the Palace." When he hesitated, both of them urged him until he finally agreed.

As Mark continued on his way, Moira said, "He's changed, Ray."

"I guess he is. Any man with his job is going to get harder."

They idled along, wasting time for almost an hour, and then made their way to the Palace Restaurant. Mark walked up just as they got there, freshly shaved and wearing a light-weight brown suit with a clean white shirt that made his dark face look even darker. He greeted them more cheerfully, and they entered the Palace. The restaurant was crowded, but Ray had reserved a table, and led the way to it. There were fresh flowers in a vase and a white tablecloth. "Why, Ray, how nice!" Moira exclaimed.

As she leaned over to smell the blossoms, Ray shrugged. "I wish I could have come up with an orchestra so we could have some music with our dinner—but that'll have to wait until we get back to Boston." He had gone to some trouble to get the flowers, having hired a Mexican to go out and gather them. His keen awareness of the nicer things set him apart from most of the men in the West.

"You never brought me flowers when we ate here," Mark jested. "But then, you don't want to marry me, either."

The other two laughed as they sat down. They ordered their food, and as they waited Mark slowly relaxed, letting Ray carry the burden of the conversation. Without seeming to, he gave close attention to Moira—as did every other man in the room. In a country starved for women, any woman would have been an attraction, but with her dramatic good looks, Moira was like a splash of color in an otherwise dreary world. Mark was a little puzzled, for he couldn't discern much depth of affection between the pair. They certainly enjoyed each other's company, but he saw no sign of any deeper emotion in either of them. Ray, he knew, kept his emotions hidden, but it was his judgment that Moira Ames was a woman of extremes. It seemed strange to him that she displayed so little feeling for the man she was going to marry.

He told them about his trip as they ate, mentioning a brush

with five young Sioux warriors, and her eyes fixed on him. "You have such a dangerous job, Mark."

"Not as dangerous as my last one—that one landed me in a Mexican prison," he smiled. "And certainly not as dangerous as the job I had before that."

"What job was that?" she asked.

"I worked for Robert E. Lee," he smiled. He started to say something else but stopped when he saw Lola come in through the front door.

Moira caught his glance, and at once said impulsively, "Ask her to join us, Mark."

He hesitated. "She'd probably be uncomfortable, Moira."

"Nonsense!" Ray said briskly. "I'll do it myself if you're too bashful." He got up and walked over to where Lola was standing. "Lola, Mark just got in. Come and join us, won't you?"

He expected her to refuse at first; it was plainly written in her eyes. But she accepted. "That would be nice, Ray."

Mark rose as Hayden led her to the table.

Moira bubbled enthusiastically, "Sit down, Miss Montez. You can keep these two from bullying me."

Lola sat down and the two men took their places. "I think they are more likely to fight over you than do any bullying, Miss Ames," she commented with a faint smile.

"I hope not!" Ray exclaimed, and he turned toward Mark. "We almost came to that a few times at the Point, didn't we? Remember Alice Glover, the Major's niece?"

"I'm trying to forget that little incident," Mark said with a grin. "She had each of us ready to go after the other with a saber—and all the time she was laughing at us."

Hayden laughed at the memory. "She was secretly engaged to one of our instructors all the time. But I never faulted Alice for putting us through the hoops, Mark. That's the way the game is played between men and women."

Moira scolded him with a smile, "That's right—always blame the woman for your own foolishness." They kept up a light conversation until the food came, and when they were finished with the meal, Moira asked as they idled over coffee, "What will you do now, Miss Montez?"

Mark had wondered the same thing, but had not wanted to

ask. It seemed a little crude of Moira to bring up the matter of Lola's profession, but he saw no sign that she meant anything by it. Lola shrugged, saying mildly, "I haven't decided yet."

Ray said, "Julesburg will be a ghost town in a few weeks. That's what happens to all these end-of-track towns. When the railroad workers move on, there's nothing left to keep a town going. Why, think about what a hummer North Platte was—and yet there's not two hundred people there right now!"

"I'll be going back East in a week," Moira said. "My father's sending his special car. If you have any intentions of going that way, I'd be glad to have you accompany me on the trip."

It was a strange thing for the aristocratic girl to suggest, but somehow it didn't come out as hospitable as it might. Lola only shook her head slightly, saying, "That's very kind of you, Miss Ames—but it's unlikely that I will be going that way."

Ray had missed the underlying exchange between the two women. "Well, that leaves only two choices, Lola," he commented. "Either stay in this town—or follow the track." He got to his feet, apologizing, "I'm sorry to go, but I need to meet Reed in thirty minutes. He'll probably want to see you first thing tomorrow, Mark."

"All right."

Moira also rose and prepared to leave. "I'm glad you're back, Mark. Miss Montez, nice to see you again."

As soon as Ray led her outside, Moira said, "Are you worried about Mark?"

"Worried?" Hayden looked puzzled. "What's wrong with him?"

"Oh, Ray!" she snapped impatiently. "Can't you see what's going to happen? With only one woman to every three hundred men, how long do you think a man like Mark Winslow will be able to keep away from a woman like that?"

"I think Mark's old enough to handle himself, Moira," he said in surprise. "But what if they did fall in love? She's a beautiful woman."

"She's a dance hall woman," Moira said in exasperation, her pace picking up so that he had to lengthen his strides to keep up. "Mark is a man who could go to the top. Look at how fast he's come with the Union already. Father says that General

Dodge thinks there's nobody like him. But if he marries a dance hall girl, that will end it all."

Hayden stared at her. "Why are you so concerned?"

"I hate to see a man like Mark wasted," she snapped. "And I'm disappointed in you, Ray. After all, Mark's your friend. You should warn him about her."

"Why, I couldn't do that!" he said in astonishment. "In the first place, it's none of my business. The relationship between a man and a woman is their own business, Moira."

"Yes . . . but he's not in love with her. He's lonely, and she's beautiful—and available. If he mistakes that for love, he'll be throwing his career away."

"I don't agree that she's 'available.' Lola Montez is hardly a loose woman."

Moira gave him a swift glance. "I take it from that that you tried your luck with the Union Belle, darling?"

They argued about it all the way to her hotel, and when she left him abruptly, he went to his meeting with Reed thoroughly disturbed. Although her attitude puzzled him, he finally shrugged and resolved to put it out of his mind.

Mark and Lola had watched the pair leave, and Mark asked, "Anything I can do to help you, Lola?"

She shook her head, and getting to her feet, refused, "No, Mark. Thank you for the offer." No longer hungry, she wanted to get away, for the encounter had displeased her. Moira Ames obviously disliked her, despite all her outwardly generous gestures, and she wanted to leave. He stood and followed her through the doors, and would have gone with her to her boarding house, but she said, "Thank you for inviting me—but it wasn't wise." Something came to her eyes that he could not understand, and she put out her hand. "Good-bye, Mark."

"Well . . ." he hesitated. "I'll see you again." She shook her head, and turning, walked along through the gathering gloom without a backward look, not stopping until she had closed the door of her room. She took off her hat, washed her face with the tepid water from the pitcher, then went over and lay down on the bed, staring at the ceiling. She had stared at it a great deal over the past two weeks, and the dissatisfaction that had been growing steadily in her came stronger than ever.

She had reached a dead end in Julesburg, and now that the town was on the verge of drying up, she had no energy to decide which direction to take. There was nothing for her in the East—and not for one moment did she entertain the idea of going back to her old life in Texas. As the tinny sounds of the saloons came to her through the open window, she thought despairingly, *There's got to be more to life than this!* Now that she had escaped her life in Texas, an elusive idea, a concept of a better life, floated to her.

She began to weep, silently, letting the tears roll down her cheeks in the darkness. Finally she grew still, and, too tired to get up, she lay there and drifted off into a fitful sleep.

A knock at the door brought her awake with a start, and she came off the bed to stand before the door. "Who is it?"

"It's me, Shep. Can I talk to you?"

She hesitated. He had never come to her room, and it disturbed her to think that he might have wrong ideas. Nevertheless, he was the closest thing to a friend she had in Julesburg, so she said, "Just a minute, Shep." She walked to the basin and cleaned her face before opening the door. He filled the frame with his huge bulk, and when she stepped back to admit him, he seemed to make the already tiny room even smaller.

"What is it, Shep?" she asked, going to the lamp and turning up the wick. She had not seen him since Cherry had left town, and had assumed that the bouncer had gone with him. "Sit down."

He shook his head, and she noticed that his hazel eyes were bright with excitement. "Lola, I think I have a line on your pa."

Lola stood very still, her face both shocked and expectant. The amber light of the lamp showed her features relax in relief, and her lips opened in surprise. Shep nodded, smiling slightly. "May be a bum steer, but I kept thinking about that picture. Near drove me crazy the way I couldn't quite remember. I had sort of given up on it, but two days ago I run into Nick Bolton. He works for the railroad, but I ain't seen him in a few months. Well, Nick knows every hand on the Union payroll, or pretty near, so I got to talking to him. Didn't have the picture of course, but I described him and told Nick his first name was Jude."

"Did he know him, Shep?" Lola interrupted quickly.

"Well—yes and no. If I'd had the picture, the guy mebbe could have done more. But he reminded me about a fellow I seen back at Grand Island—that's where Cherry first set up his tent. His name was Jude, all right, and I guess he's the one that rang my bell when I seen the picture. His name's Jude Moran and he's a foreman for one of the right of way gangs. They stay way out in front, so most of 'em don't get back to town too often. I never seen him after Grand Island, but Nick says he's with a gang out past Cheyenne."

Lola stood there, soaking in his words. "I've got to see him, Shep."

Yancy said cautiously, "Well, you can go back with me, Lola. I ain't said nothin' to Cherry about all this—but I know he wants you to come back to work at the Wagonwheel." His rough features were inquisitive, and he spoke what had been on his mind. "Why didn't you come along with us when we left, Lola?"

"Cherry was getting too possessive."

"Guess that had to come. Cherry's always had a way with women." He thought hard, then shook his head. "Cheyenne ain't much, Lola. It'll be booming in a few weeks, soon as Casement changes his construction site from Julesburg to that town. Mostly tents right now, and a few shacks. Dunno where you'd stay or whut you'd do. And this fellow Moran, he may not be your pa." A thought came to him, and he added, "I remember him because he was a preacher of some kind. Came into the Wagonwheel once and tried to preach a sermon. I had to take him out, of course."

His words brought a sudden excitement to Lola, and she said, "That sounds like him, Shep! My mother left him because he was crazy over religion." She began to walk back and forth, thinking about what to do, and finally shook her head. "I want to go, Shep—but there's no way. I won't go back to Cherry, and any other saloon would be just as bad."

Shep Yancy's face was scarred from a lifetime of fighting his way, but he possessed a store of shrewdness, and now his hazel eyes were alert. He said carefully, "Lola, I got an idea. May not be what you'd like, but I figured you wasn't going to go back to work for Cherry. He was pressin' you pretty hard; I seen that comin' on."

He paused, and when Lola saw that he was reluctant to go on, she asked, "What's your idea, Shep?"

He shrugged and began, "I'm one of the roughs, Lola. You know that. I been taking care of myself since I was twelve and most of the time in pretty hard places. Sometimes I think I been a bouncer in every low-down joint in the country—and I'm getting tired of it. I don't know nothing else, Lola, and I'm too dumb to learn, I guess."

"No, that's not true, Shep," she shook her head. "You could do something else if you wanted to. Now, what's the idea?"

"Well, I've been watching things at Cherry's joint, and I noticed that there's some fellows who don't like that kind of place. They come there because it's all there is—but what they'd really like is a small place where they could play cards, maybe even have something to eat. A place where they wouldn't have to be afraid some drunk would let go with his Colt, you know what I mean, Lola?"

"Well, I guess so," she said slowly. "Are you thinking of opening your own place, Shep?"

"Aw, Lola, I'm not smooth enough for that—but if you'd work with me, I think the two of us could have a good thing."

"Me?" she exclaimed. "Why, Shep, I don't know anything about running a saloon!"

"Maybe not, but I do," he said quickly. "Now hear me out, Lola, before you say no. What I got in mind is a small place, with one good-sized room for a small bar and a few tables. A kitchen in the back for cooking, and a waitress to do the serving. Then we get about three or four smaller rooms off to the side, where a fellow could bring his friends and have a quiet game and a good meal. Make it real nice, you know? There ain't never been nothin' like that in any of the construction towns!"

"But would it pay, Shep?" Lola asked doubtfully. "Would there be enough men who'd come to a place like that?"

"Why, we won't know till we try, Lola," he said spreading his big hands wide. "But I got a stake and I'm willing to risk it. I been gambling all my life, but this time I'd be gambling on myself—and on you—instead of the turn of a card."

"What would I do, Shep?"

"That's my big idea, Lola," he said, and excitement came into his voice. "We'd call the place the Union Belle Casino. And you'd sort of be the hostess, see? You could deal some blackjack, but mostly if you'd just be there, it'd make the place different. I can take care of the bar and boss the cook, and I can handle any trouble that comes along—but I want a place with class—more of a club than a saloon, don't you see?"

Lola said impulsively, "I'll do it, Shep! I've been walking the floor for days trying to figure out what to do, and I think this is it. I've even got a little money to put into it."

"Lola, that's great!" Shep was so excited he reached out and put his huge hands on her shoulders, and his eyes gleamed. "Come on, let's go get something to eat. We got plans to make, girl!"

Lola picked up her coat, and as they left the room, she asked, "What about Cherry? Will he get angry if you start your own place?"

"He never took me to raise," Shep shrugged. "Anyway, we won't be taking much of his trade—just the high-class part." They left the boarding house, and as they walked down the street he spoke rapidly, full of plans and bubbling over with excitement. "I figure Casement and Reed will move to Cheyenne in two weeks, about. There's a building there I got spotted. It's just what we need, Lola! Used to be some kind of storehouse, but we can throw up some partitions, put some rugs on the floor and hang some chandeliers, and we're open for business!"

"The Union Belle Casino," Lola mused. "It may work, Shep. We'll give it our best try, won't we?"

"How about we go fifty-fifty, Lola? Partners?"

"All right," she smiled and shook his work-hardened hand. "Partners it is. When can we leave?"

"In the morning. I can rent the place and fix up one of the rooms for a bedroom for you, Lola. We can make it real nice. And we'll hunt up Nick Bolton and show him that picture of your pa."

They ate supper, and the next morning left on the work train. Shep had made some sort of arrangement with the conductor, and they had a seat in a car packed with Irish laborers, most of them with headaches from their activities the night before.

As the train huffed and moved in short jerking motions out of the station, Lola looked out at Julesburg, feeling no regrets at leaving. She turned to Shep and gave him a smile. "Here's to Cheyenne and the Union Belle, Shep!"

He nodded happily, and the train picked up speed, clicking over the rails, straining forward toward Cheyenne.

CHAPTER TWELVE

A DIFFERENT KIND OF PREACHER

★ ★ ★ ★

"It looks great, don't it, Lola?"

It was late Saturday afternoon and Shep was standing in the middle of the main room of the building he and Lola had labored over for three weeks, his face oozing with pride and satisfaction. "There won't be nothing like the Union Belle any closer than St. Louis!"

Lola straightened her aching back, took a careful survey of the room, and agreed. "It does look nice, doesn't it, Shep." Then she smiled ruefully, adding, "It ought to look good. We've broken our backs and spent almost every penny we had on it."

She thought back to how dismal the old building had been three weeks earlier. When Shep had brought her into the gloomy old warehouse, her faith in the project had faltered, for all she could see was dirt, cobwebs, and rough walls. But Shep had been so enthusiastic that he had carried her along. They had hired four Mexicans and had labored along with them to transform the barn-like structure into what it now was.

Lola sat down at one of the new tables, poured herself and Shep a glass of lemonade, and admitted, "I'm a little scared, Shep. If this thing doesn't work, we're in trouble."

Shep sat down and drained his glass, helped himself to more lemonade, and gave her a smile. "Aw, Lola, it's gotta work. This is the fanciest place in Cheyenne."

They both sat there drinking the tepid lemonade, looking around at the interior of the room they had invested so much of themselves into. It was not overly large—thirty feet wide and fifty feet long. The walls were freshly papered and all the wood-work gleamed with fresh white paint. The ceiling was high, giving the whole room an air of spaciousness not found in most frame buildings in western towns. The floor had been in good shape, but even so they had scrubbed hard to clean the heart pine until the grain was visible.

The fixtures and furniture had come from Max Dietrich's saloon, the Red Devil, in Julesburg. Shep had discovered that Max was going back East and had bought his entire stock. Since Max's place had been the fanciest in Julesburg, the price was steep, but a bargain nonetheless. Along one side ran a high bar made of walnut that gleamed richly in the light of the six chandeliers, and behind it ran a mirror that reflected the entire room. Several of Max's large pictures of scantily dressed saloon girls had been vetoed by Lola, despite Shep's wish to display them, but she had kept landscapes, which now hung along the walls. Eight round tables and matching chairs had been stripped of their old finish and now gleamed under several coats of varnish.

A door at the back led to a small kitchen where they could hear the Chinese cook, Chen Song, humming happily as he banged his pots and pans together. Along one inside wall was a door that led to four smaller rooms. Three of these contained tables that could be used for cards or eating, and the fourth Shep had made into a bedroom for himself. Yet another door in the hallway led to narrow stairs and a large attic. This had been converted into Lola's living quarters, and was composed of one large bedroom with a window looking down on Main Street, and a sitting room with a sofa and a pair of rockers.

"I was talking to some of Reed's surveyors last night," said Shep, still sipping his lemonade. "They say it won't be more'n a week or ten days before Casement pulls out of Julesburg and sets up here. We got this place done just in time, I reckon." The sound of footsteps could be heard outside, and the front door opened to admit a tall, fair-skinned man of about thirty. "Hey, Nick," Shep called out. "Come on in and wet your whistle. Lola, this is Nick Bolton. Nick, this is the girl I told you about, Lola Montez."

Bolton pulled off his hat to reveal curly yellow hair. "Pleased to meet you," he said in a high tenor voice.

Lola smiled and got to her feet. "Glad to meet you, Nick. What'll it be?"

"Some beer would cut this dust in my throat, I reckon." She got him a full schooner and he drank it thirstily. "Thanks, Lola." He looked around the room and nodded. "Real fancy!"

"Yeah, we been workin' hard on it," Shep acknowledged. "You hear anything about when Reed and Casement are gonna move the main camp from Julesburg to Cheyenne?"

"Next week," Bolton told him. "This town will be swarmin' when they make the move." He took another sip of his beer, and gave Lola a searching look. "You got that picture Shep was tellin' me about?"

"It's up in my room," Lola said eagerly. "I'll get it." The two men sat and talked as she left.

When Lola returned, Nick studied the picture carefully, then nodded. "Sure, this is Jude Moran. He's lost some hair and gained quite a few pounds—but I'm pretty sure this is him." He gave the picture back to Lola, adding, "He's bossin' a crew that's working on the right of way. They usually stay out for two or three weeks at a time. Then the boys get restless and have to come into town for a little recreation."

The two men sat there watching Lola, and she was conscious of their attention. "I think he may be a relative of mine, Nick. Could I go out where he's working?"

"I guess you could," Bolton nodded. "But I ain't sure just where they are right now. I asked Mack Travis, one of the surveyors about him, and he said that Moran goes and has a religious service every Sunday over at Fort Russell. The Sioux come into the Indian Agency there, and the way Mack told it, Moran gets them together and preaches at them." Fort Russell was the U.S. Army post two miles north of Cheyenne.

"I'll borrow a wagon tomorrow, and we'll take in the preachin' if you want, Lola," Shep offered.

Lola said quickly, "Oh, thank you, Shep, I'd like that."

Bolton asked no further questions, but commented with a

slight smile, "What's Cherry say about you leavin' him, Shep? He mad?"

"Nah," Shep shook his heavy head. "He offered me a raise, but I told him I wanted to be the boss for a while."

"Hear there's likely to be fireworks if Winslow tries to pull a stunt like he did at Julesburg," Bolton observed. "Cherry Valance ain't likely to sit around and let that happen again. I hear he's been makin' some plans for Winslow with all the other saloon owners."

"We wasn't invited to that party," Shep said. "But it don't surprise me none that he's bent on takin' revenge. Cherry's used to havin' his own way, and he ain't a feller who forgets anybody who gets to him. He's like a Sioux, Nick. He'll be good for a year, never sayin' a word, and then when you think he's all calmed down, he'll put a knife in you."

Bolton nodded. He drank the last of his beer, then got to his feet. "Like I say, I could be wrong, but I think Moran is the man you're looking for, Lola."

He turned and left, and Shep said, "You sure you want to go to Fort Russell, Lola?"

"Why, of course. That's why I came here." Lola gave Shep a look of surprise. "Why do you ask that?"

Shep lifted his heavy hand and tugged at his whisker-covered chin. He was not normally a thinking man, but he had considered the possibility that things might not turn out as his friend hoped. "Oh, I dunno, Lola. But most of the time when I look forward to something and then get it—somehow the gettin' never turns out like I expect. You say this man is your pa, but you ain't seen him in what—twenty years?"

"I don't remember him much, Shep," she answered, her eyes doubtful. "My mother left him when I was four, so I don't really know what I expect. The only thing I know about him is that he's always been religious. That's why my mother left him. She said he drove her crazy trying to reform her."

"Yes, well, that's the way with some people," Shep agreed. "And from what Nick says, he must still be about the same."

"He may be—and I may not want to have anything to do with him," Lola admitted slowly. Then she rose to her feet, looking pensive. "But I do know one thing, Shep. I saw a letter he wrote, and he asked about me, wanted to help me, he said. So I've got to at least see him. What time do we need to leave in the morning?"

"Well, Indians are never in a hurry," Shep observed. "Guess we can leave about eight. That ought to be enough time to get there for the preaching."

Shep went off after supper, and Lola went to her room. Even though the furniture was old and rather worn, she had come to feel that this space was a citadel. She sat in a rocking chair looking down on Main Street, realizing that the peace that lay over the small town was about to be broken by the invasion of construction gangs. Already over twenty saloons and gambling houses were in place along the street, and though they were quiet now, in two weeks the street below would be a river of shouting, jostling men determined to plunge into vice with the same energy they used to lay rails.

Finally she went to bed, and for a long time she lay there thinking about Jude Moran. Somehow the thought of meeting him frightened her. She could not understand why, for if he were not the kind of man she hoped for, all she had to do was turn her back and walk away. But lying there in the darkness, Lola realized suddenly that a hope had been building up in her—a hope that her father would bring some sort of stability into her rootless life. The longing for love that had been in her since childhood was stronger than ever. The men that were drawn to her could not offer the pure, selfless love she so needed. They sought her only to satisfy their own selfish appetites. She knew there had to be more to love than fleshly desires, more to life than aimlessness, and as she drifted off to sleep, she hoped her father might be able to give her some answers.

She rose at dawn and found Shep already up and moving around. After fixing and eating a large breakfast, she changed into a simple gray dress and wide-brimmed straw hat with a matching ribbon. Shep grinned at her. "We look just like respectable folks, don't we, Lola?"

She noted that he wore a freshly pressed dark blue suit and a pair of highly polished black boots. "Well, that's what we are, Shep," she smiled. "You look nice."

He ducked his head at her compliment and pulled his coat

back to show her the .44 he wore, saying, "Guess most folks don't wear a gun to church, but you can never tell. Might be a few young bucks along the trail who could give us a hard time."

The August sun burned down on them as they rode along the dusty road that led to Fort Russell. Shep talked animatedly about the prospects for the Union Belle, and although Lola responded, her mind was on the situation that lay ahead of her. By the time they pulled into the stockade wall, she was keeping a tight rein on herself, and said in what she hoped was an idle tone, "Not a very pretty place, is it, Shep?"

He looked at the unpainted buildings that formed a double line inside the walls and shook his head. "Army posts ain't much to look at, and that's a fact. This one looks better'n most of them, though." He drove the wagon to a hitching post, got out and helped her down. "Guess we'd better find out where the preachin' is gonna be." He stopped an undersized corporal who was walking idly along the building. "Hey, corporal, where will the preachin' be this morning?"

The soldier gave them a curious look, then waved his hand to a large building across the parade ground. "Over in the storeroom," he said. "You come in just for that?"

"Why, course we did," Shep said, emulating surprise. "And you ought to be there yourself, boy. Lots of temptations in this part of the world. Young fellow like you needs a good dose of religion to keep himself out of trouble!"

The corporal shook his head in disgust. "I ain't had a good temptation in so long, I probably wouldn't know what to do with it," he muttered, then left them, wandering down the sidewalk.

"Looks like part of the congregation is already here," Shep said, leading Lola across the hard-baked earth. He indicated ten or twenty Indians who were outside the storehouse watching them. Shep sized them up and told her quietly, "Agency Indians, most of 'em. The wild ones won't come in except in winter when their bellies get empty." He stopped outside the door and asked a middle-aged Indian, "Preaching started yet?"

The man grunted and gave a slight nod, his obsidian eyes emotionless. At that moment, singing began to come from the interior and Shep opened the door for Lola, saying, "Guess we're just in time."

The room they entered was stacked from floor to ceiling with everything from food supplies to cavalry gear, but the inner part of the room had been cleared. There were no chairs, so Lola moved with Shep to stand in front of a large shelf filled with uniforms. There were about thirty or more Indians standing in the center of the room, most of them women and children. At the far end a man stood behind a desk that held a heavy-looking Bible.

The preacher was a large man, almost six feet tall and weighing close to two hundred pounds. His large hands, bulky shoulders and heavy legs gave him a durable look. He noticed them as soon as they walked in, and examined them with a pair of dark blue eyes. His reddish hair was thinning in front, and a short red beard framed a firm, pointed chin set in a square face. He sang a song that Lola had never heard before in a strong baritone voice. Few of the Indians were making any attempt to sing, but he sang five or six verses with great vigor.

Lola had come merely to see Jude Moran, not for any religious motivation. She had never been to any service other than Mass, and she stood there watching Moran carefully, marveling over the strangeness of the setting. The Indians stood stock still, even the smaller children, watching the preacher with solemn faces. Only a few of them made any attempt to join in the singing, but that did not seem to bother Moran. He sang the first song at least five times, then two others before he finally paused and picked up the thick Bible from the table in front of him.

He nodded toward an Indian in white man's clothing, saying, "I wish I could speak your language, but Little Wolf will help me out." The Indian repeated this for the congregation. He spoke rapidly, the words guttural and from the throat, then paused, looking expectantly at Moran.

"This is the book of the Great Spirit," Moran said, holding the Bible high for them to see. "In this book, He tells us why trouble comes. The Great Spirit says that once there was no trouble, that He made the world good." He proceeded slowly, pausing periodically for Little Wolf to interpret, putting everything into terms the Indians could grasp. Lola had never read the Bible, and as Moran went on, she found herself listening carefully to the simple story. "There were plenty of buffalo to eat, and no winters when the women and children cried because there was no food. No one ever got sick—and no one ever died. Men and women walked with God, and obeyed Him. But we know that the world is not that way now. Sometimes sickness comes. All men die, even young children. War comes and the best of the young men are slain. Men are often liars and thieves. The world we live in now is not good. Why is that?"

Moran waited until Little Wolf finished speaking for him, then opened his Bible and read, "All have sinned and come short of the glory of God." He began to tell the story of Adam and Eve in the garden, how they fell and what that meant. Lola noticed that the congregation still showed no outward sign of interest, yet they were watching Moran carefully. It occurred to her that some of them were probably thinking that most of the evils that had come to the Sioux had been brought by white men like Moran—men who had taken their lands and were killing all the buffalo.

Moran concentrated on the Indians, yet more than once his quick blue eyes touched on the two visitors. He spoke of how every man needed something within his heart to fill the empty space. He pointed out that life was more than this world, and then he raised his voice slightly, saying, "The book of the Great Spirit tells us all of this—but it also tells of what He has done. The books says that even though men have been disobedient to Him, the Great Spirit loves them. But someone has to pay for the way that men have sinned against Him. Who can pay for the bad things that all men have done?"

The preacher paused, looking over the room, and then he smiled and said, "Let me read what the Great Spirit has done. He has found one who can make all men good." He opened the Bible again and read slowly, "For God so loved the world that he gave his only begotten Son, that whosoever believeth in him should not perish but have everlasting life." Then he closed the book and spoke about the saving power of Jesus Christ.

Lola found herself listening to his words carefully. Her religion had never been more than a ritual. When she was younger, she had gone to church and tried to be good, yet had never connected Jesus and His cross with her own life. Jesus had been a statue on the wall of the church, and the cross had been an ornament she had worn around her neck. But as the preacher spoke about the blood of Jesus and His sufferings on the cross, an uneasy feeling began to grow in her.

"Every man and woman, and every child needs peace in his heart," Moran continued. "But the only way to find that peace is through the Lord Jesus Christ, the only Son of the Great Spirit. He says in the Bible that if we give up our wrong-doing and cry out, we will be forgiven of all our bad deeds, and we will have this peace." He closed his Bible, stepped out from behind the pulpit and asked, "Would any of you like me to pray with you, that the Great Spirit will forgive you all your wrongs and give you peace in your spirits?"

Lola cast a quick glance over the room and saw that three of the Indians, two women and one older man, had their hands lifted. She wondered what Moran would do next, and watched carefully as he went to each of them and prayed a simple prayer. It was not like any prayer she had ever heard, for she was accustomed to the memorized prayers she had been taught by the nuns as a child. But this man spoke to God as he would speak to a friend! With the old man he said simply, "Oh, God, you know this man's heart. He wants to be forgiven. He wants to know your love and peace. As he calls on you, I ask that you hear his prayer. Forgive his sins as you have promised, and let him be accepted into your kingdom. I ask this in the name of Jesus Christ."

Lola saw that tears were rolling down the old man's face, and Moran said, "God bless you! I can see that God has saved you. Is that right, my brother?" The old man apparently understood some English, for he nodded his head, and said, "Yes—Jesus God—He is good!"

Moran looked around and said, "I will be here for the rest of the day. If I can help any of you, come and talk to me. Now, let us pray. . . ."

After the prayer, the Indians began to file out. Shep said, "Come on, Lola. Let's meet the preacher."

Lola's heart was fluttering, but she forced herself to accompany Shep, who went right up to Moran. "Mighty fine preaching, Brother Moran," Shep said, putting out his hand. "I'm Shep Yancy. Me and this lady own a saloon in Cheyenne. Thought we might be in need of a prayer now and then, so we come to hear the preachin'.'"

"Glad to know you, Yancy," Moran nodded. "I'll be starting a church in Cheyenne soon. I hope you both will come."

Shep nodded. "My mama always took me to church when I was a little feller, but when she went on, I kind of got out of the habit." He stood there, noting that Lola remained silent, then said abruptly, "Say, I gotta go pay a call on an officer while I'm here. Maybe you can look after the lady for a spell?" He turned without waiting for an answer and left.

Lola knew he had done so to give her a chance to be alone with Moran, but she wished fervently he had not! She felt awkward and had not the faintest idea of what to say to this man.

Moran said, "There's some cool water in my office. Why don't we go have some of it?"

Lola stood there uncertainly, then decided to bring the matter out into the open. "I'm Lola Montez," she said, watching his face carefully.

Moran blinked his eyes and rubbed his hands together—but he responded quietly, "Yes, I thought you might be. You look exactly like your mother did when she was your age."

Lola's heart beat faster and she could not think of a thing to say. She had come thousands of miles to find this man—and now that she stood before him, she didn't know what she expected of him.

Moran saw her difficulty, and smiled. "Come along. We can talk better at the office."

She nodded and followed him out of the warehouse and down the line of buildings. He paused at a door, stepped aside, allowing her to enter. The room was small, containing only a desk, two chairs and some rough shelves nailed to the wall. There was a pitcher of water and several glasses on the desk. "Sit down, Lola." She took her seat, and he poured two glasses of water and handed one of them to her. "It's not very cool, but it's wet." He drank his water, and she took several sips that helped open up her parched throat.

"You're a very beautiful young lady," he began. "I've wanted to see you for a long time."

"I—I found a letter you wrote to Mother before she died,"

she said. "That's why I left Texas and came to find you."

"I was real sorry about your mother. How's your sister?"

As she told him about Maria, Lola regained some of her composure. She had been half afraid that he would be like a loud, shouting preacher she had seen once in Mexico—a red-faced man who stood in the middle of the streets and told people they were going to hell. It came as a relief to discover that he was not at all like that. She liked the way he didn't pressure her, and she wondered if her mother's description of his religious fanaticism had been warped by her own unhappiness with her marriage. She had always known her mother cared nothing for religion, and now Lola realized that she had not even been a good woman. Now, facing her father, she began to suspect that all the talk about his pushiness had been simply a reflection of her mother's rejection of his way of life.

She found herself speaking of her brother-in-law, Ramon, and though she didn't say a great deal, Jude's eyes showed a quick understanding. "Just as well you got away, I think," he said. Then he asked, "Who is this man you're in business with?"

Lola hesitated, not knowing how to defend her position. There was no way to make owning a saloon acceptable in his sight, she realized, so she said evenly, "When I left Texas, I only had a little money. I had to earn a living, so I took a job dealing cards with Cherry Valance in Julesburg. Shep worked for him, and he was very kind to me. When Cherry left Julesburg, I had to do something, so Shep suggested we go into business. That's all he is to me—just a friend."

"I see."

Lola braced herself, waiting for the sermon on the evils of saloons she was certain would follow. She was prepared to get up and walk away as soon as it started, but he sat there regarding her with a calm expression on his face.

When he did speak, he did not even mention saloons. "For a long time, Lola, I've wished there was some way to help you— but it's not been easy, with the way your mother felt about me. But now that you're here, I hope I can do more." He gave her a shy smile, adding, "I've never remarried, and I don't know the first thing about being a father—but I'd like to see you from time to time."

"I would like that, too," Lola said. She got to her feet and said, "Will you be in Cheyenne much?"

He rose with her. "Quite a bit," he nodded. "I've decided to lay off work for a while. I've saved up some money, and as I said to Yancy, I'm going to try to start a church in Cheyenne."

She expected him to pressure her to come, but he said only, "Maybe we can have supper together once in a while."

"Yes!" she said eagerly. "That would be nice."

He walked outside with her and they found Yancy leaning idly against the side of the trading post. Lola shared her news at once. "Shep, this is my father, just as I hoped."

"Well, sir, you got a mighty fine daughter," Shep said quickly. He was somewhat awkward as he faced Moran, and he seemed to have trouble finding what he wanted to say. Finally he shrugged and said bluntly, "Preacher, saloons is all I know. Been raised in 'em and I've seen the worst. But I wanna tell you that Lola here ain't no saloon girl. I been watchin' her, and bad as I am, I can spot a good woman when I see one. What I mean to say is, you don't have to worry about her. Her and me is friends—and I'm keeping an eye on her."

Moran smiled and put his hand out. "I think my daughter is very lucky to have a friend like you, Shep," he said heartily, "and I appreciate your concern." Then he nodded and said, "I'll see you both in Cheyenne."

On the way back to town, Shep said, "You know, that's not a bad fellow—your dad. He ain't much like the hell-fire-and-brimstone type." He spoke to the horses, adding, "I might just like to hear a little more of that preaching, Lola."

Lola thought about Jude Moran and smiled. "He's not what I expected, either, Shep." She sat there for several moments, then added softly, "But he's what I hoped for!"

PART THREE

CHEYENNE SUMMER

★ ★ ★ ★

CHAPTER THIRTEEN

A NEW SEASON

★ ★ ★ ★

The combination work-passenger train strained as it huffed up the valley of the Lodgepole toward Cheyenne. Mark sat loosely, his long legs across the opposite seat, watching dust-devils form and dance along the desert. This was April, and spring had come late this year of 1868. A gusty wind boiled against the car's sides and scoured down the aisle, laying its burning edge on him. On the plain a band of antelope rushed up from a coulee, then scudded away into grassy hills that stretched away endlessly.

Conductor Jamie Lord passed by, glancing at Mark. "Be in Cheyenne in ten minutes, Mr. Winslow."

"All right, Jamie."

As Mark began to pull his gear together, he thought of the task that lay in front of him. This April marked the beginning of another construction season. The Union Pacific's steel had stretched 240 miles across Nebraska from North Platte the year before, stopping eight thousand feet high in the snowy jaws of Sherman Summit, just beyond Cheyenne. But now with the arrival of spring, ten thousand men of all kinds—graders, steel layers, bridge builders, gamblers, freighters, gunmen, ex-soldiers, tradesmen, mule skinners, cowhands, doctors, lawyers and politicians—were set to join in a great tidal wave from Cheyenne to see the end of track for another turbulent, wicked year.

They're ready for it, Mark thought, looking the passengers over. They had a buoyancy that made them impatient with the long ride, and he had it himself. The fifteen-hour ride on the train from Omaha had been intolerable, and now he stretched his muscles, anxious to get on solid ground. He made his way through the car, stopping several times to talk about the work ahead with men who grinned and spoke to him. Many of the men had the ruddy faces and tuneful, lilting talk of Ireland. Nearly all were war veterans, and in their cowhide boots, formless store suits and round-brimmed hats, they made a rough show, but Winslow knew them well. They were the kind of men who could stand the bitter blast of winter and the merciless heat of the desert sun better than any others. He had learned during his apprenticeship the previous year that they could throw their shovels down, pick up their stacked guns and fight off the Cheyenne and Sioux when they made their lightning swift raids on the track.

Mark moved down the aisle, swaying with the motion of the train, and came to a stop beside two men. "Hello, Cherry," he said, stopping to pay close attention to the men. It was a way he had, changing quickly from a lazy attitude to sharp attention. He ignored Lou Goldman for the moment, concentrating the full power of his gaze on Cherry Valance.

"Hello, Winslow," Cherry said. "Been in Omaha?"

"For a month." The train was slowing down now, and all around him men were scraping their boots along the floor as they got to their feet. They laughed and cursed, shoving one another with animal-like good humor, but even as they filed by Winslow he did not take his attention from the two men. "Guess things will pick up in Cheyenne now," he said idly.

Valance studied him, weighing the words as if looking for some hidden meaning, then nodded, "Always that way. Main Street is packed now. New places will have to move to the edge of town."

Jamie Lord came by shouting, "Cheyenne! Everybody out for Cheyenne!"

Mark nodded, shifted his grip on the suitcase in his hand, and turned to leave. "I'll see you later, Cherry."

Goldman glared at him, then said to Valance, "Real friendly, ain't he now?" The hazel eyes of the gunman were half-closed, and his thin lips turned upward in a sour grin as he watched Winslow step down and move through the crowd. "Always good to know exactly what you're up against. That's your man, Cherry. As long as he's around, we're out of business."

Cherry didn't answer. He drew on the long thin cigar, expelled the smoke, then nodded briefly. "Let's get off this thing. I'm sick of it."

Goldman rose and followed Valance down the aisle, but after they stepped down, he pressed the matter. "Cherry, wake up! It ain't like you to let a man whip you like Winslow did in Julesburg last summer. All the others are waitin' to see what you'll do. And so far, all you've done is smile and be polite." Goldman's wire-thin frame showed as the wind molded his shirt to his body, and he touched his gun in a habitual gesture. Winslow disappeared down the street and Goldman shook his head. "He's in our way, Cherry, and you don't seem to know it."

Goldman's words grated on Valance, and he said irritably, "Shut up, Lou, will you? You think I don't know about Winslow? We've had to handle others—but this one is another breed of cat. We'll take care of him, but it'll have to be done right. If we miss, we'll have him right on our back, and I don't fancy having an Indian like him jumping at me."

Mark glanced back to see the two men watching him. After he had run Valance out of Julesburg the two had seldom met, but it was just a matter of time before another collision occurred. But he was not a man who worried about the future, so he filed thoughts of Valance away and looked around at Main Street, noting that every square foot of space was taken, and several side streets had branched off east and west. It was a roughly-built town, made of canvas and unpainted wood for the most part, and an edge of half-suppressed violence that ran just beneath the surface.

As Winslow passed by Valance's Wagonwheel saloon, the big tent seemed to breathe as the breeze caused the canvas to lift and fall, then he turned off Main Street toward the Union Pacific's offices. He walked quickly, pausing slightly when he passed a freshly painted wooden structure with an ornate sign swinging on wrought iron chains in front. The Union Belle's clean and inviting exterior contrasted sharply with its surroundings.

He had an impulse to turn and enter the front door, but instead he picked up his pace and made his way down the street. It was a hesitation that was unlike him, and he examined it. He had been in the place more than once during the past months, but had never felt comfortable. Lola was polite, and he liked the quietness of the place—yet something in the way she looked at him was troublesome. He shrugged off the irritation, then moved toward the low, flat buildings that housed UP's offices.

Materials were stacked high alongside the buildings, ready to be shuffled to the end of track. Mark entered the larger of the three buildings and was greeted by a short, heavy man who grinned at the sight of him. "Well, lookee here at what's blowed in!" He came over and shook hands with Mark. "Glad to see you."

"How've you been, Josh?" Mark asked. He put his suitcase down and smiled at the smaller man. Joshua Long had a red moon-face and a pair of bright blue eyes. His job was to move the supplies to end of track, and he lifted his voice, "General— Winslow's back!"

A door swung open to Mark's right and Jack Casement came out, in a hurry, as usual. He was a wiry man, small like a terrier. Little as he was, he was always willing to fight it out with any of the thousands working under him. He had a full rust-colored beard and a pair of bristling eyebrows. "What's doing in Omaha?" he asked abruptly.

"It looks good, General. Your brother Dan's got stuff piled up so high that Omaha looks like a freight dump. Ferries are working twenty-four hours a day. He says you can get eighty cars of material a day."

"Not enough!" Casement snapped. He was a dowdy, scrappy man, and he gave a discontented shake of his head. "We'll need at least a hundred—and even that won't be enough."

"Oh, come on, General!" Josh Long argued. "This is the year we whip the daylights out of Central!"

Casement paced up and down the floor, unable to keep still. "Mark, Reed wants to see you. Get on over to the hotel."

"What's on his mind, General?"

"Nothing to grin about," Casement scowled. "Get going, and tell him that he's got to get more material if he wants that track laid."

Mark picked up his suitcase, nodded, and left to make his way back to Main Street, where he entered the Strand Hotel and asked for Reed. "Room 210, Mr. Winslow," the clerk said. "You want a room for yourself?"

"Not sure yet, Ed," Mark said. "I'll let you know." He moved down the short hallway, and as he passed the door to the saloon, he heard his name called, and turned to find Jeff Driver and Dooley Young coming toward him.

"Well, look what the cat drug in, Jeff!" Dooley said loudly. His smile was hidden behind his huge moustache, but he slapped Mark on the shoulder. "Finally got tired of loafin' and come to help me and Jeff do the work, I see."

Mark grinned. "Hello, Dooley—Jeff. You two look rested up."

"Not much doin' for a fact, Mark," Driver said.

"Well, come on up with me to see Reed. I've got an idea our resting days are about to come to an end." He led the way up the stairs, found the door, and rapped on it. "Sam? It's Mark."

"Come on in," Reed said, getting up from the small desk.

He was a smallish man, with a close-cropped beard. "Just get in?"

"Yes. Casement said you wanted to see me. I found these two sopping up whiskey downstairs."

"Aw, Captain, that's not so!" Dooley shook his head. "I was jest watching Jeff to see that he didn't drink too much."

Reed grinned at the pair, then turned serious. "Well, I've got bad news. Our schedule's been wrecked, Mark. The plan for '68 was to locate to Salt Lake and lay steel as far as the Wasatch range. But two days ago I got a wire from General Dodge. He's dropping his work in Congress and he'll be here within a week."

The three men suddenly looked hard at Reed. Driver had started to light a cigarette, and paused with the match burning. General Dodge was law to all of them.

Reed walked to the window, looked down, then came back to say drily, "Well, the order now is to make our location lines final all the way to Salt Lake in thirty days, and to Humboldt

Wells, two hundred twenty miles west of the lake, in another sixty days. Also, we've got to cover the whole line with men regardless of the cost, and get into Salt Lake with steel as fast as possible. It makes no difference where the snow catches us this year, you understand? We have to keep on."

"Five hundred miles of steel and no stops?" Mark asked, shock in his face. "That's a tall order, Sam!"

"What's it all about, Reed?" Driver asked. He lit his cigarette and drew in the smoke. "What's the big hurry?"

Reed shrugged his shoulders, then moved his cigar around in his mouth. "Under the first plan, the Central was to build from Frisco east to the California line and the Union was to build west from Omaha and meet them there. We all knew that Huntington and Crocker and Stanford would never stop at the California line. Now they've persuaded the Secretary of the Interior that the Central is a sounder line than the Union, so it should get the lion's share." He puffed on the cigar, adding in a grudging voice, "They've done a great job. Put the Sierras behind and they've got all the level stretches of Nevada in front."

"And we haven't even reached our heavy work in the Wasatch chain," Mark muttered.

"Which we'll hit in the dead of winter," Reed nodded glumly. "And now Central's sprung a surprise. It intends to beat us into Salt Lake. If it succeeds it will block us out of our only logical terminal and dictate what the Union will have in through traffic. We're whipped, Mark," he added.

Mark was thinking hard. "Yes, if they can do it. If we lose, our whole financial structure folds up. There's no revenue to be had out of a road running nine hundred miles across a desert without a terminal."

"Right!" Reed nodded. "The government will listen to the road that gets to the lake first. That's why we've got to get to Salt Lake first regardless of cost—regardless of anything. And we've got other troubles. The Indians are sore and they're going to hit us."

"Yeah, shore as a cat's got climbing gear!" Dooley broke in. "And I been hearin' about troublemakers in the construction gangs."

"Guess we know who put 'em there," Driver said. "And the

gamblers have already made their boast they intend to take control of the end-of-track town this year. Valance is gone, but he'll be back to ramrod the thing."

"Came in on the train with me," Mark nodded. He moved restlessly around the room. "Sam, what's first on your list for me to do?"

Reed said, "See if you can find out what the Indians will do. You'll have to go to Fort Sanders and talk to Black Horse. Maybe he'll help us some. Get back here as quick as you can."

"All right." Winslow turned and started for the door. The three men left the room, and Mark said, "I'm hungry. See you two later."

"Nope," Dooley said promptly.

Mark stared at him. "What do you mean—'no'?"

"I mean no," Dooley said. He gave Driver a sharp look, saying, "He ain't heard yet."

"Heard what?" Mark said shortly.

Driver said quietly, "General Dodge took a trip last year to Julesburg—before you cleaned it up. He didn't like what he saw, so he told Reed that the railroad's going to back up its authority in all end-of-track towns this year. Reed sent word out to all the joints that you're the man to clean 'em up if they don't mind their manners."

Mark stared at him. "How do you know all this?"

"Why, they made the mistake of lettin' Shep Yancy in on it," Driver grinned. "I guess they figured since he'd been a bouncer for Cherry he was all right. But Shep and Lola don't need the town wide open to run their place, so he passed the word."

"Who'd he tell?"

"Why, he told Lola," Jeff said. "And she told me."

Mark studied Driver's dark face with a new interest. "I didn't know you and Lola were that close, Jeff."

Driver shrugged his shoulders, saying, "Well, I spend a lot of time at her place."

Dooley broke in quickly, "At the meeting, the gamblers decided to put you down if you interfered with them like you did at Julesburg. Which is why Reed told me and Jeff to baby-sit you this year."

Winslow looked down at Young and grinned suddenly. "You

had any baby-sittin' experience, Dooley?"

"Aw, Captain, I'm an expert," the little rider grinned. "You ain't forgot how many of us Youngs they was back in Virginia, have you?"

"I never did know exactly how many there were," Mark said gravely. "Every time I rode by the house, kids were pouring out every door and every window."

"Shorely! Ma and Pa took the scripture serious where it says to replenish the earth! Why, we had every kind of baby at the same time."

"How many kinds are there besides boy babies and girl babies?" Driver inquired.

"Why, you ignorant Yankee!" Dooley exclaimed. "There's arm babies and lap babies. And then there's knee babies and after them there's porch babies. After which comes a yard child, and then a set-along child."

"A set-along child?" Driver asked curiously. "What's that?"

Dooley stared at him and explained condescendingly, "A set-along child is a baby that stays put on a quilt at the end of a row of cotton. I thought everybody knowed that!"

Driver and Mark both laughed, but then Mark said, "Well, I guess the kind of baby-sittin' you'll be doing will be a little different. I hope you got rested up while I was in Omaha, because from what Sam Reed says, I don't guess any of us is going to do much sitting until we hit Salt Lake." He turned and left the room, the two men on his heels. "I'll check in and then we'll get some supper."

"Best food is at Lola's place," Driver said as they walked down the stairs. "Her and Shep got a Chinaman who can cook like nothing you ever seen."

Mark hesitated, then nodded. "Let me get a room and we'll give it a try." He got a room, put his gear inside, and then the three of them walked outside into the gathering darkness of the windy night. The boardwalk drummed with loud feet and the racket of bands playing and barkers calling out, "Come over here and give us a bet!" burst out of the saloons. They could hear the ringing of a switch engine's bell from the depot, and a blast of the steam whistle split the night air from time to time.

The Wagonwheel was jammed, Mark noted as they passed.

"Cherry's making lots of money," he commented as they moved by it.

"Like always," Jeff shrugged. "The track hands work like slaves all week and just can't wait to get to town and put it in Cherry Valance's pocket."

"Total depravity," Dooley said. "Man is a poor lost sinner headed straight for the pit. And that there's good, sound Foot-washin' Baptist doctrine in case you two heathens don't recognize it."

"You a Baptist, Dooley?" Driver asked in amusement.

"Why, I was a feeler," Dooley stated solemnly.

"You was a what?" Driver demanded.

"A feeler." As they reached the door of the Union Belle, Dooley explained, "At the baptizin's in the creek, somebody's likely to get washed away if they step in a deep hole. So a feeler is the one who goes out and feels around to be sure there ain't none." He sighed deeply and shook his head. "I swear, Jeff Driver, you're as dull as a widder woman's axe!"

They entered the brightly lit room, and as always Mark was struck with how different it was from the other joints in Cheyenne. There was a hum of voices and the sound of laughter from a group of men playing cards at the rear, but none of the ear-shattering noise that filled the other places. Cigar smoke floated on the air, but the aroma of meat cooking was the prevailing scent, and Mark quickly announced, "I'm starved."

"Come on," Jeff said. "Let's grab that table by the kitchen." He led the way and the three of them sat down. At once a young woman with a quiet face came to stand beside them. "Hello, Maureen," Jeff said. "What's good tonight?"

The girl was no more than twenty, and although she wore a blue dress that left her shoulders bare, it scarcely resembled the flashy, low-cut gowns of most saloon girls. "Chen Song made a wonderful beef roast, with new potatoes and green beans."

"Sounds fine." Jeff looked at the other two and they agreed. "Bring us three orders. After she left with their order, Jeff leaned back in his chair. "This place is doing great."

Mark looked up to see the bulky form of Yancy coming across the floor. He stopped and looked down at them. "Hello, Winslow. Didn't know you were back in town."

"Just got back today," Mark said. He looked around at the busy room, saying, "Looks like you and Lola are running a good business."

"Yeah, it's worked out better than I thought," Yancy nodded. He was wearing a gray suit with a string tie, but no tailoring could disguise the bulky muscles. He still looked like a bouncer, Mark thought, but he seemed friendly.

"You look great, Shep," he said.

"Shore do," Dooley nodded. "If you drop dead we won't have to do a thing to you."

"I don't guess you have any trouble in here," Mark smiled, looking around the room at the placid scene.

"Oh, once in a while a rough one comes in," Yancy shrugged. "But they don't stay long." He laughed and his big face broke into wrinkles. "I try to look like a big shot, but I still feel like a bouncer," he admitted cheerfully. He moved a step closer and lowered his voice, "You get the word about what Cherry and his friends got in store for you?"

"I heard. Thanks for the warning."

"Aw, it was Lola who told Driver," Yancy said.

Mark looked around the room. "I don't see her, Shep."

"She usually comes in about this time for supper. I'll tell her you fellows are here."

He moved away and Dooley observed, "He ain't as big as a mule—but then, he ain't a heck of a lot smaller, either. I reckon he's all right."

The meal arrived, and as they ate Mark listened while his two companions talked—mostly about the war. They carried on a constant debate over the battles, and since both of them had gone through most of it, they had strong opinions. Mark always kept out of the arguments, and neither Young nor Driver ever lost their tempers. They were arguing about the Battle of Gettysburg when Mark saw Lola come into the room.

She looked across and caught his eyes. "Hello, Mark," she said, coming over to their table. "Shep told me you were here."

The three men got up, and Mark said, "Hello, Lola. Please, sit down and have something to eat with us."

"I'll just have pie and coffee," she said, and the four of them sat down. "You've been gone a long time," she said. "What have you been doing?"

"Just chores," he answered. Her presence did something to him, and he was annoyed at himself. She was wearing a white dress with puffy sleeves, fitted at the waist and bodice. Her olive-colored skin glowed under the tint of the chandeliers, and her black hair was wound around her head like a shining ebony coronet. Mark was so enthralled with Lola's beauty, he hardly noticed the pie the rest of the group was savoring.

Driver, he saw, also kept his eyes on Lola, and he thought with a jolt of surprise, *Why, Jeff is smitten with her!* The thought disturbed him, though he realized nothing could be more natural. With women so scarce, most of the male population of Cheyenne was probably mooning over Lola's beauty.

After the meal, Dooley got up and said, "Jeff, we got to go down and help Josh get them cars ready to pull out by sunup."

Driver did not want to go, but Young pressured him. "You heard what Reed told us. Now, come on." He grinned at Mark and said, "Captain, please don't get yourself shot tonight! Me and Jeff will only be gone mebbe two-three hours, so keep yore head down, all right?"

"I'll do my best, Dooley," Mark nodded.

The two marched out, and Lola asked, "What was that all about?"

Mark shrugged. "I guess you know, Lola." He looked at her and added, "Thanks for the warning—about Cherry's intentions to rub me out."

Lola shook her head. "It's serious, Mark. Shep says so, and he knows. You've got to be careful."

"Forgot how," Mark said idly, seeming to be thinking of something else. "In the war, at first, I went around ducking under a log everytime I heard a gun go off. And I wondered how the more experienced men could just walk around like nothing was happening. I thought they were brave and I was a coward." He looked up and his gray eyes were thoughtful as he added, "But that wasn't it, Lola. You just can't hang on to an emotion forever. Pretty soon I heard so many bullets that I just got used to them. You never think they're going to get you."

Lola knew that look in his eyes, and she shook her head.

"You mustn't be careless, Mark," she said urgently. "Cherry may have polished manners, but he's a killer."

"Sure. I know that."

Lola realized that he was not to be warned, and she sat there silently. Finally she said, "Do you remember when we almost froze to death in that cabin, Mark?"

The memory of their close call returned to him, and he nodded. "Sure. It was a pretty close thing. But we made it."

She put her hands together and looked at them. Then she lifted her dark eyes to his and smiled. "I'll never forget that time, Mark. It was hard, but somehow it was—it was different from anything that ever happened to me. We were close to death, but I never felt so alive in my life."

He smiled and nodded. "That's the way of it, Lola. You don't know how precious life is until you come close to losing it." He looked around the room and said, "Is this what you want, Lola?"

She knew at once what he meant. "Oh, Mark, it's better than what I came from. You know that."

"I heard you found your father," he said quietly. "I didn't know you were looking for him."

Lola saw the hurt expression on his face. "Mark, I should have told you, but after we left Texas things—went wrong."

He knew she spoke of the time he'd kissed her. The moment still burned in him, and he said, "Well, I'm glad you found him. I hear he's a preacher."

She smiled, her eyes glowing. "Well, he is—and of all the things I didn't want, it was to be preached at. But we've become very close." She paused for a moment, then added, "I go and listen to him preach sometimes. And Shep goes with me—and even Jeff went."

"Maybe I could go," Mark smiled at the thought, but then his brow creased, and he shook his head. "My folks are wonderful Christian people," he murmured. "My grandparents, too. Guess I've missed all that somewhere . . . the war, maybe."

Lola said quietly, "I missed it, too, Mark." A sadness touched her and she asked quietly, "Do you think if someone misses his way, he can ever get right again?"

"My grandfather says you can," Mark nodded. "He was a real rowdy one in his early days. Wound up in jail and nearly died. But he came through it." He thought about Christmas Winslow, his grandfather, and said quietly, "I wish I could see him again. He was something!"

"You'll probably meet my father," Lola said. "I've told him how you helped me."

"Did you tell him all of it?" Mark asked.

"No. Just that I couldn't have gotten away without your help." She sighed and said, "Mark, why do we always have to end up talking like this? Why can't we just forget the past—the bad part of it?"

"I don't know," he shrugged, then asked, "Have you seen Ray Hayden lately?"

"Why, he's been gone for a month, Mark. But Jeff told me that he's due back any day."

"I wonder if he and Moira got married?"

"I didn't hear about it." Lola hesitated, then said quietly, "Mark, I know Ray's a friend of yours, but . . ."

She paused, and he prompted, "What is it, Lola?"

"Well, maybe I shouldn't say anything, but isn't he supposed to be engaged to Miss Ames?"

"More or less."

Lola bit her lower lip, then shrugged. "I thought he was too—friendly for an engaged man."

"You mean he was chasing you?" Mark asked.

"Yes."

Mark thought about it, then shrugged. "Ray's always been a ladies' man. And strictly speaking, there's no formal engagement between him and Moira. Don't worry about it."

The thought still troubled her, he could see, but she dropped the matter. "All right, Mark."

"If he bothers you again, let me know, okay?" He got up to go, saying, "I've got to leave for Fort Sanders at dawn. Better get some sleep."

"Come back soon, Mark—and I wish you would come to hear my father preach." A smile lit up her face, and she said, "If a saloon woman can go, I think the town bouncer can, too."

He grinned, and the smile made him look much younger. "I'll take you up on that. A hard-nosed one like me'd give your father a real challenge!"

He left the casino, and for a long time Lola sat there watching the door. Finally Shep ambled over and said, "I told him about Cherry, but he's a tough one to scare."

"Yes, he is, Shep—but he's not tougher than a bullet fired from a dark alley."

Shep thought about that, then said, "No, no man's that tough." Then he asked curiously, "Lola, what's between you two?"

"Nothing, Shep," she said quietly. "We just seem to have a way of hurting each other." A thought crossed her mind, bringing a sober look to her dark eyes. She got up suddenly and went over to the blackjack table, smiling at the customers mechanically.

Shep watched her for a long time as she sat there, then finally muttered, "Winslow's not the only tough one in this town." He walked over and took a seat where he could watch over his little domain.

CHAPTER FOURTEEN

THE FALL OF A MAN

★ ★ ★ ★

"I'm glad you made this trip with me, Moira," Ray said. "It's pretty rough leaving the comforts of Boston for Cheyenne—but the worst of it was leaving you."

The two of them had come in on the afternoon train the day before, and he had let her persuade him to accompany her on a horse ride in the early morning coolness. He hated to get up early, but she had prodded him into it, and now they were walking their horses along the banks of Crow Creek, a small stream that encircled Cheyenne before meandering down to join the South Platte River. Over to the west the Rockies began to lift their heads toward the clouds, and the desert ran off to the east to such a distance that it was almost impossible to tell where the land ended and the sky began. They had seen several small bands of antelope, and as they crossed the bubbling creek, two deer sprang up and fled in long bounding jumps.

Moira was startled by them and pulled her horse up suddenly, but she watched the floating leaps of the animals with admiration. "How beautiful!" Turning to Ray with a smug smile, she said, "Now, wasn't that worth getting out of bed for?"

He shifted in his saddle, standing in the stirrups to relieve his aching muscles. "I wouldn't get out of bed in the morning to see every antelope and mule deer in the territory," he complained, adding, "but it's worth it to see you all fresh and pretty." He was a man who would always turn a phrase when a pretty woman was concerned, and he was pleased when he saw his words brighten her eyes.

"It's so different out here, isn't it?" she said, touching her horse lightly with her riding crop. "Living in a city, you can't see very far, but out here in the desert you're aware of how big the world is." Her green eyes swept the open spaces, soaking up the vista, then stopping to scrutinize the horizon. "Look, Ray—is that some sort of a signal, that smoke over there?"

He turned to look in the direction of her gesture, studied the spiral of white smoke that rose straight up in the still air. Glancing around, he noted that another column of smoke was rising a few miles to the right.

"Could be an Indian sign," he said. "But I don't know what it means."

"I suppose Mark would know."

At her remark, Ray frowned and shook his head. "I doubt it. Mark's good at cleaning up these end-of-track towns, but it takes a real scout to read smoke signals." He changed the subject. "I'll have to get back soon. Reed wants me to go to Sanders and talk to Major Steers about obtaining more troops to protect our track laying crews."

Moira looked up, noticing the intensifying heat of the sun, and said, "I'll be sunburned if I stay out in this heat too long." She turned her horse back in the direction of Cheyenne, and added in a tone that seemed idle, "I suppose that's one advantage the Union Belle has, with that dark skin of hers. She can take the heat better than most women."

Ray shot a quick glance at her, wondering if her words were more pointed than they seemed. He had seen quite a bit of Lola before going to Boston, but had said little to Moira about it. He had been crestfallen that his advances to Lola had been deftly rejected, although he was the kind of man who would always view rejection as a challenge.

"I guess most of the men in town are wild about her," Moira continued, turning to look at him. "She's very pretty."

"I guess she is," he murmured.

"You guess she is!" Moira laughed. "Come, now, Ray, that

tells me more about how you feel than anything else you could have said!"

"What do you mean?"

"Why, you can no more help paying attention to women than you can help breathing, Ray," she said. "You don't *guess* whether or not a woman is pretty, you take one look and know everything about them!"

"Why, Moira, I didn't know you thought about me in that way," he said with some agitation in his features. "You make me sound like a womanizer."

She laughed again at his instant defense. "It's the way you are, the way you'll always be. You see women as prey. It's their job to run away, and it's your job to pursue them. It's all a game to you. If they get away, you shrug your shoulders and try again. If they don't get away, you've got another notch to cut into your belt."

He rode along, considering her words, then said, "You know me pretty well, Moira, but then, you're a smart girl. I just hope you don't have it in your mind that I think of you that way—as just another woman. Because that's not so."

Moira studied him, taking in his handsome face. "You're too good-looking, Ray," she commented. "And you've had too much success with women."

The edges of his lips turned up in a smile. "Yes, and there's another one of us on this ride who's in a very similar position."

They both laughed, and Moira nodded, "Exactly right. Both of us are spoiled. I expect that's why I can't make up my mind about us."

He wanted to press the issue, realizing that she had just expressed the truth about how she felt about him. But he was wary, knowing that she was not a girl who could be pressured. He had made progress with her during his stay in Boston, having taken time from his heavy work schedule to spend it with her. He had been around women enough to sense that she was poised on the verge of making a decision, and he had been delighted when she had decided to come along with him to Cheyenne. But despite Moira Ames's poise, she was still vulnerable and as shy as a deer at a waterhole. One wrong move, he understood, would frighten her away, so he restrained the urge that rose in him to press her to marry him.

"You're the only woman for me, Moira," he said simply. "No man in his right mind would ever think of another woman when he had you."

His simple compliment seemed to touch her, and she smiled up at him. "That's very sweet, Ray."

The heat continued to rise and they turned their horses to head across the flat countryside. Eastward and northward, the land rose into the rolling, broken contours of the Black Hills, while off to the south lay the heavy peaks of the Medicine Bow range. When they dismounted in front of the stable at eleven o'clock, both of them were thirsty and tired. Moira handed the reins of her mount to the hostler and said, "I'm tired after riding for just a few hours. Think what it must be like to pound spikes for ten hours a day under this sun, Ray."

"It takes a tough breed," he nodded. He led her to the hotel, asking as they walked, "Have you heard what the Central's using for labor?"

"No."

"Chinese gangs," Ray said. "Charlie Crocker couldn't get enough hands, so he tried fifty of them. Wes Odum was there, and he said it was a sight to see them! They don't weigh more than a hundred and twenty pounds apiece. Nobody thought it'd work out, but it did. They work well as teams, Wes said, and they get thirty-one dollars a month. The word is that there are over five thousand of them at work on the Central."

They turned into the hotel, and Moira paused before going up the stairs to her room. "It's odd, Ray. We Yankees pride ourselves on being independent, but we can't even build a railroad without the Irish and the Chinese." Then she turned to mount the stairs. "Thanks for the ride."

It was an abrupt departure on her part, the sort of behavior that irritated Ray Hayden. He was accustomed to women who were more pliant, and as he went to his own room and cleaned up, a restless irritation began to grow in him. He dressed in fresh clothes, lit a cigar and left the hotel. A poorly cooked meal at a newly opened cafe put an edge on his rising temper.

"Boston spoiled me," he muttered under his breath as he left the meal half-finished and walked down Main Street. A stack of paper work awaited him at his office, but instead of turning toward the Union's offices, he went into the Wagonwheel.

At midday the huge tent had few patrons, and there was a cathedral-like air about the place, owing mostly to the high peaks of canvas that muffled the sounds from the outside and lent a cool impression of darkness. Only a few of the many clusters of lamps were burning, a single bartender stood behind the long counter, idly polishing a glass. "Hello, Mr. Hayden," he nodded. He reached back and poured a shot glass full of the amber liquor without being told, and said, "Not much doing today."

Ray drank the whiskey, then slid it across the bar for a refill. The restless spirit inside him grew, and he asked, "Any games in back, Ed?"

The barkeep nodded. "One. Cherry's in it. Guess they'd be glad for some fresh blood."

Hayden drained his drink, paid for it, then made his way to a section at the rear of the tent that had been partitioned off by a wall of rough lumber. Passing through the opening, he followed the sound of voices and came to stand before a door. When he knocked on it, a voice said, "Come on in," so he pushed the door open and entered the room.

"Glad to see you, Ray," Cherry said at once. "Pull up a chair—but watch these birds. They're highway robbers!"

Ray dropped into a chair, nodding at Phil Castleton and Archie Bleyer, the two men he knew. "Meet Jason Wallford. And Jason, this is Ray Hayden."

"Glad to know you, Hayden," Wallford nodded, putting out his hand. He was a small man, but his grip was strong as Ray took his hand. He was well-dressed and a large diamond glittered from the ring finger of his right hand. He was not over forty, and his brown hair was carefully combed.

"Hayden's one of Sam Reed's top men with the Union Pacific, Jason," Cherry added.

The information brought a quick look from Wallford, and he said, "That so?" He put a thin cheroot between his lips, savored it, then nodded, "You fellows are doing a fine job. Figure to beat the Central to Salt Lake, I take it?"

Ray studied the man, saying, "Got to do it." Wallford was not a typical citizen of Cheyenne. He had the look of a professional man, but something about him refused to be cataloged.

As the game went on, it became obvious that he had money, for he lost several large pots with no apparent care. He traveled the country quite a bit, for he named several cities, including Boston and New York. Casually, Ray tried to trip him up, saying, "The Paxton Hotel in Boston? I thought that burned down a couple of years ago. The one over on Jefferson?" He had stayed in the Paxton recently, so he well knew it was still there.

"No, that was the Regent, I think," Wallford answered. "The Paxton is on State, not far from the Court House."

The game was a pleasant one, especially in view of the fact that Ray won over two hundred dollars. The restlessness left him, and as always when he won at cards, he became effusive. Soon he found himself talking about the Union and the problems that lay ahead, and more than once he referred to General Dodge in a personal way.

Castleton and Bleyer left at two-thirty, and a little later Cherry said, "Well, I've got to get ready for tonight." When he left the table, Wallford poured two more drinks, lit another cigar, and the two men sat there talking, mostly about railroading—a subject that seemed of great interest to Wallford.

Ray had taken enough liquor to dull the fine edge of his mind, but he realized as the talk went on that there was more than idle curiosity to the man's interest in the progress of the Union. Ray thought suddenly, *He's too sharp to waste his time on the Union. I've got something he wants.* He knew the type well, and was on his guard. Wallford was smooth and had the manners of the East, but something in his thin features and the glitter of his eyes warned Hayden that underneath his manner lay a carnivore.

"You know a lot about the railroad business, Jason," he said idly. "More than most people."

"Yes, I do," came the answer instantly. "As a matter of fact, I have an interest in several lines—one in Texas and another in Rhode Island."

"And another in the Central Pacific?" Ray shot the question at him suddenly, and was pleased to see a break in the smooth countenance of the man.

Wallford's thin lips turned upward in a smile, and he nodded. "You're too clever for me, Ray."

"I doubt that. You've managed to pry quite a bit of information out of me about the Union."

"Most of the things you spoke of are general knowledge," Wallford shrugged. "But I confess that I was pumping you." He put the cigar to his lips, puffed it slowly, then asked, "No offense, I hope?"

"Certainly not." Ray shook his head, and then he smiled and added, "But if Sam Reed finds out I've been playing cards with one of Central's spies, I'll be selling shoes for a living."

"No problem there," Wallford shook his head in a positive motion. "Nobody here knows I'm with the Central." He studied the younger man carefully, then said, "You're a pretty knowing fellow, Ray. It takes a clever man to get a secret out of me."

The compliment pleased Hayden. He took a drink, then grinned. "When I tell Reed you're here, Jason, you won't be much use as a spy, will you?"

"No, I won't." Wallford considered Hayden, then said in a muted tone, "But that's only if you tell who I am."

"You think I won't?"

"I don't know," Wallford said, holding his steady gaze on Hayden. "I don't know you well enough to know what you'll do. You may be one of those men who are blindly faithful to the company they work for."

A trace of irritation in his tone, Ray replied, "I think I'm as loyal as the next man, Wallford."

"Why, to tell you the truth, Ray," Wallford mused, "I'm not a great admirer of loyalty—at least not to a company." He put out a forefinger and began to draw circles in the damp tabletop, deep in thought. Finally he looked up and grinned, "To my mind, there's only one true object of loyalty—and that's myself."

Ray was of the same opinion, and so were most other men he knew, but he had never heard it stated so bluntly. It was customary to talk about loyalty, but he had long ago learned that when the pinch came every man looked first to his own skin. He stared at Wallford and asked evenly, "Are you trying to buy me?"

"Certainly," Wallford nodded. There was no trace of shame in his face, and he laughed at the expression on Ray's face. "Are you really so shocked at that, Hayden?" he jibed. "Surely this isn't the first time you've bumped into the rough underside of the business world?"

The easy manner of Wallford disarmed Ray, and he shook his head. "No, it's not the first time, but—"

"The only difference is that I don't bother to disguise what I want. I want to be rich. And I will be." He examined the end of his cigar, then trained his dark eyes on Ray. "I'm a very selfish man, Hayden. No nobility in me. I want to live in fine houses, have the best to eat and the best to wear. I want to have men saying 'Yes, sir' to me, and I want power." He smiled and spread his hands wide. "I don't think that's too much to ask, do you?"

Hayden stared at him, fascinated by the man, but suspicious. For once in his life he was sure that another human being shared the selfishness that formed the core of his own philosophy, but he quickly recovered by saying, "All very eloquent, Jason, but I still intend to let my employers know about you."

"That's as it must be, of course," Wallford nodded. "A man must look out for himself." He got to his feet leisurely, put out his hand and smiled. "I've enjoyed your company, Ray. I don't like many people, but I do like smart people—and I think you're smart." He picked up his hat, put it in place, then shrugged. "Telling Reed about me will change nothing. I'll move on, but someone will take my place. And even if they don't, you know the slim chance the Union's got of beating the Central. The Central's tunneled through the mountains and has got nothing but flat country ahead. And I heard you say earlier that the Union will hit the worst grading of all in the dead of winter. There's no way you can lay track through those mountains in ten feet of snow, Ray, and everybody knows it."

"It can be done," Ray insisted.

"And if it is done, will it make you rich?" Wallford demanded with an edge to his voice. "No, you'll get a salary and the big boys will get the cream." He moved toward the door, but when he got there, he turned and nodded. "If you decide to inform Reed of my mission, Ray, I suppose this will be our last meeting. If you don't—we'll need to have some more conversations. Forgive my blunt manner, but if you come with us, you won't be just an errand boy. I can see already that you're going to have trouble being loyal to your employers." He laughed and strolled out of the room, shutting the door behind him.

Ray sat there for fifteen minutes, going over the conversation.

"I've got to tell Reed at once," he said—yet he didn't get up. When the barkeep came in to clean the table, he rose and left the Wagonwheel. But when he got to the office and found Reed poring over survey maps, he said only, "Sorry to be late, Sam." All afternoon he worked with Reed, and more than once he almost blurted out the truth about Wallford, yet he did not. When he left the office at five, he went to his room and sat staring down at Main Street for two hours, revving up for the night. But he heard little of the raucous noise, for in his head he kept hearing Wallford: "I want to be rich. I want to be powerful." Finally he rose and began to shave, but before he was finished, he stared at himself in the mirror, finally slamming the washstand so hard the pitcher rattled. "Well, by heaven, I want the same thing!" Saying it seemed to free him, and he immediately calmed down and finished shaving.

★ ★ ★ ★

Although it was almost five o'clock in the afternoon, Cheyenne still sweltered under the full force of the blistering summer sun. The force of the dry heat surprised Moira as she stepped out of the relative coolness of the hotel. She blinked, then moved out into the merciless glare, wondering again why she had not fled to the comforts of Boston weeks ago. She was a city woman, accustomed to ease and culture, and as she made her way along the crowded boardwalk, resentment rose up in her at the sight of the crude street.

The population had soared, and now the town was so crowded it was erupted with dissonance. She saw soldiers, gamblers, peaceful Indians, and a number of Mexicans. As she stepped through the ankle-deep dust to cross the street, a painted woman in a fancy dress gave her an impudent look. The saloon woman wore a dainty little derringer at her waist, and her lips curled up into a smile when a man strode over to take her arm.

Moira watched as they disappeared into one of the saloons, and thought of the article in the crude newspaper she had read earlier:

In Cheyenne there are men who would murder a fellow human for five dollars. Nay, there are men who have already done it, and who stalk abroad in daylight unwhipped of justice. Not a day passes but a dead body is found somewhere in the vicinity with pockets rifled of their contents. But the people generally are strangely indifferent.

Her thoughts disturbed her, and she shook them off, turning down the side street that led to the UP offices. As she drew closer, the activity increased, and she had to pick her way past huge dumps of steel and ties. A train steamed in, saturating the air with the screech of brakes and the hiss of released steam. She stood to watch as a carload of tracklaying materials was muscled from a sidetrack by sweating, red-faced laborers, then picked up by the engine. Even as it disappeared from the yard, the workers loaded the next flatcar with steel, fishplates and ties.

The dust settled on her face, and she dabbed at it with her handkerchief as she pushed her way through the door under the large UNION PACIFIC sign. The air inside remained hot, but it was a relief to be out of the blaze of the afternoon sun.

"Why—Miss Ames, I'm surprised to see you out in this heat." Josh Long left his desk and came over to greet here. His round face was flushed, and he mopped it with a soggy red handkerchief, adding, "I guess you want to see your father?"

"Is he in, Josh?"

"Sure is. He's been talking with Mark Winslow—but I know he'd want you to go on in."

"Thank you, Josh." Moira moved across the office, passing through the door without knocking. "Hello, Father," she said, seeing the two men leaning over a desk, peering at a map.

The men straightened in their chairs, and Ames said, "Too hot for you to be out, Moira. This sun will cook you red as a lobster."

"I can't stay in that room all the time," she said, then turned her eyes on Winslow. "Hello, Mark." There was a flare of interest in her eyes when she smiled at him. She was accustomed to men paying her much attention, and his distant manner piqued her. "You've been quite a stranger lately."

"Blame my boss," Mark shrugged. "He's about to run all the tallow off me."

Ames shifted his huge bulk, shook his heavy head slowly,

saying, "You're going to have worse, Mark." He touched the map with a heavy forefinger. "Things aren't improving. Durant has gone crazy, I think. Look . . ." He traced his finger along a spidery line and anger touched his plump mouth. "He's gone behind our backs and changed most of the lines we agreed on. Claims he laid out new lines to save money."

"I guess we know what'll happen to any money Durant saves," Winslow remarked. "He's made a fortune already on the UP."

"You're right there—and everybody knows it."

"Wait and see what Dodge does to him, Mr. Ames," Mark said. "He'll nail his hide to the wall."

"Maybe, but Durant is clever," Ames said heavily.

Moira said, "You're more worried about this than I've ever seen you, Dad." She had not noticed before how much weight he had lost, but now his expensive suit hung on him loosely. The dark circles under his eyes and lines fatigue had etched into his broad face made her somewhat nervous. "Is it really so bad?"

Ames shrugged. "I haven't said much to you or your mother, Moira, but I've mortgaged the shop to the hilt. Can't get another penny from the bankers on it. If the UP loses out to Central, we'll be out on the street."

A shiver ran through Moira, for she had accepted her opulent and extravagant way of life with little thought. Now fear rose up in her, but she covered it quickly. "You'll do it, Father," she smiled and took his arm. "What you need is something to eat. Let's go get supper."

"Isn't Ray supposed to be in later?"

"Not until seven." She took his arm, then gave Mark a warm smile. "Come along. I want to hear about Ray's misspent life when you two were younger."

She brushed aside his protests, and the three of them left the office and made their way to Cheyenne's main street. Ames, accustomed to making decisions, announced, "We can get a private room at the Union Belle," he said. "I need a little peace and quiet—and the food's good."

Moira gave Mark a quick look, started to remark that he would have another chance to see his Mexican lovely—but suppressed the comment before it was spoken. Instead, she chatted with the two as they made their way down the still-empty street. The whiskey-seeking Irish laborers wouldn't make their appearance for another two hours. The three of them went inside and Mark spotted Driver sitting at a back table, talking to Lola. He looked up and briefly acknowledged the newcomers, then returned his attention to Lola, whose back was to them. Shep Yancy moved away from the bar to meet them. "Good to see you, folks. You like a private room?"

Ames nodded, and Yancy called out, "Maureen—" The waitress appeared at once and led them to the short hall, then opened a door to a small room containing a round table and eight chairs.

They sat down, and Maureen asked, "Would you like to have something to drink before your meal?"

"None for me." Ames never drank, but he said, "You two have something if you like." Mark asked for a beer and Moira ordered a glass of wine. After the girl had brought their drinks and taken their order, she left.

"Now," Moira said with a glint of humor in her green eyes, "I want to hear the truth about you and Ray when you were chasing women during your wild days at West Point."

"You'd be bored to tears," Mark smiled. "We worked ourselves to death and there wasn't much time for ladies." He sat there idly, his legs outstretched and his tall frame relaxed. He had the knack of going slack when circumstances permitted, and he did so now.

Moira was a clever woman, and soon she led him into reminiscing about his days at the Point, and the father and daughter listened with amusement as he recounted some of the escapades he had been involved in.

Maureen brought the meal—pork roast, new potatoes, gravy, fresh bread, and a green salad. They ate slowly, Ames putting his food away absently, his sober face relaxing as he smiled at Mark's stories. Winslow's company affected her father as she'd hoped, and after the main course, they lingered over fresh peach pie and coffee.

Finally Ames heaved himself up, saying, "I'm going back to the office. Want me to walk you back to the hotel, Moira?"

"Oh, I'm sick of that room, Dad!" A slight smile flitted across her features, and she said coyly, "Mark can take care of me. He doesn't mind having a woman on his hands—according to rumors."

"Rumors created by Ray Hayden," Mark nodded. "That man is building up his faithfulness at my expense." Then he added, "I'll stay with her until Ray gets in."

"After that you'll have to go out to Camp Six right away, Mark," Ames said in parting. "Some sort of trouble there. Take care of it."

He left and Moira studied Mark thoughtfully. "What will you do about that, Mark? The trouble, I mean."

"Don't know," he shrugged. "See what it's like when I get there. Never pays to plan too far ahead, Moira."

She got to her feet and he rose. "Let's take a walk. I'm tired of being inside."

They left the small room and passed through the now busy bar. Jeff Driver was still sitting at a table with Lola, and Moira sinisterly drew Mark to a halt. "Why, hello, Lola," she said in a syrupy sweet voice. "The meal was *very* good."

Lola looked up, sensing at once that the remark was superficial. She took in Moira's tight grip on Mark's arm, and her possessive air. "Thank you," she said. "We're always glad to have you." She watched the pair leave, and when she looked back at Driver, a different expression clouded her face, one he couldn't read.

"Make a good-looking couple, don't they," he said. "Too bad she's Hayden's girl. I think Mark would like to court her."

"You think that?"

"Just an idea." Driver leaned back in his chair, considering her. She was wearing a black dress that matched her raven hair, with small rhinestones around the scoop neck, her only ornaments two pearl earrings and a green haircomb. She was aware of his attention, knowing that someday he would speak out, but was uncertain as to what her answer would be. She smiled pleasantly and they continued to talk, but her mind stayed with Mark and Moira.

The object of her thoughts walked slowly down the street, shielding Moira from the swell of people beginning to flood the town. "Getting crowded," he remarked. "Have you ever been to the old Spanish church?"

"No. Is it close?"

"Not far." He led her off the main street, down a quieter one, following it past the business section until they reached a grove of cottonwoods that sheltered a small stone building with a cross on top. "Oldest building in Cheyenne, I think," he said. A low stone wall ran along one side of it, and he said, "Want to sit down?"

"Yes," Moira nodded. She sat down, and he hesitated, then joined her. "It's such a small church," she remarked.

"It was originally for the Indians." The sound of tinny music floated to them from the saloons, and he looked toward the sound. "Guess the missionaries never thought there'd be anything like Cherry Valance's place this close."

The air was cooler as the sun began to drop beneath the outlines of the town. Moira leaned back, looking at the church, then at Mark. "You're a strange man," she said impulsively. "Everyone talks about what a hard character you are."

"My job," he shrugged.

"What will you do when the railroad is finished?"

"Another railroad, I suppose." He gazed at her and asked, "What will you do, Moira?"

She laughed suddenly and put her hand on his arm. "I may be in the poor house, if Dad is right." She didn't seem worried, however, and in the falling darkness she seemed to glow. Her light hair and green eyes picked up the last lights of the sun, and he was aware, not for the first time, that Moira Ames was perhaps the most beautiful woman he had ever seen.

Suddenly he was uncomfortably alert to the power of her beauty, and he rose to his feet. She had not missed the expression on his face, and with an impulse, got up and moved closer to him. She said nothing, but buried hungers raced through Mark, and without planning it, he reached out and put his arms around her. If she had resisted, he would have released her at once, but she lifted her face and leaned against him. When he kissed her, she responded eagerly, and Mark knew he could not hide his desire for her.

Mark's grip tightened around her as the passion heightened, and she put her hands around the back of his neck, wanting the moment to last forever. Then suddenly her lips slid aside, breaking the tension, and he reluctantly dropped his arms and stepped back.

"You did that very easily," Mark remarked quietly.

She had been stirred by the kiss more than she wanted to admit. "That's what you wished, wasn't it?"

"Yes."

"And you're thinking I'm easy, aren't you?"

"No. I'm not thinking that." He tilted his head down to catch her eyes, then added, "I'm thinking of Ray."

"I'm not married to Ray!"

"You're going to marry him, aren't you?"

"I—I don't know." She was disturbed by the scene, her agitation obvious in the nervous manner she twisted her hands. "He wants me to."

"And what do you want?"

She was suddenly aware that her feelings for Ray were even more confused than she had thought. Almost angrily, as if he had accused her of something wrong, she said, "Don't pick at me about Ray, Mark!"

He studied her, not understanding what was behind her words. The entire scene had affected him deeply. "I guess we better get back to town, Moira."

She took a deep breath, getting control of herself, then came up with a smile. "Don't you trust me, Mark?"

As they moved away from the wall, tracing their way back toward the town, he said, "No . . . and I don't trust myself, either. But I know one thing, Moira. Ray's a friend of mine. He loves you, which means you're off bounds for me."

Moira walked beside him, annoyed for some reason, but not completely understanding why. When he left her at the hotel, she moved to the window and watched as he made his way down the street. When he turned in the direction of the Union Belle, she shook her head in an angry gesture, and without thinking, picked up a book from the table beside her bed and threw it against the wall.

Neither of them had noticed Hayden as they had returned to the hotel. He had come back to town and inquired at the Union Belle for Moira. Jeff Driver had smiled and mentioned that she had left with Winslow. A potent flash of jealousy had flashed through him, and he had lurked across the street from the hotel waiting for them to return. When they came into sight, there was something in their attitude that angered him. He watched them go up, and left at once for the Wagonwheel.

He stayed at Valance's saloon, drinking steadily for two hours, and getting thoroughly drunk. It was at that time that Jason Wallford came to sit beside him. Wallford had been observing him carefully, and now he said quietly, "Been thinking things over, Ray?"

Hayden looked up, and when he spoke it was with the carelessness of a drunk man. His blurred eyes tried hopelessly to focus on the powerful man beside him. "Yeah. I'm ready to listen, Jason."

"Fine. Come along and we'll see what we can work out." As Wallford led the way through the crowd with Hayden stumbling along behind, he caught Valance's eye, and nodded slightly. Valance smiled and watched as the two men disappeared.

"Like a lamb to the slaughter," the saloon owner said quietly. When he turned back to his game it occurred to him that he'd just seen the fall of a man. Hayden's move proved once again that his philosophy was sound—every man was for sale.

CHAPTER FIFTEEN

THE SHEPHERD CALLS

★ ★ ★ ★

Jack Casement's troops marched across the plains steadily throughout May and June, leaving the shining rails behind as a monument to their progress. The big knock-together ware-houses bulged with railroad fittings, materials, and provisions. Tie contractors had a thousand men busy up on the Black Hills slopes, cutting good hard pine and spruce and hemlock in an attempt to trim the cost of hardening the flimsy cottonwood. In their camps along the Laramie, Medicine Bow and North Platte rivers, huge stocks of ties and bridge timbers accumulated, ready to be floated down to the grade.

Cheyenne flourished. The call for labor had gone East, bring-ing trainloads of restless Irishmen, some of them fresh out of the steerages of Western Ocean immigrant packets, eager to join the veterans who whiled away their final weeks of idleness in dining, gambling and fighting.

Cheyenne was Julesburg all over again, but a bigger, more vigorous place, sure of its destiny. General Dodge called it the gambling capital of the world, noting that "Every known gam-bling device is in lucrative operation there." The hundred foot span of the lavish Wagonwheel Saloon contrasted sharply with the ten by fifteen shack that served as the U.S. Post Office, a clear measure of who controlled the town. In addition to the saloons and gambling houses, there were six bonafide theaters, and at least seventeen "variety halls"—usually a saloon, a theater and a house of prostitution combined under a single roof. The Cheyenne newspaper, *The Leader*, ran a daily column under a standing head, "Last night's shootings," and a local magistrate, Colonel Luke Murrin, levied a ten-dollar fine on any man who drew a gun on another inside the city limits, "whether he hit or missed."

The result was that Cheyenne's reputation spread far and wide, a stink in the nostrils of the godly. If Julesburg had billed itself as the most wicked city in America, the depths of Cheyenne's depravity could be judged by the fact that visitors revealed an almost compulsive tendency to describe it in terms of the regions below the earth.

Even the tolerant made jokes about it, one of which concerned a conductor whose train was boarded in western Nebraska by an obstreperous drunk. When the man loudly announced that he "wanted to go to hell," the conductor immediately sold him a ticket to Cheyenne.

After Editor Samuel Bowles of the Springfield, Massachusetts *Republican* visited Cheyenne, he commented, "Hell must have been raked to furnish them and to Hell they must return after graduating here."

Yet under all the tawdry glitter and the evil capering lived the solid, sober citizens who had also followed the Union Pacific into town. On January 5, 1868, with the thermometer standing steady at twenty-three degrees below zero, the newspaper noted that Cheyenne's first public school building was dedicated.

Another event transpired in Cheyenne, but there were no notices in *The Leader*. In a small frame building on the east side of town, Jude Moran had his first service. There were only seventeen people there, most of these Indians who had come over from Fort Sanders for the event. Lola had not been there that morning, but on the following Monday morning her father paid a visit to the Union Belle. Shep and Lola were having coffee, and Yancy offered at once, "Well, if it isn't the preacher. Come and have some breakfast, Reverend."

"Already had mine," Moran smiled. "But some of that coffee would be good."

"Maureen—bring some fresh coffee for the parson," Yancy called out. Turning back to Moran, he said, "Hear you quit the Union Pacific."

"That's right. I'm going to start a church here in Cheyenne." He looked at Lola and said, "You're looking fine, Lola."

She felt awkward, not knowing yet what to call him, but smiled anyway, saying, "I hope the church does well."

"I'm not much of a preacher," Moran shrugged. "All my life I've had to muscle things around. Guess I know how to get work out of men . . ." He took the coffee that Maureen brought, then laughed, "Sometimes when I'm preaching I have a notion to grab some heads and knock them together like I did as a foreman."

"Well, you got the muscles for it, Parson," Shep grinned.

"I guess—but brawn won't do it for what I'm after. You can whip a shoddy worker—but that never changes his heart. And that's what's got to happen before a man or a woman can get right with God."

Lola studied him as he talked, fascinated by the thought that he was her father. Other than her eyes, she saw none of him in her physical appearance—her mother's Spanish blood dominated those traits. But somehow she felt at ease with him, and by the time he got up to leave thirty minutes later, she asked, "Please, come by and have supper with me tonight."

He stared at her, caught off-guard, but a flush of pleasure rose to his cheeks. "I'd sure like that."

After he left, Shep said, "He's a fine fellow, Lola. He's certainly no one to be disappointed in—I'm glad he's your pa."

Moran came back that evening for supper, and the two of them enjoyed each other's company. Lola was once again apprehensive that he would try to force his religion on her, but he said nothing about it. He had been all over the West and they sat sipping coffee while he told her tale after tale. He was a natural storyteller, and she was content to sit and listen. It wasn't until ten o'clock that she began talking about herself.

Moran toyed with his coffee, letting her speak at her own pace. He felt guilty about neglecting his daughter, and listened as she spoke of how hard it had been living with her mother and sister in the cantina. Even though she didn't complain, her manner betrayed how difficult it had been. He sensed the goodness that was in her, and rejoiced in it, marveling that God had kept her from the low life of the saloon.

It was nearly midnight when Lola finished her story. She had been staring down into her coffee cup for a long time when she said softly, ". . . so it was Mark who got me away. If it hadn't been for him, I guess I'd still be there."

"But you rescued him, too," Jude said quietly. "Maybe God saw that the two of you needed a boost, and put you together."

The sound of his voice startled her, and she sat up quickly, a faint flush in her cheeks. "I . . . I've never told all that to anyone," she admitted.

"I'm glad you're here, Daughter," he said. "God has watched out for you. That's been my prayer since I held you in my arms the first time, when you were just a baby." His brow suddenly contracted, and he shook his head. "I've grieved all my life over what happened. I loved your mother—but she never loved me, I guess."

"It wasn't your fault," she said quickly. Putting her hand on his, she smiled. "I've wondered about you all my life. Now I've found you."

Giving her dainty hand a tight squeeze, he said huskily, "I thank God for keeping you safe." Then he stood up. "This has been the best evening of my life. I hope we can do it often."

"Yes," Lola agreed, getting to her feet. The moment of parting was awkward, and she made it lighter by saying, "I'd like to visit your church next Sunday."

"Well, you know how much I'd enjoy that," he smiled, leaving the restaurant with a final wave of his hand.

Lola lay awake for a long time that night thinking of the unique evening. Jude Moran provided the part of her life that had been missing—the stability that she had always longed for and never had. Not once in all her years of growing up had she felt the security that had come to her during the simple meal with her father. Without realizing it, she had built up a wall of defense to protect herself from the life that had surrounded her at the cantina. Everyone she knew had been a potential betrayer—but Jude Moran was safe. As she drifted off to sleep, she basked in the knowledge that he wanted only what was best for her.

She thought often about her father as the week passed, though she didn't see him again. On Sunday morning, she put on a simple blue dress and left the Union Belle. The quietness of the morning washed over her as she made her way along the boardwalk, and she regretted that the demands of her work kept her from enjoying the peaceful morning hours. The streets seemed almost deserted. Only a few horses were tied to the hitching posts, and she saw fewer than a dozen people on her journey.

Following her father's directions, she made her way down one of the side streets at the edge of town, and found the building he had described. It was an unpainted one-story affair, like most of the other buildings in Cheyenne, and in front of it two wagons and a dozen or so horses filled the space at the hitching post. The sound of singing greeted her as she approached the door. She hesitated for one moment, then resolutely pushed it open and stepped inside.

She saw her father standing beside a table at the front of the room. A short, red-faced man was leading a song vigorously, and her father came at once to her side. He was smiling, and said, "Why, it's good to see you, Daughter. Let me find you a seat." The room was fifteen-feet wide and less than thirty-feet long, but it was full of people. Over half the congregation was Indian, and she saw at least two white families with smaller children. He led her to a seat close to the front, then left her. She found herself standing between a short squatty Indian who studied her intently, and Jake Kilrain, a tall man in his late forties. Jake was a foreman for the Union and came to the Union Belle frequently.

"Hello, Lola," Jake said cheerfully. "Glad to see you."

For the next twenty minutes, Lola listened as the song leader, Joshua Long, another railroader she knew, led the singing. Joshua came into her place with Jeff Driver fairly often, and his bright blue eyes caught hers and he gave her a smile. He had a clear tenor voice, and threw himself with gusto into the singing. Lola had a good voice and a quick ear, and because Long sang each song several times, often calling out the words before they sang, she was able to join in. Her clear contralto swelled with the voices of the men, and Long gave her a nod of encouragement, saying once, "Fine! Fine! We need some ladies to help us with these good old songs of Zion!"

The singing was not polished and the setting was rough—but as Lola stood there in the crowded room, she began to be affected by some quality that she could not explain. Most of the songs were simple, and all of them were about Jesus. Lola knew Jesus Christ only as a statue she had seen on the walls of a church, but the vigorous words that composed the songs that morning said he was more than that. One of the songs stirred her greatly. It spoke of the death of Jesus, and for the first time in her life she thought of Jesus as a real man, suffering real pain. The first verse ran:

When I survey the wondrous cross
On which the Prince of Glory died,
My richest gain I count but loss
And pour contempt on all my pride.

And the second verse spoke of the physical details of the cross of Jesus:

See from his head, his hands, his feet,
Sorrow and love flow mingled down;
Did ere such love and sorrow meet
Or thorns compose so rich a crown?

The song stirred something in Lola's heart, and to her surprise, she found her eyes growing misty with tears as the song went on, for the death of Jesus had become more than a dry, dusty historical fact, or part of a crucifix on the wall.

Finally Josh stopped and said, "We'll sing just one more song. It was written by one of the most wicked men who ever lived—a man named John Newton. Newton lived a terrible life of sin, and became a slave trader. But God reached down and saved him, and Newton wrote this song about the grace that could save the worst of men. It's called 'Amazing Grace,' and I guess all of us can join with John Newton in thanking God for His mercy in saving us."

Amazing grace, how sweet the sound
That saved a wretch like me.

I once was lost, but now am found,
Was blind but now I see.

Josh belted the words out, and soon Lola found that she could join the simple melody. But the lyrics troubled her—especially the word "saved." Josh had said that Newton had been "saved," but that meant nothing to her. *Saved from what?* she thought. Nevertheless, she found her heart touched by the words as Josh led them through the other verses.

Twas grace that taught my heart to fear,
And grace my fears relieved.
How precious did that grace appear
The hour I first believed.

But it was the last verse that moved her most—perhaps because the breaking in Josh's voice made it difficult for him to sing.

When we've been there ten thousand years
Bright shining as the sun,
We've no less days to sing God's praise
Than when we first begun!

"It's going to be wonderful when we leave this old world," he concluded with a tearful smile. "Heaven is nearer than we think!" Then he turned and said, "Brother Moran, come and preach the Word of God to us."

A feeling of awe had touched Lola whenever she saw her father, and it came again now, stronger than ever, as he picked up his Bible, opened it, and began to read. He was not particularly impressive in manner or appearance—yet at the same time there was a dignity in him that captivated her as she listened.

"Our text is found in Luke's gospel, chapter fifteen." He waited while those with Bibles thumbed through them. Lola felt a touch on her arm and turned her head to see the stocky Indian on her left shoving a tattered Bible at her. Not certain of what he wanted, she stood there helplessly until Jake Kilrain reached over and took the Bible. He ruffled through it expertly, found a page and handed it back to her, pointing to a line just as her father started reading.

"What man of you, having a hundred sheep, if he lose one of them, doth not leave the ninety and nine in the wilderness, and go after that which is lost until he find it? And when he hath found it, he layeth it on his shoulders, rejoicing. And when he cometh home, he calleth together his friends and neighbors, saying unto them, Rejoice with me; for I have found my sheep which was lost. I say unto you likewise joy shall be in heaven over one sinner that repenteth more than over ninety and nine just persons which need no repentance."

Jude began to speak in a quiet voice, saying, "Not all of us have had flocks of sheep to care for, but we've all lost something. Maybe you've seen a huge flock of sheep and wondered how one shepherd could keep up with so many of the creatures. Well, in a human way, I don't think one man could know all that many sheep very well—but in this story that Jesus told, the shepherd knew all of his sheep personally. So when one of them got lost, wandered away from the flock, the shepherd's heart went after him. He was more concerned over that one lost sheep than he was for those that hadn't strayed off."

Jude was a good storyteller, and as he continued telling of the plight of the sheep and the determination of the shepherd to save him, Lola found herself caught up in the tale—and when she glanced around, she saw that the other hearers were equally entranced. When Jude began to make an application of the parable, she found herself moved to the heart.

"This shepherd," Jude said, looking over the crowd, "who is he? Why, he's the Lord Jesus Christ! Just like the shepherd in the story left to find the lost sheep, Jesus left His home in heaven to find His lost sheep! I imagine His Father said, 'Son, those humans that we made—they've all wandered away from the fold. Every one of them is going to die and go to hell if somebody doesn't bring them back!' And I expect the Lord Jesus answered, 'Father, I love them too much to let that happen. I'll go down there myself and get those lost sheep!' And He took off his royal robe and laid it to one side, and He took the golden crown off His head. And while all the angels watched, He left the glory of heaven! Stepping down from star to star, He came to a stable in Bethlehem, and there He became a little baby. And the one who had had a heavenly Father but no earthly mother, now had an earthly mother but no earthly father!"

Lola was fascinated by the account of Jesus leaving heaven. She unconsciously leaned forward as Jude continued.

"But who was the poor lost lamb in the story?" He looked around and smiled a little. "Well, I reckon that was me, folks. I was the one who wandered away from the fold. And it was you, too, and every man and woman who ever lived. We all left God and went into the wilderness. I wouldn't want to tell you the things I did when I was a lost man. I was a wicked man—a lost sheep! But Jesus found me, Praise the Lord! He came down and washed me in the blood and forgave all my sins!"

Jake Kilrain said, "Amen!" and Jude began to speak more fervently. Lola clenched her hands tightly together as he quoted many scriptures and shared several illustrations. He read one scripture, "All have sinned and come short of the glory of God," that burned into her heart so strongly she would have left had she not feared calling attention to herself. She sat there waiting for him to finish so that she could get away, promising herself that she'd never come back.

Finally Jude lowered his voice. "How can we get right with God? That's the big question. Well, Jesus is looking for you. He's still the Good Shepherd. But you have to want Him like He wants you. That's what it means to be saved, friends. When we admit we're sinners, and when we ask God to forgive us—that's when Jesus goes to work. He comes into our hearts, making them all clean, and then every day we get up and say, 'Jesus—don't let me stray off! I'm one of your sheep, so please keep me safe.' "

Then Jude continued, "Some of you are lost sheep this morning, just like I was. And maybe some of you are pretty miserable. If you want Jesus to forgive all your sins, wash you white as snow, and walk with you all the way to heaven—why, He's ready! We're going to pray now, and all you have to do to get right with the Lord God is just kneel down and ask Him to save you. Turn from your sins—then believe in Jesus, the Good Shepherd."

Lola was suddenly caught between two great desires; her first impulse was to get out of her seat and run out of the room. But something was pulling at her—and she was afraid of it. She wanted to fall on her knees and pray, but her heart was filled with fear. There had been no war in her spirit when she had knelt before the statues in the little church in Mexico. Her hands trembled and her legs were so weak that she could hardly stand. Tears began filling her eyes, so she closed them quickly, trying futilely to ignore the emotions that pulled at her.

Moments passed, and she was aware that some were kneeling. She looked across the room to where her father knelt beside a young man and took that opportunity to leave. Jake Kilrain, seeing her turn to go, said, "Come back again, Miss Lola."

She fled the room, almost running, and the bright sunlight blinded her as she stepped out of the dim light of the church into the street. Quickly she made her way back across town and entered the front door of her saloon with a gasp of relief. Shep and Maureen were sitting at a table eating sandwiches.

Shep said, "Hey, Lola, come and have some lunch," but she shook her head and left the room without speaking.

"That's odd, ain't it now?" Shep murmured. He looked at Maureen, "I reckon Lola's a little upset."

"She told me she was going to hear her father preach." Maureen turned her gaze to the doorway where Lola had disappeared. "She looked pale. I wonder what happened?"

Shep shook his heavy head. "I'd say she got too much hellfire-and-damnation talk—but her pa ain't in that line." He took a bite of his sandwich, chewed thoughtfully, then mused, "Maybe she's got religion. I've seen some who took it that way."

Maureen thought about that, then shook her head. "I hope not, Shep. If she got religion, she'd have to close this place down. And I'd be back at the Wagonwheel again—or maybe worse."

Yancy looked across at Maureen, thinking of how she'd come to work at the Union Belle. He'd found her on the street one night, knocked unconscious by some man. He'd picked her up and carried her into the Union Belle, where Lola had cared for her until she was well. She never dared to mention the name of the man who'd beaten her, but when Lola asked her to stay and work as a waitress, she'd accepted eagerly. She had worked hard, and though many men approached her, she had shown no interest at all.

Now Shep said, "Maureen, you ought to get married. This is no life for you." He surprised himself, for he had decided long ago to let people do what they pleased. But there was something in Maureen's quiet face that drew him, so he added, "Plenty of men would be interested."

"I already know what men are interested in." Maureen had an oval-shaped face, and her features were pretty, rather than beautiful. There was a playful spirit in her that she covered with a rigid manner, as if afraid to let that part of her show. Shep had noted it, however, and so had Lola, who had said once, "Shep, someone has hurt that girl so bad she cries on the inside."

Now Yancy saw that Lola's observation was correct, for Maureen's lips were tight as she added, "I was excited once when a man was interested in me—but that was a long time ago, Shep." She shook her head in an angry motion. "Now all I want is to be let alone!"

Shep said carefully, "Why, you can't crawl into a hole and live small, Maureen!"

"It's better than getting stepped on."

Her words were as bitter as the angry light in her eyes, so Shep kept his answer brief. "Not all men are bad. But I guess you'll have to learn that for yourself, Maureen." Then he looked upstairs toward where Lola's room was located, adding, "But I agree with you on one thing—I hope Lola don't get religion. I'd have to go back to bouncing for Cherry if she did!"

After a while, Lola came down and Yancy could tell she was depressed. Her face was pale, and when he asked, "You feel all right, Lola?" she simply nodded.

But later that afternoon, she grew more talkative and mentioned that she had been to church.

"Good sermon?" Shep asked.

Lola shrugged her shoulders, and he saw that she was having trouble. "I guess so." She paused, then added, "It bothered me some, Shep."

"I guess good preaching does that, Lola. And your pa is a good one." He studied her, then asked innocently, "You think you might join the church?"

She shook her head immediately. "No, not me." She looked around the barroom, and there was a sadness in her dark eyes. "I guess this is where I belong, Shep. At least I know this world. Not a lot of happiness in it—but I'm safe."

Shep bit off the end of his cigar, lit it, then said, "Know what you mean. I thought of getting religion more than once, myself. But what would a fellow like me do then, Lola?" He reached over and patted her shoulder awkwardly with his huge hand in an attempt to cheer her.

"Don't worry about it, Lola. I guess we'll come out as well as most."

Her eyes looked unhappy. "Not much satisfaction in life, is there, Shep?"

He blew a puff of blue smoke at the ceiling, then said, "It sure beats the alternative!"

CHAPTER SIXTEEN

SHOWDOWN AT FORT SANDERS

★ ★ ★ ★

Cheyenne was coming awake for another roaring night as Mark rode in along with Jeff and Dooley. They guided their horses down the street, threading their way through the flood of shouting men until they reached the hotel. Mark dismounted, but the other two kept their seats.

Dooley watched Winslow slide from the saddle, noting that he moved slower than usual. "You reckon you can keep out of trouble long enough for me to fill up my mouth at the cafe?" he asked. He gave Driver a sly wink, adding, "You shore done lost a step, Captain. Why, back when you was in the war, it wasn't nothing for you to walk the company down to its ankle bones!"

Mark gave a quick grin. He face was etched and lined with fatigue—the week-long trip along the right of way had been hard on all of them. "I was younger then," he replied. "I'm going to wash up and sleep the clock around. Put my horse up, will you?"

"See you tomorrow," Driver said, and the two turned their horses toward the stable, leading Mark's tired mount along. An hour later both of them pushed their way into the Wagonwheel and bellied up to the bar.

"Why don't we go to Lola's place?" Driver complained.

"We can go there later," Dooley nodded. "I'm feelin' a mite touchy, Jeff. And Lola runs such a high-toned place, I'm scared to chew tobacco or spit in there. Anyway, I want to see what the talk is—and this is the place to do it."

"All right," Driver nodded, "but I'm going over to the Union Belle to eat pretty soon." The two of them lounged at the bar, listening to the conversations around them and letting the fatigue dissolve. Neither of them drank much, and it didn't take them long to pick up on the latest gossip from Cheyenne. Driver finally motioned to Dooley and the two of them started for the door.

Lou Goldman had been sitting at a back table with Dent Conroy, watching the pair. As they started to leave, he got to his feet and made his way across the crowded floor, intercepting them. "Driver, you can drink your liquor someplace else from now on." He had not forgotten that Driver had pulled a gun on him, and had primed himself to make the man crawl.

Driver halted, turned to face the gunman, and said, "I'll drink where I please, Lou. You know that."

The wiry frame of Goldman tensed, and several men scurried out from behind him. Goldman was a sinister figure with his white hair and pale hazel eyes, but Driver didn't flinch. He had heard stories of the man's skill with a gun, and while he was not afraid, he grew very watchful.

"You can do your drinking at the Union Belle," Goldman said. He grinned and taunted Driver, "You been runnin' around after Lola like a love-sick kid. Everybody knows that."

"Keep your mouth shut, Goldman," Driver returned at once.

Goldman grinned more broadly. It was the kind of situation he liked, and he gave a look around the crowd. "Why, you boys see what he's doin', don't you? He's trying to pick a fight with me. Now I don't stand for that—besides, everybody knows what kind of a woman Lola is." He watched Driver's lips tighten, and added, "Why, I can tell you about Lola. She. . . !"

"Goldman! You're a dog!" Driver said. His left hand hovered over the gun at his side, and his eyes narrowed. The music in the bar broke off quickly, and the place was filled with sudden movement as men scrambled to scurry from behind the two men.

A silence fell on the room, and once again the people of Cheyenne waited for trouble. There was no doubt about Goldman's intentions, for he was rigid and ready to draw. But he drew the moment out, saying, "Well, boys, there it is. Driver just won't have it any other way. Go on and make your pull, you joker! It'll be the last thing you ever do!"

"Hold on, Lou!"

Cherry Valance appeared from behind Goldman. He put himself between the two men. "Get out, Driver."

Goldman protested in a stern voice, "Cherry, don't interfere!"

"I'm the boss, Lou," Cherry shot back, then said, "Everything's under control folks—you can go back to what you were doing. Start up the music, Larry!" The band broke into a lively tune, and as the crowd, deprived of action, turned to other things, Valance said, "Come on, Lou."

Goldman followed him sullenly, watching as Driver and Young went out the door. He threw himself down in a chair, slammed his fist on the table and cursed. "Why didn't you let me nail him?" he demanded.

Valance was cool as he sat down. His smooth face was unruffled as he began to deal himself a hand of solitaire. "Because I don't want to get Winslow stirred up. If you shot his man, he'd pull the place down inside an hour."

"I can handle Winslow!"

"You can handle Driver, maybe, but Winslow's another story." He lifted his eyes to glance across the room. "As long as he leaves us alone, we're all right. But if things break, I want Winslow to go first, not Driver or anyone else!"

Cherry sat there idly for the next hour until he saw Hayden enter. Getting to his feet, he went to meet him. "Come to my office, Ray," he said quietly. "Got something for you."

Hayden followed him and when they were alone, Cherry pulled out a bottle and motioned to a chair. "Have a seat, Ray—and a drink."

"All right." Hayden was wearing an expensive suit, and there was a new diamond stickpin in his tie.

"How were things in Boston?" Cherry asked, taking a drink.

Hayden drained the glass, picked up the bottle and filled it again. "Busy. Things are a mess for the Union. Brigham Young is giving them some ultimatums. It looks like either Dodge or Reed will have to go deal with the old goat."

"What's their schedule look like?" Cherry demanded. "Wallford's gone someplace, sniffing around, but he'll want to know what you've got as soon as he gets back."

"Depends on what happens when Durant and Dodge lock horns. Did you know Grant's coming to referee that meeting?"

"No."

"Fact. He's on his way to Fort Sanders now. Reed and Dodge are there, and Durant rode out on the same train I took." He studied Valance, then said, "I need some cash."

Cherry walked over, opened his safe, and came back with an envelope. "Wallford said to give you this. He wants to know the possible trouble spots up ahead. I think he's got the idea of planting troublemakers in the crews."

Ray stuffed the bills in his pocket carelessly, then got up. "Guess I'll play a little poker."

Valance smiled. "Better go see that lady of yours first, Ray. I'd bet she wouldn't like to be kept waiting."

Hayden laughed. "Make her wait, Cherry. Women love a man who won't give in to them."

He left the room. "Fool!" Valance muttered as he went back to close the safe. He knew that Hayden would lose most of the money he had received at the poker table; he always did. He and Wallford had agreed to pay him well for that reason.

After they had left the Wagonwheel, Jeff and Dooley shouldered their way along the packed street to the Union Belle. The place was crowded, so they took a table over against the wall. Dooley eased back in his chair, noted that Lola was dealing black-jack, then said, "Well, Jeffrey, that was somewhat of a tight squeak. That Goldman was primed and set to fire."

"Wonder why Cherry stopped it?" Jeff asked.

"He ain't ready for the balloon to go up, son. It wasn't no act of charity, not that sucker! Now Goldman ain't got no sense. Why, if brains was dynamite, he wouldn't have enough to blow his nose! But Valance is slick—and tough, too. Puttin' him down would be like putting a wildcat in a croaker sack."

Driver sat there, listening idly to Dooley ramble on, but his eyes kept returning to Lola. Dooley noticed the direction of Driver's gaze, but said nothing. Finally Lola rose from the table to join them. Both of them stood up as she took her seat, and as they sat down, she said, "Jeff, I just heard about the trouble you had with Lou Goldman."

Driver shook his head and smiled. "No trouble, Lola."

"That's not what Bob Horton said." Lola's lips were pressed tightly together as she added, "He said that you got into a row with Goldman over me and that there would have been a shooting if Cherry hadn't stopped it."

"Why, Lola, it wasn't—"

"Jeff, listen to me," Lola said intently. "Don't try to keep men from talking about me—especially Goldman. Don't you realize he was just using that for an excuse to get even with you?"

"Maybe so," Jeff admitted. "But I won't tolerate that kind of talk about you."

Lola leaned back and studied Driver. He was an attractive man, his dark features regular and rugged. There was a stubbornness in him she admired, and a sense of humor as well, but she wished that he would not pursue her so doggedly. She sought for a way to tell him it was hopeless, but nothing came to her. Finally she shook her head and gave up. "Where have you all been for the last few days?"

"You bring her up to date, Jeff," Dooley said, getting to his feet. "I'm gonna go play me some cards." He left the two and went to the poker table, where he played a leisurely game. He won a few dollars, but his mind remained on Jeff Driver. He watched the two talk, then Driver finally got up and left the room. *Hate to see him riding for a fall,* Dooley thought as he left the table. *But it's plumb clear that Lola's not got him on her mind.*

He encountered Shep Yancy, and the two talked for a while. "Town's pretty much wide open," Yancy said. "I been expecting Mark to put a stop to some of it, but he ain't."

"Been gone for a week," Dooley nodded. "Maybe he'll take care of that chore now he's back." He yawned and said, "I'm so tired you could scrape it off with a stick!"

"Go on up to my room," Yancy said.

"Don't want to put you out."

"I'm leaving as soon as we close down. Going over to Benton."

"Thinking of settin' up there, Shep?"

"It'll be the next construction town," Yancy nodded. "Cheyenne will be quiet enough in a few weeks. Go on and take the bed."

"Why, I reckon I will, Shep. Much obliged."

Dooley went at once to the room, pulled off his boots and gunbelt and flopped down on the bed. He went to sleep almost at once, and for three hours did not move. He awakened almost as suddenly as he had dropped off, realizing that he was hungry. Rising from the bed, he moved out of the room without putting on his boots and made his way into the main room of the club. It was empty, but he saw a faint light coming from a crack toward the rear of the room. He moved toward it, stopping when he heard a faint sound.

Carefully he pushed the door open. A woman sat at the table, her head on her arms, her shoulders shaking with her sobs. Dooley at once tried to retreat, but the door squeaked, and the woman jumped up and faced him, giving a small frightened cry.

"Aw, now don't be scared, Miss," Dooley said hurriedly. He saw that she was the waitress who worked for Lola.

"Who are you?" she demanded. Tears streaked her pale cheeks. Her large brown eyes matched the mass of hair that fell around her shoulders.

"Jest ol' Dooley Young, Miss. Shep let me have his bed for the night while he went to Benton."

"Oh." The girl relaxed and turned away from him. She stood there so long that he didn't realize at first that she was crying again. He stood by helplessly, finally moving closer to touch her on the shoulder.

"Miss—if there's anything I can do—?"

He was taken off guard when she suddenly turned and leaned against him. Her shoulders shook as great sobs racked her body. He held her gently, saying nothing, thinking, *I'd like to perforate the sucker who brought this on!*

Finally she grew still, and then drew away. "I'm . . . I'm sorry," she whispered. "I guess everything just caught up with me."

"Sure," he nodded, and tried a small smile. "I guess most of us would like to cry, but like my Uncle Seedy used to say, 'I'm too big to cry and it hurts too much to laugh.' "

She gave him a strange look, and then a glimmer of a smile showed on her tear-streaked face. "That's the way I feel, I guess."

She turned to go, but he said quickly, "Say, would you mind helping me fix some sort of a snack—maybe some eggs? I been on the trail for a week, and I woke up starving to death."

"Well—I suppose so."

He pulled a high stool up next to the bar and began telling her stories as she pulled a pan from a shelf and proceeded to fry him half a dozen eggs. Dooley Young was an entertaining man, and she wound up having a cup of coffee with him as he ate. Her face seemed to soften as she smiled at his tale of a ring-sided gouger he had shot in the hills, and he noted that the hardness he had seen earlier was gone.

Finally he was finished, and she said, "I've got to go now."

"Thanks for the supper . . ." He paused and said, "I don't know your name."

"Maureen," she said, then turned to go.

He reached out to pat her arm as she passed, and she whirled to face him, pulling herself into a defensive posture.

Dooley blinked, and said immediately, "Just wanted to say, Maureen, that I'm sorry for whatever it was made you cry. If I can do anything—?"

She looked closely at him, then shook her head. "No," she said quietly. The smile had disappeared and he read misery in her eyes. "There's nothing you can do, Mr. Dooley."

When she left, he stared at the door, his cheerful expression gone. He wondered again who had driven her to such a point as he left the kitchen.

★　★　★　★

Mark was roused out of a sound sleep by a loud knocking on the door. He slid his hand under the pillow, pulled the .44 out, and left the bed to stand to the right side of the door. "Who is it?"

"Reed."

Mark tossed the gun on the bed, turned the key, and stepped back to let his boss in. As usual, Reed wasted no words. "Get your pants on, Mark. We've got to be at Fort Sanders quick as we can get there. Meet me at the station; I'm running a special just to get us there."

Mark scrambled into his clothes, slipped on his gunbelt and left the hotel. When he got to the office he found Reed waiting for him, standing beside a huffing engine pulling only one passenger car. The two men got on, and at once the wheels began to spin, leaving Cheyenne at a break-neck speed.

Reed sat down and glanced moodily out the window before saying, "Grant's going to be at Fort Sanders. There's going to be a showdown tonight between Durant and Dodge. If Durant has his way, Dodge will be out—and that'll mean the Central Pacific will win all the marbles."

Mark stared at Reed. "I didn't know Durant was strong enough to challenge Dodge head on."

"He's feeling pretty secure. Ames hasn't been able to find any money back in Boston. He's mortgaged his plant to the hilt, but that's not enough. So Durant figures he can call the shots. He's got some money lined up, and he'll use that as a lever."

The thought of the Union Pacific going under had not occurred to Mark. "Why am I coming?" he asked.

"Dodge said to bring you."

The two men talked about the company's problems until the train pulled in at Fort Sanders, where Hayden waited to meet them. His face was flushed, and he said quickly, "Better get down to headquarters. Grant got here an hour ago and they're due to start pretty soon."

The three men got in the wagon, and Hayden filled them in on the events, but it was apparent that nothing had happened yet. "Everything depends on Grant," Reed murmured.

They pulled up in front of the headquarters house of General Gibbon and saw that the participants were standing stiffly in front of the house, posing for a picture. The group broke up and moved inside the house as Mark and the others strode toward the building. Dodge motioned to the three men and led them inside where Mark found a side window to stand beside.

Dodge stood with his back to one wall, his temper evident in his speech and the tension on his face. Grant, Sherman and Sheridan sat down, expressionless. Durant, Mark saw at once, was already half-angry, his small fingers plucking at his Vandyke beard.

Dodge said, "I want to make my position very clear."

They all looked at him carefully, especially Grant and his two generals. It was obvious to Mark that there was a rapport between the men, for Dodge had been a commander for Grant during the war. Men grow to either trust or hate one another in that setting, and it was clear in the way Grant gave Dodge his full attention that he trusted him.

"When I laid out the lines for the road, I did so with the government commissioners in mind. I wanted what they wanted—a line that would be sound, built for traffic and not for subsidy. As long as I am in charge, that is the way it will be. I will not have private contractors agitating for changes that make profit for them." He turned then and looked directly at Durant, biting his words off. "I will not have Durant sending his own set of engineers out to set aside my orders."

"I think I must remind you, General Dodge, that the investors are paying for this project," Durant snapped. "And since they're spending the money, they are entitled to any changes which will bring in more revenue."

Dodge's eyes grew flinty. "The Credit Mobilier contracts are tainted, Durant. You and your 'investors' are feathering your own nest at the expense of a sound line."

Durant shrugged his thin shoulders. "Still, private money is building this road. It's a gamble. We may all lose everything. And I want to remind you that this money is a loan that we must repay to the government. It's not a gift, as you seem to think, General. The Credit Mobilier is under a terrible strain—if it collapses there won't be a transcontinental road."

The air was thick with antagonism and distrust. Grant looked at Dodge, then at Durant, finally asking, "What about that, Dodge?"

Dodge said, "I want the private investors protected. Sherman Ames is one of them, and he's played fair because he wants the road built right. I tell you now, I cannot have either private contractors or financial interests dictating the layout of the line. I can't fight the battles back East. As long as I'm chief engineer, neither Durant nor any other man will interfere. If the changes Durant has made stand, I'll quit."

A silence built up, and everyone watched Grant. He had no real authority with the Union Pacific, but all knew he would be the next president. Two years earlier, Grant had given Dodge a furlough from the army to become the Union's chief engineer. He sat there quietly for a long time, then said, "The government expects this railroad to be finished. The government expects the railroad company to meet its obligations. And the government also expects General Dodge to remain with the road as its chief engineer until it is finished."

Durant got the message. Color came into his pale face, but he was a clever man and would not display his anger here. He made a quick change. "I withdraw my objections. We all want General Dodge to stay with the road."

The meeting ended abruptly, and the participants headed for the special train that was to take Grant and his party on their way. Before leaving, Dodge called Reed, Winslow, and Hayden to one side. "The soldier vote insures that Grant will be our next president.

But in the meantime, President Johnson hates us. We're out of money, and I don't know if Sherman Ames can raise any more."

"What are our orders, General?" Reed asked.

"Keep laying steel! We'll beat the Central if I have to lay the ties with my own hands. Mark, you take care of any trouble. I don't want any holdups. Put a tight lid on the construction towns, and if the workers get out of hand, pound them into the ground."

"All right, General Dodge," Mark nodded, his face serious. "You can count on it."

Dodge and Reed moved away, and Mark said, "Ray, you understand what this all means?"

"I think we all do," Hayden nodded. "Durant will cut our throat if he can."

"No doubt." They walked back to Ray's wagon to wait for Reed.

Hayden asked idly, "You see much of Moira while I was back East?"

An impulse to tell Ray about his walk to the church with Moira rose in Mark, but he knew his friend would never understand. After all, he didn't understand it himself. He nodded, saying only, "We had supper a couple of times."

"Good thing I'm not jealous," Ray said evenly. "I remember how we used to try to steal each other's women."

"That was a long time ago."

Hayden studied Mark, then let it go. He knew what he would have done had the cases been reversed, and he had been alone with Mark's girl. It never occurred to him that any man would miss a chance with a beautiful woman out of loyalty to a friend. He had built himself a little system years ago, and it said, "Take what you can get—no matter what." Now as Reed returned and climbed into the wagon, he thought, *I've got to have more money from Jason—and I need to persuade Moira to marry me right away.* It was significant that the two matters foremost in his mind were of equal importance.

CHAPTER SEVENTEEN

END OF TRACK

★ ★ ★ ★

"What's wrong with you, Lola?" Shep asked. "You've been mooning around for days. You feelin' poorly?"

The two were taking a break from the books they had been going over that early Monday morning.

"No, Shep. I feel all right." She took a sip of coffee, leaned back in her chair and closed her eyes.

He studied her face, then said suddenly, "I know what's wrong with you. Maybe you ain't noticed it, but every Sunday you get this way. You go to hear your dad preach, then for two, three days after, you go creeping around like a sick cat." A look of concern washed across his broad face, and he asked anxiously, "You reckon maybe you're tryin' to come down with a case of religion?"

Lola opened her eyes and gave him a slight smile. "No, I don't think that's it, Shep. Most of the time I don't understand what my father's talking about when he preaches. Maybe I'm just dreading all the trouble it's going to take to move from this place."

"Aw, it won't be so bad, Lola. I already got us a place rented at Benton, and this time we've got lots of help to fix it up." Cheyenne was in its last days as a construction point; within a week Casement would move his site to Benton, which would fill up just as Cheyenne and Julesburg had. Then it too would dry up when the wave of workers moved with the end of track toward Utah.

A thought struck her, and she said, "Someday, Shep, the railroad will be finished. There won't be any more towns like this one or Benton. What will we do then?"

Yancy was not a man of great forethought, and a look of surprise came to his eyes. "Why, I never think that far ahead, Lola. I guess we'll open a saloon someplace, like this one."

The thought displeased her, and she shook her head. "There's got to be more to life than running a saloon, hasn't there?"

"Man has to do something, Lola—and a woman, too. What's the difference between running a saloon and running a general store?"

"Oh, I don't know, Shep!" Lola rose and began to pace around the room, agitation in her face. "Maybe none—but when I look ahead and think of doing this for the next forty years, it scares me."

Yancy nodded as if something had been confirmed. "It's what I thought, Lola—you've been listening to your dad. All preachers think about is getting a robe and a crown—going to the glory land. But most of us are more interested in the here and now than we are in settin' around on a cloud plucking at a harp some time way off."

Lola stopped her pacing, came over and put her hand on his thick shoulder. She had grown genuinely fond of the big man over the weeks they had worked together. He was rough and had often led an evil life, but he had let none of that come into their relationship. Now she smiled down at him and said, "Maybe you're right, Shep. After all, I'm a lot better off than I was at the cantina back home. Lots of clothes and money—more than I ever thought. I'm even my own boss. Not many women can say that." She shrugged her shoulders, lifted her chin and said, "Let's get the bookwork done. I want to go out for some fresh air today."

"I can finish it, Lola. Why don't you let that handsome lieutenant from Fort Sanders take you for a buggy ride? Do you good and would sure give him a thrill."

"Maybe I will, Shep," she smiled as she turned to go. "I'll be back in time to open up tonight."

She went to her room, changed into a simple pearl gray dress and a pair of sturdy calfskin boots. Before she left, she looked in the mirror to adjust the small hat she had donned, then picked up a parasol and left the Union Belle. It was the middle of July, but the heat of summer was modified, and as she made her way along the street she enjoyed the bright sun and the cool morning air. It would be hot later in the day, but snow lurked in the mountains that lay on the horizon, and all too soon it would fall on the land, freezing the earth and turning the grass to a shriveled brown.

There was really so little to do in Cheyenne that after visiting the three stores that had anything a woman might want, she was perplexed as to what to do. The town picked up some momentum as the sun rose, and she heard the sound of the engines huffing over in the direction of the Union's stockpiles. She made her way through the dusty street, drawn by the activity, and as she turned a corner, she saw Jeff Driver coming toward her on a fine gray horse. His eyes lit up when he saw her, and he dismounted at once. He lifted his hat, saying, "Why, Lola—didn't expect to see you here."

"Hello, Jeff." She smiled at him, confessing, "I'm stealing the day off." A thought came to her, and she asked mischievously, "Why don't you take me for a buggy ride?"

He brightened up, then just as quickly grew gloomy, "Can't do it, Lola—not today. Got to ride to the Fort on an errand for General Casement." It was the first time she'd asked him to do something with her, and he flirted with the thought of getting someone else to go to Sanders—but Casement had been pretty anxious. "Say, I'll be back by three or four this afternoon. Put that ride on hold, will you? We can go down to the river and have a late picnic. Real pretty down there when the sun goes down."

"All right, Jeff."

He grinned and said, "I'll run on then—probably ruin my horse getting there and back."

Lola watched him leave at a gallop, and felt a moment of concern. He was in love with her, or almost so, and she had no feelings of that sort for him. It disturbed her to think that she

234

might have given him false hopes, but it was too late for such thoughts now. She walked toward the loading area, and for a time stood there watching the men load the steel and ties on the flat cars.

They were noisy, yelling at one another, and with the clanging of steel and the thumping of the ties on the cars, she was caught by surprise when a voice behind her said, "Hello, Lola."

She turned to see Mark with Moira Ames and Ray Hayden. Hayden asked, "What brings you down here, Lola?"

"Oh, I was just out for some air."

Moira said innocently, "I suppose it does get tiresome breathing that stale smoke in a saloon all night."

There was nothing wrong with the remark, but Lola sensed the unkind intent in the other woman's gaze. "That's right, Miss Ames."

The whistle of the engine blew shrilly, and Mark said, "Moira wanted to see the end of track, Lola."

"Come along with us, Lola, if you've nothing else to do," Ray suggested. "You haven't seen it, have you?"

"No, but—"

"Oh, come on," he insisted, and looked at Mark. "It'll be all right, won't it?"

"Of course." Mark nodded and added, "Come along before we get left behind."

Lola had apprehensions, but the thought of a boring afternoon prompted her, and she smiled, "I'd really like to see it."

The four of them boarded the work train, and Mark led them to some seats in a passenger car filled with the usual quota of Irishmen bound back to the grading camps. Moira and Ray sat down together, and when Lola seated herself by the window, Mark took his place beside her. Ray exhibited less cheerfulness than usual, Lola noticed. He sat idly listening as Mark pointed out some of the sights, and there was something in the way he looked at Mark that was not his customary good humor. Moira was the most animated of the four, her greenish eyes sparkling with excitement. She spoke more often to Mark than to the others, and it crossed Lola's mind that perhaps she and Ray had had a quarrel.

Mark got up once and went to the barrel for water, bringing

back two glasses for the women. When they had finished their drinks, he stood there, swaying with the movement of the train, his interest caught by Lola's expression. As Ray was explaining the difficulties that lay ahead, Mark noted the way her mouth stirred. She had a womanly fullness behind a smiling reserve, a richness that he had always admired. She looked up, caught his gaze, but said nothing. As he turned and went back to replace the glasses, he was aware that the wall he had unintentionally created between the two of them was still in place.

Moira had not missed the look that had passed between the two, and she studied the pair as Mark came back and sat down. She had long ago decided that Mark Winslow was one of the most interesting men she had ever known, and his refusal to pursue her—especially after the kiss at the church—piqued her. She had grown tired of men who fawned over her, and she was determined to elicit some sort of response from Winslow.

She began to pay more attention to him, and when the train stopped, it happened that Mark handed her down from the high step, and she took his arm quite naturally as they made their way to the construction area.

"I guess you're stuck with me, Lola," Ray said evenly. There was a sour note in his voice, and his eyes followed the pair as they walked in front. "I can't decide if my best friend is trying to steal my woman—or if my woman is trying to steal my best friend," he commented, seeing that Lola was watching him closely.

"I think it's neither, Ray."

"You're sure of that? I'm not." Ray's eyes narrowed and he shook his head. "You think that Mark decided to walk with Moira? Not likely. She's handled men so long that it's automatic, Lola. She's a romantic—no matter how much she denies it."

"Some women have to flirt a little, Ray. Especially women like Moira." That sounded critical to her own ears, so she added quickly, "She's accustomed to having men drawn to her. It doesn't mean anything."

"You're half right, Lola. Moira is used to manipulating men. But like I said, she's a romantic at heart. She's seen all types of Eastern men, conquered them all. But Mark is a pretty romantic figure. The man who tamed Julesburg and all that. The strong heroic type—just the kind to offer a new challenge to a girl like Moira."

Lola shook her head. Mark and Moira had stopped to wait for them, so she admonished softly, "Don't let that kind of thinking control you, Ray. Mark's not a man to steal his friend's woman."

He gave her a swift look, but said, "Ah, but you're taken with him, too, Lola. You're no judge of what he'll do."

She couldn't respond, for they came to stand beside the others, getting a full view of the work. This was Casement's capital city—a formless, dusty, confused affair lying across the sun-blasted Wyoming plain. The long boarding train stood on a siding; the shacks and warehouses and corrals and shops that fed materials to ten thousand men stood in formless rows under a pall of alkali whipped forty feet into the sky. Great dumps of steel and ties lined the right of way, and wagons and men crossed and recrossed the powder-churned earth. A material train slowly backed along the rails, stopping at the very end of steel. Half a dozen soldiers squatted under the false protection of a tin-roofed lean-to, their faces broiled black.

"Come along," Mark said. "We'll see better over there." He led them to a small hillock ten feet high where they could see the activities of the track gang directly under their eyes. The rush of the steel truck and its galloping bay horse; the runout of the rails; the bronze voice of the steel foreman yelling "Down!"; the clanging fall of the rails and the swift attack of the sledges beating the spikes home all fascinated Lola. Her eyes were filled with the scene, and she moved closer to Mark as a material train heaved forward another length of track, funneling black smoke into the sky.

"They work so hard!" she exclaimed.

"They work hard and they play hard," Mark nodded. "That's why they get out of hand when they hit town. But they're the only kind of men who could swing a sledge or hoist forty pounds of steel in this heat."

"I don't think—"

Her statement was not finished, for a gunshot laid its flat sound across the hot windless air, followed by a closely grouped series of explosions.

From a small coulee a column of Indians burst forth, almost hidden by the cloud of dust stirred up by their angular, long-maned ponies. They raced down on the steel gang as the construction engine's whistle set up an intermittent hooting. The crews dashed across the grade to where their rifles were stacked. The soldiers rushed out of the lean-to, knelt and began firing. The Indians, holding to a single wedge-like column, bore straight down upon the camp.

"Get Moira under cover!" Mark yelled at Ray, then grabbed Lola in his arms and jumped from the small hillock. He went down on his knees and rolled awkwardly to cushion her fall. He saw her face grow pale, but she let go of him at once. He pulled her up and pushed her against a pile of ties.

He drew his gun and waited, and a few seconds later a bullet struck the tie above Lola's head with a solid thunk. The Indian column rushed through the camp, shooting at random. The fire quickened as the Irishmen got their rifles unlimbered, and Mark said to Lola, "Those Indians can't stand up to that kind of fire."

He was right, but as the line wheeled, the column passed by the section of ties where they hid, and a lone Indian spotted the pair. He wheeled and aimed his rifle at Winslow, who raised his pistol and got off a single shot. The Indian pulled the trigger, but Mark's slug had taken him in the chest, driving him back and spoiling his aim. He fell to the ground in a heap of blood, and the rest of the column drove by, leaving the camp, followed by heavy fire from the workers and the soldiers.

Mark turned to tell Lola that it was over, and shock ran through him as he saw her lying on the ground. "Lola!" he cried out, and fell to his knees beside her. She was on her side, and as he pulled her over, he saw that the bodice of her dress was already soaked with bright crimson blood. A bullet had taken her high to the left, and he ripped the dress from her shoulder, whipped a handkerchief out of his pocket, and placed it over the hole, shouting for help.

When Ray ran around the corner, his face scared, Mark said, "Tell that engineer to get us back to Cheyenne quick as he can."

"Is she—"

"She's hit hard—now get going, blast you!"

Mark picked up Lola's limp form and made his way to the

train. Men crowded around, but he yelled, "Get out of the way!" He climbed aboard the train, followed by Moira, who was white as flour. Ray came in saying, "I told him to tear the tracks up." He looked down into Lola's face. "How is she, Mark?"

Winslow gazed down at Lola. He continued to hold the compress in place, although she had not opened her eyes. "I don't know," he said tightly. His dark face was set in a rigid cast, and all the way back to Cheyenne, he silently held Lola in his arms.

The whistle signalled their arrival, and Mark commanded, "Ray, go to Doctor Innes's office. If he's not there, find him. Have him waiting when I get to his office with Lola."

"Right!" Ray ran to the door, dropped out as the train slowed, grabbed a horse tied to a post and drove him at a dead run out of the yard.

"Can I do anything, Mark?" Moira asked tremulously.

He gave her a strange look as he came to his feet. "I guess not, Moira. It's up to the doctor now. And God," he added in afterthought. He moved down the aisle carrying his burden carefully, and out toward a wagon. "Get in and help me hold her," he said, and Moira climbed up obediently. He lifted Lola up, and the blood from her wound stained the front of Moira's dress. "Hold that compress in place, Moira," he said, then took up the lines and drove the wagon slowly into town.

CHAPTER EIGHTEEN

A LOST SHEEP IS FOUND

★ ★ ★ ★

Doctor Innes came out of a doze with a snap of his wiry neck. He had been leaning back in his chair, his graying head against the wall, when the sound of boots coming up the steps to his office jerked him from a fitful nap. As the door opened, he lowered his chair, got to his feet and asked crankily, "When did you two get back?"

Mark came into the room, his face filled with fatigue, and Driver looked even worse. They had just come in from the desert, as the fine dust on their clothes testified. Mark ignored Innes's question, demanding, "How is she, Doc?"

The dowdy physician stared at him without answering, then pulled a bottle out of the drawer of his desk. He turned it up, let the liquor go down his throat, then shut his black eyes as it hit his empty stomach. He corked the bottle and returned it to the drawer before he answered.

"No good, Mark."

Innes rubbed his eyes, then added, "If we could just get the fever down, she'd have a chance. But she's got pneumonia now—or almost."

"It's been three days, Doc," Driver said almost angrily. "You said then it wasn't so bad."

Innes glared at him, his fiery Scots temper flaring. "I'm not

God, man! I said it wouldn't be hard to get the bullet out—and it wasn't. But the slug was in a bad place, and it carried some fragments of her clothing when it went in. That brought on an infection that caused a fever, and now it's going into pneumonia." He glared at the two men, yanked the drawer open and took another drink from the bottle.

"Be quiet, Jeff," Mark said. "Doc's done all he can."

His manner pacified Innes, who threw his hands up in a gesture of desperation. "There's not much we doctors can do. Set a bone, take a bullet out, help a baby into the world. But you two were in the war. You know how often a man would get hit— maybe just a minor wound. But something would go wrong and he'd die."

Both men had their memories of such things, and Jeff asked heavily, "Do you reckon she's going to die, Doc?"

Innes bit his lip, trying to find some nice way to say what he felt. But he was a blunt man, feeling that honesty was the best way. He nodded and admitted quietly, "Aye, lad. It breaks my heart to say it—but she's headed that way."

Silence fell on the room for a minute, then Mark asked, "Do you need anything? Medicine—more nursing help?"

"That girl Maureen, she's a natural-born nurse," Innes said, stroking his chin. "And I've been a mite surprised at the Ames woman. It was my thought that she was no more than a spoiled brat—but she's been a help. No, Mark, it's out of my hands. Out of anybody's hands—except God's."

Winslow's face was thoughtful. He finally said, "You know, she saved my life once. I was a gone coon, and she nursed me through it." He bit his lip, and the sadness in his eyes flared into anger. "And here I am, can't do a thing for her."

Innes's eyes were on Mark as he pulled on his coat. He had wondered about the man's concern, and the remark he'd just made cleared some of it up for him. Driver, he had readily discerned, was in love with Lola, but there was something in Winslow's face that made him wonder about the man's feelings. "Come along," he said, picking up his black bag. "I'm going to check on her now. Maybe the fever's broken."

The three men walked out of the office and down the steps, turning toward the hotel where Lola had been installed. They entered and Ernie greeted them, "Hello, men." He hesitated, then added, "Been hoping Lola would be better this morning."

Mark nodded, but said nothing. They climbed the stairs to the second floor, and Innes went into a door, followed by the other two. Maureen was sitting in a rocker staring out at the street. Her face was drawn, and she shook her head saying, "She's no better, Doctor Innes. Fever is very high."

Innes said briefly, "Let me have a minute with her," and crossed to an adjoining door. Innes had commandeered two rooms, one for Lola and another for those who cared for her. Maureen tucked her hair in place, then said, "She woke up just before dawn. I think she had some kind of a nightmare."

"She say anything?" Mark asked.

"No—not really." Maureen thought, then added, "She was out of her head, but I thought once she was asking for her father."

"Has he been here much?" Driver asked.

"Oh, all the time," Maureen said quickly. She bit her lip, then added, "I don't think too much of men—but that man's been hurting for Lola. He's here most of the time, in this rocker. I ran him out last night. He nearly collapsed, he was so exhausted, so I made him promise to get some sleep."

Innes came back into the room, his features grave. "You can come in—but she won't know you," he warned briefly.

Mark and Jeff stepped inside, followed by the doctor and Maureen. Mark had not seen Lola for two days, and shock ran along his nerves as he leaned forward to see her face. The fever had eaten away her flesh, it seemed, making her face skull-like. Her eyes were sunken and her lips almost white and very thin. He stood there looking down at her silently, struggling against the blind futility that gripped him. He was a man of action, ready to match his muscles and his skills against anything. He had lost many times in various struggles, and bore the scars, both inside and out, but he had always been able to fight. Now no amount of fighting could help the wasted form that lay before him. He thought back to the time when he had been the sick one, of how she had cared for him, and his eyes began to smart. He shook his head, turned away and left the room.

Driver followed him, stopping long enough to ask, "Doc,

when will you . . . know something?"

Innes knew that was not the question Driver had intended to ask, but he made no attempt to hide the facts. "The fever had better break in twenty-four hours. If it doesn't she could go into convulsions, and weak as she is . . ." He broke off and went back into the sick room.

"I'm going to get drunk," Driver announced suddenly. He glared at Mark and added, "Fire me if you don't like it."

"He's in love with her, isn't he?" Maureen said after he had gone.

"I guess he is, Maureen." Mark pulled his shoulders straight, drew his mouth into a thin line and left the room without saying another word.

Maureen went in to stand beside Doctor Innes. The struggle that was going on in the slight form beneath the covers had made them close. "I'm sorry for Jeff," she whispered. "He's going to go crazy when she goes."

Innes nodded, then added, "Lola's made some good friends. I reckon Winslow's hurting about as bad as Jeff. He just won't let it crack that surface of his." He moved away from the bed. "Where's Moran?" he asked as Maureen followed him out into the other room. "First time I've been here that he wasn't underfoot."

"I made him go get some sleep."

Innes started for the door, then turned to say, "I never knew a human could pray so long. That man never stops."

Maureen agreed, and he asked, "You don't believe all that does any good, do you, lass?"

Maureen hesitated, then shook her head. "No—but I wish I did."

"Now that's a strange thing to say—but I know what you mean."

Doctor Innes left, and Maureen sat down in the chair. She thought about Jude Moran and his prayers, and wondered, as she had often done of late, how her life could have been different if her own father had been his sort.

★ ★ ★ ★

"I hear the Union Belle's not going to make it, Ray." Cherry

Valance was standing at the bar drinking with Hayden. He shook his head, adding, "I admire Lola. She's a straight one. Too bad."

"She's not dead yet," Ray said quickly.

Cherry observed him closely, then commented casually, "Miss Ames has been sticking pretty close to her. That surprises me a little."

It had surprised Hayden as well, but he merely said, "I didn't think she had it in her."

Cherry surveyed the crowd. "We're moving to Benton next week. It ought to be the biggest town yet. What will Winslow do?"

"Dodge told him to clamp the lid down."

"You heard him say that?"

"Sure I did."

Cherry frowned, his lean face intent. "I think he'll try to shut us down right off. Find out if that's what he's got on his mind."

Ray stared hard at the saloon owner. "That I can't do, Cherry. Mark and I are pretty close."

"How do you plan to work that? You've been taking plenty of money, Ray, but now that the chips are down, you're starting to fold. I don't think Wallford will like it."

"He can like it or not. I won't have Winslow killed." Hayden downed his drink, turned and left without a word. He'd had too much to drink, he knew, but he couldn't seem to help it. The money he'd gotten from Wallford had gone to the gambling tables, and he cursed himself for a fool as he went toward the hotel. *How did I ever get into this thing?* he wondered, as he had many times. When he was drunk, he hated himself, but as soon as he was sober he half believed that he had had to join up with the Central. He thought of that now as he entered the hotel, nodding at Ernie. *The Union's going down the drain. It wouldn't make any difference if I stayed loyal or not. A man's got to look out for himself.*

He knocked on the door and Moira answered it. "How is she?" he asked as he entered, the stale smell of whiskey accompanying him into the room.

"No change." Moira moved away to stand by the window. "What have you been doing, Ray?"

"Nothing much." He came close and tried to put his arms

around her. She did not move away, but there was a lack of response that angered him. He pulled her close and kissed her. She refused to return his attention, and he stepped back with a helpless gesture. "You sure don't make a man feel very welcome, Moira."

She gave him a steady look that made him wonder what was in her heart, and then she said, "I'm sorry, Ray. But this is a pretty poor time for romancing."

He was a man who hated to be challenged, but he knew he was behaving badly. "Of course, Moira. You're right."

"I guess it's been getting to me," she murmured, almost as though speaking to herself. "I've never thought much about death. Dying was always something that happened to old people—or at least to somebody I didn't know." She shook her head, and a line of fatigue furrowed her brow. "Now, sitting here hour after hour, watching her die. . . ."

He nodded and said quickly, "It was like that for too many men during the war. But maybe she'll take a turn for the better."

"Doctor Innes doesn't think so. He's pretty honest, Ray. He said tonight that she wouldn't last more than a day or two at most."

Ray shook his head. "She's a fine woman, Moira. I've never known one quite like her." The temporary sickroom made him feel uncomfortable. "I'll see you in the morning. Are you going to stay here all night?"

"Maureen will take my place at midnight. Good-night, Ray."

He did not try to kiss her again, and when he reached the street, he was more depressed than ever. He didn't want to go back to the Wagonwheel, so he bought a pint of whiskey and went to his room to drink himself to sleep.

Moira spent the next few hours sitting in the chair, checking from time to time on Lola, bathing her face and trying to detect any change. At midnight, when Maureen came into the room, Moira said, "She's getting worse, Maureen. I think her father ought to be here."

"I'm surprised he isn't back," the girl said. "He's never been gone this long before."

"I'll send someone to find him." Moira left and sent word to Mark to have Lola's father found, then went to bed, tired and low in spirit.

* ★ ★ ★

Mark came into the room to find it very crowded. Maureen, Jeff Driver, Shep Yancy, Moira and Dooley Young were all there. It was late, nearly midnight, and he said, "I've tried every place I can think of, but I can't find a trace of Moran."

He had gotten Moira's message twenty-four hours earlier and had exhausted every resource. He leaned against the wall, stared at the floor and then closed his eyes. For the next twenty minutes no one spoke at all.

Doctor Innes came out of the other room, asking Mark, "You find him?"

"No." Mark looked up and asked, "Is she dying?"

"Yes."

Mark studied the doctor's face for some trace of hope. Finding none, he said, "I'll go look some more." He started for the door, but it opened abruptly and Jude Moran walked in. He looked ten years older than he had the last time Mark had seen him, but there was a strange light in his bright blue eyes.

Doctor Innes said, "Where the blazes have you been, Moran? Get in to your daughter at once."

"All right," Jude said quietly, moving slowly into the adjoining room.

"She won't know him—but I'm glad he came anyway," Doctor Innes said grimly.

Mark straightened up and wordlessly followed Jude into the sick girl's room. He stepped inside the dimly lit room and closed the door behind him.

Jude stood beside Lola. He turned and examined Mark carefully. There was a strange peace in his face, and he smiled unexpectedly. "Glad you came in, Mark."

Mark searched for something to say. Finally he spoke huskily, "She's a fine girl, Jude."

"Yes, she is," Moran agreed. He looked more closely at Mark, then asked, "Are you a believer, Winslow?"

Mark shook his head. "No."

Moran's smile did not change. "No matter. You will be some day, I trust." Then he picked up his daughter's hand and held it gently. For a long time, it seemed to Mark, he stood there looking down at her, then he said, "I know you don't believe in prayer—but God has been speaking to me."

Mark had always been suspicious of those who claimed to hear from God personally, but there was something in the quiet manner of the man that held him silent.

"I've been out in the desert for a long time, fasting and begging God to save my girl," Jude said, still looking down at Lola. "And there was nothing. God was gone and the heavens were brass. I almost lost my faith, Mark. But then—just a little while ago, the word came to me—clear as print. I was crying, lying on my face in the dust, and God said, "Go tell your daughter to get up, for I will heal her.""

Mark stared at Moran, but there was no mark of emotional disturbance in his manner. "You believe you heard from God, Jude?"

"I know it." There was an air of total assurance in him, and he turned back to the still form of Lola. He did not raise his voice, but said in a conversational tone, "Lola in the name of Jesus Christ of Nazareth, you are healed."

There was the faint sound of a piano from one of the saloons, and it seemed to magnify the silence of the room. Mark swayed slightly, waiting for Jude to say more, but the preacher just stood there, a smile on his face.

Then Mark looked down—and he saw the faint flutter of Lola's eyelids! The movement was barely perceptible, but it was real.

"Daughter, open your eyes," Jude said. He reached his hand out and brushed her forehead gently, adding, "You have been touched by the Lord, Lola."

Mark stared in disbelief as Lola's eyes opened. He had been in the room once before when the fever was high, and her lids had opened. But there had been no recognition in them. Now she was looking up at Jude, and her lips moved faintly. "Father—?" she whispered.

"Yes." Jude knelt down beside her, and she moved restlessly. "Do you know me?"

"Y-yes," Lola said, and her voice was stronger. She looked over his shoulder and saw Mark. "Mark—it's you!"

Mark licked his lips, but could not say a word. He had never felt so strange in his entire life, and as Lola struggled to sit up, he watched dumbfounded as Jude pulled her into a sitting position.

Jude asked, "Lola, you've been very close to death. Did you know anything at all?"

She hesitated, then said slowly, "I knew I was dying—and I was so afraid! It seemed like I was being pulled down into a deep, black hole. I tried to scream—but I couldn't." She touched her face with a gesture of wonder, then lowered her hand. "And then I heard you calling me—and it was like you put your arms around me." She thought and then said, "But there was someone with you. I couldn't see him—but he was there."

"That was the Lord Jesus," Moran said. "He's the one who brought you back."

She stared at him, then her eyes filled with tears. "I—know. Once I saw Him, when I was dying—I remember now!"

Jude said, "Daughter, would you like to have Him with you always?"

Lola's lips parted, and she nodded wordlessly.

"He's been waiting for you. You're one of His lost lambs, daughter. Now, just tell Him how you've strayed—then ask Him to make you His own."

Mark watched as she closed her eyes and for a few moments she prayed silently. Then she opened her eyes, and breathed, "I—I love Him so much, Father!"

Mark turned and left the room, unable to stay longer.

"Is she gone?" Innes demanded at once.

"Go see for yourself."

Innes gave him a baffled glance, then disappeared into Lola's room.

"What is it, Mark?" Moira asked, her eyes enormous.

He shook his head, and then all of them except Mark went to the door. They found Jude standing with his back against the wall as Doctor Innes held his hand on Lola's brow, an expression of disbelief on his face. "Temperature's normal—completely normal!" he said hoarsely.

He took his hand away, then stared at Lola. "How do you feel, girl?"

Lola looked up at him, her face thin and wan, but her dark

eyes clear. "I feel very weak, Doctor—but I am not sick anymore."

Innes stared at her, then shook his head. "I've never believed in miracles—but it looks like I'll have to rethink my position."

Moira stepped back and watched as the doctor gently examined Lola, but she could see that the crisis was over. She turned and left the room to stand beside Mark.

"It's wonderful, isn't it?" she said quietly. "I never thought it could happen."

"Jude did," Mark said. He looked back at the door and seemed to see beyond it. Then he shook his head and added, "Lola will never be the same again. I saw it in the war lots of times. Those that almost died were changed. Some of them lost their courage, but others seemed to just get more."

"From the look on her face," Moira said thoughtfully, "I'd say that Lola hasn't lost any courage."

"No." Mark thought hard, then nodded and said, "They may still call her the Union Belle, but I'm not sure she'll ever be what she was—a woman dealing cards in a saloon."

If he had heard what Lola had just said to Shep, he would not have been too surprised.

Shep had come to bend over and take her hand, and she had said, "Shep, you've lost your partner."

"What's that, Lola?"

She smiled up at him, a joy in her face that he had never seen, and she said with full assurance, "Jesus Christ brought me back from death, Shep. From now on, I'll be serving Him."

"But—what will you do, Lola?" Shep asked in confusion.

Lola looked at her father, who returned her smile, and said, "I'll be doing whatever God tells me to do, Shep!"

PART FOUR

THE GOLDEN SPIKE

★ ★ ★ ★

CHAPTER NINETEEN

A NEW LIFE

★ ★ ★ ★

Lola came out of the hotel, stopped and took a deep breath, then exclaimed to Jeff, "Oh, it's good to be outside!"

Driver looked at her, considered the color in her cheeks and the excitement in her eyes, and commented, "You look good. Lost a little weight, maybe."

It had been two weeks since her close brush with death, and the days had been long for her. She had steadfastly held to the idea that God had pulled her back to life. Doctor Innes had suggested to her and her father that maybe it wasn't a miracle, saying, "If it was a real miracle, wouldn't you be completely healed, up and around at once?"

But Lola had already found the answer to that. She had said calmly, "Now Doctor, don't forget, you were the first one to announce that it was a miracle. I believe God saved my life—and now He's doing another miracle in healing my body."

Jeff had been by to see her several times, making the trip from Benton, but Mark had been on the run, carrying out orders for Dodge and Reed. Maureen had taken every moment away from the Union Belle to stay with her. Even Moira had been by from time to time, less often as Lola improved.

Jeff asked, "When will you be moving on to Benton?" Shep Yancy had opened up a new version of the Union Belle in the latest town, and Jeff had been there several times. "It's a fancier place than the one you had here. Shep is anxious to have you back."

Lola took his arm, saying, "Let's walk a little bit, Jeff." He adjusted his pace to hers, and she didn't answer his question at once. Instead, she commented on the changes in Cheyenne since the construction workers had left. "It's so quiet! I've been watching out my window at night, and it's like another town since the workers left."

"It is another town. When you pull six or seven thousand people out of a small town, it makes a difference. Some of these hell-on-wheels towns dry up and blow away after the railroad leaves." He looked down the nearly deserted street. "But Cheyenne won't blow away. It's got a good start."

Lola listened as he spoke, enjoying the sun and the faint breeze. The long days in bed had done something to her, for she had never been forced to inactivity in all her life. As the hours passed, she had slowly learned to be alone with herself, and much of the time she spent reading the Bible. The Scriptures had been a bit confusing at times, but her father had been there to guide her. It fascinated her to learn how relevant the Book was despite the ancient language, and once she had exclaimed in delight, "Why, Father, it's just what I need! I can't get over how it seems to have been written just for me!"

She had learned to read and to ponder the truths in the Scripture, and to her complete astonishment, prayer became an exciting part of her life. In the past, prayer had always been a time of mumbling set, formal petitions, and when she discovered that if she waited, God would fill her spirit with His presence, her whole outlook changed.

Her new way was, of course, a delight and a joy to Jude Moran. He reveled in her growth, and the two spent hours and entire days together. It was an answer to prayer for him. For years he had prayed for Lola, and now she was with him—and even better than that, she was walking with God!

Jeff interrupted her thoughts by mentioning Benton again. "Think you'll be able to leave here and join Shep in a week or so?"

She hesitated only for an instant, then said, "I won't be going back to the Union Belle with Shep, Jeff."

"You won't?"

"No. I'm going to live with my father."

Driver thought about that and nodded. "I guess I figured you might do something like that. Mark said so right after that night your father came in and prayed for you."

"I've been thinking about it since then," Lola said, "but I was unhappy in the Union Belle before that. It seemed like such a waste to me, Jeff. I grew up in a saloon, and that was all that seemed to be in store for my future. I was more unhappy than I thought, I guess, but since God gave me my life back, I've known that nothing will ever be the same."

Driver gave her a careful look, wondering what her decision would do to his own intentions. "Let's go sit down by the well." He led her to an old well with a bucket and dipper under an alder tree, and they sat down on a bench built of rough slabs from the sawmill. He dropped the bucket, pulled it up, and brought her a dipper of the cool water. She drank it thirstily, then he went back and had a drink. When he returned and sat down beside her, there was a hesitancy in his manner that drew her attention.

She waited patiently, for she had learned that Jeff was slow to make up his mind. He was a ruggedly handsome man, and she appreciated his steadfast qualities. Now he took a deep breath and turned to face her, saying, "What about me, Lola?"

She knew instinctively that he had spent a long time coming to this point, and now she was disturbed. It was a thing that she had foreseen, but hoped would never come about. "You've been wanting to ask me that a long time, haven't you, Jeff?" she asked with a slight smile.

"I'm pretty slow about most things, I guess." He looked down at his brown hands, then up again. "I've never met a woman I wanted to marry before. But if you'll have me, Lola, I'd like to take care of you. I don't have much—but you'd never starve and you'd never know meanness from me."

It was a simple declaration, honest and to the point, like Driver himself, and Lola hesitated, not wanting to hurt him. "Any girl would be lucky to have a man like you, Jeff," she said slowly. "But marriage is such a big step."

"Don't you care for me at all, Lola?"

"Oh, yes—yes, I do, Jeff!" She put her hand on his arm, her eyes filled with concern. He thought he had never seen her so beautiful. Although she had lost weight during her illness, in his eyes that made her no less attractive. Her eyes looked large in her thin face, warm and gentle. "But I've got to make you understand how it is with me." She struggled for words, then seemed to find them. "Before I found God, Jeff, I made all my own decisions. But now—it's not like that anymore. I've been reading in the Bible a lot, and it says that when we come to know Jesus Christ, we have to do what He says."

The thought puzzled Driver, and he asked, "How do you know what Jesus wants you to do?"

"Why, some of it's easy, Jeff. The Bible makes many things clear—for example, Jesus commanded His disciples to get rid of anything that would keep them from being close to God."

"Like what?" Driver asked, curious and trying to understand this new Lola.

"Oh, lots of things," she said. "It's not always the same for people, Jeff. One person may drink too much, and that would keep him from God. But others don't have any problem with that." She hesitated, then confessed, "One thing that God pointed out to me was my love of money. I grew up without anything, Jeff, and when I started to make quite a bit of money in the saloon with Shep, I liked it. I liked buying lots of clothes— things like that. But for the last few days I've been reading in the Bible about how possessions don't mean anything—not really. And in my spirit God kept saying, 'You don't need anything but Me.' "

Driver stared at her. "You really think God told you to get out of the saloon business?"

"Yes, I know it. And that's why I can't give you an answer, Jeff—not right now. There's a verse in the Bible that says, 'Ye are not your own, ye are bought with a price.' So I can't marry you— or any man—unless I know that God wants me to. I may never marry at all."

Jeff said heavily, "That's pretty hard on me, Lola. I love you more than you think."

She was touched by his simple declaration, and said gently,

"Jeff, I admire you so much—but until I find out what God wants for my life, I can't allow myself to make any decisions about marriage." A humorous thought struck her and she laughed. "I'm going to Benton to help my father with his church. I'm probably doing you a favor—keeping you from getting saddled with a lady preacher!"

He forced a grin, saying, "I guess that would put a strain on a man, wouldn't it? Maybe I could take up the offering." Then he sobered and said, "I'm glad for you, Lola—that you're out of that saloon. And I'll be around."

She knew his meaning at once and said, "That's good to know, Jeff." She rose and the two of them continued their walk, Driver sober and restrained and Lola thinking of Benton and what her decision would mean.

A week later, her father came in a wagon and the two of them, along with an Indian deacon, loaded their things and drove to the new settlement. She was cheerful and happy, glad to be leaving Cheyenne and anxious to begin their new life. When they drove into Benton, Jude said, "There it is, Lola—and a more sinful place never was, I do think."

"It looks a lot like Cheyenne," Lola offered, looking at the tents and hastily thrown up shacks that composed the main street. "I see Cherry's set up in grand style."

"Sure. He'll be where the workers are, to drain them dry." He drove down Lincoln Street, the main avenue, turned off onto a side street, then brought the wagon to a stop in front of an ancient structure that had been several things in its day, including a stable, but now bore a hand-painted sign over the door: CHURCH OF BENTON. "Guess that sounds a little proud, like it was the only church," Jude said as he helped Lola down. "But as of now, it's true enough. Come on in. Keep in mind that it's not a fancy place, like I've warned you."

They entered and Lola saw the first floor was empty except for a number of slab benches and a table at the front. "Bare essentials," Jude grinned. "But more than John the Baptist had. There were nearly thirty here last Sunday, and I'm looking for more tomorrow. Now, come on and we'll get you settled."

He led her to what had once been a hayloft. "This will have to do," he said apologetically, drawing back a blanket that hung over an opening. She entered to find a rather large room with one window that was evidently new. The unpainted walls smelled of pine. There was a bed, a table and an old cedar chest. "Best I could do, Lola," he said quickly. "Can't get a room in this town for love nor money."

"Oh, Father, it's fine!" she said, and put her arms around him and kissed him. I'll bet you did all this yourself—put in the window and all."

"Well, it's hardly the Crescent Hotel. Pretty rough for a young lady."

"It'll be fun fixing it up," she said firmly. "Anyway, we won't be here long, will we?"

"No, that's right. Just until Casement moves to the next campsite—which will probably be Bryan, according to Mark."

"Well, we're pilgrims, aren't we? I like what the Scripture says about Abraham, that he was looking for a city not made with hands."

He looked at her fondly and said simply, "It's good to have you here, Lola. I was getting pretty lonesome—nobody to share things with."

"I'm happy, too, Father," she smiled, then said briskly, "Now, let's get unpacked, and you can show me the town."

By Sunday she had seen what there was of the town, and had even met four families who lived in the area and had encouraged them to come to church. When the service started, the place was crowded with a mixture of Indians, workers, and townspeople. Josh Long was there, his ruddy face beaming at the crowd, and to Lola's surprise, Mark and Dooley came in while the singing was going on. She was sitting on a chair to one side, facing the pulpit, but when they came in and took a back seat, she grew nervous. When Josh asked her to sing, she rose and sang a cappella one of the hymns that she had become fond of. Her voice was clear and sweet, and the congregation leaned forward to listen. When she finished, a man said, "Now that's good singing! How about another one, Missy?"

She sang another, then when asked for a third, laughed and said, "That's all I know," and sat down.

Jude got to his feet and preached a short message on the grace of God, ending with, "We all want to see God working in our lives, and sometimes we think it can't happen. But it can. I want my daughter to come and tell you what God has done for her. Lola—come and share your experience with these good people."

Nothing had been said about this, and Lola felt a flash of fear, but Jude smiled at her, nodding, and she got up and walked to the table, where she turned and faced the audience. She had a clear view of Mark's face as she began, "I was raised in a saloon. . . ."

In plain speech she related how she had left Texas and come to the midwest seeking her father. She said, "I had a friend who helped me get away from there, and I thank God for him every day." As she said this she looked directly at Mark and smiled, then went on to tell how she had become owner of a saloon. By the time she got to the part where she was dying, there wasn't a sound in the house. Most of them knew Lola, for they had come from Cheyenne to the new town. She had been a legend, the Union Belle, the woman who had no emotions. Now they listened as she told how her father had prayed for her as she lay dying, entranced by her testimony of how she had sensed the presence of God and been pulled back from death at the last moment.

"God saved my life," she concluded, "and then He saved my soul. I will never stop thanking Him for His mercy. And if there is one of you who has a burden bigger than you can carry, like I did, let me say in the words of John the Baptist, 'Behold the Lamb of God that taketh away the sin of the world.' He is able—I know He is!"

She sat down and a wave of "amens" swept over the crowd. Jude came to the front and closed the meeting, with a call for prayer, and to his pleasure, a dozen people came forward, kneeling on the bare floor. Two of them were women, and when he nodded at Lola, she went to pray with them. One was an older woman whose husband was very ill, and Lola prayed earnestly with her for God to heal his body. When the woman rose, her eyes were wet, and she said as Lola hugged her, "That's such a comfort!" The other woman was young, no more than seventeen, and was so distressed she could say almost nothing. Her face was pale and her lips were white as she clamped them together. Finally Lola heard her whisper, "I've been so bad!" and little by little the story came out—an age-old story of a girl seeking a little excitement and color, and finding herself used by a man looking only for gratification. Lola understood at once that she was pregnant and afraid to tell her family. She prayed for her, then put her arms around the girl, whose name was Lena Sills, and whispered, "Come back tomorrow, Lena. We can talk more then. Maybe I can help." Lena hugged her as if she were her last hope, and as she left, there was a tiny glimmer of light in her eyes.

Finally the last inquirers had gone, and Lola looked up to see Mark and Dooley coming to her. Dooley said, "Miss Lola, that was one sockdologer of a testimony! Made me want to hit the glory trail my own self."

Mark said, "I'm glad to see you. You're looking well."

"I feel fine," she smiled. "You two look worn out."

"Been working hard," Mark said.

"That's gospel!" Dooley nodded. Then he shifted his feet and said in an unusually restrained manner, "You reckon you could go by and see Maureen, Miss Lola?" He pulled at his heavy moustache and there was a worried light in his blue eyes. "She ain't doin' well a'tall."

"Why, I'll go this afternoon," Lola said at once. "What's wrong with her?"

"Aw—I dunno," Dooley muttered. "She's all mixed up in her mind. But you can help her if anybody can." He ducked his head as if he had revealed too much, then said, "Gotta run now."

When he had left, Lola said, "Come and see my new place, Mark." She led him upstairs, proudly displaying her room that she had fixed up with curtains, and the small dining room where she and her father ate.

"It's not very fine, but Father and I are comfortable." She picked up a pitcher and poured him a glass. "Lemonade. Not cold, but it's wet."

He sat down and sipped the tepid drink, listening as she chatted on about the move to Benton. She was, he saw, not the same woman he had known. She had lost the defensive side of her spirit; now there was a freedom and an air of expectancy in her voice and her expression that was good to see. He commented on it when she finally paused in her speech.

"You're happy, aren't you, Lola?"

Her lips parted slightly and she turned her head to one side. "Yes, I am," she said as though finding the thought strange. "I've always been—well, sort of afraid. Now I never seem to worry about things."

He marveled at the health that glowed in her cheeks, thinking of how terrible her features had been as she lay on the bed in the hotel. He wanted to find out more about her experience, but something kept him from asking. She noted his reticence, and said, "Have you seen Moira lately?"

"No, she went back to Boston. Ray's been mooning around like a lost hound."

"She surprised me, Mark," Lola said. "I thought she was a totally selfish woman, but I was wrong. Maureen told me how she helped nurse me. And afterwards, when I was myself, we had some good talks. She's spoiled, but that's just a surface thing. The real Moira is just waiting to love someone—to give up everything for them."

He stared at her, interested in the statement. "I guess you see something in her that other people miss, Lola."

"We talked a lot one night. She's really afraid of some things."

"Doesn't show much."

"No, she's clever," Lola agreed. "But there's a penalty for being rich and beautiful. She told me she is never sure if a man likes her for herself or for her father's money."

Mark said dryly, "She may have a chance to find out. I hear that her father is about to go down the drain. He's sunk all his money into the Union, and if it goes down, he'll go down with it. Then Moira won't have to worry about whether men like her for her money."

Lola was disturbed by the news. "Is that going to happen, Mark? I mean, can the Union Pacific really fail?"

He nodded, and there was a gloomy light in his eyes that was not typical of his spirit. "It could. The Central has done most of its hard grading, and we'll be getting to the worst of ours in the dead of winter."

She thought about that, then said, "What about you, Mark? What will you do if it all fails?"

"I'm used to failures, Lola," he answered with a shrug. "That's one thing that stands out about my life—I've experienced failure often—both in war and in peace. Failing gets to be a habit."

"No, I don't want you to think like that, Mark," she insisted. "You've got so much to give. Look what you did for me!"

He grinned, the memory of past days coming very strong. "Do you still have that man's outfit you wore when we were run out of Mexico? I'd like to see you in that rig again."

She laughed with delight. "No, I don't have it." She sobered and said, "I think of that time often. It was terrible, but it was a good time, too."

"Until I messed it up," he said.

She quickly said, "Mark, you have to forget that. I have. You must remember how frightened I was then. I'd been fighting men off since I was a child almost, and when you kissed me, I just gave my fears free reign. You can see that, can't you?"

He looked evenly at her. "What if I tried to kiss you now?"

She rose and said, "I might not like it—or I might. But either way I'm not afraid anymore."

He had risen with her, and now he saw that there was a courage in her, a fearlessness that was new. He smiled and said, "I may try you out on that someday—but Jeff Driver would probably shoot me if he found out. What are you going to do about him?"

"Nothing, Mark. Not right now." Then she said with a boldness that shocked them both a little. "What are you going to do about Moira?"

He stared at her, then asked, "What makes you think I have to do anything, Lola? She's Ray's girl."

"Oh, Mark, I know you better than that!" She shook her head, then added, "I'm not judging you—but you're not the best at hiding your feelings—and like I said, Moira and I had some long talks."

"She's Ray's girl, and that settles it."

"Things aren't always neatly arranged, Mark," she said gently. She wanted to say many things to him, but refrained. She did add, "Ray's in with her, in his own way, but he's not a steady man. You know that."

"He'll be all right," Mark said stubbornly. "He just isn't sure of himself yet."

"Exactly right—and that's what bothers Moira. She needs a strong man, and Ray hasn't given her much proof that he's what she needs."

Mark shook his head. "It would be a poor sort of man who stepped in between a friend and his woman."

She saw that he was blind to Hayden's faults, so she changed the subject. "What's wrong with Maureen, do you know?"

"Not really. I think she's getting mixed up with some man— the wrong man, according to Dooley's version."

"I'll go by and get it out of Shep."

"Hope you can help her. I think Dooley's got a vested interest." Then he said, "I'll be leaving tomorrow. But maybe I'll be back in time for church next Sunday. Thanks for the lemonade."

"It's good to see you, Mark." She put out her hand, and he took it with surprise. She laughed at his expression. "Don't worry, I'm not going to force my attentions on you! But thanks for coming—and for all the things you've done for me."

He left then, and all the way back to his room, he wondered at the changes in her. He thought about what she had said about Ray and Moira, but finally decided she was wrong. *Those two will be just fine.*

★　★　★　★

September came, and found the end of track past the Red Desert and into the desolation of the Bitter Creek region. Following that dry and meandering stream bed, the road ducked its way through one geologic fault after another. On the fifteenth it left Rock Springs Station and pressed into the Bitter Creek Canyon. On the twentieth it broke into the Valley of the Green River, only to find it filled with the tents of another hell-on-wheels waiting for the thirsty construction men. On the twenty-seventh the road rushed over a river's gorge and reached Bryant, which roared overnight into a full-sized town. Directly ahead the rugged mountains waited. Salt Lake lay two hundred miles west, with winter and nothing but heavy mountains ahead.

Mark met with Reed that night and studied the rolling hills. "Where's Central now?" Mark asked.

"Coming up the Humbolt, two hundred sixty miles from Ogden."

"Sixty miles farther from Ogden than we are—but they've got nothing but level ground to cover. Our heavy work's just started. We're going to get snowed in ninety days from now. They could beat us, Reed."

"It depends on Sherman Ames. He'd better come up with a lot of money, because it's going to take a bundle to put the tracks down in the dead of winter!"

CHAPTER TWENTY

THE NOOSE IS SET

★ ★ ★ ★

Winslow rode into Bryant, made his way to Reed's office, and entered the warm room soaking wet. A driving rain had caught him on his way back from a trip that had stretched from two weeks to five. Reed and Casement looked up from the location maps they were examining to take in his two-week old beard and the gaunt features. "You look like you've been pulled through a knothole, Mark," Casement grinned. "You do any good?"

"I don't know what you'll think. I got the ties." He slumped down in a chair, throwing his long legs out in front of him.

"How much?" Reed asked.

"From ninety cents to a dollar and a quarter a tie, at the siding."

Casement swore, "We ought to be getting gold spikes at that price!"

"I told Mark to get the ties no matter what they cost. We're not in a position to bargain," Reed said. "How about the bridge timbers?"

"Be waiting for you at Echo Canyon."

"Where've you been all this time?"

"With Dodge. I went with him to see Brigham Young. We had to tell him it was impossible to build into Salt Lake City."

He smiled and added, "He went off like a keg of dynamite. Preached a sermon in the tabernacle scorching the hide of the Union and practically called Dodge a devil."

"What'd Dodge do?" Reed was amused.

"Why, he broke the news to Young that the Central wasn't coming that way either. Made it pretty clear. The next Sunday Young preached another sermon, which touted the Union as Utah's best friend. All in all, Brigham Young got a good deal. Dodge promised to use his Mormons as laborers as much as he could."

"Glad that's out of the way," Reed said with relief, then his face sobered. "Hate to greet you with bad news, Mark, but things have gone crazy around here. You've got to do something about the saloons."

"They've forgotten Julesburg," Casement snapped, his terrier face angry. "You've got to set them down—a few funerals won't do any harm!"

Mark nodded but showed no concern. "I'll take care of it, Sam."

The two older men regarded him with interest. Both had learned to trust him, but there was something about Winslow's present attitude that troubled them both. He was not as alert as a man should be when walking into a dangerous situation. Casement tried to warn him. "Cherry and his boys haven't forgotten what you did to them at Julesburg, Mark. They'll nail you to the wall if they can."

Reed said, "Jack's right. You watch yourself."

"Driver and Young around?" Mark asked. "Looks like they're going to have to work with me on this job."

"They're out at Number Two Camp. Jack Rich has had some trouble out there," Casement shrugged. "Should be back by now."

Mark dragged himself out of his chair. "Guess I'll take a moment to get cleaned up before I straighten out this town." He left the office, rode to the stable, then got a shave and a haircut. The rain was still coming down at five, so he ducked into Caleb Marsh's Cafe. The owner met him with a smile. "Hello, Mark, good to see you."

"Hello, Caleb. How've you been?" He took a seat, gave his

order and read a two-week old paper while the food was being prepared. He was enjoying his meal when Dooley and Jeff came in. Both of them were wet, and they looked out of sorts to Mark.

He briefed them on his trip, then asked, "What's the trouble at Camp Two?"

Dooley shook his head. "Dunno." It was unlike the small man to be so sparing in his speech, and Mark examined him more carefully. In all the time he had known Dooley Young, he had always been the most cheerful man Mark had ever seen. During the war, when all was lost and there was nothing left but hurting, it was Dooley who had grinned and kept the rest of the men in Mark's regiment from giving up.

Mark looked questioningly at Jeff, who shook his head in a warning gesture. "Somebody's been put in that camp to cause trouble, Mark. The men won't work. That's not like Irishmen."

"No, it's not." Mark picked up his coffee, sipped it, then said, "We'll take a ride out there tomorrow."

Dooley finally spoke up, "You need me for anything, Mark?"

"No. Just be ready to leave early." As soon as Young left, Mark asked, "What's biting on him, Jeff?"

Driver said, "Remember that girl that helped nurse Lola— Maureen. Dooley's fallen for her like a ton of bricks."

"Does she like him?"

"I don't guess so, Mark. Not enough anyhow. She quit working for Shep and went back to Cherry's joint. Shep told me she's picked up with the same gent that beat her up and left her in the street—fancy gambler named Bob Dempsey." He pulled his hat off and set it on the seat carefully. "She's a pretty girl—but she's no judge of character."

"You talk to Dooley?"

"You ever hear of one man having any luck givin' advice to another one about a woman?"

"No, I never did. But he'd better get over it. I hear the gamblers have gone too far. Reed wants us to clamp the lid down on the rowdys, and I don't want Dooley to have his mind on a woman while we're trying to do it."

Jeff gave Winslow a careful look. "You're a hard nut, Mark. I don't suppose *you'd* let personal ties get in the way of *your* job.

But some of us don't work like that. We can't turn ourselves on and off like we was a faucet."

Mark stared at him, taken aback at Jeff's words, for he read some sort of personal message in them. "What would you have a man do, Jeff? When we marched off to war, we had to put everything in a box. If we lived, we could go home and open the box. But you know as well as I do that a man can't do a job well when he's got his mind on something else." He tried to explain it more clearly, for there were few men he liked better or trusted more than Driver. "That doesn't mean a man has to put aside love in order to perform his job. It isn't right for a man to love his work more than his wife. A man needs to have both, but he should bear in mind that they're not the same thing, so it's important to keep them separate."

Driver stared at him, then nodded slowly. "I guess you're right, Mark. I'm no expert on women."

"Well, that makes two of us," Mark shrugged. Then he got to his feet and said, "Guess I'll go get some sleep."

Driver said, "You ought to go by and see Lola and Jude. They've got their church set up in a tent down Orange street."

"They all right?"

"Sure." Driver grinned and said, "They keep moving their church right along with the Union Pacific. I told Jude he ought to name it The Union Pacific Church." He ducked his head, and when he lifted it, there was a slight flush in his cheeks. "I—I've been going pretty regular—to their church, that is."

"Well, that's good," Mark said. "My folks are Christians— and my family tree is loaded with preachers. I know I haven't been the man they'd want me to be." He clapped Driver on the shoulder and added, "But you should stay with it, Jeff. Every man needs God."

He left Driver and turned to go to his room. The rain had stopped, and on an impulse he turned and made his way down Orange street until he came to the tent with a cross perched on top. He ducked through the flap, calling out, "Anybody home?"

A thin rectangle of light at the back of the tent appeared, and he saw Lola peer out at him.

"Mark!" She ran to him, delighted by his unexpected visit, and took his arm, pulling him toward the back. "Come with me to the kitchen. Have you eaten?"

"Just had supper." He stepped into a section of the tent that contained a wood stove, a table, and three chairs and one cot.

"Let me treat you to a piece of the cake I made today—and some fresh coffee."

She chattered as she got the coffee and cake, then sat down and leaned on her elbows, watching him as he ate. She had regained some weight, he noticed, and no sign of her illness remained. Her dark eyes caught the yellow flare of the lantern, and her cheeks glowed with health. He ate slowly, and she told him about the church, describing the move from Benton and sharing how many people had been converted in Bryant.

"They say this town kills a man a day," she said, "just like the other track towns." The thought sobered her, but in another moment her smile returned. "Thankfully, at least that many again have come to know the Lord since we've been here."

"I've thought about the two of you a lot," Mark said, the light returning to his eyes. They sat there talking for an hour, and it occurred to him that he had not spoken so easily in years. His companions during the war and on construction crews had always been men. But sitting and talking intimately over coffee with Lola, Mark felt a twinge of regret. *Some men get to enjoy this kind of thing all the time*, he thought as he relaxed in his chair.

"Jeff told me about Maureen," he said later. "Too bad. I guess you've done all you can."

"I talked to her until I was hoarse," Lola said. "But she's got a blind spot where Dempsey's concerned. He's good-looking and has a lot of money—a real ladies' man. I've seen enough of them to spot one."

"I'd have expected Maureen to see through him. She's been around that sort before, I suppose."

Lola shrugged, grief in her eyes. Mark recognized the same compassion for others in her that he admired so much in his parents. "Dooley's taking it pretty bad," he commented.

"I know. I'm praying for her, Mark. God's able to open her eyes."

Her easy statement made him feel uncomfortable, for it marked the difference between her way and his. He stirred and asked, "Ray been around?"

"Oh, yes. I see him once in a while. He's been going out to the camps quite a bit." She hesitated before continuing, "I got a letter from Moira last week. She's coming here with her father on business soon—next week, I think."

The subject was a little touchy for both of them, and Mark decided to leave, saying, "Got to go to bed. Dodge has ridden me ragged the past few weeks." She stood up and he was suddenly aware of how small she was. "You're not very tall, Lola," he said, almost as though he were speaking to himself. "My youngest sister is about your size."

Lola smiled up at him. "I wish I'd had a brother like you, Mark. Were you two close?"

"Not as close as we should have been." He thought back to his life in Virginia before the war. "Patience or Pet, as everybody calls her, is the youngest in our generation of the Winslow clan. I'm the oldest in the family, and I was a pretty brash young man. I'm afraid I didn't pay too much attention to my baby sister." There was a sadness in his voice, and he said softly, "Why do we let things go by us, Lola? I love Pet—but I can't remember ever telling her so."

"I'm sure she knows it, Mark," Lola said. "Don't think of the past. You can't change it. Where is your sister now?"

"Still in Virginia. She's married to a fine man. Got two kids and another on the way."

"Why, then you can demonstrate your love for Pet by being a good uncle to her children. Go see them. Send them little presents. You should even write Pet a letter and tell her what you've just told me."

Her eyes held him, and he murmured, "Yes, that's what I need to do." He paused for a moment, gazing into her dark eyes. "You're good for a man, Lola."

She stepped close to him, and he could see the concern written on her face. "Mark—don't let this job make you too hard. You've just come out of a war where you had to learn to kill to survive. Now you're still forced to fight."

"It's my job, Lola."

She shook her head slightly, then said, "Mark, a man is more than the job he performs. There's a soul involved, and there's only one soul in you. If you lose that, what good does all the rest do?"

He looked down at her thoughtfully. "You know, you sound a great deal like my mother, Rebekah. She's a fine Christian—just like you. I wish you could meet her." Then he said quickly, "But what kind of a man would I be if I quit? General Dodge and Sam Reed trust me. What if we all quit? Somebody has to fight the wars and build the railroads."

She stood there, looking up at him with a soft maternal expression in her face. "I know, Mark—but I hate seeing you grow hard."

He leaned forward suddenly and gently kissed her. She did not move away, but neither did she respond. He drew back, studied her, then smiled, "I warned you I'd try that someday."

"It was a friendly kiss, Mark," she said, and a smile came to her. "Now, go get some rest." She watched as he left, and then stood there for a long time thinking about the future, which seemed very uncertain.

★　★　★　★

Daylight was only a feeble line in the east when the three men rode out of Bryant. The air was cold, and Driver shivered, drawing his coat around him. "Winter coming soon."

Winslow nodded, but Dooley did not appear to have heard. He was slumped in the saddle of his gray mare, his face hidden behind his hat and his huge moustache.

They rode for four hours, stopping only to cook up some bacon and coffee, then resumed their journey. It was after two when Driver announced, "There she is." He pointed to a crest where a camp scored the sky. "I can't figure out what's going on. Nobody's working that I can see."

They rode through a street that marked the middle of the camp, and Mark observed quietly, "It smells like trouble. Where's Joe Riley?"

"Over there." Jeff led the way to the end of the street, a line of sullen workers watching them. Mark spurred his horse suddenly, and the animal's quick jump startled the ill-tempered, suspicious men.

The three rode past them and came to where Riley, the foreman, waited for them. He spoke as they dismounted. "Come on inside. Got some grub left from dinner." The three tied up their horses and stepped inside the tent to find Riley facing them, worry on his face. Never unwilling to fist it out with any of the men who worked for him, Joe Riley's expression betrayed an uncharacteristic fear.

"What's going on, Joe?" Mark asked quietly.

"The men refuse to work. They gamble and gripe all day, then get drunk at night." Riley hesitated, then lowered his voice. "Had a man killed last night."

"Who was it?"

"Mason, one of my foremen. He was trying to get the men to work, and last night somebody drilled him." He shrugged helplessly. "Mark, you'd better tell Reed to send in the soldiers. I'm leaving in the morning."

"What are you afraid of, Joe?"

Riley was a tough one, but there was something in the situation he didn't like. "It's a set-up, Mark. Somebody's put some troublemakers in this camp. They'll make it rough on anybody who tries to settle things down."

"We can't send soldiers to every construction camp," Mark said sharply. Then he added in a kinder tone, "We'll see what happens in the morning."

"Did you know Lou Goldman was here?" Riley demanded.

That drew the attention of all three of the men. "No, we weren't told that," Mark said, surprised. "We'll wait until morning to leave all the same."

"Do what you please. I'm pulling out. I'll get you some blankets and a place to sleep."

Mark made no move that day, but he could feel the eyes of the railroad men on him. The pressure began to affect him, and he longed to throw himself into some sort of action, but he remained cautious. Later, when they were all lying in their blankets, he told the others, "We've got to stop this. Somebody's spending a lot of money to tie up this camp. If we let it get by, they'll hit every camp we've got."

"Goldman's here—and he didn't come for no tea party, Mark," Dooley said. "He's probably got some of his low-down friends here."

"I guess—but we've got to take care of whoever tied this

camp up," Mark said. He slept fitfully, and the three of them arose at dawn.

The red, raw embankment of the right of way ran directly in front of the camp, and the men gathered around it. "Now, let's find out who's keeping the crews from working," Mark said, and walked to where the men waited.

As they drew close, Dooley moved closer to Mark. "That's Tap Brand there. He's no Irishman. He's a bouncer for Roy Spicer. I seen him kick a man to death back in Benton."

Mark noted Brand's squat figure, his huge shoulders and close little eyes. He also noted Lou Goldman and three other men who were not workers watching carefully. There was no sense in waiting to make a move, so he said, "Tap, get to work or hit the road."

Tap stared at him and cursed. He started to raise his hands to attack, but Mark sprang across the space that separated them, cracking him in the mouth with a right hand that drove him backward to the ground. He rolled over, got to his feet and spit out a tooth. The crimson blood ran down his chin, and he squinted and came toward Mark, his hands lifted. He had been a pug somewhere, Mark realized, in addition to a barroom brawler. He came in jabbing with his left, his right fist cocked and ready. Mark took the left on his forearm, waited for the right, moving his head slightly when it came while reaching forward and grabbing Brand's head. Lowering his head, he pulled forward, smashing Tap in the face with his skull. The sound made a noise like that of a hammer hitting a melon.

Tap fell to his knees, but he was still dangerous. Grabbing Mark's feet, he pulled them and fell on him with a bear-like embrace. He was as powerful as a gorilla, and Mark knew he would lose if he didn't get free. With a burst of strength, he rolled the bruiser off and got to his feet. Brand was up in an instant, and paused to shake the blood from his face. "Bust him up, Tap," Mark heard Goldman say.

Mark knew he had to end the fight now or get beaten. He was no match for a boxer, especially one who could use thumb-gouging tactics. He didn't wait for Tap to move, but went at him head on. Mark's fist caught him full in the throat before he could move to defend himself, and he fell to the ground gagging and rolling into a fetal position. The sound of his choking agony was sickening, and Mark's own face paled.

Finally Tap struggled to his feet, but when he tried to talk, he could only make raw cawing noises—like a crow. He was in terrible pain, but Winslow showed no mercy. "Hit the road, Tap," he said. Then he turned to the silent crowd. "Nobody can make you work," he said, "but we can make you leave the camp if you don't want to lay steel."

A voice said, "It's time to work," and that triggered the crowd. The belligerence vanished and they moved away quietly, murmuring about the fight.

Mark turned to face Goldman. "Lou, get out of camp—or make a fight of it."

Goldman laid a murderous glance on Mark, but he noted Young and Driver standing to either side of Winslow like a pair of cocked guns. Although the desire to kill burned strong in him, he was not fool enough to take on the three of them. He shook his head, swung up into his saddle and rode away.

"You've made Goldman take water twice, Mark," Jeff pointed out as they mounted their horses. "He won't be able to stand that for long. So watch yourself."

Mark's reply betrayed no trace of fear. "It'll be us or them soon enough, Jeff. Some of us will have our numbers coming up."

Dooley looked toward the dust that marked the progress of Goldman and his men and spat. "Like as not we done plowed up a snake, Captain. You've pushed Cherry and his crowd pretty hard. He's gettin' froggy—and this play might make him jump."

Mark considered the dust cloud, but shook his head. "There's more to this than the gamblers. All they want is the towns wide open. Whoever put the troublemakers in this camp wanted the Union Pacific crippled. Nobody wants that more than the Central."

"In that you're probably right, Mark," Driver admitted. "Been too many 'accidents' and unexplained breakdowns here—and this isn't the only camp where the men have gone sour."

"Still—Goldman and Tap are Cherry's men," Dooley put in.

Mark nodded. "Sure, but it's my guess that somebody's paying Valance for doing a wrecking job. The trouble he's stirred up has hit at the Union's most vulnerable spots. This stretch of line is critical; we need it done at once. And what about the timbers that got burned over near Bear River? Why those particular timbers and not some others? We could have replaced any others, but those were made to order—we'll be at a dead stop until we can replace them."

"Whut you gettin' at, Captain?" Dooley demanded.

An angry light glowed in Mark's eyes. "We've got a leak. Somebody is tipping off whoever is behind Valance to how to hurt us the worst."

His words sobered the other two, and as Mark spurred his horse to a faster gait, he continued, "I'd like to hear what Cherry says to his boss about this scrape. My guess is they'll cook up something pretty raw to make up for it."

★　★　★　★

"You're going to have to do better, Lou."

Jason Wallford did not raise his voice, but his small black eyes were cold when he looked across the table. Ray sat directly across from him, flanked by Valance and Bob Dempsey, a dapper man with coal black hair and a trim moustache. Goldman, his clothing covered with fine dust, was standing a few feet away, his hazel eyes still angry. He had come into Valance's office and informed them of the fiasco that had taken place at Camp Two.

Wallford shook his head. "I'm paying you plenty, Cherry. If your hired hands can't cut the mustard, get rid of them and hire some who can."

Goldman glared at Wallford, but clamped his lips together. He was a man with few complexities. His one fixed idea was that he could stand up to any man in the world, and yet twice Winslow had backed him down.

The door opened and Maureen came in with a tray of sandwiches and several schooners of beer. "I brought the lunch, Mr. Valance."

"Put it on the table, Maureen," Cherry said absently. His mind was on Wallford, and he did not notice the soft look that the girl gave Dempsey. As she began laying the food out on a round table, he said, "You've got your money's worth, Jason."

Wallford threw down the cards he still held in his hand and

his voice grew louder. "You don't know what's going on. This isn't a game of horseshoes where you get points for being *close*. It's all the marbles—or none! Whoever gets to Ogden first will get the terminal. The other road will have a thousand miles of track ending up no place." There was a streak of raw impatience in his voice as he added, "If you can't do the job, Cherry, I'll have to look elsewhere."

Valance's face flushed, and he made a violent gesture with his hand, slicing the air. "You're pushing the wrong man, Wallford!" Maureen recognized the cruelty that she had seen in the man before, and she caught Dempsey's glance as she poured the beer into glasses. He saw her nervousness and gave a slight shake of his head, then smiled reassuringly.

Goldman said, "It ain't very complicated. It's just one man in the way."

"That's right," Wallford snapped instantly. "But you don't seem to have any luck with Winslow. What's the matter, Lou— you scared of him?"

Goldman's thin face grew tight, and he gritted his teeth. "I'll take care of him—don't worry about that!"

Cherry said, "There's only one way to take care of Winslow, Lou. Don't waste your time thinking about anything else."

"Sure," Goldman murmured. "I know that."

Hayden wanted to speak up, to protest, but the thought of the nice packet of bills in Wallford's pocket prevented him from saying anything. He wiped a thin sheen of perspiration from his brow.

Wallford caught the gesture and studied Hayden carefully as he remarked, "Ray, it was your idea to stop the line at Camp Two. You've done a good job—but we need something that will really put a crimp in the Union—and we need it quick."

Ray was still thinking about the threat to Mark, and he said absently, "I'll see what I can come up with. But I truly don't think the Union has a chance to beat the Central, Jason. They'll bog down in the Wasatch Mountains when they get caught in the dead of winter. Nobody could build a railroad through that kind of terrain, especially not in the middle of the snowstorms that hit that area."

"You may be right," Wallford conceded. "But we can't take

the chance. Find some weak spot as soon as you can." He smiled sardonically, adding, "You've got a pretty good thing, Ray. All you have to do is pass a word. It's Cherry and Goldman who have to do the hard work." He turned and said, "Cherry, this thing about Winslow—you'll have to take care of him."

Maureen had finished setting the table, and reached the door as Wallford spoke. He caught the expression on her face, and as soon as she left, he said, "What about that girl? She heard a lot."

Dempsey smiled and smoothed his moustache. "No problem there."

Cherry studied the man, then said, "She gave you trouble once, Bob."

Dempsey's lips formed a cruel line. He moved his heavy shoulders and said softly, "If you remember, Cherry, I taught her a lesson. She won't get out of line."

Wallford and Valance were silent for a few moments, then Valance nodded at the Central's spy. "It'll be okay, Jason. And don't worry about Winslow, Lou and I will take care of it."

"You'd better," Wallford frowned. "We're coming down to the wire—and none of us will get any cake if we don't stop the Union. It's up to you now, Ray," he added. "Get something for us quick."

Ray nodded. "I'll do what I can, Jason. Shouldn't be too hard. There are a lot of weak links—and the Union's out of money."

They broke up then, and Dempsey went at once to find Maureen. He slipped his arm around her and smiled. "How about we have us a party tonight, honey—just the two of us."

She responded with a smile and leaned against him, then a worried light came into her eyes. "Bob, what about Mark Winslow?"

He tightened his grip so that she gave a slight gasp. "Honey, you just forget all about him. Think about me, all right?"

She was frightened at the power of his grip, and replied, "Sure, Bob."

"That's my girl!" He gave her a quick kiss, then moved away. He did not see the expression that swept across Maureen's face, for he felt confident in his ability to control her. *Just needs a strong hand, Maureen does*, he thought with a smile. *Just like a high-spirited mare!*

CHAPTER TWENTY-ONE

CALLED HOME

★ ★ ★ ★

As Ray handed Moira down from the passenger car, he knew with one look that she had changed. She wore a gray wool coat with a hood that framed her face, and as he bent forward to kiss her cheek, he thought, *She's not the same as she was.* But he said only, "I've missed you, Moira."

She murmured, "It's good to see you, Ray." Then she turned to her father who was lowering his bulk off the step and said, "I suppose you'll be going to meet with Reed, Dad. I think I'd rather go to the hotel."

Sherman Ames had lost more weight, and there were lines around his mouth and eyes that had not been there the last time Hayden had seen him. He nodded absently. "I'll be along later." He put out his hand, saying, "We'll have a lot to talk about tomorrow, Ray." Then he hurried off, leaving the two alone.

"Better get in the buggy," Ray suggested, taking her arm. "It's cold out here." He walked with her to the buggy, handed her up, then mounted and spoke to the horses. As they made their way along the street, he made small talk, and she responded in kind. He listened to her words and to her tone, but there was something different in her demeanor, although he could not put his finger on it.

"Let's have a cup of tea before you go up," he said when they reached the hotel, and before she could object, led her into the dining room. "You look tired, Moira. Have you been well?" Ray asked her as soon as they were settled at a table.

She studied the tea in her cup, keeping her eyes down. Then she lifted them and answered, "Oh, I haven't been sick, Ray— but it hasn't been pleasant." Her eyes were not as bright as usual, and she lacked the animation he had always admired.

"Tell me about it, Moira."

She laughed shortly, putting her hand on his wrist in a sudden gesture. "I've had a problem solved, Ray. I've never been sure what men truly liked—me, or my father's money." She shook her head as he tried to protest, and there was a bitter light in her eyes. "Well, I don't have to worry about that anymore! Father's lost his business and is in debt up to his chin."

Ray stared at her, shocked. There had been talk that Ames was in bad shape financially, but Hayden had assumed that he would find a way to recover his losses. Immediately, Ray's mind leaped to how pleased Wallford would be when he learned about this. But he swiftly turned his attention back to Moira, aware that she was watching him carefully. He returned her gaze, his fair cheeks now suddenly tinged with a faint flush. "Are you waiting to see if I throw you off now that you're broke, Moira?"

She studied him for a long moment, realizing how little she knew about him, before conceding, "I have thought of it, Ray. You're an ambitious man. You've made no secret of that. Now it seems that my father can no longer be of any use to you."

Her assumption was exactly right, but he was the sort of man who wanted to be well thought of. His pride hurt that she had accused him of being shallow, and despite the fact that he was not at all sure that she was wrong, he let a playful anger streak his tone, and said, "I can't believe you still think I'm so low! Don't you trust me at all?" He leaned forward and smiled. "In the first place, I don't think you ought to count your father out. He's got friends, and they won't let him down. But even if that happened, it wouldn't have a blasted thing to do with what I feel for you. I love you and want to marry you and I don't give a hoot whether or not you've got a penny."

She smiled, her doubts gone. "That's good to hear, Ray." Her smile was not quite steady, and she added, "I guess the shock of all this has shaken me badly. I've always had everything—and the thought of being poor comes as quite a blow."

He got up, pulling her to her feet. "Go get a little rest," he advised. "You're going to need it—because I'm coming back for you at six to show you and the town of Bryant what a real celebration is like!"

She left after promising to meet him, and he hurried out of the hotel to the UP's offices. He wanted to be in on the talk that Ames would be having with Reed and Casement, for he hoped to pick up additional information for Wallford. He was uncomfortably aware that Moira's declaration had triggered an unpleasant chain of thought. He wanted to believe that he was honest with himself, even though he knew he played a role before others. Now he knew that his pursuit of Moira had been, at least in part, motivated by the very thing she had mentioned—her father's money and position. Now that that was gone, his ties with the Central were not just another way to gain money and position—they were the *only* way.

As he entered the office he found Reed, Casement, and Mark standing around the wood stove listening to Ames's talk. Ames acknowledged him with his eyes as he spoke. ". . . so I failed to get any more Boston money. Our only hope now is to bull the thing through—finish the line before the Central. If we accomplish that, there'll be investors standing in line to *give* the Union their money."

Reed shook his head. "We can only go so far without money, Ames. The men have to be paid—and we've got to have ties and steel."

For nearly two hours they doggedly examined the possibilities, and finally Ames said wearily, "Well, if we don't have a miracle, we're lost."

He turned, grabbed his coat, then asked, "Ray, are you going back to the hotel?"

"I'm having dinner with Moira at six, but I've got a few things to do first."

Ames nodded and left the building, Hayden taking his own leave twenty minutes later. He made his way straight to the Wagonwheel, discovered that Valance was out, and went looking for Wallford. Unsuccessful, he went to his room to clean up for dinner. *Got to get in stronger with Jason and the Central more than ever now,* he thought, and as he tied his tie, he devised the perfect way to do it.

★ ★ ★ ★

Dooley Young sat with his legs wrapped around the legs of a kitchen chair, listening to Lola as she told him about past Sunday services. He admired the strength of her hands as she mixed dough, and when she popped the bread into the oven and sat down across from him, he asked suddenly, "You reckon you'll ever get hitched, Lola?"

"Oh, I don't know, Dooley. Maybe someday." She gave him a quick look, then asked, "What about you? Do you think you'll get married, Dooley?"

The question bothered him, and he picked up the cup of scalding black coffee, held his moustache up, and drained it with a slurping sound. Setting the cup down, he shifted on the chair, then said in a serious voice, "I've follered around a few girls, Lola. Done my chasin' just like any young feller. But it never got serious."

"It's Maureen you care for, isn't it, Dooley?"

He nodded and admiration touched his bright blue eyes. "You're pretty sharp, Lola." Then he shook his head and added gloomily, "Ain't that a caution now? Here I go and fall in love with a gal that's took up with a fancy man who'll use her and throw her aside like an old shirt! He done it once, didn't he? Why'd she go back to him, Lola?"

Lola shook her head, compassion in her eyes. "I don't think there's any answer to that sort of thing, Dooley. Maybe she just thought that life was passing her by and she had to grab at whatever comfort she could find."

"She won't get none from Dempsey!"

"No, and I guess she knows that. Most of us have gone into something knowing full well we'd get hurt. But that's the way we are." The sound of the brassy pianos and shouting from the saloons crescendoed into the room. "The flesh is very strong, Dooley. When we want something and it's there, most people can't do much but take it."

"You didn't," Dooley argued.

"But I might have," Lola said quietly. "None of us knows what we're going to do. If I didn't have Christ in my heart, I might do the same foolish thing Maureen's doing." She gave him a careful look, then asked, "Have you talked to her about how you feel, Dooley?"

"Shore. But she can't see nothing but that fancy man." He looked down at the table and shook his head. "Can't blame her. I don't look like much."

"That's not true—and anyway, looks are hardly important," Lola offered quickly. "I must tell you, I've been praying for Maureen." A comical thought came to her, bringing humor to her eyes. "I asked that God send an angel to protect her. Maybe that's you, Dooley."

He grinned, the old humor spilling out as he said, "Been called lots of things, Lola—but nobody ever tagged me for an angel." He got up and said, "I need to go find Mark. Him and Jeff went out to settle some kind of stuff over at Bitter Creek. Jeff's been with him all afternoon. Tonight's my turn."

"One of you stays with him all the time?"

"They got him on their list," he shrugged. "Cherry and his bunch knows that if they want to run things they'll have to put the Captain down."

Lola's shoulders drooped, and she said quietly, "I wish he'd leave before they kill him."

"Aw, he's pretty tough, Lola. He stacked his musket at Appomattox." She gave him a confused glance and he explained. "Most of our boys got took prisoner or else quit. But some went all through the hull war. Never gave up until General Lee told us to lay our rifles down at Appomattox."

"I know he's tough," she acknowledged, "but his toughness makes him hard, Dooley. Every day he gets a little harder. If he keeps on he'll be no better than Cherry Valance and his kind."

Dooley studied her, but had no reply. "Well, he won't quit, Lola. You can bet the farm on that." Then he said, "I'm gonna go see Maureen before I relieve Jeff."

"Tell them I said to come by. I'll give them some supper."

"Yeah, I'll do that."

Dooley left and found Mark and Jeff at the office, stained

with dust from the road. "Lola says come on and eat the supper she's got cooked," he said.

Mark looked at Jeff and asked, "All right with you?" before accepting. "Be up early, Dooley. We've got to make a trip over to the Wasatch chain tomorrow."

Dooley nodded, then made his way from the office to the main street of Bear River City, shouldering his way through the crowds of workers who filled it to overflowing. The Wagonwheel was packed, but he slipped through and stood at the bar until he caught sight of Maureen, who was dancing with a red-faced Irishman. As soon as the dance was over, another man claimed her, and Dooley settled back to wait. He had not been there longer than twenty minutes when he saw Cherry Valance come through the front door of the saloon. He went straight to two men who were sitting at a back table, motioned to them, and they disappeared into the rear of the tent.

"Kind of looks like a pow-wow," Dooley murmured, scheming silently. *A man ought to be able to hear through a piece of canvas.* Impulsively, he got up and made his way out of the Wagonwheel. Walking to the side of the big tent, he looked around and saw that no one was paying any attention to him. He sauntered down the side of the canvas wall, avoiding the ropes, until he came to the back. He could hear the blaring of the band and the shouting of the crowd, and at first could not find the spot. Eventually, he heard the sound of voices and moved close to the tent, putting his ear to the canvas. He heard a man talking, but didn't recognize the voice.

". . . have to have something quick. The people out west will pay anything to see to it that they beat the UP into Utah. Now, what have you got?"

Dooley identified Cherry's voice at once. "We've got the thing in hand, Jason. Don't worry."

"You've said that before, Valance . . ."

"All right—you come out of there!"

Dooley started to wheel, knowing he'd been caught, but there was no place to run. He reached for his gun, but something struck him on the head, and a brilliant light exploded, then faded to a dull blackness as he slumped to the ground.

"Who is it, Bob?" a man asked, leaning forward with a gun in his hand.

"Don't know," Bob Dempsey said. "Let's get him inside and get a look at him." They picked up the unconscious Young, Dempsey commenting, "He's not so big, Will. Let's take him in the back way and let Cherry have a look at him."

They made their way to the back entrance, passed through a flap and found the section Valance used for his private office.

"What's this, Bob?" Valance asked as the two men deposited their burden on the floor.

At once a fearful Ray Hayden said, "It's Dooley Young—one of Winslow's men."

"We caught him snooping outside," Dempsey said. "Will saw him sneaking around, so I figured we'd pick him up. He was listening to you outside the tent."

"If he heard me," Ray said quickly, "he'll pass the word to Winslow and Reed."

"We can fix that," Cherry said idly, his eyes on Young. "We'll find out what he knows—and if it's too much, we'll stop his clock."

Ray stared at Valance, but the man's cold eyes dared him to protest. "I'm getting out of here," he announced.

Valance laughed harshly. "Ray, you like money well enough, but you got no stomach for doing what it takes to get it."

"Go on," Wallford said. "We'll take care of this one. Come back tomorrow and we'll talk some more. I like the idea you have. You're a smart man, Ray. Just hang on and you'll be in the money."

After Hayden left, Cherry asked in disgust, "Why do you keep feeding him that line? You don't like him any better than I do."

"I don't like anyone," Wallford corrected. "Even you have to admit he's useful. He's like a horse or a shovel, Cherry. We'll use him up, then replace him."

"And that goes for me, too, I guess?" Cherry grinned, shaking his head. "You're a hard one, Jason. I never saw a harder one."

Wallford didn't answer. "When he wakes up, find out what he knows. He'll have to be killed if he could get in the way."

He moved toward the door and turned to the left. He never saw the form of the woman who stood in the shadows outside Valance's office. Maureen had brought an IOU from Prentiss, one of the gamblers. She had paused when she had heard Dooley Young mentioned. Her face grew pale as she listened, and her heart beat wildly. Aware of the danger to herself if anyone caught her helping him, she slipped out of the club by a side entrance and started running.

★ ★ ★ ★

Mark and Jeff dug into the stew that Lola set before them with the appetites of two men who had not eaten since breakfast. Jude came in while they were eating and pulled up a chair to join them. "How's the UP doing, Mark?" he asked as he filled his plate.

"Got some rough sledding ahead, Jude."

Having worked as a grading foreman for the Union for years, Jude understood the problems, and as the meal went on, Mark found himself talking freely. Every now and then he would glance at Jeff, who never took his eyes off Lola—it was clear to Mark that he was still in love with her. He realized that Driver was the kind of man who would not move easily from one woman to another. A man such as Jeff would carry the grief of her rejection all his life.

Mark ventured, "How's the church doing, Jude? This is a pretty rough place."

Jude agreed, his reddish hair and beard taking up the light from the lamp. "The world's a rough place, Mark—as I suppose you know. But for the gospel, it's a more fruitful ground here in Bryant than in the most prosperous district of New York."

Mark was interested. He was a man of great vigor himself, and he saw that same quality in the preacher. "How do you figure that?"

"Because in the more genteel parts of the world, people think they're all right with God if they behave in a civilized manner. Never occurs to most people that the sin of greed is just as black to God as the sin of adultery. Out here you don't have to convince a man he's a sinner. Every one of them knows that."

"That's right," Driver said quietly. "All you have to do here is convince him he's got to do something about it."

Lola stopped and put her hand on Jeff's shoulder. She smiled at him warmly, saying, "You've changed since you made up your mind to follow God, Jeff."

Driver met Mark's astonished gaze and laughed ruefully. "Guess you never noticed. I suppose it takes a while for that kind of a thing to show through."

"I'm glad for you, Jeff," Mark said quickly. "I'm still a lost sheep myself, but I know you've done the right thing."

Lola opened her mouth to speak, but was interrupted by a loud knocking on the door. She turned and went to open it, and Maureen practically fell into her arms. "Maureen! What's the matter?" she cried.

"It's Dooley!" the girl gasped. She was out of breath from her run, her face pale. She gasped, "They're going to kill him! Mr. Winslow—you've got to help him."

Mark sprang from his chair. "Where is he, Maureen?" he demanded as he buckled on his gun belt.

"In Cherry's office! Oh, hurry!"

Mark and Jeff left the church at a dead run. They rounded the corner and plunged into the crowd that milled around, knocking men aside recklessly and ignoring their curses.

"What is it, Mr. Winslow?" Mark looked down to see Terry McGivern's stocky form running beside him. "Is it trouble?"

"Yes! Round up as many UP hands as you can get—bring them to the Wagonwheel!"

"It'll be quicker than you think!" McGivern cried out, and he wheeled and began shouting, "You Union terriers—come on for a bit of fun!" and at once men began running to join him.

Jeff pulled Mark to a sudden halt. "Wait a minute," he said urgently. "Let Terry get some of the boys here. There's just the two of us—"

"No time, Jeff," Mark snapped and rammed his way into the Wagonwheel without hesitation. Jeff followed him, his eyes pinpointing a dozen men who would obey any order given by Cherry Valance.

Lou Goldman was standing at the bar, and Mark spotted him immediately. He walked straight up to him, stopping four feet away. "Where's Cherry, Lou?" he demanded.

"Cherry?" Goldman mumbled. "He ain't here right now."

"You're a liar, Lou," Mark said. He was poised, ready to fight, and his eyes locked on Goldman. "Take exception to the remark?"

Goldman, usually a man of instant temper, had gauged Winslow's mood. He drew himself up straight, kept his hand away from his gun, and said, "No. I'll just remember it."

"Go put on a nightgown, Goldman!" Mark laughed harshly. He waited for Goldman's reaction, but the gunman clamped his lips together and said nothing.

As Mark wheeled and walked toward the rear door, Goldman's hand flashed for his gun. The clear sound of a gun being cocked prevented him from carrying out his evil intention. His head swiveled to see Jeff Driver training a Colt on his heart.

Driver remarked easily, "We played this once before, didn't we, Lou?"

Goldman saw several of his men waiting for his signal, but he never gave it.

"What we waiting for, Lou?" Dent Conroy snapped from Driver's left, more than ready to put a bullet in him.

Driver paid him no attention, but kept his dark eyes fixed on the face of Lou Goldman. "Your boss is tryin' to figure out if it's a good day to die, Conroy," he said evenly.

There was a sudden sound of shouting in the rear, and then a scuffling. Driver knew he was in a bad spot and hoped that help would come, when Mark reappeared in the opening. He had Dooley slung over his shoulder, and Jeff noticed the bloody face of the little man as Mark walked toward him.

He held Dooley in place with one hand and drew his gun with the other. "Where's Cherry, Lou?"

Goldman's face was pale, and he shook his head. "He left about ten minutes ago, Winslow. That's all I know."

A loud crash preceded McGivern and a small mob of his tracklayers as they barged into the Wagonwheel. "I've got a few of me best here, Mister Winslow," Terry said with a bright smile. He was eager to fight, and added, "Now if you'd like for me and the boys to do a little demolition—"

Mark kept his gaze on Goldman as he replied. "I'm taking Dooley to the doctor. I'll be back as soon as I get that done." A silence came over the place, and Mark's eyes seemed to glitter in the yellow lamp light. He let the silence run on until it was almost painful.

"When I come back, Lou," he said softly, but with a barely disguised ferocity, "I'm going to kill you. And Cherry, too. As for the two in the back who were doing the beating—I'm going to hang them on the lamppost outside."

Driver glanced around the room and saw that every man in the saloon was absolutely certain that Mark Winslow meant every word he was saying. Goldman said nothing, and Mark turned and stalked out of the room. Driver backed out and joined Mark, who headed for the doctor's office.

"Is he alive?" Driver asked.

"He's breathing," Mark said tersely.

They found the doctor, a tall, thin man named Sanders. Mark said, "Get to work, Doc."

Sanders took a quick look at Dooley. "I'll have to cut his shirt off. This arm may be broken." He began to work, the sight of Dooley's crushed and bloody face causing him to shake his head.

Finally he was finished, and they came out of the room into his outer office, where they found Jude, Lola and Maureen.

"Is he all right?" Maureen whispered.

Sanders told them, "He's had a bad beating—his nose is broken and some ribs are cracked—but he's better off than I thought at first."

Maureen began to cry, and Lola put her arms around her, comforting her. Jude said, "It's all over town, Mark, what you said to Goldman. Wait for a while before you do anything. Get some help."

Mark gave him a defiant look, shaking his head. "I'm going to rub them out, Jude."

"Mark," Lola said. "Don't go. You'll just end up killing each other."

Mark's face was set, and there was a cruelty in it that neither Lola nor the others had ever seen.

"Stay off the streets," he warned, walking out the door.

Mark found McGivern and a milling crowd of Irishmen. "Come with me," he said. With a yell they fell in behind him. He led them to Simms' hardware store, which was still open. Willard Simms' eyes grew large as the store filled up with the yelling tracklayers. "Get your guns out, Willard," Mark said. "The Union's paying for them."

A shout rang out, and Simms began handing out rifles, shotguns and handguns, along with ammunition. When he ran out, the rest of the mob grabbed axe handles. "Send the bill to me, Willard," Mark said, then turned and led the way down the street.

Word had gotten out, and Driver saw at once that it was going to be an all-out war. A rifle shot rang out, and a man dropped to his right. Driver pulled his trigger and laid his shot on the flash, and then a fusillade of shots broke the night air. The Union men scrambled for cover, and Mark ducked into a doorway, trying to see the lay of the situation.

Most of the shots from Cherry's men rained down from the windows across the street. "Lay your fire on that," he shouted, as soon as he had organized the track hands into some kind of orderly line. They moved down the street, some of them falling, but the shooting was too intense to last long.

"They're breaking!" Jeff shouted.

"Close up! Close up!" Mark ordered, and they continued down the road, firing at the retreating men.

It turned into a brutal slugfest, with men falling beneath the blows of ax handles or the barrels of rifles. Lights gleamed out of a second story window and several of Valance's men appeared, and began targeting the Irishmen. Mark knocked one of them back with his last shot, then others threw a withering fire on the snipers, driving them back.

The fight raged down the street, leaving dead and wounded in its path and inside the buildings. Cherry's men were pinned in and were forced to throw down their guns.

"I don't see Cherry—or Goldman," Jeff shouted.

"They're here . . . somewhere," Mark answered. "We'll search every building."

They moved down the street, but found no sign of the two men. Finally Mark relented. "All right. That's it."

"What'll we do with these birds, Mr. Winslow?" Terry asked, waving his hand at the captives.

"Lock them up somewhere," Mark said. He was weary to the bone and turned to walk away. Driver joined him, and the two men made their way slowly down the street. They were almost at the end of the main street when Lola and Maureen appeared. Without warning, a shot rang out—then another. Mark felt the hiss of one slug close to his head and pulled his gun. He heard Lola cry out Jeff's name as more shots filled the air. One of them raked across Mark's neck, stinging like a wasp, but he stood upright and began to fire at the riders who had appeared from behind a corner.

The ambush could not last because McGivern and others were coming, aiming their bullets at the men on horseback. There was an angry cry, and Mark heard Goldman's threat, "We'll get you yet, Winslow!" before the horses wheeled and thundered away.

Mark put his gun away, turned and saw Lola kneeling beside Driver. He went to her side and knelt. "Jeff—is it bad? Where'd they get you?"

Even in the darkness, by the dim light of the lanterns hanging on the buildings, he could see that Driver was shot to pieces.

"Mark—" he said weakly as he struggled to raise his head.

"Take it easy, Jeff," Mark said. "We'll get you to the doctor."

Driver coughed and blood filled his mouth. Lola wiped his face, crying silently.

Everyone was quiet, and when Jeff spoke weakly, Mark leaned forward to catch his words.

"We . . . had some good . . . times, didn't we—Mark?"

Mark nodded, his throat tight. "Sure did."

Driver's head was resting on Lola's lap, and he looked up into her face. There was no strength in him, but his gaze remained steady. "Lola . . . thanks . . . for telling me . . . about Jesus."

He took a deep breath, and his eyes closed momentarily. Suddenly, he glanced up. "Mark. . . ?"

"Yes, Jeff."

"Take . . . care of yourself."

Mark took the dying man's hand and held it. "Thanks, Jeff. You saved my life. . . ."

Jeff nodded and a smile touched his bloody lips. "Glad of that . . ." His eyes closed as pain racked through his body. Then he slowly opened them again. "Mark. . . ?"

"Jeff? What is it?"

"Take care . . . of Lola, Mark!" He tried to lift his arms, but found he couldn't. "Mark . . . try to believe . . . in Jesus!" he gasped, his eyes intent on his friend. With a final shudder, he relaxed, his dark head falling limply onto Lola's lap.

She held him as she would have held a child who was hurt, tears streaming down her face.

Mark Winslow's throat was dry. He got to his feet and discovered that his legs were trembling so badly he could barely stand. Taking a deep breath, he walked down the street, a tall, lonely figure, disappearing into the darkness.

CHAPTER TWENTY-TWO

A LATE BUGGY RIDE

★ ★ ★ ★

The bloody clash between the gamblers and Winslow's track-layers made few headlines, but the once-small cemetery outside of Bear River City looked like plowed earth for a time as the town laid nine more men to rest. The saloons that didn't close down became almost as circumspect as a town hall meeting. This was partly due to the fact that Reed and Casement drove the men night and day as they attacked the Wasatch territory, trying to get as much steel laid as possible before the winter storms struck.

But the iron-fisted control of Winslow had more to do with the demise of the saloons than the railwork. The night of violence had left Mark a hard man. When he was not out on a mission for Reed, he personally rode the streets where he would squelch the least sign of trouble with fists or guns. He treated both customers and owners alike, and when there was a shooting in Nolan Gipson's saloon, it was Gipson who was almost killed by Mark's bullet.

Dooley healed quickly and was ready to go gunning down the men who had beaten him, but Mark put a halt to that. Lola had insisted on watching over the little rider while he recuperated, and Mark stopped by in mid-morning to check on his progress. He found Dooley dressed and raring to go, despite a tender nose and sore ribs.

"Captain," he greeted Mark as soon as Lola admitted him. "Guess I'm ready for work. If I keep on eatin' Lola's cookin' I'll get fat as a possum."

Lola laughed, but remarked seriously, "You ought to wait for a while, Dooley. Doctor Sanders says your ribs aren't completely healed."

"Aw, if I felt any better I'd have to take medicine for it," Dooley said. "Lemme get my coat and I'm ready for trouble."

"You're looking tired, Mark," Lola observed after Dooley left. It was not so much fatigue, but rather a hard edge that etched lines on his face. The death of Jeff Driver had taken something out of him. His spirit weighed heavy, and his eyes were grim. And if Driver's death had taken something out of him, it had also put something in, and it was this that Lola deplored. Mark had always been a tough man, but now there was a ruthlessness in him, a quality very close to cruelty. She had heard stories of his heavy-handed application of rough justice, and now as she looked at him, she could believe it.

He answered her briefly, "Working hard, I guess."

She hesitated, wanting to say something to him, but not certain how to put it. Finally she said, "Mark, don't let Jeff's death destroy you."

He gave her a swift, intolerant glance. "You think I ought to forget it? Act like it never happened?"

"You could never do that," she said quietly. "If I live to be an old woman I'll still carry the memory of Jeff with me. That's the only way we can give him anything, Mark."

"What about the ones who killed him?" he asked harshly. "Don't you have memories of them, Lola?" Anger scored the planes of his wedge-shaped face, and he clenched his fists together. "They're alive and he's dead. You expect me to just pass that by?"

"I don't expect you to, Mark," Lola said, "but it's what you ought to do."

"Forgive my enemies? Turn the other cheek?"

She faced him fully. "That's what Jesus said, Mark. The men that killed Jeff will have to answer to God."

"They'll have to answer to me first," he said thickly. The rage that had exploded in him after Jeff's death had settled into a seething hatred that lay heavy in him, never asleep for a moment. He tried to make her understand, aware his reaction hurt her. "Lola, it's different for you. You're a woman and you have all the gentleness that a woman should have. But a man has to stand for what's right. If I let Jeff's killers go, I'd never know a moment's peace."

"And how much peace do you have now, Mark?" she asked gently, her eyes on his.

He had no answer for her. The restlessness that had driven him since the end of the war and the breakup of the old order of his life he had learned to live with. But the constant demands of his job had drained his natural good humor, and now the death of Jeff Driver had sucked him dry of the little goodness he'd possessed. He knew he had become a sour, unforgiving man—but even as he stood there, recognizing that he had none of the peace she mentioned, he had no power to cast off his driving thirst for revenge.

Lola watched as he thought, and a tremendous sadness washed over her. "I remember, Mark," she said gently, "the time you were so sick and weak you couldn't lift your head. Do you ever think of that time?"

"I've never forgotten it."

Her lips parted and there was a longing light in her eyes as she said, "I think you'll never know any peace until you are broken like that again. I don't mean physically sick. It's your spirit that's sick. You're bitter and unbendable."

He stared at her, unable to read the expression on her face. "A man has to be hard in order to live, Lola."

She shook her head quickly. "You're wrong, Mark. The only way to live is to have love—and you can't love anyone with bitterness and a lust for vengeance filling you to the brim. I saw gentleness in you once, but you've lost it." Dooley's footsteps echoed in the hallway. "You'll have to be broken before you'll ever be a whole man," she emphasized once more.

Dooley came in carrying a canvas bag and gave the two a quick look. He was a perceptive young fellow, and sensed at once the tension between Mark and Lola. He admired them both, and hated to see them at odds, so he offered quickly, "I can make it to the room on my own, Captain—in case you ain't ready to leave yet."

Mark shook his head. "I've got to go to work. I'll see you later, Lola."

Dooley came to stand before her, giving her a quick grin. "Well, I reckon you patched me up so I can get through two or three more clean shirts, Miss Lola. Let me know if I can ever do anything for you."

"I will, Dooley."

The two left, and as soon as they were outside, Dooley commented, "That gal shore does beat hens a'pacing, don't she now?"

"Sure." Mark changed the subject abruptly, saying, "You better stick around the office and run errands for Josh Long for a few days, Dooley. Let those ribs heal up."

Dooley shrugged. "It's your say, Captain—but I got one leetle call to make."

Mark gave him a swift glance. "If you're thinking about Bob Dempsey and the other scum who beat you up, you're too late. They got away in the fracas. Probably helped Cherry and Goldman murder Jeff."

Dooley considered that, then let out his breath. "Well, now, I guess I'll meet up with them someday."

"You know Maureen went back to work for Shep at the Union Belle?"

"Shore." Dooley bit his lip and finally said, "I sort of figured she'd come by and see me. If it hadn't been for her, reckon them two would have finished me off. I been wonderin' why she never come."

"Probably too ashamed of herself, Dooley," Mark said. "I talked to her a couple of times since then, and I got the feeling she wanted to see you, but was afraid of what you might think of her." He regarded the little rider carefully and advised, "Guess if you went to see her she might feel a little better."

"Yeah, I'd better do that. Matter of fact, now might be a good time." He turned and headed in the direction of the Union Belle, a determined look on his face.

Lola's words haunted Mark all the rest of that day: *You'll have to be broken before you're a whole man.* The thought troubled him, and he found himself summoning up arguments against her words. *I fought for a losing army, did time in a Mexican jail, and nearly died in a snowstorm—living only to see the railroad kill my good friends. What's it to be broken if not all that?* he wondered. But her comment about peace kept nagging at him and would not let him rest. *Some people seem to glide by through life without many troubles. Some fight from the cradle to the grave. Guess I'm just one of the last sort.*

But his uneasiness at Lola's words grew, and he stayed in the saddle constantly to avoid facing up to it, riding with Casement to survey the roadbeds that stretched now into the foothills of the Wasatch chain, returning at night to patrol the town. On Tuesday there was a flare-up in a crew working on Tunnel Number 2, and he told Reed, "It's some of Central's work, Sam. I'm going to bust them so hard they'll bleed." He had taken Dooley and Nick Bolton along, and when they got to the tunnel he identified the ringleader and knocked him into the dirt, senseless, and put him afoot for town.

Nick and Dooley watched as he mounted up and told the workers, "If I have to come back, it'll be a rope instead of a beating."

"That was pretty hard, Mark," Nick said when he joined them and they started back to Bear River City.

Winslow gave him a rough look, and he said no more. But when Mark went his own way once they hit town, Nick shook his head doubtfully. "Mark's headed for trouble, Dooley. He's got Cherry and the roughs down on him, and I don't doubt that Central's got him picked out for a bullet. Now he's making enemies of our own men." Bolton was a clear-thinking man, and he added, "You've been around Winslow a long time, Dooley. Try to slow him down."

"Ain't nothin' ever slowed a Winslow down," Dooley shrugged. "The whole blamed Union army couldn't get the job done, Nick. The Captain was fightin' just as hard at the end when the thing was lost as he wuz at Bull Run when it looked good for us. All the Winslows is like that—stubborn as a blue-nosed mule!" He touched his broken nose and added, "But he was always a light-hearted man, Captain Winslow was. Now he's going around lookin' for somebody to bite. We better stick close to him, Nick, 'cause he don't care anymore. Don't give a dead rat if he lives or dies—and that's when a feller can get hisself into a passel of trouble!"

★ ★ ★ ★

Winter was in the wind in late September, and the Union leaped the rising contours of the land at a rapid pace. The word was out that the Central, using Chinese coolies, was racing toward Ogden at a rate that might beat the Union; and Casement's Irishmen fought back by laying steel at five or even six miles a day. Good construction practice was abandoned. In the fever of hurry, ties were laid on bare earth and ballast was left for clean-up crews coming behind. Rail joints no longer necessarily met on ties, but hung between.

The steel swung up out of Bryant, struck Blacks Fork and surged on to Granger. At Church Buttes they were six thousand three hundred feet above sea level. At Piedmont they reached the huge stacks of ties waiting at Tie Siding and hit the first summit of the Wasatch Range. It was in Piedmont that Sherman Ames's Credit Mobilier contract was ended, the reverberations of Ames's financial crash already trembling. But Durant got the money and the grading went on.

Moira and Ray saw relatively little of each other, for like every other Union Pacific man, Ray was working night and day. The time they did have together was strained, though what caused it neither of them could say. The change in their relationship troubled Moira more than it did Ray, for she had more time to think about it, and she wondered why she felt so little concern over their relationship.

Something, she knew, had changed for her when she saw Mark and his Irishmen clean the gamblers out of town. The stark violence of it horrified her—yet at the same time she admired Mark for his courage and drive. Unconsciously, she compared Ray to Mark, and it was Mark who came out on top—the natural choice for a girl who relished color and drama.

Her love of excitement surfaced one Friday night when Mark joined Reed, Casement, Ames and Ray for dinner. The meal took place in one of the small dining rooms in the Union Belle, for Shep had kept to the original idea of a club even though Lola was no longer there. He met them at the door, his broad face beaming. "Glad to see you, folks! Got everything ready for you." He led them to the room, and Reed asked suddenly, "How do you get along without Lola Montez, Yancy?"

"Well, not very well, to be truthful," Shep said ruefully. "But I scrape along—and she's better off. I'll send Maureen in for your orders. Drinks are on me."

When Maureen came in, Mark had an opportunity to examine her while she was taking orders from the others. She looked calm, which was not unusual, but she had lost some weight. She had refused to let Dooley court her, but Young remained persistent. "Ain't but a matter of time," he'd told her. When she came to take his order, he smiled and treated her as he would any friend.

The wine was passed around, and the talk predictably turned to the problems of finishing the line. Casement and Reed were at loggerheads over some of the priorities, and the two of them waged a loud discussion over the problems. Tunnels were the issue, and between the two a great gulf was fixed. Reed was for more of them, while Casement argued that it was cheaper and quicker to go over the rising hills.

"The tunnels will be ready by the time your steel gets there," Reed said positively. "If we waited until you got there, we'd be held up."

"How do you know they'll be ready?" Casement demanded. "I hear they're bogged down at Number Two in Echo Canyon. If that tunnel ain't ready, we're stopped dead, Reed."

Ray lifted his eyes at this and paid closer attention. He had been drinking the wine steadily and could no longer think clearly, but he was eager to discover all he could. "Those tunnels are tricky things," he observed as the two men continued their discussion. "Just one cave-in and the whole thing's over. Wouldn't it be better to go around that rise—or go over it?"

Reed adamantly shook his head. "No. There's no way around it without laying fifty miles of track, and the grade's so steep you'd have to make a dozen Z's to get over it—no engine could travel a grade like that in winter."

Ray suggested tentatively, "Hate to put all our eggs in one basket—which is what this seems like to me."

Ames shook his head. "Let the engineers decide that, Ray. You and I need to see to it that they've got steel to lay down."

Ray lifted his eyes, started to say something, then shrugged and took another glass of wine. The information about the tunnel had opened up a new train of thought, and he said little as the dinner progressed.

The meal was served, and as he ate, Ames remarked to Winslow, "Dodge sent word you did the right thing—cleaning the trash out of town."

"I hear they're already setting up down the line," Casement put in. "Maybe this time we ought to hang a few of them before the construction gets there. Be a good example to the rest."

Ames smiled and shook his head at the fiery speech. "I suppose that would be extreme, but you can't let it get as bad as it did here, Mark."

The meal finished, Reed, Casement and Ames shoved the dishes back to spread a map on the table. They plunged at once into making plans, and Ray joined them, whispering to his fiancee, "Moira, I need to be in on this. It'll be boring for you, I'm afraid."

"Will it take long?" she asked.

"If it's like all the other meetings, it will," he said with a grimace. "Maybe I should take you back to the hotel—?"

"Oh, it's too early! Can't you sneak away?"

Ray smiled ruefully. "In a group of four, it's hard to sneak away without being noticed." He could have excused himself, but he wanted to hear more about the tunnel at Echo. Glancing at Mark, he asked, "Isn't there anything in this town that Moira could do?"

Mark shook his head and smiled. "Not that I can think of."

Ray had a thought, and said, "I saw a poster somewhere today—it said there was some sort of a meeting at Jude's church."

"Just a visiting preacher come to town," Mark shrugged. "I don't think it'd be in your line, Moira."

"Are you going?"

"Hadn't planned to."

"Oh, come on!" Moira urged. "I've heard a lot about Lola's church." She turned to Ray and smiled. "Come on, Ray. Beg off your meeting and we'll all go."

Ray shook his head. "Wish I could—but your father asked me to stay. You and Mark should go on without me."

Mark protested, "It's not your kind of church, Moira."

"How do you know?" she asked with a pout. "I'm beginning to think you're ashamed to be seen in my company, Mark. Where's that Southern chivalry I've heard so much about?"

"Oh, take her, Mark!" Ray exclaimed. "Take my buggy—maybe I can get away early and we can have a late drink after you get out of church."

Moira laughed, "You're the one who needs to go to church, Ray! A late drink after church, indeed! Come on, Mark."

"We'll drop by after the service, Ray," Mark promised as he allowed himself to be led out by Moira. When they had donned their coats, he put her up in the buggy, climbed in and headed down the street.

"This is your idea, remember," Mark reminded her. "I don't know this preacher, but I've heard quite a few Methodist evangelists. Some of them get carried away. Jude's not in that line, but if the preacher starts in on you, don't look to me for help."

She looked at him, startled, then saw that he was smiling at her. "I suppose I need to be preached at as much as anybody," she remarked. Then she added, "It's good to see you smile, Mark. You've been going through a difficult time lately." She hesitated, then added gently, "I'm so sorry about your friend who was killed. His death's been very hard for you, hasn't it?"

He gave her a surprised look, for a genuine compassion filled her voice. "Yes. It's always hard. I lost lots of friends in the war—but I never got used to it."

"And the man who did it got away?" She shook her head and said angrily, "He ought to be shot!"

Mark said, "Well, that's what I think." Then he added without thinking, "Lola thinks I'm too full of thinking like that. Maybe she's right."

Moira was silent, then said carefully, "I suppose she has to say that, being a preacher of some sort. But how can you help wanting to strike out when somebody hurts the one you love?"

"Some can, I guess—but I'm still a sinner, Moira. Wish I could turn the other cheek—but so far I've not been able to."

They reached the small church, and as Mark got out and tied up the horse, Moira grew apprehensive. "Mark, I'm suddenly afraid to go in there."

He laughed at her, his face looking much younger as he did,

reached out and caught her arm. "It'll be good for you," he proclaimed. She came out of the buggy protesting, and nearly slipped. He caught her, holding her close to keep her from falling.

She put her arms around his neck, a light of humor in her eyes as she said, "I think I'll scream until the preacher comes out, then tell him you forced your attentions on me."

Mark was very aware of her closeness, but said lightly, "Come on, woman. You need to go to church!"

They entered the church and Jude strode up to greet them, his ruddy face beaming. "Why, Mark—and Miss Ames, this is a surprise!"

He was so happy that Mark felt he had to explain. "Well, Jude, Miss Ames is bored out of her mind, so she asked if I'd bring her to church!"

"Mark!" Moira exclaimed, mortified. "What will the Reverend think of me?" She looked around and asked, "Where's Lola, Reverend?"

"She'll be a little late," Jude said. "Had to make a call. Now, you folks want to sit up front?"

"No, we'll stay in the rear lines, Jude," Mark grinned. "If this preacher is anything like Peter Cartwright, I want to be as close to the door as possible."

Jude had to grin. "Well—he is a little along those lines. But a good man all the same, and a fine preacher. You sit down and any time you want to shout, just go right ahead."

Mark found a seat for Moira, and they sat there watching the crowd file in. It was a mixture of older townspeople and some of the track layers who moved along with construction. "Jude carries his own congregation when Casement moves the town," Mark said quietly. "That fellow must be the preacher."

Moira looked on the platform to see Jude speaking with a short muscular man with a full set of black whiskers. He had piercing black eyes and a firm mouth. "He looks like he could eat nails," Moira whispered.

"Got to be tough, those Methodist preachers, out in this part of the world." Mark told her that his grandfather had been a missionary to the Sioux for years, and she was fascinated.

"He preached to the savages?" she asked.

Mark suddenly smiled at her and said, "Well, I guess so. He married one of them. That was my grandmother—White Dove."

A wave of red swept up Moira's neck, and she stared at him. "You're joking, of course?"

"Not a bit. She was my father's mother. His Indian name was Sky Blue—because of his eyes. He dropped the 'Blue' and is now known as Sky Winslow. So I guess the evangelist will have one of the 'savages' to preach to tonight."

"I—I'm sorry, Mark," Moira whispered. "I had no idea you were. . . ."

She had difficulty saying the word, but Mark just grinned. "Don't worry about it, Moira. I'm proud of my grandmother. And I got cussed out for being a rebel so much that I'm almost proud of being part Indian."

Moira was stricken, but had no chance to say more, for Lola entered. She saw them and came to say hello. "So good to see you, Moira, Mark." She didn't sit with them, and when her father called on her, she sang a song with such feeling that many in the congregation wept. After she sang, the service started, and Moira sat there taking it all in. It was a typical service of its kind—but Moira had never attended anything other than the Episcopalian Church. She was accustomed to altar boys and priests wearing ecclesiastical garb, to the chanting of slow hymns by a trained choir, and to an "address" rather than a "sermon." In the next two hours, she was treated to lusty singing, a fiery sermon punctuated by a chorus of "amens," and an altar call in which many fell on their faces, calling out for God to have mercy.

Finally Mark touched her arm and whispered, "Let's go." She rose to follow him outside. "Is the service over?" she asked as he handed her up.

"No—and it may not be for another couple of hours," he said when he got in. "Sometimes the service doesn't close at all, not in the usual way. People just stay and pray all night long." She was so quiet as they drove back, he looked at her curiously. "What did you think of it all, Moira?"

"I—I don't know," she said, quite honestly. "They all enjoyed it so much!" She laughed ruefully. "They even seemed to like it when the minister raked them for their sins." She had been strangely affected by the service, disliking some aspects and baffled by much of it. Quietly she asked, "Is it real, Mark? I've never seen anything like it."

He spoke to the horse, thinking about her question. Finally he nodded, "It's real, all right. Most of it. You get that many people together for any reason, some of them won't be sincere. But most of it is real, I think."

"Well, if that's real religion," Moira said thoughtfully, "then I don't have any."

"Why, it's just the form you're looking at," Mark said quickly. "It's not the robe or the lack of it that makes a preacher. And the kind of singing changes from place to place." He struggled to explain his meaning, "We had a fellow in our outfit, his name was Ophie Sanford. Every place we went, he went to church. Funny thing about it was—he went to any church that was handy—Quaker, Catholic, Methodist, Baptist—anything he could find. I asked him once about it, and he said, 'Why, I go to worship God, Captain—and I can do that in any church.' Which is a pretty good way of looking at it, I guess."

They arrived at the Union Belle, and Mark said, "Wait here and I'll see if Ray's finished." He disappeared into the club and was back almost at once. "They're all gone," he announced. "Guess the meeting was over quicker than Ray thought." He got in and turned the team around. "I'll take you to the hotel. Maybe he'll be there."

"I don't think so," Moira said. "He's probably in a poker game somewhere."

"Well, I'll try to find him."

"No, let him play." She didn't seem angry or upset, which struck Mark as strange.

"I'm wide awake," Moira continued, looking around at the town's commotion. "What time is it?"

He pulled out his watch and peered at it in the darkness. "Quarter past nine."

"What's over that way?" she asked, pointing north.

"Well, Bear River—and the Wasatch Mountains."

"Is the river far?"

"Couple of miles."

"It's early. Let's go see it."

"Why—there's nothing much to see, Moira. It's not a big

river." He didn't want to take her, but she was insistent, and he relented. "Well, it won't take but half an hour or so—then you've got to go in."

"All right."

He drove out of town and found himself enjoying the drive. He knew that she was bored with the life she led, and was glad he could bring her some happiness. The wind was cold, and he dug a blanket out from under the seat. "Better get under this," he warned.

She spread it over her shoulders, then threw a fold over his, and moved close to him. She laughed and said, "If you freeze, I'll be lost. I can't drive a buggy."

They soon came to the river, which was much more beautiful in the rich moonlight than it was during the day. It swirled at the feet of their horse, silver and flickering with tiny points of light, and for a long time they sat there, listening to the gurgle as the water passed over the smooth stones.

Silence consumed the night air around them, and Moira murmured, "It's so quiet, Mark!"

He nodded. "Sure is better than the racket I hear all day. And the talk." He asked without meaning to, "When are you and Ray getting married? I asked you that before, didn't I?"

She moved restlessly, and he was acutely aware of her as she pressed against his side. "Oh, I don't know, Mark. Things are so mixed up."

The silence ran on, and for some reason she was filled with a feeling of great emptiness. Lately she had become painfully aware that her life was never going to be the same as it had been, and in the darkness and the quiet, all her fears and apprehensions seemed to rush in, flooding her with a sadness that she had never dared to show anyone.

He looked down and saw that her eyes were damp with tears that gleamed in the moonlight. "Why, Moira, what's the matter?"

"Oh, Mark! I'm so unhappy!" She turned her face toward him and began to sob. Her body shook, and without volition, she leaned against him. He was taken by surprise, and instinctively put his arm around her, holding her. She had appeared so strong, independent and unrestrained that he had never sensed a weakness in her, but now she seemed like a broken-hearted child.

Finally the sobs began to subside, and she raised her face to his, tears making silver tracks down her smooth cheeks. She trembled, still in his embrace. She was a lovely woman, and he was moved by her sudden display of weakness. "Moira—" he whispered, "I'm sorry." Then she parted her lips, and with no thought at all of doing so, he lowered his head and kissed her. There was a response in her that stirred him, and for one moment he felt her desires, rich and strong as his own, awaken. Then thoughts of Ray filled his mind and he quickly lifted his head, saying, "You've had a bad time—but it'll be all right."

She gave him a quizzical look. "We've both had a bad time, Mark."

He turned the horse around and they drove back to the hotel. He got out and helped her down. "I'll put the buggy in the stable for Ray." She was standing close beside him, and she reached out and touched his cheek with an intensely feminine gesture, saying, "You've been a help, Mark. Thank you." Then she turned and walked into the hotel.

Mark got in the buggy and left, unaware that Ray Hayden stood in the shadows across the street from the hotel. He had gone seeking them, and failing to find them, had waited for their return. He had been close enough to witness the caress that Moira gave Winslow, and seeing it, he smiled grimly. He was not a possessive man as a rule, but something raked across his nerves as he saw the look she gave Mark. His own feelings for Moira had been confused, but now he was determined that he would have her—if for no other reason than to prove to Mark Winslow that he was the better man!

CHAPTER TWENTY-THREE

OUT OF THE PAST

★ ★ ★ ★

December came and with it bad weather. Snowflakes the size of half dollars drove slantwise through the early morning light as the train from the East pulled into the station at Bear River City. The full force of winter lurked just over the glittering tops of the mountains to the west, waiting like a wild beast to leap on the lower valleys.

Ray Hayden pulled his sheepskin coat tighter around his neck, stamping his feet to restore circulation. The train was late, but the message he had received in a cryptic telegram had left him no choice but to wait in the morning cold. It had said simply, "Morning train, Tuesday. J.W." Hayden had not met with Wallford since the fateful eavesdropping incident. They had exchanged coded messages twice, but now it was clear that Wallford wanted a personal meeting.

The engine turned loose a huge blast of steam and ground to a halt. People began disembarking at once, and Hayden kept back, not wanting to be seen with Wallford. Most of the passengers were laborers, with the exception of a couple of small families. He noted a fine-looking woman with silvering hair step down, take in the surroundings, then proceed at once toward the station office. Wallford descended after her, his eyes searching for Ray. Hayden moved out of the shadows of the long depot building and caught his attention. He waited until the man came to him and said with irritation, "Meeting like this isn't smart, Jason. There was talk after the trouble here that you were tied in with Cherry. If I'm seen talking to you, it'll ruin our plans."

Wallford's black eyes were expressionless. "I didn't come for conversation, Ray. The Central and the Union are neck-and-neck. You've had plenty of time to think. How can we stop the Union?" He saw Hayden hesitate, and pulled a package out of his pocket. "There's ten thousand dollars in here—and I've got another one just like it in my bag. It comes from the top—but you've got to deliver the goods. Nothing less than a foolproof scheme this time." He saw greed in the fair man's eyes and added, "And of course, if you succeed you're guaranteed a big job with the Central. Stanford himself told me, 'If Hayden delivers the goods, send him to me. We can use a man like that in the board room.' "

That tipped the scales, and Hayden responded quickly. "I've got the way, Jason." He drew a folded sheet of paper out of his pocket and opened it. Wallford examined it carefully while Hayden explained. "Here's the end of track—where we are right now. Most of the rest of the right of way lies right through the Wasatch Mountains. Now—here's Echo Canyon. We've got crews tunneling from both sides of the mountain using nitroglycerin to blast through. The plan is for them to meet somewhere in the middle. When they do, the worst of Reed's problems are over. It'll be rough laying track in the winter, but nothing stops that man!"

Wallford stared at the map, then lifted his eyes. "You're saying that the tunnel is the key to stopping them?"

"Blow that, Jason, and no work force in the world could beat the Central." Ray's voice was determined, and he added, "Put some charges in there, set them off. Do it late enough so there's no hope of re-drilling it. They can't go around it , and they can't go over it. We can't lose."

Wallford thought hard, then a smile came to his thin lips. "You've got it, Ray." He handed the money over, saying, "The rest is yours when the tunnel is blown." He watched the other man's expression, then added casually, "Of course, you'll have to do the job yourself."

Ray stared at him, startled. "Me! Why, I can't get away with that, Jason."

"Yes, you can. When the time is right, you just let me know. I'll have some help ready for you, and you can go plant the charges and blow the tunnel. You won't have to return to the Union. You can join Stanford and the others in California—right in that big board room!"

It was a development that Hayden had never considered, for he had thought he would be in on the planning rather than the action. Wallford noticed Ray's hesitation and urged him on. "You'll have to choose, Ray—and right now. Either give the money back and go down with the Union—or get on board with us at the Central."

Wallford had calculated his moves well. He had Hayden right where he wanted him, even though most of what he claimed was a lie. The Big Four knew nothing of Hayden, Leland Stanford included. There was no promise of a job, and no additional money to be had. But he knew Hayden well, and by putting the cash in his hand had drawn the man into his net. Hayden wavered until he looked down at the cash. "I'll do it, Jason," he said.

"I thought you might. You're a smart fellow, Ray. Now, I'm going to keep under wraps. I'll be staying at the hotel, doing a little gambling and keeping my ear to the ground. Give me at least two day's notice, and I'll have the explosives and the men to help you." He put a hand on Hayden's shoulder, adding, "Just a little while, Ray, and you'll be moving with the big fellows." As soon as he disappeared, Hayden left as well, going slowly back toward town. His head was bowed in the falling snow, and he was acutely conscious of the package of bills in his pocket. He was also aware of a heaviness that he could not shake off. "A man has to take care of himself!" he muttered defiantly to himself. Such had been his philosophy for a long time—but somehow it did not comfort him as he walked slowly through the falling snow.

★　★　★　★

Mark awoke as the first light of dawn filtered through his window. He had gone to bed after two in the morning, having stayed up to go over figures and grading reports with Reed. As he rolled out of bed, his eyes were gritty and he lacked his former buoyancy. He moved slowly as he dressed and shaved. He recalled the day before with distaste, for there had been a flare-up in Roy Spicer's saloon. Spicer was a borderline case, a tough man who should have been run out of town with Valance. He had barely kept within the line Mark had set, and yesterday trouble had broken out. One of his dealers had cheated some of Casement's steel layers, and in the fracas two of them had been killed by Spicer's men. Mark had gone at once, and Spicer and two of his men had put up a fight. The violence had exploded, and when it was over, all three of the troublemakers were shot—two of them fatally. Both Nick Bolton and Dooley had taken bullets, Nick through his bicep and Dooley along the side of his neck.

The realization that Dooley could be lying beside Jeff Driver in the cemetery made Mark's hand suddenly tremble—and he looked at it in shock. "Didn't know anything could make me shake," he said in surprise. "Maybe it's time to quit all this."

Lola had said nothing, but he knew that she and Dooley had discussed the incident. There was no rebuke spoken, but her eyes revealed the sadness he had caused. He finished shaving, put his razor away and slipped into his coat, turning abruptly when a knock came at his door.

He slipped his gun from under his pillow and went to stand to one side of the door, saying, "Who is it?"

A woman's voice replied, "Open the door, Mark."

He didn't recognize the voice, and was wary as he turned the key and jerked the door open, gun in hand—then he froze where he was, shock racing through his nerves.

"Since when did you start greeting your mother with a .44, Mark?"

Winslow stared at Rebekah Winslow, unable to think. She stood there regarding him as she had done a thousand times before, and his mind reeled with those memories, while at the same time trying to adjust to the sight of her.

He tossed the gun on the bed, stepped forward and pulled her into the room, his arms around her. He had not seen her since he had left Belle Maison after the war, and she seemed smaller than he remembered. She clung to him fiercely, and he felt her body move with a sob—then she stepped back and dashed the tears from her eyes. She was, he saw, as vigorous as ever, and at the age of fifty still an attractive and vibrant woman. Her auburn hair was streaked with silver, but still as curly and pert as ever.

"You look worn out, Mark," she said finally.

"Mother—what are you doing here?" he asked in bewilderment. "Is something wrong at home?"

Rebekah nodded. "It's your father, Mark. He's very ill."

Mark stood very still. "Is it his heart?"

"Yes. He's been going down for a year."

Mark nodded. "Dooley told me a little about it. I'll see my boss and we'll start back—"

"No," Rebekah said with a slight smile. "He's here—down at the station." She put her hand up and laid it on his cheek and he saw that she was fighting back the tears. "You know how your father is, Mark. When the doctor told him he didn't have long, he wanted to see all of you. Dan and Thomas were close. Pet was right there, of course—and Belle came at once. He said his good-byes—and then he said, 'Rebekah, get my pants. We're going to see Mark.' "

Mark could not hide the moisture that gathered in his own eyes. He was the oldest son and had been closer to his father than the other boys. The thought of his father coming all the way across the country to see him momentarily robbed him of speech. He cleared his throat. "He's on the train?"

"Yes."

Mark took her arm and led her down the stairs quickly. "How is he, Mother?"

"Very weak. I think he's kept himself alive on the hope of seeing you," she said. As they left the hotel and moved quickly through the snow, she told him about the trip. "Everyone's been so kind, Mark—especially west of Omaha. I informed the conductor Sky was your father, and he couldn't do enough for us. He made the caboose into a private room for Sky and me—just ran the other men right out!" Memory of it gladdened her eyes, and she went on to tell how as the crews changed, each new crew watched over them. She squeezed his arm and said, "I'm proud of you, Mark. You've made a name for yourself with the men of the Union."

Mark shook his head, unable to respond. His world was suddenly falling, and when they got to the station, he saw that the caboose had been shuffled off to the side track. Billy Thomas, one of the conductors on the line, hurried up to him, his eyes sympathetic. "I figured you might not want to be moving your father around any more than is necessary, Mr. Winslow, so I had Shorty put the caboose where you could use it for a bedroom for a spell."

"I appreciate that, Billy," Mark said, touching the man on the arm.

"Well, there's not much in the way of accommodations," Thomas offered. "Let me know if I can do anything, Mrs. Winslow," he said, pulling off his hat to Rebekah.

"You've been so kind!" Rebekah said, putting out her hand. "God bless you, sir."

Thomas flushed and moved away, and Rebekah said, "Come along, Mark," and led the way to the caboose. He helped her up, then followed her through the door. There was a fire in the wood stove, and his eyes were immediately drawn to the man sitting on a straight chair beside it.

Mark stumbled toward his father, his throat tight. Sky put out his hands, his blue eyes bright and clear, though Mark saw at once that he was very weary. "Mark—!" Sky said, and then Mark did something he had neither planned nor done since he was a boy. He put his arms out and the two men embraced. Sky's body felt thin and frail, and Mark held him gently, his eyes stinging with tears.

"Father—" he whispered, unable to say more.

Sky finally leaned back and looked at his son. His hair was silver, and there were lines of pain around his blue eyes. He reached out with one thin hand and put it on Mark's arm as if to reassure himself, then cleared his throat and said, "Well, Rebekah, are you going to miss the chance to cook breakfast for two of your favorite men?" He moved back toward the chair, his gruff voice unable to cover his feelings. "Well—sit down, son, and tell me all about this railroad. I've seen enough of it the last few days."

Mark sat down, and while Rebekah prepared bacon, eggs and coffee on top of the wood stove, Mark told the story of how the UP and the Central had raced toward Utah for two years. It steadied him to talk about the railroad, and gave him time to study his father. He was like a lamp burning low, Mark saw with grief. The straight body had bent and weakened until every move was an effort—even to remain seated in the chair took part of the reserve that Sky Winslow paid out grudgingly. Only his eyes were the same, still alert and full of humor despite the pain.

Rebekah put the breakfast on the table, and Sky pushed the food around, but ate only a few bites. Mark forced himself to eat heartily, demanding that they tell him about the family. Rebekah sat down and did most of the talking, and by the time he had absorbed the news from home, he saw that Sky was having difficulty staying awake. Quickly he got to his feet, saying, "Well, I'm a working man. Have to go check in. But I'll be back pretty soon."

Sky made no move to stand up, but reached his hand out to Mark. "I thank God that He's allowed me to see you, son," he said quietly.

Mark nodded. "I'm glad He's let me see you, too, Father. I'll be back to get you settled in later this morning. Do you need anything?"

Sky said, "I'd like to see that preacher you wrote about—Jude Moran?"

"That's the one. He'll be glad to visit with you—you two will get along well." He left then, and his mother followed him outside.

Mark paused in the cold and said, "He's very low, isn't he, Mother?"

"Yes." She was not one to hide the truth from herself or others. "He can't leave this car, Mark—but he's done what he set out to do. He wanted to see you so much!"

Mark swallowed hard, saying, "I'll send Jude by—and his daughter, too. You'll like her." He left her and walked through the snow toward the church. His mind was reeling with his father's appearance, and he knew he would have to adjust his life to meet it—but the future still lay before him in a dim uncertainty.

It was Jude who opened the door, his face showing surprise at his early morning visitor. "Come in, Mark. We're just having breakfast. Will you join us?"

"No, Jude, but thanks—I need to talk to you and Lola."

"Come on back." He led the way and Lola looked at him with a question in her eyes as they entered.

"I need some help," Mark said at once. "My parents came in on the train this morning—"

He broke off suddenly, and Lola and her father exchanged a quick glance at the strange expression on his face. "What's wrong, Mark?" Lola asked.

"It's my father," he said, and they noted his hesitation. "He's dying."

The words brought a quick cry from Lola. "Oh, Mark—!" She came to lay her hand on his arm and look up at him, compassion in her blue eyes. "How can we help?"

"He wants to see you, Jude," Mark said heavily. "He's a man of God, like you are, and I've written him about your work in the church. It'd be a help if you'd go by for a visit. They're staying in the caboose. And there are so few women here, I thought maybe you might go along to introduce yourself to my mother, Lola."

"Certainly! Certainly!" Jude said at once. "I'm sorry to hear this, Mark."

"Thanks, Jude," Mark said. "That's like you." He turned and left without a word, leaving the two alone.

"That's quite a shock," Jude murmured. "Do you know anything about his people, Lola?"

"He told me about them when we were stranded in Texas. I know he admires them more than he does anyone. His father's frailty is killing him, Father! Did you see the hurt in his face?"

"I saw it," Jude nodded. He stood in the middle of the floor, his face kind. "Mark's always been able to handle things. But he won't be able to manage this alone, will he?"

"No, he won't." Lola's expression grew tense, then she said, "I think we'd better go right away. Mrs. Winslow is probably exhausted after a trip across the country with a sick husband."

They put on their heavy coats and were soon knocking softly on the door of the caboose. Lola got her first glimpse of Mark's mother as it opened. "I'm Lola Montez, Mrs. Winslow. This is my father, Jude Moran."

Rebekah smiled, saying, "You certainly didn't waste any

time! Come in out of the cold." She stepped back to let them in. "My husband is in bed, but he'll want to talk to you, Reverend Moran." There were two small bunks built into the side of the car, and she led them to the one where her husband lay. "Sky— Reverend Moran and his daughter Lola are here."

Jude took the thin hand that the sick man extended. "I'm sorry to find you not feeling well, Mr. Winslow," he said.

"Take a chair, sir," Sky said. "I'm sorry not to be up, but you understand."

Jude sat down and began to talk to Sky. Rebekah said, "Let's have our morning coffee, Miss Montez." She poured two cups of coffee, and the women sat down on kitchen chairs. "Mark has told me about you, but I want to hear more."

Lola began a little shyly. She thought she had never seen a more attractive woman than Rebekah Winslow, and she soon discovered that the spirit of Mark's mother was no less beautiful. She found herself telling Rebekah how Mark had helped her get away from Texas, how she had became a saloon owner—and lastly a great deal about how she had found Jesus and given her life to him.

Finally she gave an embarrassed laugh. "I've never talked so much in all my life!" she exclaimed.

Rebekah smiled, wisdom in her eyes. "It's a wonderful story, Lola. God has blessed you so much. Mark doesn't say much about his feelings, but I can tell from his letters how much he thinks of you."

Lola colored suddenly and found herself unable to respond. She felt like a child in the presence of Rebekah and hurriedly began to talk of how she could help care for Sky Winslow. "You're very tired," she said. "Let me help you, Mrs. Winslow."

"Let it be Rebekah and Lola," she answered. Then for the first time she wavered and something like fear came into her eyes. "I am tired—and a little afraid." She held her hands tightly together, and her voice was so soft that Lola leaned forward to hear her words. "Sky has been holding on just to see Mark. He won't be with us much longer. I'm not afraid for him—but I'm going to be so lonely!"

Lola put her hand out, and the older woman took it, holding it tightly. Rebekah had not faltered, not since the day the doctor had told them that it was only a matter of time. She had held the family together and endured the rigors of a long journey, never once letting Sky see any grief or sorrow. But now she gripped Lola's hand with desperation, and Lola reminded her, "God will see you through, Rebekah! He won't forsake you!"

They sat there for a long moment, then Rebekah, her eyes no longer afraid, said quietly, "You have the gift of consolation, Lola." She leaned back, and they listened to Jude speak quietly and steadily, his talk filled with scriptures. "Your father will be good for Sky," Rebekah said. She looked at Lola and said warmly, "God has sent us the help we need, Lola. I thank Him for it!"

For the next week Lola and her father spent most of their time with the Winslows. Sometimes they came together, but often Lola would come alone and the two women would sit together. Rebekah found she needed someone to talk to, and the quiet girl would sit for hours listening as she went back over her life. Lola did not speak often, but as the days passed, Rebekah grew to love the young woman very much.

It was long after midnight on the last day of the week, after Sky had drifted off to sleep, that Rebekah spoke of Mark. "He's not happy, Lola," she said quietly. "He was always a cheerful boy, and no different when he became a man. The men in his unit loved him. But he's fighting some kind of a battle inside—and he's losing it."

Lola ventured, "I think I understand Mark's unhappiness. He's a sensitive man, but he's had a hard life. The war, jail, and now this terrible job! I know someone has to keep order, but Mark's not the man for it. If he doesn't stop, he'll be destroyed!"

Rebekah listened as Lola went on, and when the girl finally fell into silence, she asked what had been on her heart ever since she had arrived. "Lola, are you in love with Mark?"

Lola's hand flew to her cheek and she gasped, for she had thought her secret was safe. She felt her face grow warm, and she wanted to avoid the question. Then she looked into Rebekah's eyes, and her hand fell back into her lap.

"Yes, I've loved him for a long time, Rebekah," she said simply. "But he doesn't love me—and even if he did, I couldn't marry a man without Jesus in his life." Tears gathered in her eyes, and she whispered, "Oh, Rebekah, I love him so—and I can never have him!"

Rebekah opened her arms, and as Lola fell into them, sobbing with all her heart, she whispered, "You have been faithful to God, Lola. Now you must wait to see that He can be faithful to you."

CHAPTER TWENTY-FOUR

TEST OF A MAN

★　★　★　★

December came to an end, and there was hope that the relatively mild weather would hold. Even the cold could not stop Casement's hard driving crews. They laid track from dawn until it was too dark to see how to drive the spikes, seven days a week.

It was a strange time for Mark, the strangest he had ever known. He was either riding from point to point, putting down trouble—or he was with his parents. The caboose had been converted by Jude Moran into a real home, complete with couch, cookstove, and comfortable chairs. He had even found a piece of carpet and laid it carefully on the floor. As he had worked, he had spent long hours with Sky, and the two of them had become very close. Sky had grown weaker, but his mind was as clear as ever, and as the days passed he began to put together the facts about Mark.

"He's running from God, Rebekah," he said one night when they were alone. He was sitting up and had been reading his Bible as usual. "Just like I did."

"And God will find him just as He found you," she said firmly. "He's just strong willed." A smile came to her lips and she shook her head slightly. "It seems like I should have had at least one child who wasn't stubborn as a mule! But even the girls are that

way. Well, it certainly never came from *my* side of the family."
She chuckled, putting her hand over his. "Lola was saying last
night how much he's changed—just since we got here. She
thinks that God brought you here just for that."

Sky nodded firmly. "She's one smart girl. Pretty, too." He
stroked his thin cheeks and thought hard. "Do you think—?"

Rebekah read his thoughts. "That he might marry her? I hope
so, Sky. She's a fine young woman—just what he needs."

"I thought at times he might be interested in the Ames
woman. She's pretty enough to turn any man's head—and she's
got plenty of money."

"She's also Ray Hayden's girl—and Ray is Mark's friend,"
Rebekah said firmly. "I've heard some say that her father's lost
his money—but he's got rich, powerful friends. He won't go
down."

The subject of their conversation, Moira Ames, would have
agreed with Rebekah—on both counts. She felt sure that her
father would not lose everything, though he would never be
quite as well off as before. He had told her as much. She was
also certain that Mark would never look on her as a woman in
whom he could be interested. Not just because he was Ray's
friend, but for other reasons. It was the day after Rebekah's comment to Sky that some of this came out for the first time.

Ray had come to the hotel just after noon looking for her
father, and when he had delivered his message, Moira asked,
"Do you have time for a walk down to the store with me, Ray?"

Hayden looked at her in surprise, for she had been distant
since her return. Her voice that day was uncharacteristically gentle—even wistful. "Of course," he said. He escorted her down
to the store, waited while she picked out a few things, then
returned. When they got back to her room, she said, "Come in
and talk for a while, Ray. These four walls are closing in on me."

He was nervous, for at any time he would have to contact
Wallford and set in motion the plan to destroy the Union. He
came in and sat on the couch, listening while she spoke on minor
things. Finally she noticed that he was not himself. "Why, you're
wound up like a spring, Ray," she said in surprise. "Is all this
business of beating Central getting to you?"

"I suppose so," he muttered. "I'll be glad when it's over." He looked at her and was struck again with her beauty and charm. She had more of both than any woman he had ever known, and it came to him that in a short while he would not be seeing her again—not after he wrecked the Union, which was the same as wrecking her father. He had, of course, known that would happen, but as she moved closer, he was stirred by her as he had been during their first days of romance.

She was thinking of how weary the last months had been, and now she said quietly, "I'm so tired of all of this, Ray. After it's over, I think I'll be able to think a little straighter." She put her hand over his, and he took it at once, marveling at the smoothness of her skin. Her perfume was faint, but it came to him as she leaned against him. "Remember what good times we had in Boston when we first met? I thought you were the most handsome man I'd ever seen."

"You kept it a secret," he said with a wry grin. "I seem to remember you kept juggling me like a puppet—along with a dozen other men. But, yes, that was a great time." It came back to him strongly, the memory of those days when he had fallen in love with her. "I got so mad at you for keeping me on the string that I longed to shake you to bits and walk off and leave you."

"You should have, Ray," she said suddenly, and there was a new wisdom in her eyes. "If you'd have done that, I think I'd have married you immediately. I've always needed a strong man. I know I'm spoiled rotten, but I could be different if—"

"I've thought maybe Mark would be that man, Moira," he interrupted. "He's strong enough for you, I suppose."

She bit her lip, and silence engulfed the room. Then she lifted her eyes and said, "He's a daring, headstrong man, Ray. And I'll admit I was interested in him. He even kissed me once, down by the old church. I made him do it just to find out what he was like."

"You can do that to a man," he said with a half-bitter smile. Then he asked, "What did you find out?"

"What I already knew, Ray. He's a fine man, but not for me. For one thing, he's not my type. You've met his parents. Mark will be just like them sooner or later. It's fine for them—but I'm just not that type. No puritan in me. I'll always like the sort of life they wouldn't care for. The kind of life we had back in Boston."

He stared at her, then asked, "You said that's one reason you'd not have him. What's the other?"

She smiled and there was a wry humor in her green eyes. "Why, I saw that I could never have all of him. He's got another woman on his heart, and even if he never has her, no other woman will get what he has for her."

"Lola," he nodded. "I saw it long ago. I wonder if they'll find each other?"

Moira stood up and walked to the window, reflecting on what had been said, and Ray followed her. She stood looking down on the muddy street, then turned to face him. "I don't suppose they will, Ray. Love stories don't often turn out like they do in the books."

Hayden had been going through the worst time of his life. Since the moment he had taken the money from Wallford, nothing had been right. He knew something was terribly wrong, and for the first time in years a struggle went on in his spirit over the rightness of what he was doing. It was not a religious matter, for Hayden cared nothing for God. It was something that came from his past—from his early days at the Point and later in the war. He had hated the war, but the one thing never erased from his mind was the honor that existed between the men he fought with. They didn't call it that, of course. They didn't call it anything. But when the bugles sounded the charge, they all went forward together, the good and the bad, the courageous and the cowards. He had let that part of his life slip. Now as he was poised on the brink of another breach of his faith—and there had been many during the past years—he was afraid. He had grown frightened that if he did this thing—if he betrayed Ames, who had helped him and trusted him, and Mark and all the others who were putting their lives on the line—if he did this, he would never again be able to do a right thing. He would, he feared, lose all capacity for feeling anything in his soul. The proof of how strong this fear was lay in the untouched packet of money that he had hidden in his room. Ordinarily he would have lost most of it at the tables, but he had not even opened the package.

Hayden attempted to conceal his thoughts, but Moira saw

something of his internal struggle in his eyes. "What's wrong, Ray?" she asked gently. "Something's tearing you apart on the inside. Can't you tell me about it?"

He suddenly realized with a great clarity that he would never be able to tell her about it. It was a dirty thing, and he would carry it with him to his grave. In a burst of insight he knew that even if he did go on to Central's board room and eat off silver the rest of his days, the dead feeling that had been with him for days would not pass away.

"Moira," he whispered, "I wish that you and I could get away from here—a million miles away!" She saw the agony in his eyes and put her arms around him. He bent his head, and they clung together like frightened children.

Moira experienced a feeling of triumph as he held her. She had never been able to break through the reserve that Ray wrapped himself in. He had been charming and witty, but she had never been able to know the real man inside him. Now she said, "Oh, Ray, why haven't we ever been honest with each other like this?" She clung to him and her voice was hopeful. "We'll endure this—and then we can start all over again. Father's going to have a struggle, but you and I can help him. It'll be fun, Ray! We'll fight together and maybe fight some ourselves—but if we can cry together like this—why, it's all I've ever wanted!"

She lifted her head and he kissed her, and it was not like the first time—it was much better. She gave herself to him utterly and completely, leaving nothing of herself out. He had spent years trying to get at the woman he had always known was buried in Moira—and now that he had found her, he suddenly knew what he had to do.

He stepped back, his voice husky as he said, "My dear—I thought I'd lost you!" Then he straightened his shoulders, a determined look in his eyes, and added, "There's something I have to do—and then some things I have to tell you about myself. You may not like me much after I say them, but at least I will be honest."

He turned and left the room on unsteady legs. The scene had moved him as nothing in his life had ever done, and he walked for half an hour, thinking of her and of what he had to do. Hayden was no coward, but as he made his way to his room, grabbed the packet of money and proceeded to the saloon where Wallford passed his time, he wished fervently that he had never met the man.

He found Wallford sitting alone at a table and nodded to him. The two met outside, stepping into an alley. Ray said at once, "Wallford, I don't know how to say this, so I won't try to sweeten it." He reached into his pocket and took out the money, then extended it to the man. "Here's your cash. I'm backing out."

Wallford's eyes glittered menacingly, and he took the money and put it into his coat pocket. "Do you think that makes any difference, Hayden? You're not the only one who can blow a tunnel! You don't think I'd put myself in your hands, do you? That tunnel will be out by dark!" Without warning he pulled a pistol from his pocket and put a bullet in Hayden's chest. Ray had no time to even make a sound. The bullet drove him backward, and he fell to the ground in a motionless heap.

Wallford replaced his gun, no trace of emotion on his face as he observed the still form. "Fool!" he spat, then turned and slipped out of the alley.

★ ★ ★ ★

The warmth from the wood stove brought a coziness into the small space of the caboose, and Mark leaned back in a kitchen chair and let the weariness run out of him. He had been gone for two days, and after riding hard for eight hours through a cold, drizzling rain he was slightly fuzzy-minded as he sat with his parents and Lola. He had dismounted stiffly about noon, and the two women had pulled him into the caboose and filled him up with a hot meal, fussing over him. Now they were all listening to Sky talk of his early years—the times when he had roamed the Yellowstone country with his father Christmas Winslow.

"The Yellowstone River," he mused in a dry voice. "It's so clear you think it's a foot deep—you can see every pebble. Then you step into it and realize it's a fifteen-foot drop to those stones." He paused and the stove hissed and sputtered as the fire found a sap-rich branch, then said, "I often wondered what would have happened if I'd stayed in Oregon—or gone to the Mission to be with my father. We'd probably have missed the war way out there."

"We've had a good life, Sky," Rebekah said, looking at him him fondly. "Not many Southern families got through the war without losing a son."

He put his hand out, and she took it, holding it between her own. "I've been thinking of the wagon train, Rebekah. Do you ever think of those days? But I know you do."

Rebekah gave a sudden sly wink at Mark and Lola. "I remember how you chased around after that dancehall hussy, Rita Duvall," she said pertly. "I can remember that very well."

Sky grinned suddenly and Lola noted again what a fine-looking man he was, imagining what he must have been in his youth.

"Almost caught her, too. And she was a looker!"

"Serve you right if you'd caught the wench," Rebekah nodded. "She'd have led you a merry chase."

A thought came to Sky, and he said with surprise, "Rita was a few years older than you, wasn't she? I always think of her as she was, young and very beautiful. But if she's alive, she's in her sixties—grandmother, I'd say." He paused and let the thought linger, then shook his head. "Life goes by so fast. I was thinking last night of the time when father went to be with the Lord. He was doing the very thing I'm doing now—going over his life. He told me stories his own father had told him—about the times at Valley Forge when he nearly froze with General Washington— and how the surrender came at Saratoga. His father, Nathan Winslow, was with Washington many times, and in all kinds of weather. And he talked about his years in the mountains—and about my mother, White Dove."

"I wish I could have known him," Lola said suddenly. Then she smiled and said, "But I've met you, and that's a lot."

Sky looked at her, and they all saw that there was a translucent glow to his skin. The spirit within was bright, but they could tell that he was running down. He would often stop and hold his breath, grasping his chest, listening to the faltering of his great heart. He did so now, and they all waited—but he recovered and looked around with a smile. "Not this time," he said almost gaily.

"It'll be a long time yet, Father," Mark insisted.

"Son, I taught you better than that," Sky said with a rebuke in his voice. "Never hide from the truth. And the fact is, my turn to die has come. And except for leaving all of you, I wouldn't grieve. When my father died, he'd lost my mother, so he was like a man anxious to be off on a long journey with something wonderful at the end of it." He looked at Rebekah and said, "I'm sorry to be selfish, my dear, but I'm glad I'm going first. You're stronger than I am. I couldn't bear the thought of waking up in this world—and not having you at my side."

Tears came to her eyes, but she brushed them away. "I'll be along soon," she whispered.

Lola bit her lower lip to keep back the tears, but her eyes overflowed. Sky saw it and said in a louder voice, "Lola, stop that sniveling! Sing me that song we had yesterday."

Her throat was so tight she could hardly speak, but he kept teasing her, and finally she began to sing. She had not finished the first verse when the door burst open and they all looked up, startled.

Ray Hayden fell into the room, supported by Dooley Young. "Ray!" Mark cried out, lunging to his feet and helping Dooley put the wounded man into a chair. "Sit down—what happened, Dooley?"

Dooley shook his head. "Dunno, Captain. He staggered into the office, gut shot, but he wouldn't let us take him to a doctor—'cept he better get one fast."

"Go get Doc Sanders," Mark said, and Dooley rushed out of the car. "Take it easy, Ray. Let me see how bad it is."

He began pulling the bloody coat off, but Hayden held up a hand, gasping, "Mark—we've got to go to Echo Canyon—"

"Take it easy, Ray," Mark urged. "Who did this to you?"

Hayden's face was pale, but his eyes were clear, "Jason Wallford. He's an agent from the Central Pacific. He's been behind all the trouble we've had—and I've been working for him."

Mark grew still and stared into the face of Hayden. "Ray. . . ?"

A shudder of pain caused Hayden to shut his eyes, but he pulled himself together. "It's true. I've sold you out—you and every other man working on the Union."

Lola said, "What you have to say can wait. Let me look at your side."

"I'm not going to die," he said as she pulled the bloody shirt away. "Wallford shot to kill—but I guess the devil looks out for his own." He pulled something from his shirt pocket with a trembling hand and held it out. "Look at this—the bullet hit it and glanced off."

Mark took it and saw Hayden's thick gold watch, shattered and bent almost double. "The slug slid off and hit some ribs, but it's not going to kill me." Then he winced as Lola pulled the cloth away from the raw flesh. He had a purple bruise where the watch had been driven into his flesh, and a long ragged wound that was seeping blood. "Put some bandages on that and tie it up, Lola," he gasped. Rebekah ran to a chest and began pulling out some cloths, and as Lola bound him up, he said, "Wallford shot me because I backed out on him. He thinks I'm dead—but we've got to get to Tunnel Number Two, Mark—and quick!"

"What for, Ray?"

"Because it's going to be destroyed. Wallford told me that just before he shot me. You know what that will mean, Mark."

"We lose it all," Mark said, starting for the door. Ray got to his feet and began to follow him.

"Where do you think you're going?" Mark demanded.

There was shame in Hayden's face, but a new pride as well. "I'm going to Tunnel Number Two. With or without you, Mark."

Winslow stared at Ray and saw something in his face that he had not seen since their early days together at West Point. He hesitated, then Lola said, "Take him, Mark," and she placed her hand on Ray's arm and smiled at him. "I'm proud of you, Ray— and Moira will be, too."

Mark understood little of this, but he said, "You can't ride all shot up like that. We'll take the work engine. Lola, send Dooley after us when he gets back. Tell him to bring as many men as he can find, and to hurry."

"I'll tell him."

Mark looked at his father and mother, standing silently before them. He said apologetically, "It's another dirty job—" and his gaze shifted to Lola. "But I have to do what I can."

Sky said, "You wouldn't be my son if you didn't do your duty, Mark. I'll pray for you."

Mark turned and left the room, stepping aside to let Hayden go first. His eyes met Lola's and he started to speak, but found he could not. It was she who said, "You'll come back to us, Mark. God will keep you from harm."

He wheeled and left, and the two of them walked to the engine that sat beside the office on a siding. "You'll need a gun," Mark said, and ran into the office. It was empty except for Josh and Sherman Ames. They stared at him as he said, "Central's going to blow up Number Two Tunnel. Got any guns in here?"

Josh dashed to a cabinet, opened it and pulled out an armload of carbines. "We got plenty of ammunition. Can you drive an engine, Mark?"

"Well, I've seen it done enough."

"Used to be my trade," Josh grinned tightly and picked up one of the rifles and started stuffing his pockets with shells from a box.

"You're not going!" Mark said at once.

"We're all going," Ames said suddenly, picking up a carbine. "If that tunnel goes, it's the end."

Mark grabbed two of the rifles and a box of shells. "Then let's go."

They climbed into the cab, the two new recruits shocked to see Ray's condition. "What's happened to you, Ray?" Ames demanded. Ray gave Mark a defiant look and pulled at Ames's arm. "Got something to tell you, Mr. Ames. Come to the passenger car."

The two moved away, and Josh said, "Got a head of steam— enough to start, but pour the coal to 'er, Mark."

They were rolling out of the yard, picking up speed, when a shrill yell startled them. Mark looked out to see Dooley drive his horse at a dead run. He pulled up beside the engine and threw himself toward the steps of the cab. He would have fallen had not Mark reached out and caught him by the arm. He heaved him in, shouting, "You crazy rebel! You trying to commit suicide?"

Dooley pulled his hat down tighter, having almost lost it in the wild jump, and said, "You remember, Captain, how you went off and left me at camp when you took the boys to fight at Chancellorsville? Well, you made me miss that party—but I ain't missin' this one! Who we fightin'?"

Mark could not keep back a grin. "I guess we'll know when

we get there, Dooley. Load up those carbines while I shovel coal."

The engine picked up speed as the steam built up, and Josh gave Mark a grin. "Ain't had so much fun since I did this regular! Hope there ain't nothing in the way, 'cause I don't think we could stop in time if there was."

As they hurtled down the track, Mark wondered about Hayden. He had been shocked by what the man had said—yet he was more stunned by the fact Ray was risking his life for the Union he had tried to destroy. *Guess a man never knows what he'll do,* he concluded, and pushed the thing out of his mind. He had always had the ability to think only of the action ahead; that was what had made him a good officer. Now his mind was moving swiftly. He made a plan, or rather, it came to him fully made, and he knew at once that it was right. That also had been what made him a good officer. He could sense the right thing to do, and he never worried at it as some men did.

When they were within two miles of the tunnel, Mark said, "Take us right to the entrance of the tunnel, Josh." Ames and Hayden came to the cab just then, and there was an odd look on Sherman Ames's face.

Mark watched Ray carefully. Hayden appeared to be totally calm, unlike his usual manner.

"I don't know what we'll find when we get there," Mark said. "We'll pull up to the mouth of the tunnel and see what it looks like. There's not supposed to be anyone here, so anybody we see, will probably be the ones we're after. As soon as we stop, I'll go into the tunnel. The rest of you shoot anybody that's shooting at me."

"I better go with you, Captain," Dooley spoke up.

"You do what I tell you," Mark said harshly. "If I go down, you take a crack at it. Got that?"

Dooley nodded, his eyes bright with excitement. Then Josh said, "There she is—and there's a bunch taking cover!"

Mark grabbed a rifle and sprang to the door. He saw a group of about ten horses tied over to the left, and men scattering, taking cover behind equipment and the construction shack. A shot rang out, a loud ringing sound as it struck the steel side of the engine.

"Let 'em have it!" Mark shouted, and as Josh pulled the engine to a halt, they all scurried around to find a place to shoot from. Ames and Hayden were firing from the door and the open window, while Dooley and Josh scrambled to the top of the coal car. They lay down flat and soon were pouring a terrific fire into the men. Mark saw one of them suddenly rise up, throw his hands into the air and fall flat on his back. Another tried to change his position and a slug knocked his leg out from under him. He started crying, "I'm out of it! I been hit!" But nobody moved to help him and he pulled himself painfully along, trying to reach the shelter of a rock.

Mark yelled, "I'm going in!" He leaped to the ground as several shots struck close to him. But the onslaught from the engine increased, and he took off at a dead run toward the mouth of the tunnel. A bullet sang by his ear, and one struck the holster, turning it around, but he made a lunge and reached the shelter of the tunnel. He fell to his knees, and at once was aware that someone was in front of him. His eyes were half-blinded by the dim light, but he recognized the voice of Lou Goldman instantly.

"Now ain't this something," Goldman said, stepping closer. Mark batted his eyes and realized that Goldman had seen him drop his rifle. It lay five feet away from his feet, but it might as well have been five hundred feet. The gun at his hip had been struck by a slug and was pushed into an awkward position, almost behind his back—and he wondered if it would fire at all after being hit by the bullet.

Goldman said, "What's the matter, Winslow? Can't you think of anything to say?" He laughed at Mark, who stood up awkwardly, one foot ahead of the other, knowing that the slightest move would set the gunman off. "You been having a good time, Mark, my friend," Goldman said. "You think I was going to forget how you hoorawed me in public? Not much! You made everybody think you was top dog. Well, you've got a gun and here I am. I'm Lou Goldman, Winslow—and I'm going to put you down."

Mark saw the gun in Goldman's hand lift, and he threw himself to one side, pulling his gun at the same time. He was too slow, as he knew he would be, and Goldman's bullet scraped his ribs, knocking him sideways. Mark kept rolling, and he threw one wild shot that came nowhere near Goldman—but made him jump to one side. Mark lunged to his feet, hammering two shots at Goldman. The gunman staggered, blood staining his shirt, but he managed to fire another shot before slumping to the ground. Mark felt something strike his left leg, knocking it from under him. He sprawled in the dirt, a sharp pang running through his thigh, but he got to his feet, holding on to the wall.

Goldman lay on the ground, his breath coming in ragged gasps. He stared at Winslow with a thin, bitter expression on his lips. He looked at the gun Mark held on him and said without a trace of fear, "You take this hand, I guess, Winslow. You got the devil's own luck." He coughed, blood running down his chin.

Mark heard footsteps and turned to see Ray enter on a dead run, bullets striking around him. He pulled up short, stared at Goldman, then looked at Mark. "You hit bad?" he asked.

"Don't know, Ray," Mark said. A dizziness overtook him and he swayed, holding on to the wall. His leg was bleeding badly and he wondered if an artery had been hit.

Goldman said suddenly, "We better get out of here."

Mark stared at him. "What's the matter, Lou?"

Goldman was not a coward, but as he looked overhead he had a vision of being buried alive. It was not a thing he fancied, and he said, "Fuse is pretty short on that charge. I left no extra."

Mark took a step and his leg gave way. He sprawled on the ground and cried out, "Got to get that fuse!"

Ray said at once, "You stay here, Mark—" then plunged into the darkness of the tunnel.

Goldman stared into the tunnel, then looked back at Mark. "He'll never make it, Winslow! There ain't enough time." Goldman struggled toward the opening, but gave up, realizing his efforts were hopeless.

He looked back down the tunnel. "You know, I was bad wrong about that fellow—Hayden." His face wore a puzzled look, and his voice was very weak. "I never read a man so wrong in my whole life. . . ." His voice trailed off and he was still.

Mark nodded at the dead man—and then he heard Ames saying, "Get a tourniquet on that leg, Young. He's losing blood fast."

He felt hands on his wounded leg and opened his eyes. He tried to say something about Ray, but it was too much effort. The blackness of the tunnel seemed to open up, and he plunged into it.

CHAPTER TWENTY-FIVE

THE GOLDEN SPIKE

★　★　★　★

The wound in Mark's thigh was bad enough to keep him off his feet for two weeks. Doctor Sanders had strictly urged Dooley to keep him in bed for at least a week. "Hide his pants," he had instructed with considerable irritation when he had discovered Mark struggling out of bed.

Mark had complained, but the loss of blood had been serious. Sanders told him that if Dooley had been five minutes later with the tourniquet, he would have died, so he remained in bed, thinking as he hadn't since he'd been in jail in Mexico.

Lola had been there when he had come out of the black tunnel of unconsciousness, and he had tried to talk to her. She had placed her hand on his lips, saying, "Sleep. There'll be lots of time for talk later." Every time he woke up, she seemed to be there—or if not her, his mother. The second day he was alert enough to ask, "How's Father?"

Rebekah replied evenly, "Not good, Mark."

The news depressed him and he lay there silently, wrapped in gloomy thoughts. When Lola took Rebekah's place, he watched her as she sat across from him, her head bent as she read from her Bible. He said finally, "Things come around again, don't they?" When she looked at him with a question in her eyes, he said, "This reminds me of the time when I was sick in that shack in Texas. It seems as if you always end up nursing me, Lola." He lay quietly, fatigue and pain keeping him still. "That seems like a million years ago—yet it's clear in my mind. I can still remember every board in that shack. Funny how things stick with you."

She put her Bible aside and came to him. She pushed his unruly hair back from his brow, her cool hand resting lightly on him. She was a strong woman, filled with that inner quality that had always drawn him. Her eyes were calm, but there was a vulnerable softness to her lips that matched the gentle roundness of her cheeks. A tap at the door drew her attention. "Come in," she invited, and Ray entered with Moira at his side.

They came to stand beside his bed, and Ray asked, "How are you, Mark?"

"Going to make it." Mark noticed that there was something new in Hayden's expression, and as he studied him, he decided it was pride, self-confidence. He said slowly, "Ray, I'll never forget seeing you run into that tunnel. I'm not sure I could have done it."

Ray laughed shortly. "Yes, you could have. But look at this—" he took out his wallet and removed something from it, handing it to Mark. It was a piece of fuse, less than two inches long. "Just enough for me to get hold of," Ray said. "It seemed like they'd planted it a thousand miles down into that tunnel, Mark, and when I pulled the fuse—" He tried to grin and failed. "I just sat down and cried! Couldn't even walk I was so scared!"

Mark studied the fuse, then handed it back with a grin. "You'll never cut anything that fine again, Ray. You saved our bacon."

"I was the one who got us into trouble—" Hayden protested, but Moira interrupted.

"We've agreed not to dwell on that, Ray." She smiled up at him, and he shrugged, relieved. Moira turned her attention back to Mark, saying, "I hope you mend soon, Mark. You don't look natural lying down." She included Lola in her next words. "Ray and I will be going back to Boston soon. He's going to help my father put his business back on its feet."

"I hope things go well for you both," Lola said, and there was real warmth in her words and smile. "Will you stay on until the rails get to Ogden?"

"Sure. Somebody has to do the work while Mark lies there soaking up all the attention," Ray smiled. There was a new assurance in him, and after the pair left, Lola said, "I think they have a chance. He's not the same man—and she's changed a great deal."

"I guess finding out about Ray shook me up more than I've been in a long time," Mark said thoughtfully. "Do you really think a man can change so much?"

She nodded. "If he wants to badly enough. Now, you go to sleep." She tucked the covers over him, and he dropped off at once.

For five days he stayed in bed, then he bribed Dooley to bring him his pants. "Just want to try them on and see if I'm able to navigate," he said.

Dooley argued, but habit was too strong, and Mark dressed anyway, limping across the room while hanging on to Dooley's shoulder. "Why, I'm able to split rails!" he said proudly, but when Dooley released him, he would have fallen if the smaller man had not grabbed him and guided him back to the bed.

"Yep, I can see you're ready to fight a bear and give him fust bite," he said scornfully. "Now you git in that bed, Captain, and stay there!"

And he did, for the rest of the day, but the next day he dressed again, and it was well he did. It was almost dusk when Lola came into the room, and he saw at once she was disturbed.

"Is it Father?" he asked.

"Yes. I've got the buggy downstairs. Can you walk if I help you?"

"Let's go." He clung to her, navigating the stairs and struggling into the buggy, all the while racked by blinding flashes of pain. "I'm all right," he said quickly, though his face was covered with perspiration, despite the cold. "Get going."

She didn't speak on the way except to say, "He had a bad spell about an hour ago—very bad, Mark."

Getting out of the buggy, he slipped and grabbed wildly at her. She supported his weight, and when he was steady, she said, "I'll help you up the steps." The two of them managed the steps, then pushed the door open and went in. His mother was sitting beside Sky. She got up at once and came to him. "Be quick, son," she said, and he sat down awkwardly in the chair beside his father's bed.

Sky's eyes opened at the sound of Mark's voice. A smile came to his pale lips, and he whispered, "Glad you came, son. I—wanted to see you before I go."

Mark took the hand Sky gave him. He said, "I want you to know that no man ever had a better father."

"That's good . . . to hear," Sky said. His breathing was so faint his chest scarcely moved. "You have been a good son . . . like your brothers. I have always been proud of you, my boy . . . always."

He lay there for a full five minutes, not stirring. Mark felt his mother at his side and took her hand. They sat there silently, waiting for the end. Sky's chest suddenly heaved, and his eyes fluttered, then opened. "I'm not one . . . to force something on you, Mark . . ." he whispered. "You'll understand me. You're the only one of my children who hasn't found God. But I'm asking Him . . . to find you, son."

Mark felt a deep sorrow as he thought of his life, then that of his parents. He made a decision as he watched his father fight for breath. It was the kind of decision he'd made often on the battlefield—sharp and clear and not to be questioned or doubted. He said slowly, "Father, I've watched you and Mother serve God. Everybody I love and admire—they all believe in God." He lifted his eyes and found Lola's gaze on him, tears in her eyes.

Mark took a deep breath and said, "I will serve God—from this time on, Father. Will you believe that?"

Sky's eyes opened wide and his smile came, freely and without pain. "Yes! And will you pray with me right now?" He saw Mark's nod and began praying, the way Mark had heard him pray a thousand times—with a calm assurance that God stood right beside him. "Lord," he whispered, "I feel so close to you! Before I leave, let me see my son enter into your kingdom. . . ."

He prayed for a few minutes, and as he did, Mark Winslow opened his heart to God. First he prayed silently, then he cried out, "Oh, God, in the name of Jesus Christ, forgive my sins and make me clean!"

He felt his mother's arms encircle his neck, her tears warm

his face—and then he experienced a surge of joy that was like nothing he'd ever known. He opened his eyes to find his father smiling at him.

"Thank God!" Sky whispered. "Rebekah . . . they're all home!" he said, and he reached out his hand for her. "All the children . . . they're all home! Thank you, God. . . . !"

Mark stood up, and his mother knelt to hold the dying man in her arms. Mark hobbled away, unwilling to intrude on their last earthly moments together. He found that he could barely see for the tears that filled his eyes. "Lola?" he whispered, reaching out for her.

"I'm here, Mark." She stepped into his arms, and they stood there, clinging to each other. "I'll always be here, my dearest," she whispered.

They held each other silently as the moments passed over them. Then Rebekah was there, her head high, victory mingled with tears in her eyes.

"He's gone to be with the Lord, children. He's gone home."

★ ★ ★ ★

An American flag snapped briskly in the biting wind. The setting was sharp and desolate. Southward behind Promontory, the land rose abruptly in a long ridge clad sparsely with scrub cedar, blocking a view of the Great Salt Lake. Two engines faced each other. The straight-stacked Rogers of the Union confronted the bell-shaped funnel of the Central's Jupiter. A select group of track layers had placed a last pair of rails in position, and across this narrow space the two engines were poised. Fifteen hundred spectators crowded the scene, and Mark put his arm around Lola to protect her from the crush of Irishmen, Chinese, Mexicans and tourists. Leland Stanford awkwardly poised a sledge over the last spike of the transcontinental railroad—a golden spike.

Mark thought over the titanic struggle that had taken place during the winter storms, how the Union had laid tracks on snow when they could not lay them on the earth. He thought of Lowell Taylor, and Jeff Driver and many others who lay in graves along the right of way. Then Lola whispered, "Look, Mark! The last spike!"

Grenville Dodge had finished his speech and stepped back.

Leland Stanford took a deep breath, swung and missed!

Mark felt an elbow push at him, and turned to see Dooley's grin. He was standing there with Maureen, his bride of twenty-four hours, and he laughed, "Ain't that jest like a politician? Can't even drive a spike!"

Mark grinned, then watched as Stanford tried again, managing this time to tap the spike. The Jupiter and the Rogers, jetting out steam, slowly moved forward till their pilots touched. Irishmen swarmed over the engines, champagne bottles breaking in foaming streams over the engines.

As the cheers rang out, Mark drew Lola out of the press and led her to a small hill overlooking the scene.

"Well, that's that," Mark said. "There's never been anything in this country like it—and the country will never be the same again."

Lola asked, "Are you sad, Mark?"

"Only over the fine friends we'll not be seeing."

She moved closer and said, "We won't forget—but we have each other now. Like your parents did."

He embraced her, ignoring the whistles and yelps that went up.

"Yes! As long as we've got each other and the Good Lord, we're fine."

She returned his kiss, and they moved away from the hill. The bells and whistles of the engines followed them as they went, but they were thinking only of each other, and not a golden spike.